INTERZONE THE 4TH ANTHOLOGY

The stories we publish in *Interzone*, are nothing but figments of the imagination. Here, on the decks of the *Titanic*, which is nothing but our dream of the end of things, we are nothing but the band. We play the millennium. Four anthologies on, the tune is getting even better.

Here are the tunes we've been playing these days on the *Titanic*, as the great ship of Earth noses into the flux of things to come. For good and for ill, here are some tales of that time. Here are some stories of the foundering Mother ship, and the iceberg in the offing, and the dawn, and the journey to make . . .

Also available from NEL:

Interzone The 2nd Anthology
Interzone The 3rd Anthology

About the Editors

John Clute, David Pringle and Simon Ounsley are members of the editorial team of *Interzone*, founded in 1982. John Clute is a critic and book reviewer for the *Times Literary Supplement* and *The Washington Post*. David Pringle is the author of *Science Fiction: The 100 Best Novels* and *Modern Fantasy: The 100 Best Novels.* Simon Ounsley is an engineer and a writer.

Interzone
The 4th Anthology

New Science Fiction and
Fantasy

John Clute, David Pringle and Simon Ounsley

With an introduction by
John Clute

NEW ENGLISH LIBRARY
Hodder and Stoughton

Introduction © John Clute 1989
Story selection and Notes on the
Authors © *Interzone* Magazine 1988
and 1989
The copyright information on the
Acknowledgements page constitutes
an extension to this copyright notice

First published in Great Britain 1989
by Simon & Schuster Limited

First New English Library paperback
edition 1990

A CIP record for this title is available
from the British Library.

Printed and bound in Great Britain for
Hodder and Stoughton Paperbacks, a
division of Hodder and Stoughton
Ltd., Mill Road, Dunton Green,
Sevenoaks, Kent TN13 2YA. (Editorial
Office: 47 Bedford Square, London
WC18 3DP) by Clays Ltd, St Ives plc.

ISBN 0-450-53120-1

Contents

JOHN CLUTE

Introduction

BLINK and it's 1990. Blink again, and the great ship of the century hits its iceberg. Blink thrice, and it's dawn once more, and we have come through, as though it were all a dream. Which of course it was. Centuries are nothing but what we make of them, figments of the rage for order. Like good and evil, and Reasons of State, and blasphemy. The stories we publish in *Interzone*, taking a bead on the iceberg, are nothing but figments of imagination, either. Here on the decks of the *Titanic*, which is nothing but our dream of the end of things, we are nothing but the band. We play the millennium.

The tunes get better. In the twenty or so years of his active career, Brian Stableford has published more novels than stories, and it was only a few years ago that he began to offer shorter work to *Interzone*. 'And He Not Busy Being Born . . .', in the Second Anthology, and 'Sexual Chemistry', in the Third, are fine tales in his relentless, contemplative later manner, but 'The Growth of the House of Usher', in this volume, weds cognition and metaphor into a vision of the world beyond the millennium that is more than merely hopeful. Like the best examples of the Scientific Romance – as found in writers like Wells and Stapledon – 'Usher' gives us a poetry of future history, a music of evolution.

The last paragraphs of Lisa Goldstein's 'City of Peace' convey a perspectival vertigo not unlike that induced by Stableford's contemplative flight, but creates this effect out of a narrative that sticks calmly and toughly to a near-future Near East little different from our own – until the explosive implications of the last phrases of the tale sink in, and we are lifted, torn.

In 'The Cutie' Greg Egan takes us indoors, out of the wind of millennium, though the tale he tells so movingly could only be told of a society on the cusp of a radical disfiguring, and the claustrophobic obsessiveness of its protagonist speaks of a world attempting to turn its back on the ice. Eric Brown's 'The Time-Lapsed Man' also seems to take for granted the world which surrounds – and medicates – its wounded hero, but his progressive temporal dislocation reads like a metaphor of the innate isolation of any human animal in a world too strange, ultimately, to sense.

Appearing for the first time in these pages, Rachel Pollack's 'The Bead Woman' takes us outdoors again, but into dark woods. Set in the same universe as *Unquenchable Fire*, for which Pollack has won the £1,000 Arthur C. Clarke Award for the best science-fiction novel published in Great Britain during 1988, 'The Bead Woman' similarly sees the universe as alive, and requiring proper language from those humans who are required to mediate between the Little and the Big. And we go indoors, we shut the door behind us, we are in the traumatized closet psyche of the protagonist of J.G. Ballard's 'The Enormous Space'. It is rather like one of Georges Simenon's terrifying novels of psychic fugue from the 1940s and 1950s, and when its hero watches a visitor to his house-cocoon drive away and disappear for ever 'into that overworked hologram called reality', this reader (for one) felt a chill of recognition and envy. How good it would be to shut our eyes to the flensing in the abattoir, the maya of the hologram. And die deep inside.

But we cannot. There are not enough lifeboats. The war never ceases, there is always a berg looming, and always a new dawn glints off the eternal ice. In the work of Barrington J. Bayley, who began to publish in the 1950s, a sense of the terror of stasis and return permeates even the space operas he wrote for DAW Books, and tales like 'Tommy Atkins' are icy with entrapment. Because he has no need to change, Bayley never seems to change; he is sui generis, deeply himself, irreplaceable.

These characteristics he shares with John Sladek, who has just published, in *Bugs*, his first novel in several years; the most recent of his stories for *Interzone*, 'Stop Evolution in Its Tracks!', in its marriage of Magritte and creationism, seems to work, like so much of his best work over the past decades, as an encoding of questions it would be impossible to frame directly. Make sense? he asks the world. This? Who? Then? Not then? Then/not then? Not? Knot? Naught?

In 'Toxine', another story to be first published in *Interzone: The 4th Anthology*, Richard Calder reworks in modern dress some aspects of the myth Offenbach took from Hoffman and Hoffman drew from the deep fears of the race; his tale of redressing is poisonous, saturated, decadent as the end of the last century. And Kim Stanley Robinson, in 'Before I Wake', similarly reawakens a classical storytelling mode: the tale that is a dream: that is not a dream: that is a dream. But there is no gimmickry in the turns his tale takes, falling through.

Like the fractal caltrap it describes, David Langford's stunning 'Blit' gives off a steely medusoid glare; and one is very glad the tale is so short, because it is so dense and dangerous, and because it hurts the eyes. Like every other tale so far in the anthology, 'Blit' is set on Earth, or an analogue of Earths we might see in the clairvoyance of awakening from slumber, and it is only with the exuberantly kinetic 'Mirrors and Burnstone' by a new writer, Nicola Griffith, that we move off the *Titanic* for real, and find ourselves on a Company planet whose natives have finally come to realize that the invading humans are profoundly stupid. Griffith moves things with astonishing speed and savvy – rather like the early James Tiptree, Jr – and treats us to a classical slingshot ending designed, successfully, to make us long for more. A novel, perhaps. But 'Mirrors and Burnstone' can stand alone, without grafts. It is extremely sturdy.

In the few thousand words of 'Famous Monsters', Kim Newman creates an alternate history of the world and (more importantly) Hollywood out of hints from Wells, Burroughs et al.; an attractive alien whose cinematic monster roles capsulize a century of making scapegoats of blacks, Indians, Japanese; and sharp, poignant glimpses of the death of the clement solar system our science-fiction and fantasy forefathers dreamed of in their far-off play. A more devious alien infiltrates the plot and indeed the language of 'Driving Through Korea', becoming 'itself' in a sense the text to be read. The flowing cumulative intensity of this striking fiction, and the sense of effortlessness its telling conveys, make 'Driving Through Korea' one of the sleeper tales of the 1980s. We will remember it.

S.M. Baxter provides, in 'The Quagma Datum', the third and last original story to fit into these pages, and the first to plunge slam bang into the galaxy, as in the days of old. But Baxter is no blind space-opera recusant with biceps on his typing finger. 'The Quagma Datum' posits some intriguing arguments drawn from the physics of cosmogony, bristles with aliens, and concludes with abstractly limned but telling ironies rather reminiscent of the work of Stanislaw Lem.

And that's the record so far, after four anthologies, here in the dark of the greenhouse. Here are the tunes we've been playing these days on the *Titanic*, as the great ship of Earth noses into the flux of things to come. For good and for ill, here are some tales of that time. Here are some stories of the foundering Mother ship, and the iceberg in the offing, and the dawn, and the journey to make.

BRIAN STABLEFORD

The Growth of the
House of Usher

It was a dull, dark and soundless day on which I approached by motorboat the house which my friend Rowland Usher had built in the loneliest spot he could find, in the southern region of the Orinoco delta. There are plenty of lonely spots to be found there nowadays, after a century and a half of changing sea levels due to the greenhouse effect.

The edifice which Rowland was raising from the silt of that great stagnant swamp was like nothing I had ever seen before, and I am certain that it was the strangest dwelling ever planned in the imagination of man. It loomed out of the swamp like a black mountain, without an angle anywhere, and with no windows (though that is the fashion in modern times). Near its crown there were soft crenellations, mere suggestions of battlements, and a number of projections that might have been balconies, but the whole seemed to me languidly shapeless.

Exactly to what extent he had been inspired by the coincidence of nomenclature that linked him with the famous story by Edgar Allan Poe I do not know, but there is surely some sense in which *one* of the true architects of that remarkable tower was a long-dead nineteenth-century fantasist, even though the other was a twenty-second-century civil engineer. Rowland had always wanted to erect a House of Usher that could not and would not fall into ruin.

I was not sure, either, of the extent to which the letter summoning me here – which gave every evidence of nervous agitation and spoke of 'mental disorder' – might be construed as a kind of satire on Poe. I had never thought of Rowland as a joker, but I could not entirely believe that his protestations were serious. I obeyed his summons, of course, but I was uncertain what to expect.

I had first met Rowland Usher at college, where we studied civil engineering together. We were partners in practical classes, and we became adept together in the deployment of the Gantz bacteria which are used in modern cementation processes. These engineered bacteria, which can be adapted to almost any kind of raw materials,

1

had already wrought their first revolution, and were helping to
transform whole vast areas of land where it had been impossible
to build in the past: deserts, steppes and bare mountains alike.
While the ecological engineers were transforming the world's envi-
ronments, Gantz-inspired structural engineers were building entire
new cities for people whose ancestors had never known adequate
shelter; thanks to Leon Gantz, there need be no more mud huts –
great palaces could be raised from any kind of dirt, whether mud,
sand, or shale.

Rowland and I had been fired with a similar sense of mission,
determined to use the tools which our education provided to their
very best purpose, to play our part in a Utopian remaking of the
world, which would save it from its multiple crises. We had shared
a sense of vision and an ambition which many of our fellows lacked,
and this brought us closer together. We both became increasingly
interested in the techniques of genetic engineering involved in the
manufacture of Gantz bacteria, and dreamed of imparting new
powers to these living instruments, which would equip them to
perform more astounding miracles.

Pioneers in our field were even then experimenting with living
systems integrated into the walls of Gantzed structures, so that
houses could put down tap roots into the ground on which they
stood, to secure their own water supplies. Living systems for the
disposal of human wastes had been in use for some time, and
ingenious engineers were trying to adapt these systems to the
production of useful materials. These were the kinds of projects
which had seized our imaginations, and we often collaborated on
the design of imaginary living dwellings which would serve every
human purpose.

As I approached the remarkable house which Rowland had built
for himself, I could not help but recall these flights of fancy, and
I wondered how much progress his genius had made. The castles
in the air which I had built had been without exception edifices of
considerable beauty and profound charm. No one could say that
about the thing which Rowland had elevated from the silt of this
great swamp, which retained the blackness of that silt and possessed
an outward form that reminded me of nothing so much as one of
the great termite mounds I had seen in southern Africa, where I
had been working in recent years. The walls seemed slightly less
than solid, as though capable of a certain sluggish protoplasmic
flow, and this appearance gave me an uneasy feeling as I came to
the threshold, recalling to my mind the story of Jonah who was
swallowed by a whale.

Rowland met me at the open door and greeted me with enthusiasm. He conducted me through black, smooth-walled corridors
which curved eccentrically into the bowels of the house, to a
study where he obviously spent much of his time – there were
three telescreens, a well-stocked disc library of miscellaneous pub-
lications, an integrated sound system and two well-worn sofas.
The chamber was lighted by artificial bioluminescence, which was
oddly ruddy and subdued.

A pot of China tea was waiting for me, timed to perfection, and
we sat together drinking from small cups, exchanging platitudes.
I had not seen Rowland for more than seven years, thanks to the
reclusive habits which kept him apart from human society. I had
expected to find him changed, but in spite of his letter I was
surprised by the difference in him. He was very thin and pale,
and his hair was quite white. His voice was uncertain, sometimes
stumbling over simple sentences, and he gave the impression of
slight intoxication, though there was no wine to be seen in the
room.

I asked him if he was ill, and he confirmed that he was. Even
the most modern diagnostic computers had failed to identify the
biochemistry of its cause, despite the most comprehensive sampling
and analysis of his bodily fluids. He was continually in touch, electronically, with the medical research foundation at Harvard.

'You need have no fear for yourself,' he assured me. 'This is no
virus or other infection; the fault is integral. This is the same malady
which destroyed my father and my sister Magdalen; somehow, it is
in our genes. It seems strange, in this age when we have won such
command over the formative powers of DNA, that the cunning
double helix should still harbour mysteries, but it does. We have
not entirely conquered those inner blights and pestilences which rot
the very core of our being.'

I inferred from this rather florid speech that Rowland was suffering from some exotic form of cancer, associated with a heritable
chromosomal abnormality.

'Your sister died of this same illness?' I remarked.

He favoured me, as he answered, with a peculiar smile. 'Oh yes,'
he said. 'Many years ago, before I knew you at college. She was
seventeen years old – she was born a year before me. The disease
afflicts females more severely than males; my father lived to be
forty, and I am now forty-seven. My grandfather's sister – the last
female sufferer I have been able to identify – died at nineteen. You
will readily understand why the disease is inherited through the
male line. It is an Usher complaint, like the one which afflicted

my famous namesake. Did I not know he was a fiction, I would suspect a line of actual descent.'

I think I might have been alarmed if Rowland had told me that his sister were still alive, and had I seen her flitting ethereally through the apartment just then. This would have been one parallel too many for my tired mind to bear. As it was, though, I laughed politely.

'With Harvard on your side,' I said, 'there must be hope of a cure.'

'No,' he replied. 'I do not hope for a cure, but merely an understanding. Modern medicine has helped me to ameliorate the symptoms of my condition, but having failed precisely to identify its biochemical nature, there is no hope of permanent remission. Its origin is in the brain, which is the least understood of all the organs – perhaps the last great mystery – in this our new Age of Enlightenment. You will have noticed that my speech is affected, and my sight too – which is why, I fear, the lighting here will seem a little eerie to your eyes. The mental disorder of which I spoke in my letter is increasingly perceptible, and I know that my working days are almost over. That is why I asked you to come to me – I want to explain to you what it is that I have been doing all these years, in my solitude, while you have been helping the poor in Africa.

'I want you to get to know my house, to understand what I have achieved here. I want you, in brief, to be the executor of my will. My personal possessions are worthless, but my additions to the sum of human knowledge and creativity are not. I leave everything to mankind in general, for the joy and benefit of all future genera- tions – and you, my old friend, must convey my legacy to those heirs. There are full records of my data here, of course, but you know as well as I that the world is laden down beyond endurance with stored data, and that knowledge needs human champions if it is to be properly disseminated and developed.'

I told him that I understood (though in truth I was not entirely sure that I did) and gave him my most earnest promise that I would try to do as he wished. He was delighted by this response, but his enthusiasm seemed suddenly to weaken him, and when we dined he ate almost nothing. Soon afterwards he begged leave to desert me, and after showing me to my bedroom he left me alone, begging me to make full use of the facilities of the house and apologizing pro- fusely for not being able to give me a more thorough introduction to them.

Because the room had no window I could not ascertain whether

the threatened storm had begun, but when I lay silently in my bed
I thought that I could perceive a vibration in the dull, warm walls
that might have been an echo of lashing rain and howling wind – or
that might, instead, have been some mysterious internal process at
work within the living fabric of the fabulous structure. After a time,
I found it strangely comforting, as if it were a subliminal lullaby,
and I was carried off by it into peaceful sleep.

When I awoke the next day Rowland seemed better, and we break-
fasted together. He told me, though, that he did not feel well
enough to guide me about the house. He promised that he would
show me its wonders at a later date, and offered instead to tell me
something of the researches which had led to its construction, and
which formed the substance of his intellectual legacy.

'You may recall from discussions we had nearly a quarter of a century ago,' he said, 'that I was always impatient with the traditional
Gantz techniques which were in common use in our youth, and
which we were expected to learn in a more or less slavish fashion
in the course of our education in civil engineering.

'One of my chief interests – which we shared, I think – was the
possibility of integrating better artificial living systems into the
structure of buildings. It will not be long now, I am sure, before
biotechnologists develop methods of artificial photosynthesis, and
truly sophisticated living dwellings will not come into being until
then. Houses will one day be living machines harvesting the energy
of the sun as plants do. My house simulates, by necessity, a more
primitive kind of organism: a lowly scavenger which draws its
energy from the organic detritus of the silt out of which it is constructed. It is no more sophisticated than many sedentary creatures
which live in shallow seas, filtering food from the murky waters
which overflow them. Its closest analogues, if you wish to think
in such terms, are coral polyps, barnacles and tubeworms. Nevertheless, however primitive it is, it lives and it grows. The Orinoco
feeds it with all manner of decayed vegetable matter via the network
of filters which extends from the foundations.

'You will probably remember another of my fascinations, which
is similarly embodied in this house. Ordinary Gantz processes
involve the use of inert moulds – the cementing organisms simply bind the material brought to them, and the architect controls
the shape of what they produce by crude mechanical means. I was
always impressed, though, by the way that living organisms adapt
themselves to the construction of complicated edifices: the nests of
wasps and termites, of bower-birds and ovenbirds; the supporting

structures of corals; the astonishing forms of flowering plants and trees. I designed this house, therefore, by programming into the genes of its micro-organic creators the kind of structure it should be.

'Its main structure is, of course, built primarily from non-living tissue, like the xylem of a tree or the shell of a mollusc, but that structure retains its connections with living cells, and is formed more or less precisely by the pattern of their activity.'

'The house, then, is really a gargantuan living organism,' I observed.

'Not strictly speaking,' he corrected me. 'Its builders are micro-organisms, which associate and collaborate like the members of a beehive or the individual cells in a slime mould. If it is to be seen as a single entity, then it is a colony – a colony of trillions of quasi-bacterial cells. In adapting it for habitation, though, I do have cause to use other engineered organisms, which might be regarded as symbiotes of the elementary cells. The structure is naturally honeycombed by tunnels and chambers, but the precise design of the corridors and the rooms – not to mention the various connecting conduits which carry water, electricity and optical fibres – requires supplementary work.'

Such work in ordinary Gantzed structures tends to be carried out by de-cementing bacteria whose work is precisely the opposite of the cementers, but from Rowland's reference to 'other engineered organisms' I inferred that he was using 'worms' more akin to the artificial organisms used to pulverize rocks like granite and basalt. Most such organisms are, though vermiform, not really worms – most are the larvae of insects, akin to 'woodworm', these frequently being equipped with jaws and rasps powerful enough to cope with stone and metal.

'I have always been interested in insect larvae,' he explained, when I asked him to elaborate. 'They have in them so much *potential* – the phenomenon of metamorphosis has always fasci-nated me.'

This was an interesting sideline to the discussion, and I pursued it. 'None of the larvae which are conventionally used to tunnel through rock are capable of metamorphosis,' I said. 'They are of such a size that the insects which would emerge from their pupae would be inviable giants – incapable of breathing or of locomotion.'

'That is because Gantzian engineers have not been interested in the genes which the larvae will only switch on during and after metamorphosis,' Rowland told me. 'They have made only feeble efforts to modify such genes, and the giant insects they have managed to produce are mere grotesques. No one has tried to explore fully the real metamorphic potential of these larvae. Crudely utilitarian research into rock-breaking organisms can do no more than scratch the surface.'

'But you have gone further?'

'I have . . . taken an interest. The humble servants which help to hollow out my rooms have been my only companions for many years, and I have used them in certain unorthodox experiments quite unconnected with their more obvious purpose.'

I could see that this was a point upon which Rowland was, as yet, unwilling to elaborate. He seemed very tired and strained.

'Would it not be a good idea,' I asked, 'if we were to return to-gether, however briefly, to the United States? I know you are in touch with medical researchers there, and can transmit information gleaned from analysis of your blood and other fluids, but if you are suffering from a tumour in the brain, you surely need a sophisticated scan, which must be beyond the capacity of your own facilities.'

'Although my illness has its origins in the brain,' he told me, 'it is not a localized tumour. It is some kind of genetic defect which is capable of affecting *all* the cells, and will eventually affect enough of them to kill me, as it killed my sister. The researchers at Harvard have quite enough samples of my cells - and, for that matter, my sister's cells – in their freezers to allow them to continue examining the chromosomes for many years. Eventually, I feel sure, they will map and identify the anomaly, though by then the knowledge may be redundant as the last known sufferer will be dead – I shall leave no children of my own.

'I hope that the work done on my cells after I am dead will serve to pave the way for a successful treatment and cure. I have been doing my own research, too, using the apparatus that permits me to engineer my bacteria and my worms, to do what I can to study my own chromosomes. I have my own cryonic chambers and my own tissue-cultures – my father made the first contribution to my stocks before he died.'

'I wonder that you have not devoted your life to that research,' I said, 'instead of spending so much time on your other project.'

'Ah!' he said. 'My *other* project will assure me something worth far more than an extended lifespan – it will provide a kind of immor-tality. Even had I succeeded in curing myself I would have died after seventy or eighty years, but this house will live for centuries, perhaps for millennia. The Usher family will die out with me, but the House of Usher will continue to grow for many generations, and will be one of the wonders of this world when *your* descendants have built new worlds around distant stars. You see, my friend, that I have lost none of that Romantic imagination which drew you to me all those years ago!'

Indeed he had not, and as we talked further he waxed rhapsodic on the subject of the futures that were already nascent in the genetic technologies of the present day, his inventiveness vaulting across the centuries with talk of the miracles that godlike genetic engineers of the far future would work.

'It is not for you and me to see such things,' he told me, after some while, 'but your grandchildren will come into a world that will discover how to offer them immortality, and they will see the world transformed in ways we can hardly imagine. I will have my monument then, as Khufu has his – one of the last and greatest achievements of mortal mankind. We are members of one of the last generations to need tombs, my friend, and I intend that my sister and I shall have one of the very finest!'

His speech was becoming slurred and his tone was feverishly excited. I knew that his illness was taking hold of him, and I made every effort to calm him. In the afternoon, though, he had to leave me again, and I dined that evening alone.

The hours before I retired to my bed I spent in reading, but I was not tempted to begin the work of making my way through the discs which contained the long record of Rowland Usher's experiments. Instead, I sought solace in more familiar works – in the poetry of Blake and Byron, and (how could I avoid it?) Edgar Allan Poe. I say solace, but I really mean distraction, because the more time I spent in my tiny apartment deep in the heart of that utterly strange house, the more uneasy I began to feel about my virtual captivity. I did not like to be so cut off from the world outside and the sound of the ever-present murmur in the smooth, warm walls that surrounded me no longer seemed quite so comforting.

When I finally went to my bed I had a turbulent night, full of vague nightmares in which the imagery of Poe's poems mingled with the dreams and achievements of Rowland Usher. Conqueror Worms continually triumphed in an uncertain tragedy, from whose toils I could not escape until I woke in a cold sweat, many hours before morning.

My nightmare had had such a profound effect on me that I did not like to close my eyes again for fear of its return. I reached out to activate the bioluminescent strips that would light my room, threw back the quilt and rose unsteadily to my feet. I went to the sink on the far side of the chamber, and obtained a cup of water.

No sooner had I taken a sip than my attention was caught by a sound in the corridor outside. Though there was nothing sinister in the sound itself, I had not yet escaped the effects of my evil dream, and it drew from me a gasp of pure terror.

I knew, at the level of reason, that I ought not to be afraid, and I forced myself to go to the door and open it. Such was my state of mind, though, that it was only by the merest crack that I pulled it ajar, and as I peeped out into the corridor my heart was pounding in my breast.

The corridor was not quite dark, though its bioluminescence was considerably toned down, so that what remained was a faint bluish radiance. Because the corridor curved I could see only a few metres in either direction, and could see only one other door – that of Rowland Usher's bedroom.

That door, too, seemed to be ajar, but there was darkness within. Moving away from the door, though – just disappearing from sight around the gentle angle of the tunnel – was a human figure. I caught no more than the merest glimpse of it, but I had the distinct impression that it was a young female, perhaps fourteen or fifteen years of age. She was quite naked.

The idea that this was Rowland's sister Magdalen, somehow risen from the dead, sprang into my mind, provoked by my dream, even though I knew full well that it could not be. The power of the thought, even as I fought to dispel it, was sufficient to make me close my door again, and I found to my disgust that I was actually trembling. I – a scientist of the twenty-second century – was infected by the morbidity of the Gothic imagination! I cursed Rowland Usher and his absurd termitary of a house, and resolved to demand an explanation in the morning.

When morning came, though, the matter seemed far less urgent to me. I had slept again, more restfully, and when I awoke at the proper time my experience in the corridor seemed rather to belong to the realm of my nightmare than to the realm of reality. I honestly could not tell whether or not it had been part of my dream, and even though the cup from which I drank was still on the side of the sink, I could not take seriously what I thought I had seen. Perhaps I simply did not want to.

In any case, I asked no questions of Rowland over breakfast regarding the possibility of his being haunted by the ghost of his sister.

That day, Rowland felt well enough to conduct me on a tour of his abode, and so we set forth into its amazing winding corridors.

He showed me several other guest rooms – none of which showed the slightest sign of ever having been inhabited – and several storerooms, some of them crammed with collections of objects which he had obviously inherited from past generations, as well as hoards of his own.

There were many antique books, some with acid-rotten pages that should have decayed a century ago, some even dating back to the nineteenth century. There was a collection of minerals, one of medical specimens, one of ancient navigational instruments, and a particularly quaint assembly of display screens and keyboards from the early days of information technology. I asked if these devices were in working order, but Rowland simply shrugged his shoulders; he did not know.

When we descended into the lower strata of the house I found things much more coherently organized, and there were clearly many rooms in active use. First he showed me the laboratories where he conducted his experiments in genetic analysis and his transformations of Gantzing bacteria. His equipment was reasonably modern, though no private individual, however rich, can possibly keep up with the larger research institutions.

His fermenters, where his bacterial cultures grew, were built into the fabric of the house, and it was not until he told me their total cubic capacity that I realized how much of the house was hidden, circled by the spiralling corridors. Clearly, that space was not wasted.

I marvelled that any one man could possibly make use of the extensive laboratory facilities, but he assured me that the high level of automation made it reasonably easy. He had relatively few household robots, regarding the motile varieties as inherently unreliable examples of the mechanician's art, but some róutine activities were contracted out to service personnel who operated machines by remote control.

At a lower level still, he showed me other holding tanks, where he kept his many species of burrowing worms. Most species needed special containers of some substance which they could not break up or digest. There were observation windows which let us look in upon the creatures, though sometimes we could see little enough within because of the difficulties of providing lighting systems immune from their ravages.

Rowland allowed a few species of these worms to live free in the structure of the house, almost as parasites, because they could not damage its structure and performed useful waste-disposal functions as they foraged for food. At first it was disconcerting to come across these creatures at irregular intervals, but I soon got used to it.

'How do you direct the burrowing of the more voracious species?' I asked him. 'Surely, any kind of escape would be desperately dangerous – the worms could devour the entire fabric of the house.'

'Elementary cyborgization,' he told me. 'These creatures have little or no brain, and are guided through life by simple behavioural drives. It is a relatively easy matter to fit them with electronic devices which deliver the appropriate commands by electrical or biochemical stimulation. I handle them with great care. They cannot live, of course, on the materials they are designed to tunnel through, and their diets are deliberately exotic. I feed them what they need in order to execute a particular task, and no more. They cannot escape, and could not live wild if they did.'

Watching these curious creatures, roaming loose or in their tanks, made me slightly nauseous, though I had often seen their like before. Most were like blowfly maggots – big and soft and white, their body walls so transparent that one could see the organs inside them. Rowland's were the biggest I had ever encountered, a metre and a half in length and at least eighty centimetres in girth. Their internal organs were not themselves coloured, but were enwrapped in a webwork of blue and pink. I asked Rowland to explain this, and he told me that he had equipped their circulatory systems with haemoglobin in order to serve the oxygen needs of their organs; like us, these creatures had deoxygenated blue blood in their veins and oxygenated red blood in their arteries.

Some others looked more like elongated centipedes than maggots, being bright yellow in colour and equipped with hundreds of pairs of limbs along the length of their plated bodies. These, too, were the largest of their kind I had ever encountered, being at least four metres long, though only as thick as a man's wrist. A few of these living machines were, on the other hand, surprisingly small: there were black, hard-skinned creatures that were only a few centimetres from head to tail, though they had vast heads that were almost all jaw. Rowland informed me that these were very difficult to rear because of the enormous amounts of food they had to consume in order to work those massive jaws. In their holding tank, they were virtually submerged in high-protein fluid.

These marvels impressed me tremendously, and we spent many hours in these lower regions. He showed me something of the 'roots' which the house extended into the substrate of the swamp, and the apparatus for gathering in organic materials from the silt. He also showed me the biological batteries which produced the

house's electricity – which had a potential output, Rowland boasted, equivalent to thirty billion electric eels. Most of this, however,
remained inevitably hidden; what could be seen of the house's systems was far less, in metaphorical terms, than the tip of an iceberg.
Rowland assured me that there was much more to be seen than
could be taken in during a single day. He reeled off statistics in
an impressively casual manner, telling me that the biomass of the
house was greater than ten thousand elephants, and that if it *had*
been a single organism, then it would have been the vastest that
had ever existed on Earth.

By the time afternoon came, though, he was becoming increasingly tired, and his graphic descriptions began again to diversify
into flights of fantasy, in which houses such as this one would
gradually replace the plants and animals making up the world's
ecosystems, so that in a thousand years the entire ecosphere might
consist of nothing but organic artefacts – not merely houses but
entire cities – all locked into a careful symbiotic relationship controlled by men.

In such a world, he hypothesized, sexual reproduction would
be the sole prerogative of mankind, everything else in the organic
realm being capable only of vegetative growth or of being cloned
and transformed by human genetic engineers.

I confess that I did not find this a wholly attractive prophecy (or
speculation, for Rowland was talking of opportunity rather than
destiny), but there was something very attractive in the sheer gran-
diosity of Rowland's ecstatic voyages of the imagination, and the
magic of his ideas took a firm grip on me, encouraging my own
mind to the contemplation of vistas of future history extending
towards infinite horizons.

I joined in, for a while, with his game, and became so carried
away that I did not notice for some time that Rowland's condition was becoming desperate, and that he was on the brink of
losing his powers of motor co-ordination. He demanded that he
should be allowed to show me the upper parts of the house,
above our apartments, and uttered dark hints about there being
more in the basements than I was yet prepared to imagine, but
I had to forbid any further wandering, and in the end I had
to support him as we made our way back up to the dining
room.

For once, though, dinner seemed to revive Rowland's spirits, and
he ate a good deal. After he had rested for a while he was restored
sufficiently to conduct a longer conversation than had been possible
on the evenings of my first two days as his guest.

He set out to tell me more about the history of his researches, but soon went on to more personal matters, including secrets which he had hesitated to share with me when we were intimates in our younger days. In particular, he spoke of Magdalen, and I listened in fascination as he gradually peeled away the layers of inhibition which had hitherto concealed the inner mainsprings of his motivation. He granted me then such an insight into his character as he would surely never have conceded if he had not been certain that he was very close to death.

Alas, he was closer than he knew!

'Magdalen lived always under the shadowy threat of death,' said Rowland, his voice weakening almost to a whisper as the process of recall carried him into a trancelike reverie. 'My parents treated her with extraordinary indulgence; she was never sent to school because there seemed little point in trying to secure the kind of education that would be useful only as preparation for a later life which would not be her privilege. Instead, my father educated her himself, after his own theory, trying to equip her to obtain the greatest enjoyment from the years she actually would have. She was a beautiful child, who won the admiration of everyone, and of my father's eccentric tutelage I can say only that it seemed to work magnificently, for she was the happiest being I have ever met.

'Although I was allowed a more conventional schooling, I was also much involved in her life. My father sought to provide her with what he considered to be an ideal companionship; I, too, was a part of his scheme, though at first I did not know it. As he sought to mould her, so he sought to mould me, to build between the two of us such a bond of affection and community as to make us the lights of one another's lives. Such a uniquely close companionship he considered to be the greatest treasure which any human life is capable of discovering. I have not had cause to disagree with him in the decades through which I have lived since I lost that perfect relationship.

'I am a little sceptical now of my father's motivations. I wonder why, knowing that he was the victim of a heritable disease, he chose to have children at all. At the time, I thought the way that he took such careful and absolute control over our nurture was a measure of his heroic desperation in trying to save us from a misfortune of fate. Now I suspect that he had children precisely in order to carry out this remarkable experiment, and that we were his guinea-pigs. Nevertheless, I do know that he loved us very dearly indeed, and that the grief which he felt when

Magdalen died robbed his life, as it robbed mine, of almost all meaning.

'You see around you the extraordinary lengths to which I have been driven in my attempts to find a meaningful project in which to absorb myself. He never did find another; he lived and died a sad man, save for those years when Magdalen gave him a reason to exercise his unusual powers of creativity. You and I work with the elements of physical heredity, and cannot fully understand the difficulties which attended *his* work in delicately manipulating the psyche and the environment, but I think you can appreciate what a triumph was his when I say that I wholeheartedly believe that Magdalen's was the most joyful, the most compassionate, the most *complete* life that I think a human being might live, in spite of – or perhaps because of – its brevity.

'He taught her only those things that might stimulate her sense of beauty and her sense of wonder, to give her the fullest measure of delight in the world where her mayfly existence was to be lived. He controlled all that she saw, and heard, and felt. When I became old enough to understand what was happening, he made me his collaborator instead of his instrument, and towards the end I conspired with him in planning her last few months. We were determined that there should be no joyful aspect of human experience denied to her and we discussed carefully the question of whether it should be he or I that would introduce her to sexual love. Despite the value of his experience in such matters, the responsibility was given to me – old taboos against father/daughter incest still have some power, while brother/sister intercourse is widely accepted, and we were scrupulously respectful of prevailing social attitudes even though we had established for Magdalen a private society in which the world at large could not interfere.

'There is a sense, I think, in which the climax of my life had already passed when you first met me. You found in me a man who felt that he had already finished one life, attempting the impossible in trying to make another. All I can say is that I have done my best, and that I am proud of what I have achieved. I do not regret having become a recluse, separating myself as far as it has been practicable from the society of other men. My memories of Magdalen are far more precious to me than any other relationship with a woman or a man could ever have been.

'I realize that you are bound to think this unusual, but if you are to be the interpreter of my achievement, who must explain to the world the measure of my genius and its productions, then you must try to understand.'

Indeed, I did try to understand. He was correct in saying that in our enlightened times we are no longer so fearful of the taboos which preyed upon the consciences of our ancestors. We are no longer horrified by the idea of incest, so I was not particularly shocked to find out that Rowland had been his sister's lover. Nevertheless, the tale he told was so singular that I did have to struggle imaginatively to accommodate it. How odd and unparalleled the life of Magdalen Usher must have been!

Frankly, I doubted Rowland's assurances about the perfection of his sister's existence. I could not believe that this experiment in eupsychian engineering could possibly have been as successful as he claimed. No human being can be kept so utterly insulated from the darker side of life – from the ominous aspects of her own inner nature – as to be held inviolate from all dread, all sorrow, all splenetic impulse. Nevertheless, I did not doubt that *he* believed it, and that in his mind his sister's image must have a significance of purity greater than that of any saint or other idol.

I remembered the apparition of the previous night, of which I still feared to speak. I could not help but touch upon the subject, but felt compelled to do so elliptically, without directly saying what I had seen.

'She must be very much in your thoughts now,' I said. 'You must feel her nearness very acutely.'

'I do,' he said, dreamily. He seemed now to have been overcome by a tremendous tiredness, which carried him off into a kind of euphoric altered consciousness. Despite the fact that he had resolved to tell me his secrets, I do not believe that he would have told me any more at that time had he been in full possession of his faculties. He had surely planned a more gradual process of revelation. He was in the grip of his disease, though, and in a state of mind that few humans can ever have attained.

'At first,' he said, 'I dreamed of re-creating her. So many of her cells, including oöcytes from her womb, were taken from her even before death, to make the tissue cultures that would be used for the study of our freakish disease. I wanted to clone her, to bring her back from the dead, to make her anew. I soon realized, though, that it would be a dreadful thing to do. All the best efforts of my father and myself had gone into giving her a perfect existence within its prescribed limits. To create another of her would be to spoil our design, as if we were to take a great painting and daub over it an inferior copy. She could *never* be re-created, and to make another individual out of her genes would be an appalling travesty of all that my father and I had done.

'When I went to college, therefore, I deliberately elected to stay away from medicine, from human engineering. I went into the kind of work that would help me to transform the human environment rather than the human body. I wanted to build houses, not people – places for people to live, where they could live well, in privacy. I soon realized that it would not be enough to build the kind of houses that are now being built – I wanted to create something much more ambitious. But I could not entirely forget Magdalen, and there remained a sense in which *my* house . . . my private world . . . must in some way contain her. That was when I conceived the notion of working with the larvae.

'We are so proud these days of our own biotechnic miracles that we tend to forget nature's, and we tend to forget what a colossal bounty was made available to our early genetic engineers, in terms of the raw materials with which they began to work. I have always been fascinated by metamorphosis, by the fact that a maggot or a caterpillar can carry within it genes which code for an entirely different creature, so that when the time comes it builds itself a temporary tomb from which it will one day emerge anew.

'It struck me as a terrible waste that structural engineers should breed hundreds or thousands of new kinds of lavae to work for us, without considering that their eventual pupation would now be the end of their story. No one cared, it seemed, about the fact that these modified larvae could no longer advance to a final stage in their development, because the imagos programmed into their altered genes were hopelessly inviable.

'Thus, when I began engineering larvae for work within my house, I also began engineering them so that they *would* be able to pupate and metamorphose successfully. I knew that they could not produce giant insects, with wings and exoskeletons, so I set about reprogramming them to produce creatures that are viable at that size. The creatures I showed you today, which resemble blowfly maggots, have approximately the same biomass as a human being; they lose much of that in pupation, but can still produce something the size of a young adolescent. Mindless creatures, of course, but beautiful, in their way. They do not live long, at present, but I have laid the foundations for work which has limitless scope. In time, the engineers of the future might produce another human race.

'I have tried hard to gain sufficiently refined control over the features of these individuals, and I regret to say that I have not succeeded in producing one which bears more than a passing resemblance to my beloved Magdalen, despite using her own genetic material, but my quest has always been a hopeful one and I have derived much comfort from it. I needed *something* of her, you understand, to sustain me in my solitude . . . and they have given me that. *Something*, albeit so little . . .'

Rowland began suddenly to cough, and the cough developed into a kind of seizure.

Anxiously, I went to his side, and tried to calm him, but blood spattered my hand, and I suddenly realized that his condition was critical. His face had a ghastly pallor, and he struggled to whisper.

'So soon . . . *Magdalen!*'

It was as though the words themselves choked him. I tried to clear the blockage from his throat, to administer artificial respiration, but I could not start his heart beating again.

Within minutes, he was dead.

I checked Rowland's body for signs of life and, finding none, I called Harvard and asked to be put in touch with someone familiar with the details of his case. Then I went to another screen, and began to interrogate the data stores within the integral system. Within minutes I had a series of printed schematics which would serve as a map of the house. I located a wheeled stretcher in a nearby storeroom, and took him down to the room that housed his diagnostic computer and its ancillary apparatus. There I took the return call from Harvard. When I had manoeuvred the body into the cradle of the apparatus, the surgeon took over the remote controls, and began to check again for signs of life before continuing with the post-mortem.

This I could not bear to watch, and so I made my way back to the study where Rowland had told me his remarkable story. There, obsessed with the necessity of being reasonable, I set about the task which he had set for me. I began to inspect the discs on which he had carefully kept the records of all his experiments and all his projects.

In time, I could carry all the information away to more congenial surroundings, but I knew that if I were to do the job properly, then I would have to work in the house for at least a fortnight, in order to know exactly what ought to be taken away or transmitted electronically to my own home.

I took three further calls from Harvard, but I was not required to do anything further – the doctors there, working in association with the house's automatic systems, completed their examination, took their samples, issued a death certificate and wrapped the body in preparation for interment. By this time I had located Rowland's last will and testament, and I set in motion the legal machinery needed to put it through probate. The will provided for burial of the body beneath the house, and I knew that this was a task that I would have to carry out myself, but it was one that could safely be left for another day.

It was late when I finally dimmed the lights and returned to my own room. Midnight had long gone, but, insulated as I was from any knowledge of the setting and rising of the sun, my sense of time was confused, and I did not feel tired until I actually took the decision to stop and rest. Then, fatigue suddenly swept over me like a wave.

With darkness and fatigue came an inevitable relaxation of reason, and when I slept, my self-control – so carefully maintained by the iron grip of consciousness – was banished. I dreamed more nightmarishly than I had done the previous night, and my dreams were pure Poe.

I dreamed that I buried Rowland not in his own house but in that other – that haunted purgatory of fantasy. Our journey to the grave was through rotting passages weeping with cold slime, lit only by smoky torches whose flames were angry red. I dragged the coffin behind me, supporting only one end, and I think that Rowland somehow spoke to me from dead lips as we went, mocking my slowness.

This was bad enough, but after I had immured him in a vault behind a great metal door I remained anchored to the spot, listening for an eternity, waiting for the sound that I knew would come – the sound of the body risen from its rest, its fingers tapping and scratching at the door.

Inevitably (probably there was no real lapse of time, but simply an aching false consciousness of time passed) the sound began, and taunted my soul with echoes of dread and anguish which reverberated in my being until I felt myself literally driven insane, and howled at myself in the fury of my hallucination: '*Madman! Madman! Madman!*'

Then I woke in a cold sweat, thirsting.

And I heard, outside the door of my chamber, a faint tapping and scratching.

For a moment, I convinced myself that I was still asleep, and struggled manfully to wake. Then I could deny my senses no longer, and knew that the sound was real.

I dragged myself from my bed, feeling very heavy, my body requiring an agony of effort to move at all. I stumbled to the door, and opened it, at first by the merest crack and then – in consequence of what I saw – much wider.

There in the faintly lit corridor, prostrate at my feet, one hand still groping for the door, was what seemed to be a teenage girl.

I knew, of course, that it was not. How many human genes were in it – Magdalen Usher's genes – I could not guess, but I knew that it was but a sham, a phantasm, no more human than the maggots which would soon consume Rowland Usher's body – and one day, no doubt, my own. But still, it was a pitiful creature, and in such a form it could not help but attract my sympathies. I remembered what Rowland had said about their not living long.

Some insect 'adults' are born without digestive systems, unable to feed; they exist only to exchange genes in the physiological ritual of sexual intercourse. These creatures of Rowland's had not even reproductive organs inside them. They existed neither to eat nor to breed, being equipped only with the very minimum of a behavioural repertoire in order to serve their maker's purpose.

They existed to cling and caress, to soothe and be soothed, and that was the entirety of their existence. Like mayflies they were born and they died, innocent and ignorant of time, space and the world at large. Their universe was the House of Usher, and one can only hope that they passed their brief existence in a kind of bliss.

I was awake again now, and though startled and a little appalled, I found no alternative but to pick up the poor creature and carry her to my bed, where I stroked her gently and calmed her (I could no longer think in terms of 'it' once I had touched her).

She died before morning.

Later, I visited the caverns deep underground (but still within the living walls of the growing manse) where the free-living maggots pupated, and saw rank upon rank of grey pupae, shaped like the sarcophagi in which the Egyptians entombed their mummified dead. I watched the hatching of the humanoid ephemerae, and studied them through their brief life cycle – a mere handful of days. They did not, left to themselves, find their way into the upper parts of the house, though when I led one of them – as Rowland Usher often must have done – to my own bedroom, she knew both the way back to the deepest cellars and the way to return to the room, unescorted.

They did not really need me, I found, for it was rare that they hatched out alone. Usually, there were half a dozen alive at any one time, and they could obey their inner drives in fondling one another, achieving their fulfilment easily, comfortably, and by their own standards *naturally*.

When the time eventually came for me to leave Rowland's house, to convey his legacy to the greater world so that his methods and techniques might be employed for the betterment of mankind, I was sorry to leave these ephemerae, because I had grown fond of them, in my fashion. It was in their chamber that I buried Rowland Usher, for it was there that I found the grave of his beloved Magdalen, and I knew that brother and sister would have wished to rest side by side. I left him lightly coffined, as I knew that he would have left her, so that in time his decaying flesh might be absorbed, with hers, by the scavenging cells of the house, to become a part of its extending body, dissipated within it, united in substance if not in spirit.

When I finally came out of the house again, and found myself in the full glare of the tropic sun, I had to wrinkle my nose against the stench of the swamp, for I had become used to breathing clean and sterile air. The sky seemed very blue, its light wild and abandoned, and my eyes ached for the gentle roseate light of bioluminescence.

As the motorboat sped away toward the main stream of the Orinoco I looked back at the astonishing edifice, and saw that in this light its ebon walls gleamed and sparkled like jet, and that its softened shape resembled a Daliesque hand reaching up as though to touch the sun with molten fingers.

It was not ugly at all, but perfectly lovely.

The first House of Usher – that shameful allegory of the disturbed psyche – was burst asunder and swallowed by dark waters. In stark contrast, Rowland's house still stands, soaring proudly above the tattered canopy of the twisted trees. It is still growing, and though it stands today in a noisome swamp there will come a time, I know, when it has purified the lakes and the islands, absorbing their stagnancy into its own vitality.

I was afraid, for a time, that the mysterious canker which was implicit in Rowland Usher's being might in some curious fashion be replicated in his house – perhaps by infection as the house absorbed his mortal remains. I am glad to say, though, that in the ten years since I quit that house it has shown no outward sign of any malady, and I become more confident with every year that passes that it will truly stand the test of time.

In one of the notes which he appended to his data discs Rowland contrasts his own house with Poe's imaginary one, damning the fictitious original as a typical product of the nineteenth-century imagination and its myriad demonic afflictions. His own house, he claims, belongs not just to the twenty-second century but to the third millennium, and he hazards the speculation that its life may not even be confined by a thousand years, but may go on for ever, into that far-off Golden Age when the entire ecosphere of this planet (and who knows how many more) will be subject to the dominion of the mind of man.

We can only hope that his faith will be justified.

LISA GOLDSTEIN

City of Peace

'Hey, Yusef!' Ben said, calling to him from across the room.

Yusef looked up. He had been helping an elderly lady find a seat in the crowded Jerusalem of Gold restaurant and she was in the middle of telling him, once again, how much her feet pained her. He pretended he didn't hear Ben. Ben just wanted to pass along another complaint from the company, probably. He settled the old woman in a chair and looked around for her waiter.

'Hey, Yusef!' Ben said again. 'Over here!'

Yusef signalled to a waiter and pushed his way through the crowded restaurant. He was fine-boned, with black hair as curly as a lamb's and a neatly trimmed black beard. 'Yeah,' he said. 'What's new?'

'See that old lady dressed all in black?' Ben said quietly, nodding along one of the tables to a shadowed spot in the corner. 'The one with the veil? Keep an eye on her. I don't think she's what she seems to be.'

'No?' Yusef said. 'What is she?'

'An alien,' Ben said.

Yusef's first thought was that Ben was making some kind of joke at his expense. But Ben seemed uncharacteristically serious. And Yusef, like everyone else, had seen the pictures on television, the aliens addressing the crowded session of the United Nations. He remembered the small figure standing at the podium, saying in a deep voice, 'We come in peace,' and how the roar of applause had cut off the rest of the sentence.

'Why do you think so?' Yusef said.

'Come on,' Ben said. 'How many unchaperoned Arab women do you see wandering around the city? And how many of them take tour buses, for God's sake?'

'Maybe,' Yusef said slowly.

'No maybe about it,' Ben said. 'She, or he, or whatever, she said "Shalom" when she got on the bus, and her voice was about an octave deeper than mine.'

'Did she say anything else?' Yusef said.

22

'No,' Ben said. 'She sat at the very back, by the window. I tell you, keep an eye on her.'

'But why would an alien want to tour Jerusalem?'

'To see what's going on here,' Ben said. 'Maybe to help us out. I don't know.'

To help us out, Yusef thought. We come in peace. They had been speaking in Hebrew because Ben insisted on it, even though Yusef, who had been born in the West Bank, spoke better Hebrew than Ben. Ben had come to Israel from the United States last year. A few months ago Ben had come up to Yusef and told him that his last name was no longer Goldberg but Har-zahav, 'gold mountain' translated into Hebrew. 'This is where I belong,' Ben had said.

'Anyone else I should watch out for?' Yusef asked. He and Ben traded busloads at lunch. Ben had started in West Jerusalem and had already driven his group past the Hebrew University and the Knesset to the Jaffa Gate. They had got out at the gate and he had led them along the cobbled streets of Old Jerusalem to the Wailing Wall. After a long stop at the Wall, the high point of his tour, he had taken the tourists to the restaurant. In the afternoon Yusef would take Ben's group to the Dome of the Rock and the Via Dolorosa while Ben would retrace his steps with Yusef's tourists. They were forbidden to take their charges anywhere else for lunch; Yusef was sure the company got a large kickback from the restaurant.

'Not really,' Ben said. 'How about your group?'

'A bunch of loud kids,' Yusef said. 'Their parents want them to learn something but they don't care about that. Every time we stop they ask the soldiers for a bullet for a souvenir.'

Ben grinned. 'I can handle that,' he said. He looked at his watch. 'Time to get moving.'

'Hey, listen up!' Ben said loudly in English. Conversation slowly stopped. The few tourists still eating put down their knives and forks. 'After lunch, in about ten minutes, we'll start the tour again. Remember when we told you to memorize the number of your bus? You didn't do that, did you?' He grinned at the tourists lazily, and most of them laughed back. It was the same joke he had used the last ten times, but he made it sound fresh. 'Well, it doesn't really matter. Those of you who came with me go with my friend Yusef here in the afternoon. And those of you who came with Yusef have the great good fortune of being shown around by me this afternoon. We'll assemble outside the restaurant in ten minutes. See you then.'

Yusef went out into the hot sunlight and waited by the restaurant.

In a few minutes the tourists began coming outside, blinking as
their eyes got used to the light. A middle-aged couple walked up
to Yusef and the woman smiled at him uncertainly. 'Shalom,' she
said. Her husband looked tired. 'Is this where we meet? Are you
Yusef?'

'Shalom,' Yusef said. 'Yes, I am.'

More people came out of the restaurant and Yusef looked them
over as they slowly assembled in front of him. A young woman
wearing a T-shirt that read, 'Jerusalem – They Shall Prosper That
Love Thee,' with the word 'love' represented by a small red heart.
A scowling young man with a beard. Three fashionably dressed
women giggling together, one of whom, Yusef saw, wore screens
on her cheeks and the backs of her hands. The screens flashed
exploding and coalescing pictures, news in English and Hebrew,
advertisements, famous and unknown faces which appeared suddenly and then vanished down to pinpricks. A man and a boy
around eight years old joined them. The group looked like mostly
American Jews and that was good, because if the tour ran late they
could skip a few of the stations of the Cross. He counted the crowd:
thirty-nine. Someone was missing.

Ben called to him to say goodbye. 'Regards to your mother!' he
said. One of the first things Ben had learned in Jerusalem had been
Arabic swear words, and he had found it funny that so many of
them were about mothers.

When Yusef looked back at his group he saw a small woman in
a black dress hurry out of the restaurant. A veil covered the lower
half of her face, and a black headdress jutted over her forehead,
shadowing her eyes. There was something strange about the figure,
Yusef thought, but maybe it was just that, as Ben had said, he had
never seen a veiled Arab woman by herself. She was about the same
height as the aliens on television, a little under five feet. 'Good afternoon,' he said in English as she joined the group, having decided
that both Arabic and Hebrew were too risky. He felt disappointed
when she didn't answer.

He counted the crowd again: forty, good. 'Good afternoon,' he
said in English. 'My name is Yusef, and I'll be taking you around
for the rest of the day, until approximately four o'clock. Does anyone have any questions so far?'

'Yeah,' the eight-year-old boy said.

'Davey,' his father said. 'Shush.'

Wonderful, Yusef thought. Ben forgot to tell me about this
kid.

'We were wondering,' Davey said, undeterred, 'how come the

buses still use gasoline. How come they're not like the cars in America.'

'Well, we're not as advanced as the United States,' Yusef said. 'Sooner or later we'll have those kinds of buses too.'

'But the tanks here don't use gasoline,' Davey said. 'We saw them.'

'Davey!' the father said. 'That's enough!'

'But why?' Davey said.

'Because he's an Arab,' the father said. 'He doesn't want to hear about Israeli tanks.'

'But why?' Davey said, whining on the last word.

'Because I say so, that's why,' the father said. 'Now be quiet.'

Everyone was silent, an embarrassed silence, Yusef thought. What would Ben do? 'Okay,' he said. 'I'm going to be taking you to the Dome of the Rock and then to the Via Dolorosa, and if we have time we'll stop at the Church of the Holy Sepulchre. As I'm sure Ben told you this morning, Jerusalem is unique in that it is sacred to three faiths, Jewish, Christian and Muslim.' He began moving down the street, checking over his shoulder occasionally to make sure that they were following him. They passed tourists, beggars, merchants, Orthodox Jews with their fur hats and beards, Arab children. The small woman kept to the middle of the group, almost hidden by the press of people. He stopped at the Gate of the Moroccans, the entrance to the Temple Mount.

'The Dome of the Rock is sometimes called a mosque, but that is incorrect,' he said, facing the tourists and making sure that all of them had caught up. 'It is the third holiest shrine to the Muslims, after Mecca and Medina, because it contains the Moriah rock. The Muslims think this rock marks the spot where Mohammed ascended into the seven heavens on the horse Burak. Jews think Abraham was ordered to sacrifice Isaac here.'

They went through the gate into the open plaza of the Temple Mount, past tourists walking in groups of three and four. Yusef knew that some of these people would come over to listen as he explained the building to his charges. He led them up a small flight of steps to the façade and stopped, letting them become gradually overwhelmed by the huge walls, the ornate geometrical shapes of the coloured tiles, blue and white, green and red.

'The Dome of the Rock was built in the seventh century,' he said. 'Sultan Suleiman added these tiles which you see before you in the sixteenth century. The golden dome at the top was restored in the years 1958 through 1964.'

They looked up, predictably, to see the dome, but it was not visible so close to the façade. 'Any questions?' he asked.

The woman wearing the screens put her hand up to the façade. He liked the contrast between her bright flashing pictures and the colours of the tiles.

'Isn't this the place where Solomon's Temple stood?' the bearded man asked.

Did he sound hostile? 'Yes, it is,' Yusef said. 'The Wailing Wall, which you saw this morning, forms part of the western wall of the Temple Mount. That was part of the Second Temple, built by Herod on the site of the Temple of Solomon.'

He led them into the Dome of the Rock. The woman in black stayed in the centre of the group. For a moment he was tempted to change the afternoon's itinerary completely, to take the tourists to the neighbouring El Aqsa Mosque. If she was really a religious Muslim woman she could only go into the women's prayer rooms, not into the mosque itself. And she would have to wash her hands and feet before entering. He wondered what an alien's feet would look like. A shiver, half of horror and half of eager curiosity, went through him.

He said nothing in the quiet of the Dome of the Rock, letting the cavernous, elaborately decorated room speak for itself. His charges wandered around, looking at marble arches and stained-glass windows, Byzantine mosaics and lush Persian carpets. Even Davey was silent. The tired middle-aged man was tilting his head way back in order to see the sinuous red and gold designs of the cupola.

After half an hour he began to round up his group. 'Any questions?' he said again, once they were all together on the plaza.

'What's that other dome over there?' the woman in the T-shirt asked, and he began his standard talk about the silver El Aqsa Mosque, the moon to the Dome's golden sun. He had said the words so many times he did not need to think about them, and he was free to concentrate on the woman in black. Was she an alien? She had done nothing out of the ordinary, but for some reason he was starting to think Ben was right.

After a few more questions he led them out of the Temple Mount through Bab el Atim, one of the northern gates. 'We are going to go to the Via Dolorosa, the path that Jesus took to his crucifixion,' he said. 'Is anyone feeling tired?' He looked closely at his charges, especially at the middle-aged man and the veiled woman, but they all shook their heads. 'Okay,' he said. 'It's not a long way, but we can stop if we must.'

They started down the street. The middle-aged woman walked

next to him and he turned to look for her husband, who was lagging in the back. 'This is wonderful,' she said, smiling at him. 'I never thought I'd ever get to Jerusalem. All that history – it seems like every square foot has a story behind it.'

'Yes, it does,' he said.

'It was closed to the Jews for years, when the Jordanians occupied it,' she said. 'Oh, but I'm sure you know that. I'm being stupid.'

He smiled at her, encouraging her to go on. Maybe if he was friendly enough she would say something favourable about him to the company. He could certainly use it.

'So I guess at the back of my mind I thought I'd never be able to see it,' she said. 'But then when my husband retired and asked me where I wanted to go for our vacation I realized there was nothing to stop us. It's been open for decades.'

He nodded.

'Do you ever stop being amazed by it?' she said.

'No,' he said, warming to her a little. At twilight, when the stones reflected back the soft light and seemed to shine, he could imagine Jerusalem as the centre of the world, a just city, a city of God. A city of light. He would not have thought the woman capable of such feeling.

'I felt it the most at the Wailing Wall,' she said. 'I just stood there and cried. I made a fool of myself, probably, but I couldn't help it. I thought of all those Jews wandering the world for two thousand years, and finally being gathered back here, to the Temple. And in my lifetime. It's amazing.'

He said nothing. He had seen this display of emotion from other tourists, American Jews mostly, and he did not doubt that it was genuine. But this is my place too, he thought. This is my country. My family has lived here for thousands of years. It seemed to him that the feeling of Jews and Arabs for the land had been weighed in some ultimate scale, and that the Arabs had been found somehow wanting. But I love it here too, he thought.

They had to turn left and he was saved from having to answer. It was after two o'clock and very hot. The screens on the woman's hands flashed the temperature in Celsius: thirty-two degrees. A few of the tourists, though not the woman next to him, were panting slightly.

He led them down Lion Gate Street as it turned into the Via Dolorosa, pointing out the stations of the Cross and the Ecce Homo Arch. They turned left onto King Solomon Street after the third station – 'Here Jesus fell for the first time,' he said – and right at the fourth: 'This is where Jesus met his mother Mary.' At the sixth station they crossed a crowded bazaar street. Vendors called to them, trying to sell them soft drinks, purses, postcards, religious articles. He managed to keep his group together, making a detour around two tourists haggling with an Arab merchant over the price of a wooden table inlaid with mother-of-pearl. As he approached the seventh station he looked at his watch. It was getting late, nearly three o'clock, and they would probably want to see the Church of the Holy Sepulchre, to arrive at some destination after their long walk in the hot sun. He would have to skip the side streets to the eighth and ninth stations and go straight to the last five stations at the church.

He stopped too quickly for his group and they continued on a little way without him. 'Just a minute!' he said, calling to them. 'Everyone, stay with me!' Something hit him hard and he nearly fell. He looked around. The woman in black had stumbled against him. He reached out automatically to steady her and nearly jerked away when his hand closed around her arm. She was hard, rock hard. And she had to weigh about twice what he did to have knocked him off balance the way she had. 'Are you – are you all right?' he said automatically.

She nodded, backing away from him.

'I didn't hurt you, did I?' he said, trying to see past the headdress to her eyes.

She shook her head and moved toward the centre of the group. Why didn't she speak? He wanted to hear that deep voice, the voice that had been played over and over around the world: 'We come in peace.'

'Okay,' he said, shaken. 'Okay,' he said more loudly to his group. 'We don't have time to see the eighth and ninth stations of the Cross. We'll turn left here and continue on to the church.'

No one seemed too disappointed. Anyway they were crazy to think that Jerusalem would yield all her secrets to them in just one day. If they wanted to see more they could always come back.

They started down the street. The middle-aged woman was next to him again. 'You speak English very well,' she said. 'Where did you learn it?'

'Thank you,' he said. He was too proud to tell her that when he had started as a tour guide he used to refer to the crucifixion as 'when Jesus was crossed'. 'At Bir Zeit University, mostly.'

'How long did you go there?' she asked.

'Only a year,' he said.

She looked as if she wanted to ask him another question but had finally realized she was being tactless. And he could not tell her that

he had not quit; he had been expelled for taking part in a demonstration. If the company ever found out that he had talked about
his university days to one of his charges he would be disciplined
for trying to sneak politics into his talks. Once he had told a tourist
who had asked where he was from that he had been born in El
Khalil, and he had been threatened with dismissal by the company
for not calling it Hebron, its Hebrew name. And he was lucky to
have this job. He never tired of walking through Jerusalem. And it
was easier than picking fruit or working in a factory, the only other
things open to him.

The woman was nodding at him. Probably I've just confirmed
her impression that all Arabs are lazy, he thought. We can't even
stay in school long enough to graduate.

She started to say something else but he barely heard her. He
was thinking about his sister Asiyah. She had always been far more
political than he was, and had been the one to persuade him to take
part in the demonstration. He had not seen her since then. Had she
been arrested? Killed? No one could tell him. His mother had died a
few years ago, and he had stayed home with his father after Asiyah
was gone, wanting to speak to him but unable to. Only once did his
father break the silence, to tell him about his mother's death for the
first time.

'The Red Crescent came into town, and the doctors were trying
to get everyone to have a check-up,' his father said. 'I got your
mother to go. Neither one of us had seen a doctor since the
occupation. Well, I was all right, they said, but they said your
mother's blood pressure was far too high. Take it easy, the doctor said. Don't worry so much. And she said – you know how
she was – she said how could she take it easy with her country
occupied and her children never having known freedom . . .' His
father stopped speaking for a long time. Yusef wondered if he had
finished. 'And the doctor said if she didn't relax she would die of a
heart attack. She laughed at him. And then – and then – six months
later she was dead, just like the doctor said. A heart attack.'

Yusef nodded, not knowing what to say. He remembered his
mother as passionate, fiery, screaming at Israeli soldiers as his father
tried to hold her back. Asiyah had taken after her. In almost his very
first memory of his mother he was holding on to her skirts as they
stood by the side of the road, watching without understanding as
she stuck her tongue out at a bus filled with well-dressed people.
The bus had to have been carrying tourists, and when Yusef realized
that, a few months into his job as a tour guide, the irony was not
lost on him.

Staying home in the silent house with his mother and sister gone and only his father for company had felt oppressive, especially since he was no longer taking classes or seeing his friends at the university. He had stuck it out for a few weeks and then drifted to Jerusalem to live with his cousin. By the time his cousin announced his plan to move to the United States and leave the crazy Middle East behind for ever he had fallen in love with Jerusalem as he had once fallen in love with a woman in Hebron, and he knew every arch, every cobbled street, every tunnel and dome and spire. A few weeks later he got the job with the tourist company. He had seen his father only a few times in the intervening years.

He led his group right, past the Church of the Redeemer. A group of women stumbled past them, laughing and nearly falling, the Daughters of Dionysius. All of them had probably been drunk since mid-morning. They were Jerusalem's latest cult, but, Yusef thought, they would certainly not be her last.

They turned right again, into the forecourt of the Church of the Holy Sepulchre. He had a speech about the last five stations of the Cross and the history of the church, but he said nothing and let his charges go on ahead. Like all his tour groups they looked vaguely disappointed, having expected something grander, of the size and majesty of the Dome of the Rock. A few looked at him as if they had questions but he pretended not to see them.

Usually the bad memories stayed buried, beneath his conscious thoughts. It was the woman who had brought them to the surface, the woman with her questions about his past and Bir Zeit University. His despair fed on itself, spiralled in on itself like a whirlpool, until he could barely move. How is my father doing? Where is my sister? What will finally become of us?

The woman in black, the alien, walked in front of him towards the staircase leading to Golgotha. Was there something he could say to her, to him, to change things? But what could he say that would not be perceived by the company as propaganda?

He roused himself. He had better round everyone up or they would get lost among all the tombs and chapels and altars. He led them up the staircase to Golgotha – 'Christians believe that this is the site of the crucifixion' – and into the Rotunda and to the Holy Sepulchre itself. There was not time for anything else. They walked back outside and he counted them silently. Forty, good. 'Any questions?' he asked.

'When was the church built?' someone asked.

Yusef looked at his watch and decided there was enough time for the condensed version of the complex answer. He spoke briefly

about Emperor Constantine, the Byzantines, the Crusaders. 'Anyone else?' he asked.

'Yeah,' Davey said. 'Which one do you believe?'

'What do you mean?' Yusef said. Behind Davey Yusef saw his
father tense slightly, looking ready to clap his hand over Davey's
mouth if necessary.

'Well, we saw the Wailing Wall, and that's for Jews like us,'
Davey said. 'And that Dome thing, that's for the Muslims. And
then we saw the church, and that's for the Christians. So which
one do you go to?'

'You mean what do I worship?' Yusef said. Davey nodded. 'I
worship all of them.' He looked for the little alien and found it
standing as usual in the centre of the group. 'I think Jerusalem
shows us that people who believe in the three religions can live
together without hurting each other. I want to believe very much
that that can happen.' The alien's head was raised. He could not see
the eyes under the headdress, but he thought that it was looking
straight at him. 'In my own city, in Hebron, I knew a man who
had nowhere to live because the bulldozers came and pulled down
his house. But Jerusalem – Jerusalem is a city that tells us that it is
not necessary to act that way, that three religions can live together
in peace. Some people think the name Jerusalem comes from the
Hebrew "Ir Shel Shalom" – City of Peace.'

Davey had lost interest and was turning away. But a few people
were talking among themselves. He had gone too far. Some of
them must know that the Israelis punished suspected terrorists by
bulldozing their houses. The young bearded man raised his hand
and said, 'Do you mean to say – '

'Oh, no!' the middle-aged woman said, looking through her
purse. Everyone turned away from the bearded man to look at
her. 'Oh, darn. I promised Lillian I'd leave her prayer at the Wall.
And here it is, still in my purse. Oh, I'm so stupid.'

'Can you – can you come back tomorrow?' Yusef asked, grateful
for the diversion.

'We're leaving tomorrow morning,' she said. 'This is our last day
in Israel. Oh, Lillian'll be so mad at us.'

'Well, we could – I'll tell you what we'll do,' Yusef said. 'We
could go back to the Wall. It's not very far. And then when we get
back to the bus I'll use the radio to tell the company that we'll be
a little late so they won't worry. What do you think? Would you
mind a little more walking?'

'Oh, thank you!' the woman said. 'That would be wonderful.'
He wondered if she really believed that sticking Lillian's piece of

paper into one of the cracks in the Wall would get the prayer to God faster.

'Okay,' Yusef said. 'Is that okay with everyone? Or does someone have somewhere they have to be?'

Yusef saw people in the group shaking their heads. They had united behind the woman and her mission at the Wall, surely not the craziest quest Jerusalem had seen over the centuries.

'Yes, I do.'

At first Yusef thought a man had spoken. 'I do,' the voice said again, and he realized that it had come from the alien. The voice wasn't an octave lower than Ben's, as Ben had claimed, but it was deep, even for a man. A few people in the group looked at the small figure in black with surprise.

'You – there is somewhere you have to be?' Yusef said.

'Yes,' the alien said.

'It would take us only a half an hour, if we hurried,' Yusef said. 'I know a quick way there.'

'No,' the alien said.

'Well,' Yusef said. He shrugged. 'I am sorry,' he said to the middle-aged woman.

'It's not your fault,' she said. 'Oh, Lillian's going to be so mad.'

Yusef led his charges back toward David Street. He let the crowd pass in front of him until he was walking alone next to the alien. 'Do you – do you need some sort of – of equipment?' he asked.

'What do you mean?' the alien said.

'To breathe,' Yusef said. 'Or to walk. Is that why you have to hurry back?' He was thinking of the aliens he had seen on television, on *Star Trek*, who had needed their own atmosphere to survive.

'No,' the alien said, and turned its head away from him.

No. The word had been spoken with finality, and suddenly Yusef knew that the alien was not going to help him. A race that spanned the stars could only look with indifference at the squabbling millions on Earth. To the alien the woman's request to place her prayer in the cracks of the wall was just another quaint custom, as meaningless to it as everything else they had seen that day.

No, there would be no help forthcoming from the alien, whose promises of peace, Yusef was certain, would prove to be as hollow as those spoken by diplomats on Earth. The people of the West Bank would be dispersed to the ends of the Earth, would become the new Jews, and the irony would be lost on their conquerors. They would wander for thousands of years, strangers in new and hostile lands, and at the end of two thousand years they would come back, ravening, to take the land from whatever unimaginable people held it by then. The Dome of the Rock would lie in ruins, cracked and open to the sky like an observatory. The cycle would begin anew. He saw it all in a second, his people driven to the ends of the inhabited worlds and back by the mills of history, and he wanted to weep.

GREG EGAN

The Cutie

'Why won't you even talk about it?'

Diane rolled away from me and assumed a foetal position. 'We talked about it two weeks ago. Nothing's changed since then, so there's no point, is there?'

We had spent the afternoon with a friend of mine, his wife, and their two-month-old daughter. Now I couldn't close my eyes without seeing again the expression of joy and astonishment on that beautiful child's face, without hearing her peals of innocent laughter, without feeling once again the strange giddiness that I had felt when Rosalie, the mother, had said, 'Of course you can hold her.'

I had hoped that the visit would sway Diane. Instead, while leaving her untouched, it had multiplied a thousandfold my own longing for parenthood, intensifying it into an almost physical pain.

Okay, okay, so it's biologically programmed into us to love babies. So what? You could say the same about 90 per cent of human activity. It's biologically programmed into us to enjoy sexual intercourse, but nobody seems to mind about that, nobody claims they're being tricked by wicked nature into doing what they otherwise would not have done. Eventually someone is going to spell out, step by step, the physiological basis of the pleasure of listening to Bach, but will that make it, suddenly, a 'primitive' response, a biological con job, an experience as empty as the high from a euphoric drug?

'Didn't you feel *anything* when she smiled?'

'Frank, shut up and let me get some sleep.'

'If we have a baby, I'll look after her. I'll take six months off work and look after her.'

'Oh, six months, very generous! And then what?'

'Longer then. I could quit my job for good, if that's what you want.'

'And live on what? I'm not supporting you for the rest of your life! Shit! I suppose you'll want to get married then, won't you?'

'All right, I won't quit my job. We can put her in child care when she's old enough. Why are you so set against it? Millions of people

34

are having children every day, it's such an *ordinary* thing, why do you keep manufacturing all these obstacles?'

'Because *I do not want a child*. Understand? Simple as that.'

I stared up at the dark ceiling for a while, before saying with a not quite even voice, 'I could carry it, you know. It's perfectly safe these days, there've been thousands of successful male pregnancies. They could take the placenta and embryo from you after a couple of weeks, and attach it to the outer wall of my bowel.'

'You're sick.'

'They can even do the fertilization and early development *in vitro*, if necessary. Then all *you'd* have to do is donate the egg.'

'*I don't want a child*. Carried by you, carried by me, adopted, bought, stolen, whatever. Now shut up and let me sleep.'

When I arrived home the next evening, the flat was dark, quiet, and empty. Diane had moved out; the note said she had gone to stay with her sister. It wasn't just the baby thing, of course; everything about me had begun to irritate her lately.

I sat in the kitchen drinking, wondering if there was any way of persuading her to come back. I knew that I was selfish: without a constant, conscious effort, I tended to ignore what other people felt. And I never seemed to be able to sustain that effort for long enough. But I did try, didn't I? What more could she expect?

When I was very drunk, I phoned her sister, who wouldn't even put her on. I hung up, and looked around for something I could break, but then all my energy vanished and I lay down right there on the floor. I tried to cry, but nothing happened, so I went to sleep instead.

The thing about biological drives is, we're so easily able to fool them, so skilled at satisfying our bodies while frustrating the evolutionary reasons for the actions that give us pleasure. Food with no nutritional value can be made to look and taste wonderful. Sex that can't cause pregnancy is every bit as good, regardless. In the past, I suppose a pet was the only way to substitute for a child. That's what I should have done: I should have bought a cat.

A fortnight after Diane left me, I bought the Cutie kit, by EFT from Taiwan. Well, when I say 'from Taiwan' I mean the first three digits of the EFT code symbolized Taiwan; sometimes that means something real, geographically speaking, but usually it doesn't. Most of these small companies have no physical premises; they consist of nothing but a few megabytes of data, manipulated by generic software running on the international trade network. A customer

phones their local node, specifies the company and the product
code, and if their bank balance or their credit rating checks out,
orders are placed with various component manufacturers, shipping
agents and automated assembly firms. The company itself moves
nothing but electrons.

What I really mean is: I bought a cheap copy. A pirate, a clone,
a look-alike, a bootleg version, call it what you will. Of course I felt
a little guilty, and a bit of a miser, but who can afford to pay five
times as much for the genuine, made in El Salvador, USA, product? Yes, it's ripping off the people who developed the product,
who spent all that time and money on R & D, but what do they
expect when they charge so much? Why should I have to pay for
the cocaine habits of a bunch of Californian speculators who had
a lucky hunch ten years ago about a certain biotechnology corpo-
ration? Better that my money goes to some fifteen-year-old trade
hacker in Taiwan or Hong Kong or Manila, who's doing it all so
that his brothers and sisters won't have to screw rich tourists to
stay alive.

See what fine motives I had?

The Cutie has a venerable ancestry. Remember the Cabbage
Patch doll? Birth certificate provided, birth defects optional. The
trouble was, the things just lay there, and lifelike robotics for a doll
are simply too expensive to be practical. Remember the Video Baby?
The computer crib? Perfect realism, so long as you didn't want to
reach through the glass and cuddle the child.

Of course I didn't want a Cutie! I wanted a real child! But how? I
was thirty-four years old, at the end of one more failed relationship.
What were my choices?

I could start searching again for a woman who (a) wanted to have
children, (b) hadn't yet done so, and (c) could tolerate living with a
shit like me for more than a couple of years.

I could try to ignore or suppress my unreasonable desire to be a
father. Intellectually (whatever that means) I had no need for a child;
indeed, I could easily think of half a dozen impeccable arguments
against accepting such a burden. But (to anthropomorphize shame-
lessly) it was as if the force that had previously led me to engage in
copious sex had finally cottoned on about birth control, and so had
cunningly decided to shift my attention one link down the flawed
causal chain. As an adolescent dreams endlessly of sex, so I dreamed
endlessly of fatherhood.

Or –

Oh! The blessings of technology! There's nothing like a third
option to create the illusion of freedom of choice!

– I could buy a Cutie.

Because Cuties are not legally human, the whole process of giving birth to one, whatever your gender, is simplified immensely. Lawyers are superfluous, not a single bureaucrat needs to be informed. No wonder they're so popular, when the contracts for adoption or surrogacy or even IVF with donor gametes all run to hundreds of pages, and when the child-related clauses in interspouse legal agreements require more negotiations than missile-ban treaties.

The controlling software was downloaded into my terminal the moment my account was debited; the kit itself arrived a month later. That gave me plenty of time to choose the precise appearance I wanted, by playing with the simulation graphics. Blue eyes, wispy blonde hair, chubby, dimpled limbs, a snub nose . . . oh, what a stereotyped little cherub we built, the program and I. I chose a 'girl', because I had always wanted a girl, though Cuties don't live long enough for gender to make much of a difference. At the age of four they suddenly, quietly, pass away. The death of the little one is so tragic, so heart-breaking, so *cathartic*. You can put them in their satin-padded coffins, still wearing their fourth-birthday party clothes, and kiss them goodnight one last time before they're beamed up to Cutie heaven.

Of course it was revolting, I *knew* it was obscene, I cringed and squirmed inside at the utter sickness of what I was doing. But it was *possible*, and I find the possible so hard to resist. What's more, it was legal, it was simple, it was even cheap. So I went ahead, step by step, watching myself, fascinated, wondering when I'd change my mind, when I'd come to my senses and call it all off.

Although Cuties originate from human germ cells, the DNA is manipulated extensively before fertilization takes place. By changing the gene that codes for one of the proteins used to build the walls of red blood cells, and by arranging for the pineal, adrenal and thyroid glands (triple backup to leave no chance of failure) to secrete, at the critical age, an enzyme that rips the altered protein apart, infant death is guaranteed. By extreme mutilation of the genes controlling embryonic brain development, subhuman intelligence (and hence their subhuman legal status) is guaranteed. Cuties can smile and coo, gurgle and giggle and babble and dribble, cry and kick and moan, but at their peak they're far stupider than the average puppy. Monkeys easily put them to shame, *goldfish* out-perform them in certain (carefully chosen) intelligence tests. They never learn to walk properly or to feed themselves unaided. Understanding speech, let alone using it, is out of the question.

In short, Cuties are perfect for people who want all the heart-melting charms of a baby, but who do *not* want the prospect of surly six-year-olds, rebellious teenagers, or middle-aged vultures who'll sit by their parents' death beds, thinking of nothing but the reading of the will.

Pirate copy or not, the process was certainly streamlined: all I had to do was hook up the Black Box to my terminal, switch it on, leave it running for a few days while various enzymes and utility-viruses were tailor-made, then ejaculate into tube A.

Tube A featured a convincingly pseudo-vaginal design and realistically scented inner coating, but I have to confess that despite my lack of conceptual difficulties with this stage, it took me a ludicrous forty minutes to complete it. No matter who I remembered, no matter what I imagined, some part of my brain kept exercising a power of veto. But I read somewhere that a clever researcher has discovered that dogs with their brains removed can still go through the mechanics of copulation; the spinal cord, evidently, is all that's required. Well, in the end my spinal cord came good, and the terminal flashed up a sarcastic WELL DONE! I should have put my fist through it. I should have chopped up the Black Box with an axe and run around the room screaming nonsense poems. I should have bought a cat. It's good to have things to regret, though, isn't it? I'm sure it's an essential part of being human.

Three days later, I had to lie beside the Black Box and let it place a fierce claw on my belly. Impregnation was painless, though, despite the threatening appearance of the robot appendage; a patch of skin and muscle was locally anaesthetized, and then a quickly plunging needle delivered a pre-packaged biological complex, shielded by a chorion specially designed for the abnormal environment of my abdominal cavity.

And it was done. I was pregnant.

After a few weeks of pregnancy, all my doubts, all my distaste, seemed to vanish. Nothing in the world could have been more beautiful, more *right*, than what I was doing. Every day, I summoned up the simulated foetus on my terminal – the graphics were stunning; perhaps not totally realistic, but definitely *cute*, and that was what I'd paid for, after all – then put my hand against my abdomen and thought deep thoughts about the magic of life.

Every month I went to a clinic for ultrasound scans, but I declined the battery of genetic tests on offer; no need for *me* to discard an embryo with the wrong gender or unsatisfactory eye colour, since I'd dealt with those requirements at the start.

I told no one but strangers what I was doing; I had changed doctors for the occasion, and I had arranged to take leave once I started to 'show' too severely (up until then I managed to get by with jokes about 'too many beers'). Towards the end I began to be stared at, in shops and on the street, but I had chosen a low birthweight, and nobody could have known for sure that I wasn't merely obese. (In fact, on the advice of the instruction manual, I'd intentionally put on fat before the pregnancy; evidently it's a useful way to guarantee energy for the developing foetus.) And if any one who saw me guessed the truth, so what? After all, I wasn't committing a crime.

During the day, once I was off work, I watched television and read books on child care, and arranged and rearranged the cot and toys in the corner of my room. I'm not sure when I chose the name: Angel. I never changed my mind about it, though. I carved it into the side of the cot with a knife, pretending that the plastic was the wood of a cherry tree. I contemplated having it tattooed upon my shoulder, but then that seemed inappropriate, between father and daughter. I said it aloud in the empty flat, long after my excuse about 'trying out the sound' was used up; I picked up the phone every now and then, and said, 'Can you be quiet, please! Angel is trying to sleep!'

Let's not split hairs. I was out of my skull. I knew I was out of my skull. I blamed it, with wonderful vagueness, on 'hormonal effects' resulting from placental secretions into my bloodstream. Sure, pregnant women didn't go crazy, but they were better designed, biochemically as well as anatomically, for what I was doing. The bundle of joy in my abdomen was sending out all kinds of chemical messages to what it thought was a female body, so was it any wonder that I went a little strange?

Of course there were more mundane effects as well. Morning sickness (in fact, nausea at all hours of the day and night). A heightened sense of smell, and sometimes a distracting hypersensitivity of the skin. Pressure on the bladder, swollen calves. Not to mention the simple, inevitable, exhausting unwieldiness of a body that was not just heavier, but had been reshaped in about the most awkward way I could imagine. I told myself many times that I was learning an invaluable lesson, that by experiencing this state, this process, so familiar to so many women but unknown to all but a handful of men, I would surely be transformed into a better, wiser person.

The night before I checked into hospital for the Caesarian, I had a dream. I dreamed that the baby emerged, not from me, but from the Black Box. It was covered in dark fur and had a tail and huge, lemurlike eyes. It was more beautiful than I had imagined possible.

I couldn't decide, at first, if it was most like a young monkey or a kitten, because sometimes it walked on all fours like a cat, sometimes it crouched like a monkey, and the tail seemed equally suited to either. Eventually, though, I recalled that kittens were born with their eyes closed, so a monkey was what it had to be.

It darted around the room, then hid beneath my bed. I reached under to drag it out, then found that all I had in my hands was an old pair of pyjamas.

I was woken by an overwhelming need to urinate.

The hospital staff dealt with me without a single joke; well, I suppose I was paying enough not to be mocked. I had a private room (as far from the maternity ward as possible). Ten years ago, perhaps, my story would have been leaked to the media, and cameramen and reporters would have set up camp outside my door. But the birth of a Cutie, even to a single father, was, thankfully, no longer news. Some hundred thousand Cuties had already lived and died, so I was no trail-blazing pioneer; no paper would offer me ten years' wages for the BIZARRE AND SHOCKING story of my life, no TV stations would bid for the right to zoom in on my tears at the prime-time funeral of my sweet, subhuman child. The permutations of reproductive technology had been milked dry of controversy; researchers would have to come up with a quantum leap in strangeness if they wanted to regain the front page. No doubt they were working on it.

The whole thing was done under general anaesthetic. I woke with a headache like a hammer blow and a taste in my mouth as if I had thrown up rotten cheese. The first time I moved without thinking of my stitches; it was the last time I made *that* mistake.

I managed to raise my head.

She was lying on her back in the middle of a cot, which now looked as big as a football field. Wrinkled and pink just like any other baby, her face screwed up, her eyes shut, taking a breath, then howling, then another breath, another howl, as if screaming were every bit as natural as breathing. She had thick dark hair (the program had said she would, and that it would soon fall out and grow back fair). I climbed to my feet, ignoring the throbbing in my head, and leaned over the wall of the cot to place one finger gently on her cheek. She didn't stop howling, but she opened her eyes, and, yes, they were blue.

'Daddy loves you,' I said. 'Daddy loves his Angel.' She closed her eyes, took an extra-deep breath, then screamed. I reached down and, with terror, with dizzying joy, with infinite precision in every movement, with microscopic care, I lifted her up to my shoulder and held her there for a long, long time.

Two days later they sent us home.

Everything *worked*. She didn't stop breathing. She drank from the bottle, she wet herself and soiled her nappies, she cried for hours, and sometimes she even slept.

Somehow I managed to stop thinking of her as a Cutie. I threw out the Black Box, its task completed. I sat and watched her watch the glittering mobile I had suspended above her cot, I watched her learning to follow movements with her eyes when I set it swinging and twisting and tinkling, I watched her trying to lift her hands towards it, trying to lift her whole body towards it, grunting with frustration, but sometimes cooing with enchantment. Then I'd rush up and lean over her and kiss her nose, and make her giggle, and say, again and again, 'Daddy loves you! Yes, I do!'

I quit my job when my holiday entitlement ran out. I had enough saved to live frugally for years, and I couldn't face the prospect of leaving Angel with anybody else. I took her shopping, and everyone in the supermarket succumbed to her beauty and charm. I ached to show her to my parents, but they would have asked too many questions. I cut myself off from my friends, letting no one into the flat, and refusing all invitations. I didn't need a job, I didn't need friends, I didn't need anyone or anything but Angel.

I was so happy and proud, the first time she reached out and gripped my finger when I waved it in front of her face. She tried to pull it into her mouth. I resisted, teasing her, freeing my finger and moving it far away, then suddenly offering it again. She laughed at this, as if she knew with utter certainty that in the end I would give up the struggle and let her put it briefly to her gummy mouth. And when that happened, and the taste proved uninteresting, she pushed my hand away with surprising strength, giggling all the while.

According to the development schedule, she was *months* ahead, being able to do that at her age. 'You little smartie!' I said, talking much too close to her face. She grabbed my nose, then exploded with glee, kicking the mattress, making a cooing sound I had never heard before, a beautiful, delicate sequence of tones, each note sliding into the next, almost like a kind of birdsong.

I photographed her weekly, filling album after album. I bought her new clothes before she had outgrown the old ones, and new toys before she had even touched the ones I'd bought the week before. 'Travel will broaden your mind,' I said, each time we prepared for an outing. Once she was out of the pram and into the stroller, seated and able to look at more of the world than the sky, her astonishment and curiosity were sources of endless delight for me. A passing dog would have her bouncing with joy, a pigeon on the footpath was cause for vocal celebration, and cars that were too loud earned angry frowns from Angel that left me helpless with laughter, to see her tiny face so expressive of contempt.

It was only when I sat for too long watching her sleeping, listening too closely to her steady breathing, that a whisper in my head would try to remind me of her predetermined death. I shouted it down, silently screaming back nonsense, obscenities, meaningless abuse. Sometimes I would quietly sing or hum a lullaby, and if Angel stirred at the sound I made, I would take that as a sign of victory, as certain proof that the evil voice was lying.

Yet at the very same time, in a sense, I wasn't fooling myself for a minute. I knew she would die when the time came, as one hundred thousand others had died before her. And I knew that the only way to accept *that* was by doublethink, by expecting her death while pretending it would never really come, and by treating her exactly like a real human child, while knowing all along that she was nothing more than an adorable pet. A monkey, a puppy, a goldfish.

Have you ever done something so wrong that it dragged your whole life down into a choking black swamp in a sunless land of nightmares? Have you ever made a choice so foolish that it cancelled out, in one blow, everything good you might ever have done, made void every memory of happiness, made everything in the world that was beautiful, ugly, turned every last trace of self-respect into the certain knowledge that you should never have been born?

I have.

I bought a cheap copy of the Cutie kit.

I should have bought a cat. Cats aren't permitted in my building, but I should have bought one anyway. I've known people with cats, I like cats, cats have strong personalities, a cat would have been a companion I could have given attention and affection to, without fuelling my obsession: if I had tried dressing *it* up in baby clothes and feeding it from a bottle, it would have scratched me to pieces and then shrivelled my dignity with a withering stare of disdain.

I bought Angel a new set of beads one day, an abacuslike arrangement in ten shiny colours, to be suspended above her in her cot. She laughed and clapped as I installed it, her eyes glistening with mischief and delight.

Mischief and delight?

I remembered reading somewhere that a young baby's 'smiles' are really caused by nothing but wind – and I remembered my

annoyance; not with the facts themselves, but with the author, for
feeling obliged smugly to disseminate such a tedious truth. And I
thought, what's this magic thing called 'humanity', anyway? Isn't
half of it, at least, in the eyes of the beholder?

'Mischief? *You?* Never!' I leaned over and kissed her.

She clapped her hands and said, very clearly, 'Daddy!'

All the doctors I've seen are sympathetic, but there's nothing they
can do. The time bomb inside her is too much a part of her. *That*
function the kit performed perfectly.

She's growing smarter day by day, picking up new words all the
time. What should I do?

(a) Deny her stimuli?

(b) Subject her to malnutrition?

(c) Drop her on her head? Or,

(d) None of the above?

Oh, it's all right, I'm a little unstable, but I'm not yet completely
insane: I can still understand the subtle difference between fucking
up her genes and actually assaulting her living, breathing body.
Yes, if I concentrate as hard as I can, I swear I can see the difference.

In fact, I think I'm coping remarkably well: I never break down
in front of Angel. I hide all my anguish until she falls asleep.

Accidents happen. Nobody's perfect. Her death will be quick and
painless. Children die around the world all the time. See? There are
lots of answers, lots of sounds I can make with my lips while I'm
waiting for the urge to pass – the urge to kill us both, right now;
the purely selfish urge to end my own suffering. I won't do it. The
doctors and all their tests might still be wrong. There might still be
a miracle that can save her. I have to keep living, without daring to
hope. And if she does die, then I will follow her.

There's one question, though, to which I'll never know the
answer. It haunts me endlessly, it horrifies me more than my
blackest thoughts of death:

Had she never said a word, would I really have fooled myself into
believing that her death would have been less tragic?

ERIC BROWN

The Time-Lapsed Man

Thorn was not immediately aware of the silence.

As he lay in the tank and watched the crystal cover lift above him, he was still trying to regain some measure of the unification he had attained during the three months in flux. For that long – though it had seemed a timeless period to Thorn – he had mind-pushed his boat between the stars: for that long he had been one with the vastness of the *nada*-continuum.

As always when emerging from flux, Thorn sensed the elusive residuum of the union somewhere within him. As always, he tried to regain it and failed; it diminished like a haunting echo in his mind. Only in three months, on his next shift, would he be able to renew his courtship with the infinite. Until then his conscious life would comprise a series of unfulfilled events; a succession of set pieces featuring an actor whose thoughts were elsewhere. Occasionally he would be allowed intimations of rapture in his dreams, only to have them snatched away upon awakening.

Some Enginemen he knew, in fact the majority of those from the East, subscribed to the belief that in flux they were granted a foretaste of nirvana. Thorn's Western pragmatism denied him this explanation. He favoured a more psychological rationale – though in the immediate period following flux he found it difficult to define exactly a materialistic basis for the ecstasy he had experienced.

He eased himself up and crossed the chamber. It was then that he noticed the absence of sound. He should have been able to hear the dull drone of the auxiliary burners; likewise his footsteps, and his laboured breathing after so long without exercise. He rapped on the bulkhead. He stepped into the shower and turned on the water-jet. He made a sound of pleasure as the hot water needled his tired skin. Yet he heard nothing. The silence was more absolute than any he had experienced before.

He told himself that it was no doubt some side effect of the flux. After more than fifty shifts, a lifetime among the stars, this was his first rehabilitation problem, and he was not unduly worried. He would go for a check-up if his hearing did not return.

He stepped under the blo–drier, donned his uniform and left the

x

chamber. Through the lounge viewscreen he could see the lights of the spaceport. He felt a jarring shudder as the stasis-grid grabbed the ship and brought it down. He missed the familiar diminuendo of the afterburn, the squeal of a hundred tyres on tarmac. The terminal ziggurat hove into sight. The ship eased to a halt. Above the viewscreen a strip light pulsed red, sanctioning disembarkation. It should have been accompanied by a voice welcoming ship personnel back to Earth, but Thorn heard nothing.

As always he was the first to leave the ship. He passed through check-out, offering his card to a succession of bored 'port officials. Normally he might have waited for the others and gone for a drink; there was always a bar open somewhere, even in the early hours. He preferred to spend his free time with other Enginemen, and pilots and mechanics, as if the company of his colleagues might bring him closer to that which he missed most. This time, though, he left the 'port and caught a flyer to the city. He would seek the medical aid he needed in his own time, not at the behest of solicitous colleagues.

He told the driver his destination; unable to hear his own voice, he moved his lips again. The driver nodded, accelerated. The flyer banked between towerpiles, lights flickering by in a mesmerizing rush.

They came down in the forecourt of his stack. Thorn climbed out and took the upchute to his penthouse suite. This was the first time he had arrived home sober in years. Alcohol helped to ease the pain of loss; sober, he was horribly aware of his material possessions, mocking his mortality and his dependence upon them. His suite might have been described as luxurious, but the blatant utility of the furnishings filled him with nausea.

He poured himself a scotch and paused by the piano. He fingered the opening notes of Beethoven's *Pathetique,* then sat down in his recliner by the wall-window and stared out. In the comforting darkness of the room, with the lights of the city arrayed below him, he could make believe he was back aboard his ship, coming in for landing.

Of course, if his hearing never returned . . .

He realized he was sweating at the thought of never being able to flux again. He wondered if he would be able to bluff his way through the next shift . . .

He was on his second drink, twenty minutes later, when a sound startled him. He smiled to himself, raised his glass in a toast to his reflection in the window. He spoke . . . but he could not hear his words.

He heard another sound and his stomach lurched with sickening confusion. He called out . . . in silence. Yet he could hear *something*.

He heard footsteps, and breathing, and then a resounding *clang*. Then he heard the high-pressure hiss of the hot water and an exclamation of pleasure. His own exclamation . . . He heard the roar of the blo-drier, then the rasp of material against his skin; the quick whirr of the sliding door and the diminishing note of the afterburners, cutting out.

Thorn forced himself to say something; to comment and somehow bring an end to this madness. But his voice made no sound. He threw his glass against the wall and it shattered in silence.

Then he was listening to footsteps again; his own footsteps. They passed down the connecting tube from the ship to the terminal building; he heard tired acknowledgements from the 'port officials, then the hubbub of the crowded foyer.

He sat rigid with fright, listening to what by rights he should have heard one hour ago.

He heard the driver's question, then his own voice; he stated his destination in a drunken slur, then repeated himself. He heard the whine of turbos, and later the hatch opening, then more footsteps, the grind of the upchute . . .

There was a silence then. He thought back one hour and realized he had paused for a time on the threshold, looking into the room he called home and feeling sickened. He could just make out the sound of his own breathing, the distant hum of the city.

Then the gentle notes of Beethoven's *Pathetique*.

The rattle of glass on glass.

He remained in the recliner, unable to move, listening to the sound of his time-lapsed breathing, his drinking when he wasn't drinking . . .

Later he heard his delayed exclamation, the explosion of his glass against the wall.

He pushed himself from the recliner and staggered over to the vidscreen. He hesitated, his hand poised above the keyboard. He intended to contact the company medic, but, almost against his will, he found himself tapping out the code he had used so often in the past.

She was a long time answering. He looked at his watch. It was still early, not yet seven. He was about to give up when the screen flared into life. Then he was looking at Caroline Da

Silva, older by five years but just as attractive as he remembered. She stared at him in disbelief, pulling a gown to her throat.

Then her lips moved in obvious anger, but Thorn heard nothing – or, rather, he heard the sound of himself chugging scotch one hour ago.

He feared she might cut the connection. He leaned forwards and mouthed what he hoped were the words: *I need you, Carrie, I'm ill. I can't hear, that is –*

He broke off, unsure how to continue.

Her expression of hostility altered; she still looked guarded, but there was an air of concern about her now as well. Her lips moved, then she remembered herself and used the deaf-facility. She typed: Is your hearing delayed, Max?

He nodded.

She typed: Be at my surgery in one hour.

They stared at each other for a long moment, as if to see who might prove the stronger and switch off first.

Thorn shouted: *What the hell's wrong with me, Carrie? Is it something serious?*

She replied, forgetting to type. Her lips moved, answering his question with silent words.

In panic Thorn yelled: *What the hell do you mean?*

But Caroline had cut the connection.

Thorn returned to his recliner. He reflected that there was a certain justice in the way she had cut him off. Five years ago their final communication had been by vidscreen. Then it had been Thorn who had severed the connection, effectively cutting her out of his life, implying without exactly saying so that she was no match for what he had found in flux.

Caroline's question about the time-lapse suggested that she knew something about his condition. He wondered – presuming his illness was a side effect of the flux – if she was aware of the irony of his appeal for help.

An hour later Thorn boarded a flyer. Drunk and unable to hear his own words, he had taken the precaution of writing the address of the hospital on a card. He passed this to the driver, and as the flyer took off Thorn sank back in his seat.

He closed his eyes.

Aurally, he was in the past now, experiencing the sounds of his life that were already one hour old. He heard himself leave the recliner, cross the room and type the code on the keyboard. After a while he heard the crackle of the screen and Caroline's 'Doctor Da Silva' followed by an indrawn breath of surprise.

'I need you, Carrie. I'm ill. I can't hear. That is – ' Thorn felt ashamed at how pathetic he had sounded.

Then he heard Caroline's spoken reply, more to herself, before she bethought herself to use the keyboard and ask him if his hearing was delayed. 'Black's syndrome,' she had said.

Now, in the flyer, Thorn's stomach lurched. He had no idea what Black's syndrome was, but the sound of it scared him.

Then he heard his one-hour-past self say, 'What the hell's wrong with me, Carrie? Is it something serious?' The words came out slurred, but Caroline had understood.

She answered with words of her own. 'I'm afraid it is serious, Max. Get yourself here in one hour, okay?'

And she had cut the connection.

Caroline Da Silva's surgery was part of a large hospital complex overlooking the bay. Thorn left the flyer in the landing lot and made his way unsteadily to the west wing. The sound of the city, as heard from his apartment, played in his ears.

He moved carefully down interminable corridors. Had he been less apprehensive about what might be wrong with him, and about meeting Caroline again after so long, he might have enjoyed the strange sensation of seeing one thing and hearing another. It was like watching a film with the wrong soundtrack.

He found the door marked 'Dr Da Silva', knocked and stepped inside. Caroline was the first person he saw in the room. For a second he wondered how the flux had managed to lure him away from her, but only for a second. She was very attractive, with the calm elliptical face of a ballerina, the same graceful poise; she was caring and intelligent, too – but the very fact of her physicality told Thorn of the manifest impermanence of all things physical. The flux promised, and delivered, periods of blissful disembodiment.

Only then did Thorn notice the other occupants of the room. He recognized the two men behind the desk. One was his medic at the Line, and the other his commanding officer. Their presence here suggested that all was not well. The way they regarded him, with direct stares devoid of emotion, confirmed this.

A combination of drink, shock and fear eased Thorn into unconsciousness.

He awoke in bed in a white room. To his right a glass door gave onto a balcony, and all he could see beyond was bright blue sky.

On the opposite wall was a rectangular screen, opaque to him but transparent to observers in the next room.

Electrodes covered his head and chest.

He could hear the drone of the flyer's turbos as it carried him towards the hospital. He sat up and called out what he hoped was: *Caroline! . . . Carrie!*

He sank back frustrated. He watched an hour tick by on the wall-clock, listening to the flyer descend and his own footsteps as the Thorn-of-one-hour-ago approached the hospital. He wondered if he was being watched through the one-way window. He felt caged.

He looked through the door into the sky. In the distance he could see a big starship climb on a steep gradient. He heard himself open the surgery door, and Caroline's voice. 'Ah, Max.'

Then – unexpectedly, though he should have been aware of its coming – silence. This was the period during which he was unconscious. He glanced back at the sky, but the starship had phased out and was no longer visible.

Thorn tried not to think about his future.

Caroline arrived thirty minutes later. She carried a sketch pad and a stylus. She sat on a plastic chair beside the bed, the pad on her lap. She tried to cover her concern with smiles, but Thorn was aware of tears recently shed, the evidence of smudged make-up. He had seen it many times before.

How long will I be in here? he asked.

Caroline chewed her lower lip, avoiding his eyes. She began to speak, then stopped herself. Instead, she wrote on the sketch pad and held up the finished product:

A week or two, Max. We want to run a few tests.

Thorn smiled to himself. *What exactly is this Black's syndrome?* he asked, with what he hoped was the right degree of malicious sarcasm.

He was pleased with Caroline's shocked expression.

How do you know that? she scribbled.

Know what?

About Black's syndrome.

You mentioned it over the vidscreen, Thorn told her. *I didn't hear it until I was coming here. Well, what is it, Carrie?*

She paused, then began writing. Thorn read the words upside down: Black – an Engineman on the Taurus line out of Varanasi. After fifty shifts he developed acute sensory time-lapse. It's a one-in-a-thousand malady, Max. We don't know exactly what causes it, but we suspect it's a malfunction in the tank leads that retards interneuron activity.

She paused, then held up the message.

Thorn nodded. *I've read it. So . . .?*

She turned to a blank page, stylus poised.

How long did he last? Thorn asked, bitterly. *When did the poor bastard die?*

Quickly she wrote: He's still alive, Max.

Thorn was surprised and relieved. If the present condition was the extent of Black's syndrome, then what was to prevent him fluxing again?

He wondered at Caroline's tears. If his disease was only this minor why all the upset?

Then he thought he understood.

When can I leave, Carrie? When can I get back to the flux?

He was watching the pad, waiting for a reply. When he looked up he saw that she was crying, openly this time.

He laughed. *You thought you had me, didn't you? Discharged from the Line, your own little invalid to look after and pamper. You can't stand the thought that I'll recover and flux again, can you?*

Despite her tears she was scribbling, covering page after page with rapid, oversized scrawl.

When she came to the end she stabbed a vicious period, ripped the pages out and flung them at him. She ran from the room, skittling her chair on the way. Thorn watched her, a sudden sense of guilt excavating a hollow in his chest.

His gaze dropped to the crumpled pages. He picked them up and read: Acute *sensory* time-lapse. Not just hearing. Everything. In a few days your taste and smell will go the same way. Then your vision. You'll be left only with the sensation of touch in the 'present'. Everything else will be lapsed . . .

It went on like this for a few more pages, the handwriting becoming more and more erratic. Most of it reiterated the few known facts and Caroline's observations of Black's decline. On the last page she had simply written: I loved you, Max.

Thorn smoothed the pages across his lap. He called for Caroline again and again, but if she heard she ignored him. He wanted to apologize, ask what might happen to him. He tried to envisage the sensation of having all his senses time-lapsed save for that of touch, but the task was beyond his powers of perception.

He lay back and closed his eyes. Later he was startled by the sound of his voice, his cruel questions. He heard Caroline's breathless sobs, the squeak of the stylus, a murmured 'I loved you' to accompany the written assurance. He heard her run crying from the room, the chair tumble, the door slam shut.

Then all he could hear was the sound of his breathing, the muffled, routine noises of the hospital. For the first time in hours the sounds he heard were synchronized with what he could see.

He slept.

On the morning of his third day in hospital, Thorn's senses of taste and smell went the way of his hearing. This further time-lapse dashed any hope he might have had that Caroline's diagnosis had been a mistake.

He had not seen Caroline since her hurried departure on the first day. He had been examined and tested by medical staff who went about their business in silence, as if they were aware of his outburst at Caroline and were censoring him for it. On the third morning in hospital, a black nurse brought him his breakfast.

He began eating, and soon realized that he could neither taste nor smell the bacon and eggs, or the coffee, black and no doubt strong.

He finished his meal. He watched the nurse return and remove the tray, sank back and waited.

Two hours later he heard the sound of the trolley being rolled in, the rattle of knife and fork. Seconds later the taste of bacon, then egg yolk, filled his mouth. He inhaled the aroma of the coffee, tasted it on his tongue. He closed his eyes and savoured the sensation. It was the only pleasurable effect of this strange malaise so far.

Then he sat up as something struck him. *Two hours!* The delay between eating the food and tasting it had been two hours. Likewise the sound of the nurse's arrival.

If his hearing, taste and smell became delayed at the rate of two hours every three days – then what would it be like in a week, say, or a month or a year?

And what of his eyesight? How would he cope with seeing something that had occured hours, days, even weeks ago? He resolved to find out what had happened to Black, how he was coping. He sat up and called for Caroline.

She did not show herself for another three days.

Thorn was attended by an efficient platoon of medics. They seemed to rush through their duties around him with a casual indifference as if he ceased to exist, or as if they assumed that his senses had retarded to such an extent that he existed alone in a bubble of isolation. On more than one occasion he had asked whether he could be cured, how much worse it might become, what had happened to Black? But they used the fact that he could not immediately hear them as an excuse to ignore him, avoiding not only his words but his eyes.

On the morning of his sixth day in hospital, he awoke to silence and ate his tasteless breakfast. The sound of his waking, of the hospital coming to life around him, the taste of his breakfast – all these things would come to him later. He wondered if he could time it so that he tasted his breakfast as he ate his lunch?

He waited, and it was four hours later when he tasted toast and marmalade, heard the sounds of his breathing as he awoke.

Later, a nurse removed the electrodes from his head and chest. She opened the door to the balcony and held up a card which read:

Would you like to go out for some air?

Thorn waited until the nurse had left, shrugged into a dressing gown and stepped onto the balcony. He sat down on a chair in the sunlight and stared across the bay, then up into the sky. There was no sign of starship activity today.

He realized that, despite the seriousness of his condition, he still hoped to flux again. Surely the state of his senses would have no detrimental effect on his ability to mind-push? He had already decided that when his condition deteriorated to such an extent that he could no longer function without help, which must surely happen when his sight became affected, he would volunteer for a long-shift. He could push a boat to one of the Rim Worlds, spend a year of ecstasy in flux. It would probably kill him, but the prospect of such rapture and a painless end was preferable to the life he could expect here on Earth.

Caroline appeared on the edge of his vision. She placed a chair next to his and sat down beside him, the sketch pad on her lap. She seemed fresh and composed, the episode of the other day forgotten.

I've been wanting to apologize for what I said, Carrie. I had hoped you'd visit me before now. And he cursed himself for making even his apology sound like an accusation.

Caroline wrote: I've been with Black.

Thorn was suddenly aware of his own heartbeat. *How is he?*

She wrote: Only his sense of touch is now in the 'present'. All his other senses are time-lapsed by nearly a day.

How's he coping?

Not very well. He was never very stable. He's showing signs of psychosis. But you're much stronger, Max –

He interrupted: *What happens when his sense of touch retards?*

Caroline shrugged. It hasn't happened yet. It's difficult to say. In a way, if it does occur, it will be easier for him as all his senses will be synchronized in the 'past'. But he'll be unable to mix with

people, socialize. How could he? Their presence would be delayed
subjectively by hours, days. There would be no way for him to
relate.

He could still flux, Thorn said.

Caroline looked away. For a moment tears burned across her
eyes. Then she scribbled something on the pad:

Is the flux all you think about?

It's my life, Carrie. The only reason I exist.

She shook her head, frustrated by this clumsy means of communication. She wrote out two pages of neat script and passed them
to him.

I could understand you infatuation with the flux if you thought
the experience had religious significance; that you were in touch
with the Afterlife. But you don't even believe that! To you it's just
a drug, a mental orgasm. You're a flux-junkie, Max. When you left
me you were running away from something you couldn't handle
emotionally because you'd never had to in the past. For most of
your life, Max, the flux has provided you with a substitute for
human emotion, both the giving of it and the taking. And look
where it's got you!

Thorn sat without speaking. Some part of him – some distant
buried, human part – was stunned by the accuracy and truth of her
insight.

You just feel sorry for yourself because you didn't get me, he said weakly, trying to defend himself.

Caroline just stared at him. She shook her head. With deliberation she wrote one line. She stood up and tore off the top sheet,
handed it to him and left the balcony.

I'm not sorry for myself, Max. I'm sorry for you.

Thorn pushed the meeting with Caroline to the back of his mind.
In the days that followed he dwelled on the hope that he might one
day be able to flux again. If his sense of touch did retard, then, as
Caroline had suggested, all his senses would be synchronized and
his condition made considerably easier. He might not be able to
socialize, but that would be no great loss. His only desire was to
rejoin the Line.

On his ninth morning in hospital, Thorn opened his eyes and saw
nothing but darkness. He called for the lights to be switched on, but
instead someone spoon-fed him breakfast. He was unable to tell if
it was Caroline who fed him; he could neither see, hear, or even
smell the person. He asked who it was, but the only response – the
only one possible in the circumstances – was a gentle hand on his

arm. After his first breakfast in absolute darkness he lay back and waited.

His sensory delay had expanded to six hours now, and it was that long before the darkness lifted and he was able to see the sunlight slanting into the room. He had the disconcerting experience of lying flat on his back while his gaze of six hours before lifted as the Thorn-of-this-morning sat up and prepared for breakfast. In his vision the black nurse positioned his tray and fed him bacon and eggs. Thorn felt that he could reach out and touch the woman. He tried, and of course his hand encountered nothing.

He had no control over the direction of his gaze; his unseeing eyes of that morning had wandered, and he found himself trying to bring his errant vision back to the nurse, when all he saw was the far wall. His vision was interrupted by frequent, fraction-of-a-second blanks, when he had blinked, and longer stretches of total blackness when he had closed his eyes. The only benefit of this visual delay was that now his sight and hearing, taste and smell were synchronized. He saw the nurse lift a forkful of egg to his mouth, heard the sound of his chewing and tasted the food. The only thing missing was the egg itself; his mouth was empty.

'There we are,' the nurse said, proffering Thorn a last corner of toast. He wanted to tell her to stop treating him like a child, but that was the big disadvantage of his present condition: what he experienced now had happened six hours ago. The Jamaican nurse would be elsewhere in the hospital, the bacon and egg digested, the sounds and aromas dissolved into the ether . . .

Over the next few days he remained awake into the early hours, watching the happenings of the previous day. At four in the morning, then six, darkness would descend, and Thorn would settle down to sleep. Around noon he would wake, spend several hours in darkness, then watch the sun rise eight hours late. If the delay between occurrence and perception continued to increase by two hours every three days, as it was doing, then Thorn foresaw a time when he would be spending more time in darkness than in light.

He would be able to cope. There had been many a long period in the past, between shifts, when he had locked himself in his darkened apartment, with drink and fleeting memories of flux.

After almost two weeks in hospital Thorn began to weaken. He passed through periods of physical nausea and mental confusion. He hallucinated once that he was fluxing again, this time without the usual euphoria of the union.

The day following this hallucination he awoke early and felt the

warmth of sunlight on his skin. Eight hours later he was aware of
the sun coming up over the sea. He would have liked to watch it,
but his eyes of eight hours ago were fixed on the foot of his bed.
The frequency of his 'waking' blinks gave the scene the aspect of an
ancient, flickering movie. At least it wasn't silent: he could hear the
hospital waking around him, the distant crescendo of a starship's
burners.

Later, after someone spoon-fed him a tasteless lunch, he felt a soft
hand on his arm. He moved his head, as if by doing so he might see
who it was. But all he saw was the same old far wall of eight hours
ago; all he heard was his own breathing. He recalled the nurse's
touch but that had been light, platonic, reassuring him like a child
that everything was all right. There was nothing platonic about
this touch. As he lay there, helpless, whoever it was pulled back
the sheets and divested him of hospital garb. He shouted out in
silence, tried to fend her off – 'her' because his flailing arm caught
the softness of a breast. But he could not see the woman and he was
unable to prevent the ludicrous rape. He felt a warm, soft weight
straddle him, her breasts loose against his chest, and the sensation
was what he imagined it might be like to be taken by a succubus.

Caroline? he said. He moved his arms in a clumsy description
of an embrace, touched her familiar warm and slender body. He
was aroused now despite himself. She found him and he moaned
without a sound, ran his fingers through her black invisible hair.
He recognized Caroline's brand of love-making from the past, went
along with it as though they had never parted, and when climax
came it was as he remembered it from many years ago – a brief
ecstasy soon gone, like a second in flux but not as satisfying. Even
the unusual circumstances of the union, the fact that he could not
see Caroline, that the source of his pleasure was as it were disem-
bodied, could only intimate a greater rapture and not fulfil in itself.

The invisible weight of her lay against him now, heavy and sated
after orgasm, which Thorn had experienced through the silent con-
tractions of her body. She kissed him, and he felt salt tears fall on
his face.

Caroline . . . Why . . .?

Her lips moved against his cheek, her breath hot as she formed
words. It was like being kissed by a ghost, bestowed silent
prophecy.

In the calm aftermath of the act, Thorn began to feel revulsion.
The bizarre nature of their love-making sickened him. He felt a
return of the old guilt which he thought he had long since banished.
It was as if the union was a symbol of their relationship to date;

for years Thorn had played at loving someone whose essence was invisible to him, while Caroline for her part had wasted her life chasing someone who was for ever elsewhere.

He cried out now and pushed her from the bed. He felt her fall and almost heard her cry of pain. *Get out, Caroline! Go away!* He faced where he thought she might be, but could not be sure. *I don't want you, for God's sake! All I want –*

She attacked him then. She came at him with painful blows and slaps, and no doubt cries and accusations. Thorn was aware only of the physical violence, the punches that struck from nowhere without warning. And he was aware, too, that he deserved everything he was getting.

He lay on the bed, battered and exhausted. Caroline had ceased her attack. He had no way of knowing whether she was still in the room, but he sensed her continued presence. *I don't know why you came here,* he said. *I don't know what you want from me . . .*

He half expected another hail of blows, and flinched in anticipation. But none came.

When he thought he was alone he dragged the bedsheets around him protectively, lay back and recalled Caroline's tears on his cheeks.

There could only be one explanation for her visit.

Thorn felt himself weaken further during the hours that followed.

He waited with mounting apprehension, his body covered in chill sweat. Visually it was four o'clock in the afternoon, but the real time was around midnight. It seemed a lot longer than the delayed eight hours before Caroline entered his line of sight.

She moved out of it quickly as she came to the side of his bed. She reached out and touched his arm, and Thorn expected to feel her now, but of course her touch had startled him eight hours ago. Then, Thorn had turned his head abruptly, and now he saw Caroline full on. She wore only a white gown and nothing beneath, and she was crying.

He watched as she undressed him, and the sight of her doing this now brought a hot flush of shame and resentment to his cheeks. The sensation of her touch had passed, but as he watched her slip from her gown and climb onto him he experienced a resurgence of the desire that had overwhelmed him eight hours earlier.

The Thorn of now lay still in his bed, like a voyeur in the head of his former self. He was making love to Caroline, but, with his memories of the physical act already eight hours old, he felt as though he was watching a tacky porn-vid. He could see her, frenzied blurs of flesh and hair and tongue; he could smell her, the perfume she used and the sweat of sex that overcame it; and he could hear her small moans of pleasure, her repeated cry of his name as she approached climax.

He heard his slurred question: 'Caroline . . . Why . . . ?'

They had finished their love-making and she lay in his arms. 'Because I loved you, Max,' she had said. 'Because I *still* love you.'

He knew what happened next. Again he experienced that over-whelming sense of revulsion, brought about by guilt. He watched helplessly as he pushed her from the bed. 'Get out, Caroline!' he heard himself cry. 'Get away!' He saw her expression of pain, the acceptance of rejection in her eyes, and had it been possible he would have stopped himself saying what he said next. 'I don't want you, for God's sake! All I want – '

She came at him and hit him again and again.

The Thorn-of-now flinched, as if the blows he could see coming might indeed inflict pain upon him; he raised his arms as if to pro-tect himself.

Caroline backed off and yelled at him.

He heard himself say, 'I don't know why you came here . . . I don't know what you want from me . . .'

Caroline was crying. 'I came because I loved you, Max. I came to say goodbye . . .' She lowered her gaze and murmured, more to herself than to Thorn, 'Black died two days ago . . .'

Eight hours later Thorn lay quite still.

He deteriorated rapidly over the next few days.

The knowledge of Black's death robbed him of any will he might have had to fight. In his final hours he experienced a gradual dimi-nution of his senses. His hearing left him first – then his taste and smell, though he hardly noticed their absence. Later his vision dimmed and went out, and he was aware of himself only as a small, blind intelligence afloat in an infinite ocean.

Soon even the awareness of his physical self diminished, and then the last sense of all, the cerebral intuition of his own identity, left him too. A familiar euphoria flooded him then, and the man who had been Thorn knew, before he died, that he was being absorbed into the vastness of the cosmos he had known until now as the *nada*-continuum.

RACHEL POLLACK

The Bead Woman

There were once five Speakers who discovered a new method
of Speaking. They collected beads of different colours, sizes,
and shapes, each of the women with her own set which she kept
in a bag around her waist. When a client came to them the Speaker
would use a short branch carved into the shape of a dagger to draw
a True Ground around her and the client. Then she would draw a
smaller circle in between the two of them, a Casting Ground as the
Speakers called it, and on this she would lay a silk cloth. The client
would write down the question, the same ones clients always ask:
'Will I get fired if I ask for a raise?' 'Will my son get well?' 'Will my
husband leave his girlfriend and come back to me?'

Then the Speaker would cast her beads three times into the circle,
throwing with the left hand and picking up so fast with the right
that the fingers appeared to flicker. With each cast they saw the
patterns and lines, the faces and roads. Afterwards, rolling the beads
from one hand to another, they would break down the forms and
shapes into answers to the client's questions.

The five Speakers called themselves Bead Women. Their names
were Carla, Marjorie, Sarah, Julia and Beth. Beth was the oldest,
forty-one when she became a Speaker. Yet clients and the other
women, and even Beth herself, often thought of her as the youngest. Sometimes, if she woke up first, with the others surrounding
her, her own life amazed her. She would think she was still living with her husband and her three children. In the moment of
awakening she would think how she had to get up and mix tuna
salad for Sam and the kids. Or she would groan at the ironing
flooding out of the bedroom closet. And then she would feel Carla's
soft upper arm, or else smell the sea, invisible yet filling the house.
And she would sink deeper into the pillow, smiling as she thought
of her beads.

Slowly they became known. A man wished to start a business. One
of the women told him to travel to a certain city on a certain day
and sit in a certain coffee shop, where, if he ordered pastrami on
a brown roll, he would meet a backer for all his ideas. A woman

wished to conceive a child. The Speaker told her to eat a particular sequence of fruits and wear a red scarf around her neck while
receiving artificial insemination at a particular hour.

A man came, seeking to find the greatest hidden master of the
age. Carla cast her beads and as they fell against each other she
understood that an age is a long time, and that the master at that
moment remained truly hidden, coiled in her mother's womb.

An architect came for advice on a new project. The beads spread
out, telling the architect what offerings she could make to summon
a Benign One, a spirit who would guide the design. All those who
would pass outside the building or stand before it waiting for a bus
would hear a whisper in the walls. Those who would live or work
there would breathe more deeply the moment they passed through
the door. And they would know, as they looked out the windows,
or listened to the hiss of the elevators, that every step taken in that
building was a step towards their heart's yearning.

At the age of thirty-six years, three months, and nine days, on the
9th of September, Beth Angel Rosenbloom drove her youngest
child to day camp and her oldest to karate class. Her husband Sam
was in a meeting to discuss funding for archaeological research in
upstate New York. Her middle child had gone canoeing. Beth
drove the car into the driveway, and as she turned off the engine
she heard someone call her name. She looked around, saw no one.
When she walked to the house she heard a whisper with every step
along the flagstone path.

Inside, the whisper became a roar as the whole house began to
speak to her. She picked up her son's plastic spaceman; it told
her of a danger to the orbiting laboratory. She dropped it on the
couch, and the couch told her that Sam's project would bring him
a promotion. As she ran into the kitchen she stubbed her toe against
the vacuum cleaner. It told her of a dust storm in Amarillo, Texas.

Beth slapped her hands against her ears. On one side, she heard
Sam accusing her of desertion. On the other, a group of women
shouted her name. Beth began to cry. When she wiped her eyes
with a tissue, she saw, in the smudges of mascara and eyeliner, a
cluster of beads. A calm filled the house. A single clear note sang
in the walls. Beth Angel lay down on the carpet and fell asleep.

The Bead Women always wore the same clothes, black and white
dresses and red shoes, and on certain days a pale yellow ribbon
wound loosely about the right wrist. In the mornings they would
drink juice together, and at night they would share bowls of

diviner's soup, a thick broth filled with pasta in the shapes of letters and faces.

When they started to become known they bought a two-storey house with separate offices for all of them downstairs, and a large room upstairs where they all slept together in a huge bed hung with beads dangling from silk thread. They would lie there, with their arms across each other's shoulders, and they would dream the same dreams, or almost the same dreams, walking together through a city where all the houses spoke to them, and the streets rippled with laughter.

In the evening, before dinner, they would walk to a rock beach near their house. There they would cast their beads among the pebbles as the waves rolled up over their feet. Before work each day they would speak their names together, then cast their beads onto a gold cloth. Once a week, after all the clients had gone and they had done an offering to cleanse the house of leftover questions, they would empty their pouches (silk for Carla and Beth, snakeskin for Majorie, velvet for Sarah and Julia) and cast their beads into a copper bowl. They would tie violet scarves over each other's eyes, and then one by one shake the dish. As the beads flung together, they felt their memories shake loose. They became entwined, so that Carla shivered from a damp bedroom in Beth's hometown, and Julia's feet tapped to a tune from Marjorie's senior prom, while Sarah wept over the death of Carla's dog. Then they would reach into the bowl and each woman would find her own beads, returning them to their pouches one by one, so that piece by piece, the memories clicked back into place. On these nights they lay more closely, packed together like the parts of a single animal, gently breathing in the centre of the bed.

Beth enrolled in the State University of Oracles and Diviners. She learned to throw dice onto a blue cloth. She learned to heat up an iron rod and touch it to the shell of a dead tortoise. She learned to watch the patterns of birds scattered by bicycles in a city park. She learned to sing poems to lines of sea shells thrown onto grass. With every lesson Beth's teachers grew more suspicious at her lacklustre predictions. Beth herself found it harder and harder to shake off panic. Had she given up her family in order to memorize lists of formulas? Did she really care if someone would 'meet a tall man with black hair who will give you a present and then ask for it back again'? And when the class all stared at the surface of a pond on the back campus, and the others described lions and flowers, Beth saw only the ripples of the wind.

At the end of her second year she went to her adviser and told him she thought she had made a mistake. He agreed without stopping to cast his stones or coins, or turn over a single card. In her dorm room (where she had always felt uncomfortable at the age difference between herself and the other students) Beth packed her books and clothes. When she had finished she left a note promising to come for everything within a few days. She left carrying a nylon bag.

At the campus gates, Beth stood looking back at the students walking to class. They held books or kits under their arms; many had masks hanging loosely round their necks. One of her professors walked by, a bird specialist. Beth could just about count the lines of initiation crisscrossing his face as he stopped to investigate some tracks near the university's miniature stone circle. She raised an arm to say goodbye, but then he walked off without seeing her.

I've got no life left, Beth thought. Nothing. I threw away the only life I ever had. I just threw it away. For nothing.

A woman came to Julia. The woman's daughter was three years old and had never spoken. Was there something wrong with her? Had a spirit being, a Malignant One, seized her tongue or frozen the speech lobes in the cortex? Could she take her to some special healer (she had tried so many)? In a dream she had seen the face of the great Story Teller, Maryanna Split Sky, but she didn't know what that meant.

Julia cast her beads, once, twice, again, seeing the lines overlap, the colours as precise as tiny flashes of light. She told the woman to take the child to the skull parade in New York City on Founders' Day, the last Thursday in November. 'Go early,' Julia instructed her. 'Get a place on the edge of the sidewalk at the corner of 5th Avenue and 58th Street, in front of the toy store.' The client must wait until the papier-mâché head of Split Sky dipped down on its long metal pole. The head would bob right above the child, and at that moment the mother must clap her hands three times and say, 'Return the voice of my daughter.' Immediately, Julia said, a clown would break open the head with a silver baseball bat. Peppermints and chocolates would shower the children. She must make sure her daughter got a peppermint. As soon as the little girl had bitten into the peppermint she would begin to talk.

Hardly able to talk herself, the client kissed Julia and made a hand sign over the Speaker's head, a gesture that formed the blessing, 'Walk in the voices of our Mothers all the days of your life'. The woman was about to leave when something touched Julia. She called the woman back. Once again she cast her beads. 'Your daughter,' she said, 'will become a swindler – ' The woman gasped. 'Or – or a Story Teller.' She looked up and the two of them stared at each other in surprise.

'Can I do something?' the woman asked. 'To make her a Teller?' Julia threw the beads once more. They rattled together, broke apart. She told the woman to save the candy wrapper, bury it behind the house, and exactly one year later, dig it up, cut it into pieces, and serve it with her daughter's dinner, mixed into a pumpkin pie.

Beth walked down a flight of stairs to the train station at the foot of the hill. The station was small, with wooden arches, a favourite of industrial archaeologists. Usually, only students used it, waving their blue diviner's scarves to flag down the train. Today, however, a woman a little younger than Beth sat on the faded bench. She wore a black vinyl coat with a pink lining of fake fur. Her hair was short in back, long in front, so that it fell down over one eye. She sat there, looking past the tracks and the river, past the buildings on the other side, to the brown cliffs lit by the sun. And she cried. Ignoring Beth, she wept in a shivering voice.

Beth put down her bag. She stood looking the other way, down the track, as if the train was coming. A minute later she turned around. 'What's wrong?' she asked the woman.

The crying continued. Beth wondered if she should speak louder, or just walk away. Behind them, footsteps sounded on the stairs. The woman said, 'My girlfriend left me. She said she'd come back but she won't. I know it. I know it.' She turned to stare up at Beth. 'Is she going to come back? Is she? She said she would. She promised.'

'I don't know,' Beth whispered. She said it so softly she was sure the woman hadn't heard. 'I'm sorry, I just don't know.'

Word of the casting came to the New York College of Story Tellers. Now, Tellers have always despised Speakers. And a child's Call to become a Teller belonged legally to the Mystery of the Voice, not to be interfered with by ordinary citizens. Soon an injunction came, ordering the Bead Women, all of them, not just Julia, to show cause why they had not overstepped their legal boundaries.

The women prayed and gave blood offerings on the beach just before sunset. They pricked their fingers with silver needles, then waved them at the water so that the drops of blood turned pink in the foam. When they cast their beads among the rocks the patterns only reminded them of the Speakers' motto, 'Fly with the morning, sit with the night'. Wait, the beads were telling them. When the time comes, you will do what needs to be done.

The next day a small group of people stood outside the New York College of Story Tellers' administrative offices on Madison Avenue. They wore indigo blindfolds and they held hands, and around each of their necks hung a black bead. The next day more people arrived, and soon a circle of blindfolded men and women had surrounded the building. No one spoke. If a Teller or a visitor wished to leave or enter they dropped their hands, then re-formed the chain as soon as the outsider had passed.

Soon the press arrived, and the television cameras. Though no one in the circle spoke, the reporters found out about the injunction. They travelled to the Bead Women. They interviewed Julia and the others. They photographed them kneeling on the beach in their black and white dresses. Black beads and indigo scarves began to appear in spiritual supply shops. Student organizations declared bead days on campuses. When the word came that the court had lifted the injunction the people on Madison Avenue removed their blindfolds, hugged each other, and then left without ever saying a word. The women never found out who they were.

There were two of them and they came down the stairs in step, side by side, one in a long grey coat, the other in a leather jacket. They walked right past Beth to crouch down before the crying woman. 'Are you Alice?' one of them said. The woman nodded, and then the three went off together to the end of the platform. Beth walked as close as she dared. She saw the one in grey mark a circle with a stick from inside her coat. She saw the other one lay down a cloth. And then they all bent down with their backs to her.

Beth had never been pushy. Her mother had taught her never to annoy people, a policy she had broken only once in her life, when she left her family to enroll in the university. But now she stood over them, as if she was part of a crowd watching three-card monte on Fifth Avenue. When they untied their bags from around their waists Beth started to shake. When the beads slid into their hands her whole body drenched itself in sweat.

At the moment that they cast their beads onto the silk, Beth Angel Rosenbloom heard again that single note that had sung to her in the walls of her house. She looked down. In the clusters and spurs she saw the history of Alice and her lover. In a single black and red bead off to the lower left she saw the day Alice had stood on the platform, watching her girlfriend step onto a northbound train. And in a cluster of three beads with one above them she saw the casting itself, and she knew, before anyone spoke, that the one in grey would give the answer, and that Alice would hug her and speak to her the Blessing of the Saved.

Beth had never been a pushy woman. She watched Alice get to her feet and leave. She watched the two Speakers collect their beads and she saw the one in leather reach for the cloth. Beth grabbed her arm. 'Do it again,' she said. The two of them squinted up at her. '*Throw them.*' The one in the leather jacket cast her beads. A moment later she scooped them into her left hand, transferred them to her right, and now she and the other cast their beads together. For a long time they said nothing, only looked at the patterns, while behind them Beth wanted to scream, 'What's the matter with you? Can't you see what they say?'

And then – very slowly, it seemed – the woman in the grey coat turned her head and then her shoulders. She looked at Beth who stood trembling with clenched fists. The woman smiled. 'My name is Carla,' she said. 'And this is Marjorie. We would like you to come home with us.'

The Bead Women appeared on television and the covers of magazines. When they mentioned taking apprentices or opening a school, they had to hire a secretary to handle the mail. Offers came to publish handbooks, autobiographies, accounts of their most famous cases.

A man came to see Beth. Handsome, with a square face, wavy black hair and a long thin mouth, his looks were marred by a darkness round his eyes, as if he hadn't slept for days. He wore a blue suit that seemed not to crease no matter how he sat. It was summer, and Beth was doing her castings on the porch at the back of the house. Beyond the trees and the slight swell of grassy dunes the sea shone like a wide strip of silver in the sun.

With her stick and her cloth Beth laid the ground. When she took her beads in her hand they felt warm and sticky, as if someone had spilled syrup on them. The client had written his question, but Beth asked him to tell it to her. He ran a company, he said, which imported electronic watches from Switzerland. He had an offer to import a line of wooden toys, carved animals that ran on wooden wheels, and he wanted to know if he should accept.

Beth sighed. The Speakers' code of ethics required respect for all questions. While she slid her beads from hand to hand she closed her eyes and pictured wooden animals. They were rolling across the Atlantic, armies of them, elephants with dark faces, birds with huge wings. Beth opened her eyes. A shadow lay across the cloth. Beyond it the client sat with folded hands. Beth cast her beads.

They bounced off each other with that wonderful click, her favourite sound. She scanned for the Seven Keys: the black bead she called Darkest Mother, the faded blue she had named Ancient of Ancients, the speckled beads Sister Light and Sister Night, and the three Walkers. They all lay near the centre, a good sign. The lesser beads radiated in wavy tracks or vertical steps. The Seeker, the bead designating the client, lay touching Sister Night, right above her, as if it was sitting on her.

Beth told the client that the moment favoured expansion. He smiled, with his hands still folded in his lap. She told him a few details, and was about to send him away, when a particular line caught her eye. It looped out from the centre, small black beads curling away to a single green half in, half out of the circle. Beth looked at that lonely green lying almost beyond the bounds of human knowledge. Images came to her, a child surrounded by toys on a red carpet, a woman screaming at a man who shoved her against a wall, rows of wooden animals lined up on the shores of a lake, marching children –

The client was standing politely by his chair when Beth Angel managed to raise her head. She told him that he believed in his own reasons for importing the toys. 'But there is another reason.' And she explained how in seven years' time a boy would use these toys to build a barricade against his parents' rage. The boy would make up a game and teach it to others. Many years later another boy would stay out all night with his friends and their toys, the very night that a gas main would burst, blowing up the boy's house and everything in it. And Beth saw as well – in another line of beads – the exact reason why this particular boy needed to survive, and his parents to die. These last things she kept to herself, telling the client only that the Mother of Patterns had chosen him and taken hold of him in order to save a child's life.

He thanked Beth and shook her hand. It felt sweaty until she realized the sweat was her own. He didn't understand, she realized. She was telling him his *purpose*, and he just – She banished him from her mind as soon as he had left. She picked up Sister Night and held it pressed between her palms. Softly, she spoked the Blessing of the Oracles: 'Shaper and Mother, who ties and reties the threads of our lives, I thank you for this knowledge of our ancient lines.' Three times she said it, with her fingertips against her lips and Sister Night guarding the field of her throat.

She looked out across the lawn. Everything had fallen silent. The leaves held still, no one spoke or moved inside the house. Even the birds had gone.

That evening, when Beth told them, they all walked down to the beach. A wind had come up, bringing clouds to hide the sunset. The water looked oily. The women formed a circle around Beth, binding themselves together with a violet ribbon. They cast their beads against the stones, in honour and celebration. And yet, that night, when they lay in bed, a sadness pressed them together, as if they were all trying to hide in each other's bodies.

In the middle of the night Beth woke up. She had dreamed that she was standing on the beach, with ribbons tied all over her. They wound through the pebbles and the weeds and over the dunes, miles and miles of ribbons, stretching across the water, and when she looked up she discovered ribbons streaming from her face, all the way to the Sun.

Awake, Beth lay still for a moment, then carefully settled herself in against Carla while drawing Marjorie's leg over her own and bringing Julia's arm across her and Carla's backs. *I love you*, she thought. *I love you all so much*. For a while she thought she would cry, but she didn't. Then she fell asleep.

When she woke up all the sadness had left her. Sarah made her pancakes and Marjorie surprised her with cake. In between the bites and the laughter, she talked about the excitement and the need for humility, and whether they should let the outside world know, and what it could do for their reputation. She made jokes about special consultations with the Sacred President in which she would tell him the true and spiritual reasons why the Shaper had granted him re-election and a cooperative Congress.

But when the others left her to prepare for their first assignments, she began to wonder if it could happen again. Maybe she had only caught a stray glimpse, like someone passing an ill-arranged curtain and peeking inside only to have the curtains snatched shut by an angry hand. Clients came. She told one his meditations would improve with a new teacher and another that her son would stay with his new lover for two and a half years and then move to Texas with someone he would meet at an academic conference. But the purpose of the meditations, or the real reason the woman's son needed to live in Texas – these things remained concealed from her. It was all right, she told herself. That one time was enough.

Two days later a repeater came. He had come to Beth three times before, always with very specific questions. Now his mother was coming to visit, and he wanted to know if she was planning to move in with them. Beth cast the beads and told him his mother would stay longer than he liked, but if he didn't respond to her hints she eventually would leave and go to his younger brother. And then Beth's hand began to shake, and she wanted to bounce up and down, like a child getting a birthday present. For she could see it, written in the beads. She told him the purpose of his mother's visit, that he would get so angry he would go out every night to a local bar, and one evening he would leave behind a book he was reading, a spy novel, and halfway home he would stop and remember, but because it would be raining he would decide not to go back, and someone else would find the book and read it, and a certain scene in the book, or maybe just a sentence, would suggest an idea for a story, not a spy story, and this story would one day compel a woman in Alabama to seek help for her addiction to tranquillizers.

When the client had left – hurriedly – Beth picked up her beads in both hands and kissed them. Maybe not everyone *has* a purpose, she thought. Maybe the Shaper only takes certain people, and only at certain moments in their lives. Lets the rest fumble about, doing whatever they like.

She frowned. What did it mean that she had told the client? Would he not forget the book? Or would he leave it too soon, on the wrong night, in his eagerness to affect the world? Not possible, she thought. Her telling must have formed part of the pattern or it wouldn't have happened. 'Trust in the road,' she quoted out loud. She sat down in the rocking chair by the window. Trust in the Shaper, Beth thought. She knows what she's doing.

A woman came with a question about buying a house. The receptionist tried to send her to Marjorie, but she insisted on seeing 'Bess Rosenblum'.

The sale would go through, Beth told her. The bank would give her and her husband the mortgage, and the other couple bidding for the house would change their minds. The woman looked at the beads, then Beth. 'But what's the purpose of it?' she said. Beth said nothing. 'I mean,' the woman pushed on, 'isn't there some reason why we should live there? A secret destiny?'

Beth wanted to tell her that maybe her life didn't contain a destiny. Instead, she said, 'I'll look, but I can't promise to find anything.' She threw the beads, then again, and again. Without realizing it, she began to rock back and forth. 'Your husband will

die in that house,' she said. 'He will get some disease that will
make him grow old in weeks.'

'Oh God,' the woman said. 'Oh God.' And then, 'When? When
will this happen?'

'I don't know,' Beth said.

'You don't know? What do you mean, you don't know?'

Beth told her how the neighbours' love and loyalty would help
her husband, so that he would bless his wife for finding the house.
And because of her husband's courage a certain couple on that street
would save their marriage, and the couple's daughter would not run
away, and by staying in high school she would meet a teacher who
would inspire her to become an Earth healer, so that years later the
daughter would lead a sacred enactment to drive polluted spirits
from the Niagara River. In this way, the couple buying the house
would serve the purpose of liberating the water.

'What happens if we don't move there?' the woman said.

'Then the couple will break up and the girl will leave home.'

The client screamed, 'I don't care about them. Will my husband
live?'

'No,' Beth told her. Nothing could stop the disease. It belonged
to the purpose. If they went somewhere else, Beth told the woman,
her husband would die alone and angry, enraged at his wife without
even knowing why.

Crying, the woman said, 'Why did you tell me this?'

'I'm sorry. I'm so sorry. You shouldn't have asked.'

For two months Beth refused to see any clients. All day she sat on
the porch or walked along the beach, and at night she ate alone in
her office. At the end of that time the autumnal equinox came, the
Blessed Day of Isolation. Dressed all in black, Beth went out before
the sunrise, carrying her beads and her stick, to an old tree at the
edge of the lawn. In the dark she drew a true ground and cast her
beads. 'Bright Shaper and Mother,' she prayed, 'tell me your desire.
My voice or my silence.' Seven times she repeated these words,
and by then the sky had lit enough to see the beads. They lay all
scattered, many of them obscured by the grass. Above the centre,
against a stone, Sister Light and Sister Night lay on either side of the
Mother. Hugging herself in the damp air, Beth moaned softly. That
afternoon she told the receptionist she would take appointments.

A woman came to see Beth. She was tall, over six feet, and she
wore high heels with a brown suit with padded shoulders and a
narrow skirt. 'Someone's offered me an important commission,' she

said, 'but there's also the possibility of several smaller assignments. I can't decide which way would help my career.'

Beth cast the beads. The smaller ones fell into a pattern of a bird. Red beads at the tip suggested fire, but in the beak rested the Ancient of Ancients, the largest bead in Beth's collection. 'Take the single commission,' she told the woman. 'It will make you famous.'

'Yes,' the woman said. 'I'll do that. Thank you very much. That's wonderful news.' She leaned forwards. 'But what is the purpose of it?' Beth shook her head. 'If it's so important it must serve some special purpose. Mustn't it?'

'It'll make you famous,' Beth said. 'Isn't that enough?'

'But there must be a purpose. Can't you just look?'

Beth glanced again at the beads. 'I'm sorry. I don't see anything.'

'Do it again,' the woman said. 'I don't mind paying extra.'

'It's not a matter of money.'

'Please.'

Beth sighed. She gathered up the beads and rolled them from hand to hand. They felt sticky again, and warm, just like that first time. She threw them down. Now the Ancient of Ancients sat in the centre, surrounded by a ring of black. All the other keys, the Sisters and their Mother and the three Walkers, lay at the edge of the circle or outside it. Beth stared at the centre. Her mouth hung open, and she began to cry without even knowing it. When she turned she saw the woman sitting back, smiling, with her hands folded in her lap.

'Beth Angel Rosenbloom,' she said, 'I arrest you in the name of the law.'

No people wearing indigo blindfolds surrounded the courthouse. There were no marches or all-night castings on campuses. The story appeared once on one network's evening news as a minor item between commercials, and then vanished. Each day Carla and Marjorie and Sarah and Julia came to the court house and each day the bailiffs turned them away, saying there was no more room in the galleries. Each night they cast their beads into the copper bowl from their first days together. The beads would swirl about, and the women would dip their hands hoping to sense Beth's presence, or even stray memories left in the metal. But nothing remained of her. The police had taken away her beads.

All alone every day in her black and white dress and red shoes, with a yellow ribbon round her wrist, Beth sat upright, her hands flattened on the table. The special prosecutor, on loan from the

New York College of Tellers, charged Beth with deliberately overstepping the limits of human knowledge and trespassing in sacred territory. Beth's court-appointed lawyer argued entrapment, but he didn't seem to pursue the case very vigorously. Beth hardly listened. They had taken away her beads.

On the last day of the trial, after the jury had brought in guilty verdicts on all counts, as the judge recited the sacred formulas in preparation for sentencing, Beth noticed that the sun through the skylight cast a speckled pattern on the floor between her and the bench. It looked a little like a bead pattern, she saw. She could spot the lines between the dots and the colourings on the polished wood. It described the judge, she realized, and his problems with his mistress. She looked up at him. His voice became a series of sounds, and then the sounds coalesced into a shape unknown to the man who made them, for it belonged as well to the light and the floor. It told Beth of a daughter and how she would move in with the judge's mistress and how the two women would become Sacred Wanderers with a tribe of Found Women in the Adirondack Mountains. Beth laughed, not from the message, but simply because the real world had readmitted her.

If the judge could not see what his sentencing had done for Beth the prosecutor caught the movement of the prisoner's eyes between the floor and the judge's face. She ordered the judge to stop. She ordered the guards to blindfold the prisoner. Beth shoved and kicked them. Her lawyer tried to hold her down and she bit his finger. The guards dragged her off before the judge had even finished his sentencing.

They took Beth to a square building specially built on a flat plain, without trees or bushes or any sight of water. They led her from the car blindfolded and handcuffed. She and the guards all wore rubber-soled shoes, for in the holding cell she had created a casting out of the sounds of heels on metal combined with clanging doors. They took her to her cell, a large square room with white walls so carefully painted that no ridges or bubbles marred the smooth surface. A single window, too high for her to reach, allowed in light; a screen a few inches away from it made it impossible to inspect the sky. Double glazing kept out any sounds of birds. The bathroom was a cubicle without light. The toilet cover lifted only when she had closed and locked the door. The toilet flushed automatically when she had stepped outside and closed the soundproofed door behind her. The sink and the shower always emitted the same bursts of water, measured by computer.

On the first day Beth Angel said to herself, 'There is no way they can lock me out.' She knew now that anything, any pattern of light or sound, maybe even touch or smell or taste, could take the place of her beads.

At first, her captors tried to befriend her. They could talk to her, their orders said, as long as she clearly paid attention and responded intelligently. The conversations lasted until someone realized Beth had taught herself to memorize the noises and play them back in her mind after they left. On the day they told her no one would talk to her any more she began to study their faces, the variations in complexion, the unconscious shifting of muscles. When they realized what she was doing they began leaving her food and clean clothes while she slept.

Beth studied her food, the shapes and the colours. They gave her clear soup and she studied the steam. They gave her cold porridge and she read the lumps and bubbles. When they switched to cold broth she swallowed some and threw the rest against the wall to study the splashes. Finally they came in twice a day, wearing smooth masks, bound her arms, and fed her spoonfuls of bland soup and small square blocks of protein.

The first time they fed her she spit the food at the one in front of her. The white mask exploded into a map larger than the world. Though the guard stepped quickly out of sight Beth had already memorized the patterns. After that they blindfolded her.

The battle went on and on. They took away her shapeless white clothes when she began to unravel the thread, bite it into different lengths, and scatter them on the floor. When she bit her lip to spray blood against the wall, they came in and placed a porous gag in her mouth, open enough to let in air, but thick enough to stop her from forcing anything out. Desperate, she tried defecating in the outer room in order to read her own excrement. It belonged to the tradition, she told herself; there were ancient kings whose Speakers read every trace of body waste. But her jailers came in, cleaned the room, and put her in a straitjacket. For days they forced her to signal with her head whenever she needed to go to the toilet. Then they would take her and stand with her in the dark until she was finished.

In all their movements they had trained themselves to follow the same routine over and over. Like rigidly programmed robots they jerked their arms or nodded their heads in the same square movements.

After days of the gag and the straitjacket Beth signalled to them that she would behave. The first time they freed her she attacked them, not caring what damage she did as long as she forced them into random action. Once again they bound her, another week. The next time they let her loose she sat quietly.

She thought of creating a casting in her head; she could think of her beads, of a hand grabbing them up and throwing them. But such things would only be images, her own image. If she could have used her head, she realized, she could have spent her time interpreting her dreams. Beth had not dreamed since the day they took away her beads.

One afternoon, she stood up in her cell, turned around to address the cameras she knew were hidden in the walls, and shouted, 'What's the matter with all of you? Don't you want to know anything? Isn't anybody sick? Isn't anyone's marriage in trouble? Don't you know what an opportunity you've got here? Goddamn you, why don't you ask me something?'

She began to lose weight. She ate normally, even more than before, for she had stopped trying to force them to vary their patterns. And yet she became gaunt, weak. She hardly moved off her cot.

Outside the room, the others wondered what they could do to revive her. They put more vitamins in the food, they laced it with stimulants. For a day or two she moved around, clumsily, like a marionette, like one of them. Then she adjusted to the change and once more took to her bed. Away from the other jailers, one of two of them would cry, or pray for her, and one made a special pilgrimage to his family's shrine to beg his ancestors' forgiveness. But none of them went against their orders.

Lying on her bed, too weak to sit up, Beth thought of her children. How had they grown up? Did they think of her? She was sure Sam had remarried. Maybe they had moved somewhere. Some place far away. If she had had her beads she could have found out. She thought of the Bead Women and how they all used to sleep together. She remembered Carla rolling into her, and the way Marjorie sometimes stroked her back late at night. For the first time she wondered if she could have saved herself. Maybe if she had kept silent.

The door opened. Beth heard the click of hard heels. Startled, she turned her head. The woman stood there, the one who had arrested her. 'Beth Angel,' she said, 'there is still time. You can return.'

'Who are you?' Beth said.

'I want to help you.'

'Help me?'

'Yes. we will let you out. All you have to do is promise to stay inside the circle.' Beth said nothing. 'Is that really so terrible? You can go back to your friends. You can still be a Speaker. Just promise never to see what mustn't be seen.' She held out her hand. 'Here,' she said. 'Let me carry you out of here. We'll call the Bead Women to come and get you.'

For what seemed a long time Beth stared at that hand. She looked at the markings, the length of the fingers, the shape and colour of the fingernails. She had not seen an ungloved hand other than her own in so many months. But when she looked at it – when she looked into it – Beth shook her head.

'What is the matter with you?' the woman said. 'Don't you know that human beings need ignorance? That they desire ignorance? Do you think they want you to tell them the reasons for the things that happen to them? Do you think they want that?'

Beth looked up at her face. It was just like the hand, no pattern, nothing under the skin. She began the Standard Formula of Recognition for a divine enemy. 'Malignant One, I beg you to release me –'

'No,' the woman said, and shook her head. 'I am not an enemy.'

Beth managed to laugh. 'I don't care what you are. Go back where you came from.' She turned away. A moment later she heard the click of the woman's shoes leaving the room. She thought of Carla, and the beach, and breakfast in the big room. She thought of her beads, and she almost called the woman back. But she pressed her lips together, and stared at the wall, and a moment later the door hissed open, then closed.

Days passed. Beth no longer ate or moved. Then one day a breeze touched her skin. She turned. The door stood open to the corridor. Shaking, Beth got to her feet. She made it to the door, where she had to stop a moment, holding on to the frame. And then she stepped out, into a miraculous world of shadows and moving air, of a scuffed floor and minute noises. She heard a machine somewhere, even a voice.

Feeling her way along the wall, she reached the door. She prayed it wasn't closed, for she knew she would never have the strength to open it. It stood open, just a crack. When she pushed it it swung gently away.

Beth gasped at the colours and the shapes. There was grass and trees, and she could hear the wind, and when she looked up the sky displayed a thousand shades of blue. She heard a strange whistle and realized it was a bird. She saw it now, it circled three times overhead, and then flew away. Beth whispered, 'Thank you, great messenger. Thank you for your help and your message.' Tears prevented her from repeating it.

She moved forwards, taking small careful steps. She walked towards a tree stump, thinking to sit down and look at the Earth. But when she got closer, she saw a silk bag, and when she picked it up she could feel them all waiting for her. They were waiting to speak.

Beth sat down. She slid the beads into her hand, feeling their cool hardness. As she rolled them back and forth, alien memories teased her – a teenage hangout in a town she had never seen, a kiss from a lover she had never met – and she realized that the others were mixing their beads.

Beth slid off the stump to sit on the grass. Behind her she heard a noise. She paid no attention as she cast her beads onto the stump. She smiled at them, unhurried, simply looking. The Ancient of Ancients sat in the centre. Lines and loops radiated from it. She looked up and saw that the lines of beads ran beyond the circle of wood, over the grass and trees and into the sky. She saw beads hidden in cities and forests and under the seas. She saw how beads held together her parents and grandparents and all their ancestors, and all the people they had known, and all their acts and decisions. She saw the invention of beads, and the birth of people who would trade in them. She looked for the Sisters, and finding them she found the creation of colour, and the beginnings of motion and shape.

Beth looked another way and saw herself. She saw the years with Sam (and all the people and actions that had brought Sam into being). She saw the women, and the house, and the day Carla found the first beads, in a dark shop on an afternoon when she couldn't bear to go to work. And finally, in the centre, she saw the purpose.

One of her guards, she saw, would give Beth's story to a Teller, a woman who hadn't talked for the first three years of her life. Horrified at what had happened to Beth, the Teller would leak the story to a writer who would put it into a magazine, so that a certain woman, at a time in her life of pain and despair at her own and others' suffering, would learn of Beth Angel Rosenbloom. And she would understand that every person, every particle of dust, every star and quark, must serve its purpose. And knowing this, she would return to her own work, a map in sounds of the origin of love.

Beth picked up her beads. She understood now the reasons for her own suffering. But she understood as well that it no longer mattered, not to her. For she had seen, and if the purpose belonged to the universe, the seeing belonged to Beth. Holding the beads in her hands, she raised them to her mouth. The sun shone on her knuckles. Beth opened her hands and the beads rained onto the grass. A single note sang in the Earth.

J.G. BALLARD

The Enormous Space

I made my decision this morning – soon after eight o'clock, as I stood by the front door, ready to drive to the office. All in all, I'm certain that I had no other choice. Yet, given that this is the most important decision of my life, it seems strange that nothing has changed. I expected the walls to tremble, at the very least a subtle shift in the perspectives of these familiar rooms.

In a sense, the lack of any response reflects the tranquil air of this London suburb. If I were living, not in Croydon but in the Bronx or West Beirut, my action would be no more than sensible local camouflage. Here it runs counter to every social value, but is invisible to those it most offends.

Even now, three hours later, all is calm. The leafy avenue is as unruffled as ever. The mail has arrived, and sits unopened on the hall stand. From the dining-room window I watch the British Telecom engineer return to his van after repairing the Johnsons' telephone, an instrument reduced to a nervous wreck at least twice a month by their teenage daughters. Mrs Johnson, dressed in her turquoise tracksuit, closes the gate and glances at my car. A faint vapour rises from the exhaust. The engine is still idling, all these hours after I began to demist the windscreen before finishing my breakfast.

This small slip may give the game away. Watching the car impatiently, I am tempted to step from the house and switch off the ignition, but I manage to control myself. Whatever happens, I must hold to my decision and all the consequences that flow from it. Fortunately, an Air India 747 ambles across the sky, searching none too strenuously for London Airport. Mrs Johnson, who shares something of its heavy-bodied elegance, gazes up at the droning turbo-fans. She is dreaming of Martinique or Mauritius, while I am dreaming of nothing.

My decision to dream that dream may have been made this morning, but I assume that its secret logic had begun to run through my life many months ago. Some unknown source of strength sustained me through the unhappy period of my car accident, convalescence and divorce, and the unending problems that faced me at the merchant bank on my return. Standing by the front door after finishing my coffee, I watched the mist clear from the Volvo's windscreen. The briefcase in my hand reminded me of the day-long meetings of the finance committee at which I would have to argue once again for the budget of my beleaguered research department.

Then, as I set the burglar alarm, I realized that I could change the course of my life by a single action. To shut out the world, and solve all my difficulties at a stroke, I had the simplest of weapons – my own front door. I needed only to close it, and decide never to leave my house again.

Of course, this decision involved more than becoming a mere stay-at-home. I remember walking into the kitchen, surprised by this sudden show of strength, and trying to work out the implications of what I had done. Still wearing my business suit and tie, I sat at the kitchen table, and tapped out my declaration of independence on the polished formica.

By closing the front door I intended to secede not only from the society around me. I was rejecting my friends and colleagues, my accountant, doctor and solicitor, and above all my ex-wife. I was breaking off all practical connections with the outside world. I would never again step through the front door. I would accept the air and the light, and the electric power and water that continued to flow through the meters. But otherwise I would depend on the outside world for nothing. I would eat only whatever food I could find within the house. After that I would rely on time and space to sustain me.

The Volvo's engine is still running. It is 3 p.m., seven hours after I first switched on the ignition, but I can't remember when I last filled the tank. It's remarkable how few passers-by have noticed the puttering exhaust – only the retired headmaster who patrols the avenue morning and afternoon actually stopped to stare at it. I watched him mutter to himself and shake his walking-stick before shuffling away.

The murmur of the engine unsettles me, like the persistent ringing of the telephone. I can guess who is calling: Brenda, my secretary; the head of marketing, Dr Barnes; the personnel manager, Mr Austen (I have already been on sick-leave for three weeks); the dental receptionist (a tender root canal reminds me that I had an appointment yesterday); my wife's solicitor, insisting that the first of the separation payments is due in six months' time.

Finally I pick up the telephone cable and pull the jack on this persistent din. Calming myself, I accept that I will admit to the house anyone with a legitimate right to be there – the TV rental man, the gas and electricity meter-readers, even the local police. I cannot expect to be left completely on my own. At the same time, it will be months before my action arouses any real suspicions, and I am confident that by then I will long since have moved into a different realm.

I feel tremendously buoyant, almost lightheaded. Nothing matters any more. Think only of essentials: the physics of the gyroscope, the flux of photons, the architecture of very large structures.

5 p.m. Time to take stock and work out the exact resources of this house in which I have lived for seven years.

First, I carry my unopened mail into the dining room, open a box of matches and start a small, satisfying fire in the grate. To the flames I add the contents of my briefcase, all the bank notes in my wallet, credit cards, driving licence and chequebook.

I inspect the kitchen and pantry shelves. Before leaving, Margaret had stocked the freezer and refrigerator with a fortnight's supply of eggs, ham and other bachelor staples – a pointed gesture, bearing in mind that she was about to sail off into the blue with her lover (a tedious sales manager). These basic rations fulfil the same role as the keg of fresh water and sack of flour left at the feet of a marooned sailor, a reminder of the world rejecting him.

I weigh the few cartons of pasta in my hand, the jars of lentils and rice, the tomatoes and courgettes, the rope of garlic. Along with the tinned anchovies and several sachets of smoked salmon in the freezer, there are enough calories and protein to keep me going for at least ten days, three times that period if I ration myself. After that I will have to boil the cardboard boxes into a nutritious broth and rely on the charity of the wind.

At 6.15 the car's engine falters and stops.

In every way I am marooned, but a reductive Crusoe paring away exactly those elements of bourgeois life which the original Robinson so dutifully reconstituted. Crusoe wished to bring the Croydons of his own day to life again on his island. I want to expel them, and find in their place a far richer realm formed from the elements of light, time and space.

The first week has ended peacefully. All is well, and I have sta-bilized my regime most pleasantly. To my surprise, it has been

remarkably easy to reject the world. Few people have bothered me.
The postman has delivered several parcels, which I carry straight to
the dining-room fireplace. On the third day my secretary, Brenda,
called at the front door. I smiled winningly, reassured her that I
was merely taking an extended sabbatical. She looked at me in her
sweet but shrewd way – she had been strongly supportive during
both my divorce and the crisis at the office – and then left with a
promise to keep in touch. A succession of letters has arrived from
Dr Barnes, but I warm my hands over them at the fireplace. The
dining-room grate has become an efficient incinerator in which I
have erased my entire past – passport; birth, degree and share cer-
tificates; uncashed traveller's cheques and 2000 French francs left
from our last unhappy holiday in Nice; letters from my broker and
orthopaedic surgeon. Documents of a dead past, they come to life
briefly in the flame, and then write themselves into the dust.

Eliminating this detritus has kept me busy. I have pulled down
the heavy curtains that hung beside the windows. Light has flooded
into the rooms, turning every wall and ceiling into a vivid tabula
rasa. Margaret had taken with her most of the ornaments and
knick-knacks, and the rest I have heaved into a cupboard. Suffused
with light, the house can breathe. Upstairs the windows are open
to the sky. The rooms seem larger and less confined, as if they too
have found freedom. I sleep well, and when I wake in the morning
I almost feel myself on some Swiss mountaintop, with half the sky
below me.

Without doubt, I am very much better. I have put away the
past, a zone that I regret ever entering. I enjoy the special ease
that comes from no longer depending on anyone else, however
well-intentioned.

Above all, I am no longer dependent on myself. I feel no obli-
gation to that person who fed and groomed me, who provided
me with expensive clothes, who drove me about in his motorcar,
who furnished my mind with intelligent books and exposed me to
interesting films and art exhibitions. Wanting none of these, I owe
that person, myself, no debts. I am free at last to think only of the
essential elements of existence – the visual continuum around me,
and the play of air and light. The house begins to resemble an
advanced mathematical surface, a three-dimensional chessboard.
The pieces have yet to be placed, but I feel them forming in my
mind.

A policeman is approaching the house. A uniformed constable, he
has stepped from a patrol car parked by the gate. He looks up at the

roof, watched by an elderly couple who seem to have summoned him.

Confused, I debate whether to answer the doorbell. My arms and shirt are streaked with soot from the fireplace.

'Mr Ballantyne — ?' A rather naive young constable is looking me up and down. 'Are you the householder?'

'Can I help you, officer?' I assume the convincing pose of a law-abiding suburbanite, interrupted in that act of lay worship, do-it-yourself.

'We've had reports of a break-in, sir. Your upstairs windows have been open all night — for two or three nights, your neighbours say. They thought you might be away.'

'A break-in?' This throws me. 'No, I've been here. In fact, I'm not planning to go out at all. I'm cleaning the chimneys, officer, getting rid of all that old soot and dust.'

'Fair enough . . .' He hesitates before leaving, nose roving about for some irregularity he has sniffed, like a dog convinced of a hidden treat. He is certain that in some reprehensible way I am exploiting the suburban norms, like a wife-beater or child-molester.

I wait until he drives away, disappearing into that overworked hologram called reality. Afterwards I lean against the door, exhausted by this false alarm. The effort of smiling at the officer reminds me of the interior distance I have travelled in the past week. But I must be careful, and hide behind those façades of conventional behaviour that I intend to subvert.

I close the windows that face the street, and then step with relief into the open bedrooms above the garden. The walls form sections of huge box-antennae tuned to the light. I think of the concrete inclines of the old racing track at Brooklands, and the giant chambers excavated from the bauxite cliffs at Les Baux, where Margaret first began to distance herself from me.

Of course a break-in has occurred, of a very special kind.

A month has passed, a period of many advances and a few setbacks. Resting in the kitchen beside the empty refrigerator, I eat the last of the anchovies and take stock of myself. I have embarked on a long internal migration, following a route partly inscribed within my head and partly within this house, which is a far more complex structure than I realized. I have a sense that there are more rooms than there appear to be at first sight. There is a richness of interior space of which I was totally unaware during the seven years I spent here with Margaret. Light floods everything, expanding the dimensions of walls and ceiling. These quiet streets were built on the site of the old Croydon aerodrome, and it is almost as if the perspectives of the former grass runways have returned to haunt these neat suburban lawns and the minds of those who tend them.

All this excitement has led me to neglect my rationing system. Scarcely anything is left in the pantry – a box of sugar cubes, a tube of tomato paste, and a few shrivelled asparagus tips. I lick my fingers and run them round the bottom of the empty bread bin. Already I find myself wishing that I had fully provisioned myself before embarking on this expedition. But everything I have achieved, the huge sense of freedom, of opened doors and of other doors yet to be opened, were contingent on my acting upon that decision of a moment.

Even so, I have to be careful not to give the game away. I maintain a reasonably kempt appearance, wave from the upstairs windows at Mrs Johnson and gesture apologetically at the overgrown lawn. She understands – I have been abandoned by my wife, condemned to the despair of a womanless world. I am hungry all the time, kept going by not much more than cups of sweetened tea. My weight has plunged; I have lost some fifteen pounds and feel permanently lightheaded.

Meanwhile, the outside world continues to bombard me with its irrelevant messages – junk mail, give-away newspapers, and a barrage of letters from Dr Barnes and the personnel department at the bank. They burn with heavy, solemn flames, and I assume that I have been sacked. Brenda called to see me three days ago, still puzzled by my cheerful demeanour. She told me that she had been reassigned, and that my office has been cleared of its files and furniture.

The letter slot rattles. From the doormat I pick up two leaflets and a plastic envelope, a free sample of a new brand of chocolate. I rip it from the packing, and sink my teeth into the rubbery core, unable to control the saliva that swamps my mouth. I am so overwhelmed by the taste of food that I fail to hear the doorbell chiming. When I open the door I find a smartly dressed woman in tweed suit and hat, presumably some solicitor's wife working as a volunteer almoner for the local hospital.

'Yes? Can I – ?' With an effort I recognize her, as I lick the last of the chocolate from my teeth. 'Margaret . . .?'

'Of course.' She shakes her head, as if this trivial social gaffe explains everything about me. 'Who on earth did you think I was? Are you all right, Geoffrey?'

'Yes, I'm fine. I've been very busy. What are you looking for?'

A frightening prospect crosses my mind. 'You don't want to come back . . .?'

'Good heavens, no. Dr Barnes telephoned me. He said that you'd resigned. I'm surprised.'

'No, I decided to leave. I'm working on a private project. It's what I've always wanted to do.'

'I know.' Her eyes searched the hall and kitchen, convinced that something has changed. 'By the way, I've paid the electricity bill, but this is the last time.'

'Fair enough. Well, I must get back to work.'

'Good.' She is clearly surprised by my self-sufficiency. 'You've lost weight. It suits you.'

The house relaxes its protective hold on me. When Margaret has gone I reflect on how quickly I have forgotten her. There are no tugs of old affection. I have changed, my senses tuned to all the wavelengths of the invisible. Margaret has remained in a more limited world, one of a huge cast of repertory players in that everlasting provincial melodrama called ordinary life.

Eager to erase her memory, I set off upstairs, and open the windows to enjoy the full play of afternoon sun. The west-facing rooms above the garden have become giant observatories. The dust cloaks everything with a mescalin haze of violet light, photons backing up as they strike the surface of windowsill and dressing-table. Margaret has taken many pieces of furniture with her, leaving unexpected gaps and intervals, as if this is a reversed spatial universe, the template of the one we occupied together. I can almost sit down in her absent William Morris chair, nearly see myself reflected in the missing Art Deco mirror whose chromium rim has left a halo on the bathroom wall.

A curious discovery – the rooms *are* larger. At first I thought that this was an illusion brought about by the sparse furnishings, but the house has always been bigger than I realized. My eyes now see everything as it is, uncluttered by the paraphernalia of conventional life, as in those few precious moments when one returns from holiday and sees one's home in its true light.

Dazed by the vivid air, I blunder into Margaret's bedroom. The walls are strangely displaced, as if a team of scene-shifters have pulled them back to create a new stage set. There is no sign of the bed, and its bare mattress marked by the wine I spilled on the evening of her departure while commiserating over her dull lover. I have strayed into an unfamiliar area of the room, somewhere between Margaret's bathroom and the fitted cupboards. The remainder of the room sheers away from me, the walls pushed back by the light. For the first time I see the bed, but it seems as remote as an old divan at the rear of an empty warehouse.

Another door leads to a wide and silent corridor, clearly un-entered for years. There is no staircase, but far away there are entrances to other rooms, filled with the sort of light that glows from X-ray viewing screens. Here and there an isolated chair sits against a wall, in one immense room there is nothing but a dressing-table, in another the gleaming cabinet of a grandfather clock presides over the endlessly carpeted floor.

The house is revealing itself to me in the most subtle way. Surprised by its perspectives, I trip over my own feet and feel my heart race ahead of me. I find a wall and press my hands to the striped paper, then fumble through the overlit air towards the landing. At last I reached the top of a huge staircase, whose bannisters shrink together as I race to the safety of the floor below.

The true dimensions of this house may be exhilarating to per-ceive, but from now on I will sleep downstairs. Time and space are not necessarily on my side.

I have trapped a cat. So unnerved was I by the experience of losing myself in my own home that it takes me half an hour to realize that I have a small companion, Mrs Johnson's white Persian. While I was blundering around the Marienbad Palace that now occupies the first floor the cat entered the sitting-room through the open French window, and was trapped when a gust of air closed the door.

She follows me around amiably, waiting to be fed, but for once I am in need of her charity.

Two months have now passed. This conventional suburban villa is in fact the junction between our small illusory world and another larger and more real one. Miraculously, I have survived, though my last reserves of food were exhausted weeks ago. As I expected, Margaret paid a second and final visit. Still puzzled by my self-confidence and handsomely slimming figure, she told me that she would no longer be responsible for my mounting debts. I bade her farewell, and returned to my lunch of poodle pie.

The thought that I would never see Margaret again gave my modest meal an added relish, and afterwards I carefully set the dog-trap by the open door of the sitting-room. The untended garden with its knee-deep grass has attracted my neighbours' pets, trusting beasts who trundle happily towards me as I sit smiling in the armchair, cleaver concealed within an inviting cushion. By the

time their ever-hopeful owners call round a few days later I have
safely consigned the bones to the space below the dining-room
floorboards, a substantial ossuary that is the last resting-place of
Bonzo, Major, Yorky and Mr Fred.

These dogs and cats, and the few birds I have been able to trap,
soon formed my sole fare. However, it became clear that my neighbours were keeping a more careful eye on their pets, and I resigned
myself to a diet of air. Fortunately, the television rental company
intervened to provide a generous source of extra rations.

I remember the dour young man with the toolkit who arrived to
dismantle the attic aerial. He had made several earlier calls in the
avenue, and had parked his van a hundred yards away. I followed
him up the stairs, concerned that he too might lose his way among
those vast rooms.

Sadly, my attempt to warn him came to nothing. As he stepped
into the first of those white chambers, as large as aircraft hangars
carved in the roof of an iceberg, he seemed to realize that he had
entered a zone of danger. I grappled with him as we blundered
through that white world, like arctic explorers losing all sense of
distance within a few steps of their tent. An hour later, when I had
calmed his fears and carried him down the staircase, he had sadly
yielded to the terrors of light and space.

Three months – a period of continued discovery and few interrup-
tions. The outside world has at last decided to leave me alone. I no
longer answer the door, and there has been scarcely a caller, though
threatening letters arrive from the local council, and from the water
and electricity companies. But an unshakable logic is at work, and
I am confident that my project will be complete before the power
and water supplies are disconnected.

The house enlarges itself around me. The invasion of light which
revealed its true dimensions has now reached the ground floor. To
keep my bearings I have been forced to retreat into the kitchen,
where I have moved my mattress and blankets. Now and then I
venture into the hall and search the looming perspectives. It amazes
me that Margaret and I once lived in this vast pile and so reduced it
in our minds.

Already I can feel the walls of the kitchen distancing themselves
from me. I spend all day here, sitting on the floor against the freezer
cabinet. The cooker, refrigerator and dishwasher have become
anonymous objects in some remote department-store display. How
much longer can this expansion continue? Sooner or later the process will halt, at that moment revealing the true dimensions of the

THE ENORMOUS SPACE 85

world we inhabit, and which the visual centres of our timid brains
have concealed from us. I am on the verge of a unique revelation,
the equal perhaps of Columbus's discovery of the new world. I can
scarcely wait to bring the news to my neighbours – the modest villa
which Mrs Johnson imagines herself to occupy is in fact an immense
Versailles!

Nearby, the bones of the TV repairman lie on the yellow lino-
leum like the ribs and skull of a long-decayed desert traveller.

Somewhere a door is being forced. I listen to the grating of keys
testing a lock, then the sound of heels on the patio steps before a
second attempt to prise open the French window.

Rousing myself, I sway across the kitchen, trying to steady my
arms against the faraway washing-machine. A key turns, and a
door opens somewhere beyond the great carpeted perspectives of
the sitting-room.

A young woman has entered the house. As she returns the keys to
her handbag I recognize Brenda, my former secretary. She stares at
the dismantled dog-traps beside the window and then peers around
the room, at last seeing me as I watch her beside the door.

'Mr Ballantyne? I'm sorry to break in. I was worried that you
might . . .' She smiles reassuringly and takes the keys from her
handbag. 'Mrs Ballantyne said I could use the spare set. You haven't
answered the phone, and we wondered if you'd fallen ill . . .'

She is walking towards me, but so slowly that the immense room
seems to carry her away from me in its expanding dimensions. She
approaches and recedes from me at the same time, and I am concerned that she will lose herself in the almost planetary vastness of
this house.

Catching her as she swerves past me, I protect her from the outward rush of time and space.

I assume that we have entered the fourth month. I can no longer
see the calendar on the kitchen door, so remote is it from me. I
am sitting with my back to the freezer, which I have moved out of
the kitchen into the pantry. But already the walls of this once tiny
room constitute a universe of their own. The ceiling is so distant
that clouds might form below it.

I have eaten nothing for the past week, but I no longer dare to
leave the pantry and rarely venture more than a step from my position. I could easily lose my way crossing the kitchen and never be
able to return to the only security and companionship that I know.

There is only one further retreat. So much space has receded from me that I must be close to the irreducible core where reality lies. This morning I gave in briefly to the sudden fear that all this has been taking place within my own head. By shutting out the world my mind may have drifted into a realm without yardsticks or sense of scale. For so many years I have longed for an empty world, and may unwittingly have constructed it within this house. Time and space have rushed in to fill the vacuum that I created. It even occurred to me to end the experiment, and I stood up and tried to reach the front door, a journey that seemed as doomed as Scott's return from the South Pole. Needless to say, I was forced to give up the attempt long before crossing the threshold of the hall.

Behind me Brenda lies comfortably, her face only a few inches from my own. But now she too is beginning to move away from me. Covered by a jewelled frost, she rests quietly in the compartment of the freezer, a queen waiting one day to be reborn from her cryogenic sleep.

The perspective lines flow from me, enlarging the interior of the compartment. Soon I will lie beside her, in a palace of ice that will crystallize around us, finding at last the still centre of the world which came to claim me.

BARRINGTON J. BAYLEY

Tommy Atkins

Harry hated the time he had to spend on the factory floor. The workers there were all women and girls. Whenever he went to inspect or repair a machine he could feel their eyes on him, could sense their nudges and sneers. To make matters worse, three of the women had limbs missing.

Otherwise, in normal times, it would have been a welcome and familiar environment. The steam engine in the yard drove a jungle of roaring belts and pulleys to power mills, lathes and boring machines. On gloomy days, glowing gas jets supplemented the daylight filtering through the sooty glass roof panels. The factory produced small-arms parts, in a veritable flood which was carried away in lorries that arrived each day. Sometimes there weren't enough lorries and the crates piled up higher and higher in the loading bay. War work.

There had been four mechanics under Harry before the war. Now, as factory engineer, he had to do the routine servicing himself. He threw the clutch on the drive belt and the capstan lathe started turning. A turbaned girl slouched nearby, taking advantage of the break in her work to drag on an acrid-smelling Woodbine.

'It'll do,' he said. With an aloofness he found mildly irritating, she nodded and took her place; recalibrated the turret, turned on the sud-tap and applied the tool to the first steel cylinder, all with easy automatic skill. She would make another four hundred connecting rods before her shift was finished.

Harry's shift, though, was ending. Wearily he made his way down the aisle, his consciousness all but drowned in the noise of the huge shed and the familiar odours of oil, grime, worn leather, steel shavings and suds. This was his world; he had known it since he was fourteen. But only in the past year had it become a nightmare.

Not that anyone said anything, but the feeling was there. The feeling that something was expected of him. Something he did not want to do.

He climbed the iron steps to his office, which a wooden partition separated from the offices of the management staff. Perce Ambler, his Sunday-shift replacement, had arrived. He was carrying a large roll of stiff paper under his arm. 'Hello, Perce,' Harry said. 'Anything there I should see?'

'Nothing much, Harry. Just another poster the ministry sent.' He shifted it awkwardly with his artificial hand, but made no resistance when Harry reached out to take it from him. Harry spread out the gaudy sheet. It was the *I'm Doing My Bit* one, an example of the recent, more blatant variety.

Perce harumphed and sat at his desk, hiding himself in the reports Harry had left. How glad Harry was that it was Perce, not he, who would have to put up the poster. Perce who had done his bit, and was nearly seventy anyway.

'See you Tuesday, then,' he said, trying to make his voice cheerful. 'By the way, I've put a new bearing ring on number eighteen.'

'Right.'

The steam engine was chuffing boisterously as he made his way across the yard. It had helped make a lot of rifles, mortars and machine guns, Harry thought. Had helped kill a lot of the enemy.

He was tired. It had gone on for so long. For six days of the week he worked twelve to fourteen hours. On Sundays he worked eight hours. One day off once a month. Tasteless low-grade food. And nothing to talk about, nothing to think about, except the war.

The bullish female security guard opened the gate for Harry to step through. The dusk light, the grey drizzle, intensified the town's air of exhaustion. Apart from the elderly there were few male civilians to be seen, and even fewer who did not limp on prosthetics or display artificial hands.

Harry had noticed a tendency lately for people on the street to look permanently dazed. Fortunately there wasn't a great deal of bombing, now that the air defences had learned to keep out first the airships and then the big four-engined bomber planes. Overhead, echelons of barrage balloons hovered, flapping elephantine ears.

At the corner he bought a newspaper. WE GIVE IT TO THEM, ran the headline. 'It has been a great day for the allies on the continent,' read the leader. 'We have delivered two more hammer-blows . . .' He stuffed the paper in his pocket and continued through the town. The posters made it like walking through a gaudy but somehow tatty corridor, lurid, exhortative, stirring unnatural energy into a life that had lost it from any other source. Some, darkened with grime, were from the war's distant past. *Go, Son, It's Your Duty*, pronounced a dignified matriarch, her hand on the shoulder of an erect, serious-looking young man. *Go!* implored a diaphanously clad young beauty, gazing into her husband's thoughtful features. Marching soldiers, climbing biplanes, battleships firing gigantic guns. Women and children in an iron foundry being herded by whip-wielding alien guards in spiked helmets. *Do You Want This to Happen Here?*

Later posters made more veiled references. *How Much Does Your Country Mean to You? Will Our Young Men Stand Alone?* Pictures of clenched fists, of infantry scrambling over earthworks, of shells exploding, of awful carnage. A nurse stretching out her arms pleadingly to the spectator, while behind her stood shadowy, haunting figures of uniformed wounded.

The posters that were frankly blatant were new. There was the *I'm Doing My Bit* one Harry would have to live with on the factory floor from now on. *Who Is a True Patriot?* asked another, answering its own question with a citizen who had responded to the call and one who had not. *They Said I Couldn't Go, But . . .* a middle-aged man proudly announced, looking at where his arm had been. A young soldier on crutches looked soulfully out at Harry, a bloodstained bandage around his head, his left arm a stump at the shoulder, his right leg cut off at the knee. *I Could Still Fight, If . . .*

In fact Harry had volunteered for active service before conscription came in, but had been turned down on medical grounds. By the time standards were lowered and the age limit was raised to fifty-five, he had found himself on the Essential War Work list. He now wore a prominent War Work badge to protect him from some of the odium that an able-bodied man in civvies inevitably attracted.

From a later variant of public disgrace the badge could not save him. She stepped hesitantly from beneath a greengrocer's awning, just as he reached the top of Constitution Hill. She was quite pretty, despite some evident nervous strain, in her faded blue bonnet and embroidered blouse, over which she wore a lady's tweed jacket. A glance at the hem of her long crinoline skirt revealed the reason for her physical awkwardness. Her right leg was missing and had been replaced by the usual strut-cage prosthetic.

Her gaze flicked over Harry's body and her expression became stern as she steeled herself to an unpleasant duty. Paralysis descended on Harry. She crossed the road, almost graceful with her limping gait as she bore grimly down on him, and even as it happened it was a wonder to him how he involuntarily cooperated in his ignominy, slowing his pace and passively accepting the white feather she handed to him.

She was red in the face by now and stomped immediately away down the hill. Harry glanced around. The street was empty. But the incident had been observed by some women in the greengrocer's, who were peering at him through the doorway.

Limply he dropped the feather, and slowly began to walk again, passing by the long blank wall of a warehouse. He felt sick and resentful. Resentful that the war should press so far, should press, press and carry on pressing. The armed forces would be nowhere without people like him, he told himself. Despite all difficulties production had gone up and up, to unheard-of levels. If such levels of production could ever be maintained in peacetime, the world would be a paradise.

But in peacetime, of course, they would not be maintained. The grimy warehouse wall gave way to a hundred-foot hoarding behind which there was a bombsite. Harry realized he had been muttering to himself, and in his daze he did not hear the footsteps that approached him from behind. He only started with fright when someone bumped into him, and at the same time he felt something being shoved into his raincoat pocket. His assailant, whoever it was, rushed straight past him and hurried on, then disappeared into a side passage. All the impression Harry received was of a small, tatty man who, unlike everyone else one saw, carried no gasmask.

He stopped, and pulled from his pocket the object that had been thrust there. It was a booklet, or pamphlet. On the plain paper cover, which carried no imprint of any ministry, were the words:

ENDING THE WAR
An Explanation of the Tommy Atkins Movement

The few pages contained a cramped, badly printed text which Harry did not inspect. Instead, he replaced the pamphlet in his pocket, and continued to trudge home.

Harry's flat was about two miles from his place of work. His routine after the Sunday shift was to attend evensong at the local church, drowsing through the vicar's sermon on sacrifice and fortitude. Then he would walk home. It was not until he had eaten his meagre supper of tea, grey bread, whale-oil margarine and a scrap of cheese, that he took out the pamphlet again. He had guessed it was seditious literature, but the strangeness of the text confused him. 'The followers of Tommy Atkins were not traitors, neither were they cowards,' he read. 'They tried to serve their country and civilization *by bringing the war to an end*.' And later:

For every man taken out of the line by Tommy Atkins, an enemy soldier was also taken out. If the ruinous conflict is to end there must be neither victor nor defeated, only a mutual refusal to fight. This war, now in its twenty-fifth year, is as destructive as ever and conceivably could continue until civilization is annihilated. The original causes of the belligerency have vanished into history. The struggle continues through the obstinate habit of national pride. Meantime millions have died, millions more will die, the flower of nations has been wiped out. Each new generation is raised only to be thrown into the military mincing machine.

Our leaders view the terrible carnage with equanimity. It is not generally known that the ruling officer classes *collaborated with the enemy* in order to put down the Tommy Atkins movement. The officer classes equate any desire to end the war with treason. The treason lies not with Tommy Atkins, however, but with the officer classes who perpetuate the war. 'Reason, not treason' is Tommy Atkins's motto.

Harry's mind bounced off the disjointed and peculiar sentiments. Who was Tommy Atkins? The pamphlet seemed to presume a knowledge on the reader's part which he, for one, lacked. 'The men at the front hate the war,' it went on. 'They have been driven beyond human endurance. Everyone hates the war, except those gaining pathological enjoyment from it. But the war does not stop.'

Briefly he wondered whether he should report the pamphlet to the police. Then he went to bed.

That night Harry dreamed again of his brother Terence, missing in action six months before. His name had not appeared in the prisoner lists; he had to be presumed dead.

He was dreaming of how Terence might have died. Harry was dreaming of mud. Terence was floundering in it, bogged down and sinking, futilely struggling. No one was there to help him. His backpack pressed him in further, but he couldn't release it. As he disappeared, he was still clutching his rifle.

In the dream's confusion Terence then became the veteran who had talked to Harry once, invalided out and spending the rest of his life in a wheelchair, sunning himself in scrubby parks. He had described to Harry the great swathe of mud that, after a generation of fighting, swayed to and fro across the continent, a fatal wound in the landscape and full of unsuspecting pits and deeps, composed in part of blood and excrement and rotting bodies. It was poisonous, too, because of the gas that was dissolved in it. 'A million dead in one battle,' the veteran had said, 'and all for another mile of mud. You don't hear of Field Marshal Henry these days, do you? Course you don't, 'cos they carted him off to the gentlemen's home. Lorst his reason, he did, after they told him where the regiment he sent out had got to. Gorn, they told him. Gorn in the mud. All smashed and blown up and drowned. They never did bring any bodies back.'

Terence was in the wheelchair. Terence was sinking, the evil-smelling muck closing over him, sinking and suffocating, alone in the darkness.

Harry awoke with a start. A noise had aroused him, approaching rapidly from the southeast. It sounded like a motorbike, except that it came from up in the air. It was quite different from any aeroplane engine he had ever heard. Steadily it grew louder, until it passed directly overhead. Then, abruptly, it stopped.

He got out of bed and peered curiously through the folds of the blackout curtain. Searchlights were weaving across the sky. Suddenly, to the west, red flames leaped up from the blacked-out city, accompanied by a loud roar.

There had been no ack-ack, so he could have just witnessed the crash of an experimental plane. Fire engines clanged in the distance. He stared at the glow for a while, then stumbled back to bed and slept fitfully till dawn.

Harry rose at his usual time and pottered about the flat for a few hours. This was the one day per month that he had completely free, but he was so used to being at work that staying at home had come to seem aimless and depressing. Sometimes he told himself that having a family might have made a difference to him; but one way or another he just didn't seem to be the marrying type.

At midmorning, gas mask slung over one shoulder, shopping bag in his hand, he went out. The day was sunny and he felt glad to get into the open air. He had forgotten all about the strange pamphlet. It came as a shock when, at the same spot near the top of Constitution Hill, the same shabby little man stepped out and barred his path.

'Still gotcher white fevver then?'

Harry looked at the apparition, speechless. The stranger's hair was overgrown, his clothes ragged. He still carried no gas mask. He spoke again, in a flat, brusque voice.

'Yer bruvver wants ter see yer.'

Harry felt himself go pale. 'Don't talk rubbish!' he spluttered.

''E wants ter *see* yer, I say. *Terence* wants ter *see* yer.'

'Terence? You know my brother's name?'

'I know a lot mate, more 'n you do I dare say.' He glanced nervously up and down the street. 'Let's get aht of 'ere afore we're spotted. In 'ere, quick.' He skipped into the mouth of a narrow alley. When Harry failed to follow he stopped and turned.

'You comin' or aintcha?'

'What are you trying to do?' Harry said firmly. 'My brother is missing in action. You can't take me to him.'

The other chuckled without any trace of humour. 'E's missin' orl right. Missin' an' over 'ere. Sod yer, then. Do wotcher bleedin' like.'

He turned his back on Harry and trotted rapidly down the alley. It was confined on one side by a brick wall and on the other by a board fence. He stopped, seemed to do something to a piece of planking, and then slipped through and was gone.

Harry stood bewildered. He was repelled by the man's coarse language, frightened by the whole incident. But, he realized slowly, he could not let it pass.

He would have to find out.

It was with a feeling of dread that he let his feet take him down the alley. He spent nearly a minute finding the plank that was fastened by only one nail, and more seconds passed while he learned how to dislodge and swivel it.

A cleared bombsite, thick with weeds, lay beyond the gap. The area was fully screened from the surrounding streets – on three sides by the ubiquitous hoardings, and on the fourth by the warehouse wall opposite. In a far corner the demolition squad had left a mound of rubble. Harry was just in time to see the scruffy little man disappear behind it. He set off in pursuit, stumbling on the uneven surface, snagging his feet in the weeds. Skirting the rubble heap, he saw a tarpaulin sheet weighted down with bricks and earth. It had been drawn back to reveal concrete steps descending into the ground.

Harry crept nearer. A murmur of voices came from the cavity. At the bottom, in shadow, a sackcloth screen covered the entrance to what he supposed was a cellar.

As he stood swaying on the brink his boot sent a fragment of concrete rattling down the steps. The voices instantly stopped. The sackcloth moved, and a pale face peered worriedly up at him, clearing once he was recognized.

'Well, well! Somebody ter see yer, Sarge! Yer'd better come in, mate.'

Showing no will of his own, Harry descended the steps while his 'guide' held the sackcloth aside for him to enter. He found himself in a dank, dirty, ill-smelling chamber, lit by a single candle whose glow picked out patches of white mould on the walls. Besides the little man there were two others in the cellar, and they had turned on the packing cases on which they sat to watch him enter. He did not know the one with the soft, haunted eyes, but he knew the other. It was his brother Terence.

His brother Terence. Alive. But not only that. It came as an almost equal shock to Harry's consciousness to see Terence out of uniform. He was clad in a soiled raincoat beneath which there showed a frayed cardigan and a grimed shirt with the collar missing. Like his companions, he looked no better than a tramp.

To be out of uniform, even when on leave, was against military law. Terence rose, offering his hand with incongruous casualness. He was younger and taller than Harry, and had always been the stronger, but now he looked ill, his face pasty and gaunt. 'So glad you could make it, Harry. By God, you look as if you'd seen a ghost. Get my brother a seat, Jenkins. And I dare say the stores would stretch to a brew-up.'

Alive and out of uniform . . . Harry found himself limply shaking his brother's hand. He flopped onto a crate the little man pushed behind him.

Terence reseated himself. 'You haven't got a fag on you, have you, Harry? We're all gasping.'

He nodded and handed over a packet of five Woodbines, refusing one himself and telling Terence to keep the remainder. He was in a funk. Already the sweaty, mildewy atmosphere was choking him. He could smell the unwashed men. He was struggling for breath, suffocating in the gloom. He didn't know how they could stand to live like this. They shared out three smokes from the packet and lit them from the candle flame, bending towards it in turn. Terence took a deep, shaky drag, then coughed for a while before he spoke again.

'This is a bit of a shock for you, I dare say, Harry. I gather they told you I'd been killed in action. They do that. Still, there might be a grain of truth in it from their point of view. We *are* presumed dead, with any luck. Drowned at sea.'

'At sea? You were coming home?'

'Yes . . . for secret courts martial. They had to do it that way – too delicate a matter to be dealt with in the open, in the field. That would be to risk further disaffection. The firing squad would have been secret, too. You'd have been none the wiser. As it was, an enemy sub saved them the job. Got us a mile or so offshore. There were two or three hundred prisoners and crew on board, I think. Probably a dozen made it to the beach – including

us three, so meet my fellow survivors and companions ever since:
Private Jenkins, who you've already bumped into, and Bombardier
Parcival. You've heard of Laurence Parcival, the poet?'

Harry barely glanced at the third man, merely wondering in
passing why an established literary personage did not hold a commission, though for his part he failed to recognize the name. He
was surprised to hear of an enemy sub operating in coastal waters.
The Navy claimed to control them absolutely.

Still, both points paled to insignificance compared to the import
of what Terence was saying. 'I'll come straight to the point, Harry,'
he hurried on. 'I take it you read our booklet? Good. You'll want
to know more details.' He puffed nervously on his Woodbine,
appearing distraught, though Harry was aware that in fact his
brother was scrutinizing him closely.

'No denying it, it was all a bit of a shambles. You can guess why.
Oath of secrecy or not, you can't keep a large-scale conspiracy under
wraps for very long. The officers got wind of it, an investigation was
under way – what were we to do? Let the movement be crushed, and
get shot for planning a mutiny into the bargain? Or play our hand?
We drew up a rule of thumb: we called out any sector where support
for Tommy Atkins was 40 per cent or more. There were only a few
of those, but we gambled on their setting an example. Once the
thing got going, we thought, it could spread like wildfire. Well,
we were wrong. High Command moved like greased lightning.
We'd shot a few officers to make things worse, which wasn't in
the plan. We were sealed off right from the start. Then they sent
the special forces in. You never heard of those, I'll bet? They are
real bastards, psychopathic killers – held in reserve specifically for
dealing with mutinies. They went through us like a dose of salts.
There weren't too many of us left to ship over the water.'

He paused, and lowered his voice. 'That's it, really. You do realize
that we're trusting you, Harry? What can you do for us?'

'Do?'

'A friend of Parcival's helped us at first. She even helped us get
the booklet printed. But she's been arrested, and the books seized.
We only just got away in time. We've been stealing to eat.'

The acrid tobacco smoke had revived Harry a little. He looked
up, misery in his face.

'And the enemy?' he said. 'Did you bother to think what *they*
would be doing, while you downed arms?'

They stared at him.

'Haven't you understood anything?' Terence demanded in anguish. 'This was a mutiny that crossed the lines! The 40 per cent

I mentioned had to be on *both* sides — it couldn't have worked otherwise! What's more, it was put down on both sides in exactly the same way! One side tipped off the other — we're not sure which.'

He sighed, speaking more calmly. 'It's in the booklet, Harry. Tommy Atkins is an international peace movement, recruited from the lower ranks of all the belligerent armies. If we achieve parity, we can take away the power of the officers. After all, the generals can't do a bloody thing if Tommy won't obey them.'

Seeing the look of bewilderment on Harry's face, Terence suddenly laughed. 'I get it! You don't believe it's possible to cooperate with the blokes on the other side. All I can say is, that shows how much of a civilian you are, Harry. It's one of the High Command's constant headaches. When the front becomes static, informal truces break out all up and down the line. That's why they try to keep things moving. Big attacks, constant artillery barrages or gas carpets, sneak night attacks — it's all to stop Tommy making friends with Fritz. But he does just the same. There have to be quiet spells. Even in a big push — what happens if a squad moves into a ruined village and finds an enemy squad there? You think they start shooting? Only if there are officers around! Better to trade rations.'

'It can't all be like that.'

'You're right, it isn't. But it happens. And some of us got to see who the real enemy is. There have been peace movements before — they all failed because they were civilian. Only Tommy has the ability to make the war stop, if he can make up his mind to it. What's the matter with you? Aren't you with us?' Terence's voice became desperate. 'Perhaps you need to be out there. You should see the bodies hanging like dirty rags on the barbed wire, thousands of them. You should see young boys going mad in front of your eyes, days after arriving. There's no way to describe what it's like. The docs admit it's beyond human endurance. That's why every man takes five grammes of diazine every morning — the anti-shock drug. You need it in your system or you just can't face it.'

Harry had never heard of diazine. By now his senses had adjusted themselves to the mephitic cellar, and the cigarette smoke was easing his breathing. An eerie glow seemed to surround the men. Jenkins was busy with a primus stove and a tin can. Bombardier Parcival had been watching the exchange, smoking quietly, otherwise still as a statue. Now he rose to his feet.

'Let me try, Terence,' he said gently.

Harry saw how amazingly tall and slender he was when standing. His poetical face hovered in the gloom, dark eyes almost glowing. He seemed untouched by the wretchedness around him. Head bent as though to avoid the low ceiling, he began sauntering to and fro, the Woodbine dangling negligently from his fingers.

'They say the war will destroy civilization,' he said. His cultured accents suggested social origins which reinforced the enigma of his lowly army rank. 'Myself, I disagree; it would have happened already. I'm afraid something worse is happening. Society has gone through the point of exhaustion, has recovered, and has learned to live with the war *permanently*. If we can't stop it, it won't stop. Ever.'

He raised his cigarette to stare at the glowing tip. 'It's a curious phenomenon when you think of it. A war as damaging and futile as this should have ended long ago. If they had any intelligence at all the respective governments would have arranged an armistice. But they haven't. They can only think of victory. They're gripped by patriotic mania, as is nearly everyone else – except those who have it rubbed off them at the front, and even there . . . In truth, our revolt was on a very small scale. And many of those who joined us did so for the wrong reasons.

'I wonder if you realize just what's happened to us all. What can one say of a society that sends its sons out to be killed by the million, for generation after generation? People are actually proud to have their sons blown up at the age of seventeen. What's the explanation? Really, it's simple. Man has a natural instinct for conformity. It's what makes large societies possible. We have many names for it, mostly approving: social discipline, patriotism, solidarity, a sense of responsibility, or simply the ability to organize. But there's the darker side, the readiness to accept irrational belief, to stifle conscience in the name of some arbitrary "cause", the tendency to automatic obedience. In the past there have always been individuals who were immune from this kind of conditioning and who formed their own attitudes. They acted like a leaven in society. Now their number dwindles. Guided by crowd emotion, society is learning a mode of behaviour more resembling the social insects: the ants, bees and termites. The ruling classes are unable to break free of it, so there's only one hope: to appeal to those at the bottom of the pyramid.'

'Thass right,' Jenkins crowed, 'the toffee-noses won't do nuffin'. Courst, the bombardier's a bit of a toffee-nose 'isself.'

'Are you saying the war will last for ever?' Harry asked, puzzled. 'That's ridiculous. In fact it seems to be running out of steam at the moment. Our new push isn't as big as the earlier ones.'

Parcival spoke firmly. 'It *will* last for ever, and technically speaking it's only at the beginning. Operations *have* been on a smaller scale recently, but that's because both sides are busy developing new weapons. Already the enemy has flying bombs our ack-ack can't bring down. Only battle-theatre weapons at present, but when they have the range to reach the Home Counties the bombing and gassing will start all over again. "The planet rolls through space, war fixed eternal on its face.""

Is he quoting his own poetry? Harry asked himself disdainfully. Such high-flown ideas seemed out of place, and they embarrassed him.

Terence coughed, as if realizing that his friend's didactic manner had made a poor impression.

'I had taken it for granted we could count on you, Harry.'

'Well, you shouldn't take it for granted. *You* may spit on patriotism, but some of us still have time for it.'

He paused. 'I don't know what makes you imagine I *would* think that way.'

'But that's simple.'

No one spoke. The silence seemed interminable, and Harry became uneasy.

"'E's just a bleedin' Cuthbert after all!' Jenkins yelled suddenly.

'I'm *not* a Cuthbert!' Harry startled himself with his own furious reaction. 'I tried to enlist right at the start! Even before conscription!'

'Then wotcher doin' wiv *these*, mate? An' *these*?'

Jenkins was rushing at him, punching him on the arm, kicking his shin. 'Like yerself too much, don'tcha?' Suddenly the little man seemed to go into a paroxysm. He ripped his clothes open and cast them off, to reveal a scrawny torso. In a parody of a body-builder's stance, he raised thin arms and flexed puny biceps.

'Why ain't one o' these *yours*, then?'

Harry averted his eyes on seeing the circular scars visible at both shoulder joints.

'Ahhrr, that's nuffin', I've had all four done.' Jenkins was relishing the moment. 'Lovely it was, too, when they put the grenades among us.'

Now Terence was moving; parting, with deliberation, his raincoat, his cardigan, his shirt, pulling the garments down over his right shoulder. There, too, a circular scar could be made out under the grey dirt.

'It's a woman's, actually,' he said casually. 'Nearly as strong as the other one now. Remarkable how a female limb toughens up on a man's body.'

'Even the bloody women got more guts 'n you!' Jenkins jeered.

Harry hung his head. The two men covered themselves.

'Well, that's why we thought you were one of us, Harry,' Terence told him. 'You haven't submitted. You've resisted all the social pressures to conform, and that indicates a strain of individuality in you.' Slowly, he added, 'Of course, perhaps it's for a different reason.'

'What do you mean by that?' Harry muttered resentfully. He glanced at Jenkins. 'You think I'm a coward too?'

'Only you know the truth about that.'

Terence gazed at him coolly. 'Limb donation is largely what keeps the front manned, you know. If Fleming hadn't discovered nerve-grafting the scale of casualties would have forced the war to a standstill years ago. The bombardier is being fanciful when he says it will last for ever, of course. But it will outlast our lifetimes. It isn't just limbs now, either. Killed-in-actions are being cannibalized for anything they've got intact – kidneys, livers, stomachs, hearts. And there's talk of the Medical Corps working on something new: organs grown in test tubes. Eventually, no matter how badly smashed up you are, the surgeons will be able to patch you together and put a gun back in your hands.'

'All right, I'll bring you some clothes,' Harry said dully. 'And some rations. But only once, do you hear? From then on, stay away from me . . .'

Perhaps he hadn't spoken loudly enough. No one seemed to have heard him. Jenkins' voice floated past, saying gently, 'I don't fink 'e'll do, d'you, Sarge?' And Terence was murmuring something in response.

With a scraping sound Terence moved his crate closer. 'Never mind. Let's have a mug of tea before you go, eh? To show no hard feelings? We'll make it a drop of the hard stuff in better times, what?'

'Yes, I suppose so.' Harry felt desperate to get out of the cellar, but by now there was a strong smell of brewing tea. Soon Jenkins was pouring it into tin mugs which he handed round.

'Bottoms up,' Terence said cheerily. 'To an end of it all.'

The tea was greasy and strong, its bitterness overlain with the sweetness of condensed milk. It warmed his stomach as he forced himself to drink. His brother, to his vague surprise, began talking reminiscingly of their boyhood, and of the exciting days when the war had begun. Everyone had been in favour of it, then. No one had expected it to drag on, and on, and on.

He put the mug down still half full. Jenkins glanced at it. Harry started to rise, but he felt dizzy, much dizzier than he had earlier. He flopped back on to the crate, feeling a film of sweat form on his brow. Terence had stopped talking. They were all watching him, Parcival with his distant schoolmasterly look, Terence and Jenkins more closely.

Something in the tea. Their faces, the whole cellar, blurred. His unfocused gaze went to the brightest thing: the candle flame. Hazy and large, it filled his dwindling consciousness, before he fell at their feet.

When Harry awoke and blearily opened his eyes, he became aware of sunlight. It was shining on the concrete floor against which his cheek rested. His head ached, and it was some time before he forced his gaze into focus.

Still unsteady from the effect of whatever drug he had been given, he clambered to his feet and stood swaying. The sackcloth screen was gone from the doorway, and the sunlight streamed down the steps and across the threshold. Gone too were the mugs of tea, the primus stove, and all the meagre signs of occupation. Only the packing cases remained.

Clearly Terence and his friends were better organized than they had let on. Was there nothing here as evidence of their presence? Yes: on the case which had served as a table was a little mound of congealed candle grease. But Harry touched it, and it was cold and dusty.

He drew a deep breath. His dizziness went. The box that contained his gas mask, its strap still slung over his right shoulder, bumped against the concrete doorpost as he hauled himself up the steps and stood thankfully in the open air. As he was about to move off he spotted his shopping bag lying some yards away among the weeds, where he supposed he must have dropped it in his excitement.

He picked it up and luckily was able to remember where to find the loose plank in the hoarding. Minutes later he was walking down Constitution Hill.

There, the familiar posters hit his brain. The sky pressed down, putting a lid on the world. At the bottom of the hill, he froze.

The woman who had handed him the white feather was standing on the other side of the road.

Harry's heart began to beat fast at the memory of his humiliation. She was quite unmistakable, in the same tweed jacket and crinoline skirt that she had worn the day before. She looked at him and seemed to recognize him, for she glared accusingly before turning to limp off with an embarrassed air.

He felt a sudden impulse to go after her and thrust the Tommy Atkins pamphlet into her hands, much as she had forced the white feather on him. 'You should read this,' he would tell her. 'It might change your mind about a few things.' He went as far as digging into his raincoat pocket for it.

But it wasn't there.

He must have left it in his room. Funny, he remembered putting it in his pocket before he left.

But why would he do that?

He stood there with his hand in his pocket, fingering the absence. He gazed around him, and for the first time the gaudy exhortations on the hoardings struck a note of normality. The scene in the cellar was beginning to seem hallucinatory, dreamlike. Three impractical idealists – mutineers, rather – cowering like rats. Wearing other people's limbs! Making a mockery of sacrifice! How different from the Terence he had always imagined, fighting and dying for his country without complaint!

With these thoughts, a luminous suspicion invaded the recesses of his mind. The person he had talked to could not possibly be Terence. The cellar he had just quit had been empty. There was no smell of men or Woodbines, and none of the detritus that human occupants leave behind them.

Yet no more than an hour or two had passed, judging by the position of the sun, since he had left his flat.

Then there could have been no Tommy Atkins pamphlet either. And if there was no Tommy Atkins pamphlet . . .

My God, I've been cracking up, he thought. *I'm having a nervous breakdown.*

Terence was dead. There could be no doubt of it. Reported missing in action, and not turning up on any prisoner list. Terence had died in the mud, where his body was not found. And Harry, driven half mad by repressed guilt, demented and hallucinating, had somehow found his way to a deserted cellar, and had passed out or simply fallen asleep there. He supposed he had suffered the civilian version of shell-shock (though many doctors denied that there was any such thing as shell-shock; it was only an excuse for cowardice).

The white feather, he told himself. *It all started with the white feather.*

For the first time in months he felt calm. The sensation was as if he had lit a gas mantle and revealed a darkened room he had never seen before. With it came a feeling of triumph and of over-whelming relief. He had weathered the crisis. He had refused to identify with those enticing phantoms, had rejected their shadowy rationalizations. He had regained control over his own mind.

And the war *would* end, yes, when there was victory for one side or the other, that much was obvious. Acting automatically, he found himself following his daily routine of buying a newspaper on the corner. He stood there as he scanned the lead story. It was again of the big push, the imminent final breakthrough as the press would have it. But Harry had heard a dark rumour. It was whispered that the 'big push' was really a last gasp, absorbing all the reserves. If it failed, there was not enough to hold the enemy back.

Shocking support for the rumour came in a paragraph at the bottom of the front page. *'According to unconfirmed sources, the suggestion to train servicewomen for the front line has once again been raised in cabinet.'*

The idea horrified Harry as much as when he had first heard it, several weeks ago. Surely it could not come to that! The most shameful and desperate resort of all – to send women into battle! Wasn't it enough that so many women were already willing to –

There were other rumours, of course, some of them officially encouraged. Such as that the enemy had a restitution scheme for his millions of war disabled, planning to requisition limbs from a conquered population. The story was widely accepted. After all, popular opinion had it that such reparation should be forced from the enemy without mercy, when victory came.

Harry could not really conceive that the war could be lost. His country's will was too strong. The nation would bear any sacrifice. Folding up the newspaper, he thrust it in his raincoat pocket and walked on. Soon he was entering the High Street, halfway along which was a sign he knew well. It hung over the pavement outside the registration office of the Donation Service, and it bore the symbol of that service: a solitary burning candle. No longer was it a torment and a rebuke. A warm haven beckoned, now that the decision was made. How much more life would mean to him once he had the feeling of pulling his weight with a community making every effort. He imagined himself greeting Perce Ambler with a new joviality. How foolish he had been to exclude himself from such comradeship! He saw himself on the factory floor, respected as a man, safe from sneers and silent insults.

Coming closer and closer, the burning candle seemed suspended from the pressing blue sky, its wax dripping like blood on to the pavement.

JOHN SLADEK

Stop Evolution in Its Tracks!

Creationists are seldom colourful, exuberant characters. Their name, which ought to remind us of burgeoning life, somehow calls to mind the dusty relics of another age: celluloid collars, tent meetings, barns bearing giant advertisements for laxative. For the most part, the colourful and the exuberant have deserted this unprofitable philosophy.

One exception is Professor Abner Z. Gurns, founder of the Gurns Institute for Advanced Creationist Studies. Gurns is known for other things besides creationism. There was 'prayer-wars', his patented defence system employing, he claims, a crew of the lesser angels to defuse godless Soviet missiles in flight. Before that there was his attempt to translate the Bible into a virus, for inoculation of the whole world . . . And before that, his planned expedition to raise Noah's Ark, which he believed to have sunk 'somewhere near the East Pole'.

If Professor Gurns has a place in history, however, it will most likely be that of the father of modern creationism. Few have done as much for this controversial field as Gurns; no one has established anything remotely rivalling the Gurns Institute.

I went to interview the professor at the Institute, a cluster of modern buildings on a bluff overlooking the sturdy little town of Stove Bolt, Tennessee. The building containing Gurns's office is a no-nonsense structure of glass and steel, the kind that might pass elsewhere for a school of business administration. The only visible clue to its higher mission is the motto carved above the entrance:

WHEN ADAM DELVED AND EVE SPAN
WHO WAS THEN AN ORANGUTAN?

I waited for the professor in a bland anteroom. The only unusual note was a large framed photo on the wall. It showed ants eating a red rose. The title, I saw, was 'Paths Untaken'.

While I waited, I glanced through a selection of Institute tracts ('The Great DNA Fraud', 'Fossils – God's Joke on Darwin?'). Somehow they didn't go with that disturbing photo.

I found myself trying to form a picture of my host. Based on a couple of blurry news photos, I imagined him to be a quaint fellow in a celluloid collar and rimless glasses, sporting a watch-chain on his snuff-stained vest. The watch would be set to Central Standard Time.

On the contrary, Professor Abner Gurns turned out to be a boyish thirty-year-old with a crew cut and an athletic handshake. His white lab coat was open to show a sweatshirt with a picture of William Jennings Bryan (in a celluloid collar).

'I was trained as a scientist,' he explained. 'For years I struggled with the so-called theory of evolution, trying to make sense out of it. Heck, if it was in the textbooks, it just had to be true, right?' His boyish grin appeared.

'Well, something happened one day that hit me like a ton of assorted lightning rods. It made me see that Darwin's theory of evolution is nothing but hogwash and hokum! The American public – heck, the world public! – had been deceived for a century. It was time to take off the blinders and do some real science. So I came out here and founded the Institute.'

He led me into his office, where a glass wall showed the grassy bluff and the tiny town of Stove Bolt far below. Why had he picked this place for his institute?

'Because Stove Bolt is the place where in 1923 they held the famous Snopes Monkey Trial – the first great victory for Creationism in our century.'

What was his discovery? Professor Gurns sat on the edge of his desk and explained.

'I was studying fossils night and day, spending my days at the Natural History Museum, my nights hitting the books. Trying and trying to make sense out of evolution. Then one day on my lunch hour I wandered out on the street and got knocked down by a bus. When I got up, everything seemed strange. The people were strange. I saw purple hair. I saw this short blind man wearing a derby. He was leading this tall man who played on the derby with drumsticks. I saw a dog on wheels. Then this yellow cab pulled up, and I looked inside – *and the whole back seat was filled with one gigantic cabbage.*'

I asked the professor what all this meant to him.

'It means that nothing in the fossil world makes sense. I got more wisdom from one hairline fracture than from years of studying! I learned that we have to take fossils for what they are, and stop trying to piece them together into a story. Evolution is a fake.'

He picked up a flat stone from his desk and held it in both hands. I saw that it was an ammonite, a common fossil.

'You know, Darwinists always accuse us of not studying the fossil record. That just ain't so. Speaking as a scientist, I have always been primarily interested in the fossil record – that is, the fossils themselves, and not what a bunch of Darwinists try to tell me about the fossils.

'They claim that fossils show evolution – one animal turning into another. Hogwash! There is not one fossil anywhere that shows one animal turning into another. *Every fossil you can find is perfectly still – not moving or changing at all!*'

He put down the ammonite and picked up what looked like a soup bone. 'This here bone comes from one animal and one animal only, am I right? Speaking as a scientist, am I right?'

I had to agree.

'Okay, then. Anybody who tells you this here bone came from two or three animals has to be a darn fool.' His eyes narrowed, and he waved the bone like a club. 'A fool or an atheistic Darwinizer!'

A bell rang somewhere. He looked at his (ordinary digital wrist-) watch. 'I got a lecture right now. Come along and sit in.'

I followed him to the Wilberforce Auditorium, where perhaps a hundred students were seated, eager to receive his message. I sat to the side where I could watch them. They seemed a pretty typical bunch of kids, though slightly subdued.

'Speaking as a scientist,' he began, 'it just beats me how anybody can believe in the evolutionary fairy tale for five minutes!' There was some nervous laughter and applause.

'Evolutionists will tell you how some little old amoeba evolved itself into some bigger bug, and how that evolved itself into a fish, and so on, right up the scale until the ape evolved itself into a man. But there's two things wrong with that cockeyed story.

'In the first place, the amoebas never evolved at all. They're still here! Speaking as a scientist, I can vouch for that! I have looked down a microscope myself and seen them. They look like this.'

He showed a slide of blobs. 'Still the same little critturs they was when Noah marched them aboard the ark, two by two.'

When the murmurs of amazement had died down, he continued: 'In the second place, apes could not evolve into humans for a very simple reason: *there are no apes.* The things we call apes in zoos are nothing but men dressed up in hairy suits. I myself have visited a theatrical costume place where they rent such costumes. There they are, hairy suits *with nobody inside.*'

He showed several slides: a gorilla suit hanging on a rack, a man getting into the suit, the man wearing the suit minus the head, and a gorilla. The class murmured louder, apparently angry at the duplicity of the Darwinists.

A boy wearing a DON'T BE A MONKEY'S UNCLE sweatshirt put up his hand. 'Sir, how can they lie to us like that? Isn't it unconstitutional?'

'Lying breaks an even higher law, Vern,' said the professor. 'Not that Darwinists care about that. But let's move right along to *survival of the fittest*. Can anyone tell me what that is supposed to mean? Yes, Sue Bob?'

A girl wearing a DON'T GO APE FOR DARWIN sweatshirt stood up. 'It's circular reasoning, sir. They claim the ones who survive are the fittest. Then they try to prove this by pointing to the survivors – must be fit, because they survived.'

'Exactly, Sue Bob. Can anybody imagine anything more ridiculous than survival of the fittest?'

Loud laughter and some applause.

'All over the country, folks are jogging and riding bikes, going to fitness centres, all to keep fit – but do they survive? Heck no, they all die eventually, same as everyone else. The fit shall perish with the unfit. Why, old Methuselah lived a lot longer than any jogger, and we know for a fact, he never rode a bike in his life.'

The professor now seemed to be in training himself. He strode back and forth energetically as he talked, he flailed his arms, pounded the lectern, and spoke at times so rapidly that it was difficult to keep notes. There are, he said, five unanswerable arguments for Creationism:

'One. **The universe is one grand design**. Nucular physicists see electrons going around the atoms.' (So do nuclear physicists.) 'Astronomers see planets and stars and stuff going round the sun. Everything goes round and round like the wheels of a watch.' (This baffled many students until the professor used a large plastic model to demonstrate that watches once had wheels inside.)

'The same careful planning shows up in the animal and vegetable kingdoms. A banana is easy to peel because it was made for peeling. Fish can swim, which is lucky, because they are invariably found in water. Our two ears are located on different sides of our heads to give us stereo hearing.

'All of this design implies a designer – not to mention a team of draughtsmen and production engineers. Butterflies and flowers come in lots of pretty colours, so a team of interior decorators are probably involved somewhere. Or take birdsong, which requires not only a composer, but an arranger, a producer, and a musicians' union.

'Two. **You can't evolve a sow's ear into a silk purse**. In other words, there is just no way that a simple crittur can make itself complicated. You might as well expect a gas mantle to turn into a chocolate grinder.' (The professor explained these items.) 'Life is just what you make it, not something else.

'Three. **The great giraffe debate**. Atheistic Darwinizers may try to claim that the giraffe went around stretching its neck up to eat leaves from the trees for a few generations, and this made its neck grow longer. The real truth is, giraffes didn't need to stretch at all, because their necks were already so long. Besides, what about dolphins? They live in the depths of the oceans where there are no trees at all.' (This puzzled me and still does. I tried to ask the professor to elaborate on it, but nearby students told me to hush my mouth.)

'Four. **Everything invented by the Creator has some use**. Even a duck-billed platypus proves that the Creator had a fine sense of humour. What other use could it possibly have?

'Five. **All of the atheistic communists in Russia believe in evolution**. Enough said.'

Professor Gurns concluded his lecture by offering to thrash anyone in the room who still believed in Darwinism. That brought applause and cheers from the students.

Among the students lingering after class to ask questions was a girl student wearing an EVOLUTION – NON, MERCI sweatshirt.

'Professor, are you absolutely sure ontogeny doesn't recapitulate phylogeny?'

Gurns stood in silence for a moment, holding his large watch model. Then he said, 'Darla Jeanette, I wish you could rephrase that question.'

'Well, they say that during pregnancy, a human foetus looks at different stages like a fish, then a frog, then . . .'

'I don't see any point in dragging in talk like that, pregnancy and foetuses,' he replied. 'Young girl has no need to know about that stuff, no need at all. You tend to the fossil record, and leave the pregnancies to me.'

The professor then conducted me to the Deluge Lab, where a magnificent full-size replica of Noah's Ark had been constructed. After hanging up his watch model in the corner, he explained what was going on here: Creationist graduate students were packing the ark with pairs of stuffed animals, to prove that all the species would fit inside.

But as in all toy arks, the giraffes seemed to be giving trouble. Researchers were climbing ladders to take measurements of two stuffed ones.

'Maybe Noah laid them down,' someone suggested. 'They'd fit pretty good laid down.'

'But their legs spread out a lot,' someone else complained.

'Maybe Noah sawed off their legs. Hey, why not? There's nothing in Genesis says they had to have all animals with legs.'

'Now, now, boys and girls,' said Professor Gurns. 'I'm sure you can come up with a better answer than that.'

Back to his office, where the professor showed me a model of the Institute, with planned future development.

'We're still *evolving*,' he said, with another boyish grin. 'But seriously, we need to add a few departments to fill in all the gaps. For instance, we need some professional help in classifying the fossils of sea critturs. You know, fish fossils have been found way up on mountain slopes. The only explanation is, Noah's Flood covered even the highest peaks. We aim to prove that, once we get set up with our own Department of Marine Biology. It'll go right over here. We've already got a genuine marine to run it.

'Over here will be our anatomy department, plenty of work there, too. We need to study how the leopard got his spots, how the camel got his hump, how the whale got his throat, and all like that. Then there's the whole question of Adam and Eve's navels, a subject for some serious contemplation.

'And this area will be the new department of geophysics, to help prove how the earth is flat. For that, we'll need lots of surveying equipment, maps and so on. Probably need to buy some time on a satellite and get some real clear pictures of the earth from way high up. We like to be up to date, you know, use the latest technological – '

Footsteps came pelting down the hall. The door banged open and a student barged in, out of breath. 'Professor, come quick! The giraffe is on fire!'

As we all hurried back to the lab, the student explained. One researcher, attempting to shrink one of the stuffed giraffes slightly with a heat gun, had set it ablaze.

By the time we arrived, the fire was out, and students were opening skylights to dissipate the smoke. There was little visible damage to the animal itself. However, the great plastic model watch had melted and sagged.

As I left the Institute for Advanced Creationism, I looked out over the bluff, where students were flying kites shaped like glossy French loaves. Down below lay the town of Stove Bolt. I could just make out the little red courthouse where, more than sixty years before, the Snopes Monkey Trial had struck the first blow for Creationism. In that trial, a monkey named Snopes had been successfully prosecuted under Tennessee law for possessing an opposable thumb — a blasphemous imitation of human kind.

The Darwinists had been doing well in the trial until the very end. When the defence lawyer began his closing remarks, the jury was distracted by strange humming noises coming from within the courtroom fireplace. The humming was not like human humming, but the humming of steel rails. Finally the jury gave up all pretence of listening, and indeed the lawyer stopped speaking. All were transfixed, watching the dark hollow of the fireplace, waiting for an express train to come screaming out of the darkness and thundering through the tiny room.

RICHARD CALDER

Toxine

She lay amid the lumber of my grandmother's attic: a dead princess, used, discarded, forgotten, in the ruin of her dark tower. Her name was Toxine. After school, I often retreated to her shadows, to contemplate her broken beauty and comb her long, long hair. I had discovered her shortly before my thirteenth birthday, during a year in which my parents seemed for ever abroad. Business, they said. Her incorruptible porcelain flesh consoled me. For generations my family had dealt in antiques, and the attic had proved a graveyard for the unsaleable. But why had no one bought Toxine? Perhaps she would have been too expensive to repair; perhaps she wasn't the fashion. Beyond the trapdoor, she had awaited an admirer, a lone thing of loveliness in a world of Victorian junk. She had awaited me.

I attended a large comprehensive in Notting Hill. Staring at my book, flushed and intent, I'd discern, not a line of algebra or a spelling exercise, but a confusion of limbs lit by a shaft of light from the eaves; a sister, abandoned like me. Dressed for her first ball, her blood-red gown was emblematic of her martyrdom. The lips too, and fingernails long as a mandarin's, were incarnadined, so her body seemed one sensuous wound. But her eyes were not those of a victim: they were murderous. Green, and made of a luminous enamel, they glowed catlike in the gloom. She smelled of cat, her perfume the musty, electric scent of damp streets and brief couplings. A choker, half-obscured by inky locks, proclaimed her name. It would appear in my school books, on my desktop, on playground walls; and I would taste it upon my tongue as I ran home each evening to the sanctuary of the attic, to the hours between supper and bed. Toxine, Toxine, Toxine.

My father (though premature senility later effected a sea change) subscribed to a William Morris-type socialism, and insisted that the son of an antiquarian should be educated at a state school, alongside fellow artisans. School was an ant-nest, a midden. I remember Daz, so called because of his dandruff: a fat blubberball of a boy, my chimera and persecutor. I was consumed with plotting his demise. A poisoned wine gum? A sniper-shot from my customized Webley?

Or an assassination squad funded by the huge reserves of my piggy bank? But I was a shy, bookwormy child whose resources were purely mental; it was my shyness, interpreted as supercilious conceit, which made me so unpopular. I was called 'Lord Snooty' and boys with goblin faces would jeer and poke, while their doxies applauded, giggling. A few gum-chewing little whores kept my nascent sex dreams company (Trace and Trish, was it? Or Trash and Treeze?), but they were insufficiently doll-like, too grossly human, to inhabit those dreams for long. I was alone; my comfort, Toxine. She had sentenced my heart to a lifetime's infatuation. In my classroom reveries I would arrive at school with her on my arm, to the wonder and envy of all; and she would tell everyone how I had awoken her, just like the Sleeping Beauty, how clever I was, how we would live happily ever after. But school, with its wretched abundance of reality, prevailed, while Toxine and all that was marvellous lay dead. Toxine, I knew, must live.

Each night, after combing her hair, I rehearsed her resurrection. I laid her out; bathed her; lit candles at her head and feet. One, two, three, four candles. Then, with necromantic tools gleaned from a Meccano set, I would sit cross-legged by her side and ponder the necessary surgery. Lifting her dress above the waist revealed a panel in her abdomen, which, when removed, left her disembowelled, her pretty, clockwork innards submitted for my appraisal. She was horribly complex, a glittering bellyful of cogs, springs and wheels that granted me no favours. Toxine, you were maddeningly coy. My hands shook and faltered. Before this unknown country I at first did no more than clean off rust and oil the atrophied vitals. My astonished science master, subject to after-hours interrogations, proved an inadequate guide; I learned more from my Saturday afternoons in the public library, reading everything indexed under 'clockwork' and 'dolls'. I was soon confident my beloved would respond to more earnest overtures. But my exploratory sessions, conducted with screwdriver and knife, which would begin with such a rush of delight as I plunged my hands into her metal womb, ended, invariably, with her stomach ruptured and exploding like an overwound watch. Such delicacy! In the candlelit garret, reassembling those precious elements of life, my hands would again explore her dark interior. Ours was to be a hopeless courtship.

On my morning walk from Chepstow Villas to school I would look back at my grandmother waving goodbye and at the roof of the big, patrician house where my fairy princess was entombed. Soon, soon, I'd murmur. So besotted was I, so eager to see her walk, I forgot my loneliness, the bullyboys, the adolescent sluts, forgot even Mum and Dad (across the Atlantic, I had overheard, devouring each other); I was obsessed with knowing her mysteries, of uncovering the secret life of machines. But I also forgot precocity has its limits. The mechanism that had once animated Toxine was beyond the understanding of a thirteen-year-old; and my attempts to revive her who was more cat than girl, more machine than cat, more beautiful than all, continued to be shamed, each attempt accompanied by that explosion of belly parts, the familiar haemorrhaging of porcelain and steel.

Academically, I prospered. I swotted with the fervour of a novice who has glimpsed the life to come; but salvation lay behind a veil of unknowing, perpetually out of reach. I plundered alarm clocks, carriage clocks, cuckoo clocks, to transplant the components I had wrecked; I smuggled her ratchets into metalwork lessons, to be re-bored and soldered. Tox, Tox, why didn't you rise from your bier? Why did you stare at me, glass-eyed and dumb? Despairing, I would wander through school after last bell, through deserted classrooms, playgrounds and corridors, the fading light of that distant autumn conjuring phantoms from the dark: the goblin faces of my enemies leering from behind bike sheds; of *fillettes fatales,* spiteful and vain; and Daz, above all Daz, his face smirking into my own, babbling, 'Little dolly daydreams is dead, dead, dead, little dolly daydreams is dead.'

After months of effort I acknowledged my failure. Toxine lay unrestored. I surrendered; she had suffered my ignorance enough. I sealed the belly panel upon craftsmanship defiled by my incompetence. If her mechanical heart were to beat, it would be elsewhere, in a limbo reserved for the inorganic, an artificial paradise denied to me. All that was left was to comb her silky locks (they were real silk) and gaze upon her tirelessly until grandmother called me to bed; or else to lie by her side, she exhausted by disappointment, I by guilt. Sometimes I thought she mewled, her sphinxlike eyes burning with reproach; sometimes I thought her ruby lips trembled on the brink of resolving her riddle. But she was a tease, rewarding my devotion with silence, offering herself only to freeze at my touch. My arms about her tiny eighteen-inch waist, the red silk dress crushed beneath me, I would caress her dislocated limbs, her cracked porcelain breasts, in intimacies cold as the oncoming winter.

When snow began to fall and I took blankets to our eyrie my grandmother became anxious, especially when I caught a chill. I ignored her admonitions, her suspicious looks, and stayed faithful to Toxine. I variously explained my excursions as sorting out jumble for the school fête, or observing the stars with my telescope. My grandmother, an arthritic old woman, was unable to climb the attic stairs and could not verify these excuses.

My vigils grew prolonged. Often it was so cold I thought I might fall asleep, my head next to hers, never to wake up. It would be sweet. One night, tucked beneath several blankets, my drowsiness became irresistible. Snowflakes drifted down from the rafters, speckling her sable hair. She seemed to wear a crown of ice. Behind us, a rocking-horse broke into a canter, spurred by the north wind. A stuffed parakeet bristled. I looked into those Byzantine eyes, elliptical and grave, and in their luminous depth saw a land, a happy land, where there was neither tears nor pain. A city, with walls of porcelain and wax, descended from the sky. It was toytown, city of ceramic, bisque and cloisonné, where girls with geisha-white faces and the eyes of snow leopards danced like figurines atop a music box, danced before their master, the King of Clockwork. City of dolls, of cats, of machines. Come away, I heard her whisper, come away, O human child! I held her tight, falling over and over into a jade-green sea; but as I fell, her voice changed; it became querulous, imperative, so that, starting awake, I drew back from her and, looking up, saw the outline of my father in the dark. 'What *are* you doing?' he said.

Toxine was the creation of an unknown craftsman apprenticed to Peter Carl Fabergé. It has been speculated that he was a Frenchman who worked in Fabergé's London studio between 1890 and 1900. Toxine was the sole evidence of his eccentric talent. To construct an android, an automaton, in the manner of Jacques de Vaucanson, Jaquet-Droz, *père et fils*, Frederick of Knause, and the Maillardet family, to revive and better their technique, seemed to have been his passion. But these eighteenth-century masters, who had inspired him to realize such a perverse simulacrum of the female anatomy, had not influenced his treatment of the sex's loveliness. In demeanour, Toxine had been infected by her time: a parody of womanhood who belonged, in the history of taste, to the *fin de siècle*. The pale, consumptive flesh, tinderbox eyes, and red, vampiric mouth – all that high romanticism concealing the classically tempered innards – was an amalgam of certain women painted by Moreau, Toorop and Klimt. She was a swansong of the Decadence, her beauty that of innocence betrayed and of crime discovered; at once Ophelia, daughter of water and lilies, and that vicious chit, Salomé. That her pedigree had been unrecognized, and that she had remained uncatalogued for nearly seventy years, represented, for my father, a handsome and unlooked-for profit; for me, an incomparable loss.

My mother was still in New York. Dad had been alarmed at receiving a letter from my grandmother detailing his son's increasingly odd behaviour, namely, the boy's interludes in the attic. He had returned to investigate. And now Toxine sat in the back of our shop in the Portobello Road, lost. The night before she vanished, to be auctioned at Sotheby's, I stepped out of bed and stole downstairs. There was much I wanted to say. I promised I would find her again, that I would bring her back and nurse her to health. 'O Mademoiselle!' I whispered, kissing her cheek. 'They won't defeat us. Not Daz, not my parents, no one. I won't fail you again. Ever!' Next day my father told me about the divorce.

My progress to adulthood was uneventful. Publicly, at least. Following the sale of Toxine I was placed in the care of a child psychiatrist, who, after some months, reassured my father that my fetishism – he cited, predictably, 'domestic crisis' – would pass. It did not pass; I learned to hide it, so that from school to university my life was notorious only for being so bland. My inner life, that attic of the skull dank with dreams of mechanical girls, was uncharted. To all, I remained the ridiculous youth who spent his evenings alone with his books. No one knew what drove me to study the voluptuous laws of mechanics; what rendered me my facility with machines. But I knew: it was my guardian angel, Toxine. Nightly, she spoke to me. She said, 'Build me flesh, a body wherein I may dwell and again be yours . . .' My father, mindful of my supposedly cured fixation, was disturbed to see me poring over back copies of *The Connoisseur*. One day he discovered, at the bottom of my wardrobe, several monographs on historic automata; these, along with my hopes for a lathe, calibration instruments, or anything that might have again bruised my mind, were summarily destroyed. With the annulment of his marriage (my mother had settled in Detroit with some bastard called Hank), Dad had taken a morbid interest in my welfare. At last, either sensing my anxiety and fearing it would lead to a breakdown, or told, perhaps by a doctor, that I should be humoured, he indulged my entreaties, and a boxroom above our shop became my studio. Of course, in financing what he considered to be a therapeutic hobby, Dad never suspected the extent to which my work was Toxicological.

I took up my dark, secret task with fluency, for the loved one guided my hand. My output – clowns, acrobats, singing birds, and other exotica – was modelled on eighteenth-century examples: homages, mostly, to Vaucanson. I produced so many, my room itself began to resemble a *tableau mécanique*. Though little more than crudely engineered bagatelles made of tin and cardboard, my juvenilia, in three years, acquired a sophistication that impressed the entry board at Brunel. 'Shh!' I'd hear as I lay in bed. 'It's me, Toxine. I'm waiting. Make me walk and talk. I can't stand it any more. Make me kiss you. Make me!'

But it was not until my grandmother died and we were installed in her grand mansion that, with the benefit of a larger workshop, an inheritance and my father's increasing pliancy (he had begun his descent into mental squalor), I could attempt my androids, TX1 through 7. I limited myself to constructing their motors, hydraulics and servomechanisms; the bodywork, which I designed, was contracted out, at fearless expense, to Royal Doulton and Wedgewood. I disdained electronics; though forced to concede the advantages of a few circuits and switches, I imitated, whenever possible, the technology of the age of steam. To that age the species *Toxine* owed her origin, her inventor a steam-driven man. What a titan he had been, that disciple of Fabergé: he had translated the idiom of his eighteenth-century counterparts into that of the modern world; he had industrialized clockwork. I was jealous. He had been as familiar with the principles of advanced metallurgy as with the entrails of a clock. I wanted to understand him; to become him.

At college, I read of the great Victorian engineers and wondered how their skills might complement those of antique horologists; I studied bridges, tunnels, canals, the art of the cantilever and girder, asking how such examples might apply, say, to Vaucanson's flautist or the chess-player of Kempelen; I read the mechanistic philosophers and the works of Samuel Smiles. My first creation, a thing of cams and cranked shafts, died at birth, her body too frail to withstand the violence of her own organs. I called her Tristesse. My second android was strengthened by wire mesh, which ran like an unseen arterial grid beneath her porcelain epidermis. She was a silly, skittish thing, and I called her Taratata. Tressaillement, my third, was a confection of masterful clockwork and sweetly sculpted lines. Her gears were exquisite. She was outshone, however, by Topaze; and Topaze, in turn, by the three sisters who were the culmination of my art: the Mesdemoiselles Tonique, Toison and Trésor. On these robots I lavished gowns of crimson silk, carmine lipstick and verdant mascara. Their beauty was bittersweet. To none could I give the name Toxine. Accomplished as they were, spoilt and flirtatious, ready to prink, prank and pout at the turn of a key, the Toxine Experimentals palled before the beauty of their original. I remembered Toxine through a child's eyes, as a vision of first love. Craftsmanship alone could not recapture her; nor could those who aped her embody the uniqueness of her charm. My dolls, though technically sound, displaying complex locomotive functions despite the brittleness of their flesh, were spiritless replicas. I took a hammer to them. Poor things, by the time I sat my finals I had reduced you all to smashed crockery. It was not enough to possess the outward form: I desired the soul: that ghost in the machine, that quintessence of clockwork, that elusive twist of pitifulness and crime. How to distil? How to quantify?

I wandered through the late-night streets as I had once wandered through school after last bell: in despair. Traversing Oxford Street, I would follow girls overwrought with make-up swanking home from discos and pubs, seeking among them, in some mechanical gesture, some artifice of fashion or speech (O women are most beautiful when like machines), the answers to my hopelessness. But neither they nor the shop-window dummies, whose street this was, and to whom I turned with longing, offered counsel. Returning to my bedroom, while the house was still, I would review the ranks of little porcelain friends I had amassed over the years: antique and distant cousins of Toxine. Hidden beneath the bed was my Barbie collection. Sindy, too, was well represented. I owned dozens of these mannequins, each one altered to resemble Mademoiselle T. I would dye the nylon hair black, dress them in red, stain the sun-tanned flesh white and, with a dash of fluorescent paint, award them green pussycat eyes. But these china and plastic confidantes were as powerless as the street girls who understudied for machines to tell me where lurked the soul of my love. In my studio, spreadeagled upon a workbench, a slaughtered doll offered herself for repair. I could not move. I had begun to admit that I was to be left with only memories: images of a boy shivering in a cold, damp attic, embracing the automaton he would have died for.

Ten years passed, and memories decay. Toxine no longer spoke to me. I had failed as a child to restore her, as a man to rebuild her. My promise was unfulfilled. Burnt-out, my affective life void, I spent the days in my derelict workshop surrounded by the remains of would-be brides and empty bottles of whisky. After graduating I had studied industrial design at the Royal College of Art. It seemed inevitable that, with my knowledge of the mechanical aspects of the human form, I should excel in the design of prosthetics. My patents bought me respite from this world, a retreat from the banality of the herd. But drink, drawn curtains and the roughshod years could not wholly bring respite from Mademoiselle. A month might pass by when her presence was all but exorcized; then her face would again taunt, and I would nervously fondle a cog, a wheel, some scrap of silk rent from a red ball gown, begging her, Don't leave me, don't leave me, while she would even then grow indistinct, claimed by the forbidden zone of the past. After such a visitation the craving would begin. My blood hollered for a machine. Any machine. And I would flee the house to the showrooms of Dixons and Currys, to ponder computers, microwaves, TVs and cameras, to gaze upon stereos and VCRs, admiring their lovely man-made surfaces – modern-day correspondence of china and bisque – while surreptitious fingers delved into intricate silicon innards. Unsatisfied, frustrated, I would loiter in bookshops furtively thumbing the pages of car-repair manuals, the manifestos of Marinetti, or science-fiction novels with covers boasting chrome-plated robo-women with bellies of electrical flex. Later, I might find myself in the suburbs outside an industrial estate, where a workforce (if I was lucky, a workforce of young females) would be arriving for their shift, punctual as the Jacks of an old town clock. And life for me would have remained like this if I had not met with an epiphany, an apparition that was to salvage the past, recall me to my responsibilities, to my life's work, and bring my pilgrimage to an end.

My father came to spend much of his time in a sanatorium near Bournemouth, and I found it necessary, after so long an absence, to re-enter the world and attend to our affairs. The shop was in decrepitude; and I, who had been so prodigal with my inheritance, was in debt. In hope of mitigating the urgent but atrocious task of becoming a penny-wise bourgeois, I advertised for an assistant. The salary was meagre and, to compensate, the incumbent was to be offered free lodgings. The boxroom above the shop – the room that had been my boyhood studio – would be suitable. I saw only one applicant.

It was as I climbed a step-ladder, my back to the door, to dust a row of 'Waverley' novels, that the air filled with the scent of oil, ball bearings and the mildewy aroma of cat. I turned, and the recognition was terrible. Name, Height, Age, Weight, Distinguishing Characteristics. Beata Beatrix! No; but almost, almost. The exterior had been maltreated: raven hair, shorn and punkishly spiky; depraved chocolate-box face (that same face of Dresden china) ill-used; and the clothes – a flamboyant display of Oxfam chic – were appalling. But I saw beyond these ravages into the sacred heart of her design. And it was unflawed. Her languid, Art Nouveau lines had been traced from a drawing by Mucha; her eyes, feline and tinged with corruption, were like emeralds set by Lalique into the head of an ivory nymph;

and when she moved it was with a stiff robotic gait, accompanied by an almost audible whirr of clockwork. (My expertise with artificial limbs informed me that, beneath those full-length skirts, she sported callipers. I later learned that polio, contracted while on holiday abroad, was the cause.) An unwomanly eighteen-year-old, with childish hips and breasts, she had run away from home to live in a Golborne Road squat 'full of bizarros and rififi. And I've had enough of bizarro boys,' she'd sigh. 'I'm no sideshow. What's that? Was I *safe*? Tell it to Johnny. Tell it to Johnny Impaler.' Tina, or Tinkerbell, or Tink, as she claimed her friends called her ('because I'm just *so* mignonesque') was thus grateful for the asylum the job offered and was soon resident above the shop. Each day, as I watched her totter about like an expensive toy slightly damaged, I radicalized my methodology. I knew, now, the way ahead.

This was the illumination: Pygmalion had been wrong. I should not have sought to give life to stone and metal, but endeavoured to raise mankind to the level of the machine. The beloved had returned in a moment of grace; she lay within that human frame, moaning to be free. It would only take me to subvert the host body, to discipline and correct its imperfections, to *mechanize* it, and Toxine would again be mine. Scruples? No; I pitied Tink. Not for what I was to do to her; I pitied her the burden of her humanity. After closing up shop Tink and I sometimes drank at a nearby wine bar called the V. Berg. Once, when she had got very drunk, I learned that, like me, she was motherless. Slurred Tink, the sad and crippled, who was never to talk so again: 'It all began when Mummy died. I was thirteen. At first – when he touched me – he'd make a joke of it. Sometimes he'd say he was sorry and wouldn't speak for the rest of the day. Then things got bad. Serious. He said how much he missed Mum, how much I was like her. Monday, Tuesday, Wednesday . . . His way of loving me, he said. And I always thought it was *me* doing wrong instead of *him*. Then one day – Pow! Zap! Crash! I broke everything in the house. And I wrote in lipstick on the wall: Impaler! Impaler! Then I left. Just got up and left . . .'

Unhappy sister. Too well she knew the sadness of the flesh. I would lie awake, alone in the sterile vastness of my house, and think of her, also alone, in that doll-sized room above the shop, and dreaming, what? That she would never go to the ball? That no prince fair would kiss her rosy lips? I would save her. I would elect her to the mechanical realm, where there is neither tears nor pain. And there I would love her, for through her glowed the luminous soul of Toxine.

I began work. 'Coffee, Tink?' I asked the evening I closed shop for ever. An hour later she rested beneath a mountain of barbiturate-induced sleep. I carried her to her room and stood at her bedside, trembling. A colossal wardrobe loomed above us, an accusing sentinel, the room otherwise bare. Like a cast, the human part of her had fallen away; what was left was an Ur-Toxine, a neglected masterpiece to be retouched and restored. How beautiful she was, deconstructed, bereft of sense and pain; but more beautiful by far was her potential. She would put on a new skin of alabaster; the hair would again flow as a black subterranean stream; and the eyes, reigniting like green lanterns, would guide me home. Secure behind locked doors, I removed her clothes and measured her for conversion.

I did not dare transport Tink to my workshop; I feared the curiosity of the mob; and so, as she slept, dosed with whatever I could buy from the dealers of Brixton and Piccadilly, I set to transforming our bolt hole into the studio it had once been. Day and night I ferried equipment, Chepstow – Portobello, until Tink's room was a satanic mill primed to realize my desires. Though I removed the wardrobe I had still to knock down a connecting wall into an adjacent bathroom to accommodate the influx of machinery (a fraction of my total stock); but, despite this lack of space, I proceeded unhindered. Arms, legs, torso arrived from my contractors, while I, as always, concentrated on the microengineered nerves and sinews that would allow my china doll to walk. Part of my conversion therapy entailed keeping Tink in a persistent vegetative state: the higher functions of the cerebral hemispheres repressed; the reflexes in the brain stem intact. When fitted with the carapace of reinforced porcelain that was to be her bodysuit, her feeblest movement would activate the touch-feedback relays in the joints, providing the genius of animation. Her sensorium undermined by drugs, I theorized that her reflexes would be susceptible to posthypnotic suggestion; that, indoctrinated while she slept she would, when tossed a scrap of consciousness, obey my commands. At least, so I theorized. My *métier* was engineering; I had always felt distaste for the life sciences; and my thoughts on how the mechanization of her body might prejudice her executive will were, I suppose, fanciful. I knew only she must never, never wake. Not fully. To regulate her somnolence, the exoskeleton was to incorporate a motorized drip and a catheter, to feed my pretty zombie a liquid diet of vitamins, protein and soporifics: a regimen for a new body, a new life; a life to be afforded every luxury. Her second skin would be lined with velvet and tailored so that no moving part chafed the soft engine inside; a waste-disposal unit would be discreetly placed. As she evolved beneath my fingers, I imagined myself presenting her with bouquets of rose and poppy, a red limousine, a retinue of cats (cat-maid, cat-butler, cat-chauffeur); I would deny her nothing.

In one month my initial labours were over. Tink was encased in a tight-fitting porcelain shell, her cardiovascular system awash with sleep. 'Let me introduce you,' I said. 'Tink, this is Tox; Tox, Tink.' But they were not yet as one. I now scoured couturiers, theatrical outfitters and jewellers to buy the accoutrements that would make the transformation complete. I ordered a ball gown of scarlet taffeta, a wig of long, black silk and a choker with her name picked out in malachite. I had discovered, late in the course of manufacture, that Tink wore contact lenses. Blessed serendipity! From a specialist in the Charing Cross Road I bought a duplicate set in bright, opaque green, and had them coated with luminous film. Dressed in the opulence in which I remembered her, her pillow sunk beneath a cascade of hair, and with her own green eyes enhanced by science and blazing like Will-o'-the-Wisp, it but remained for me to glue on her long steel fingernails, and paint them and her bee-stung lips a bloody red, and Toxine was reborn.

September the third. Feast of the nativity. I bought champagne and a birthday cake I had had baked in the shape of a letter T, put on my best suit, and played selections from *Coppelia* and *The Tales of Hoffman* at full volume. I recall it rained that afternoon, but towards evening the skies cleared and we were bathed, in our bower of bliss, by the warm rays of an Indian summer. Tink had gone, her body reconstituted; only Tox remained. Her soul, to which Tink had long played host, had been distilled into a vessel fit for the headiest of tinctures. When shadows began to curl about the bedposts, setting her eyes on fire, I adjusted the valve beneath her chemise, denying her blood its accustomed soma. I lit the candles (one, two, three, four candles) and sat down to await her quickening. I waited an hour, then tried some elementary commands. She did not move. I waited.

Between nine and ten o'clock the champagne must have dimmed my brain, for I became suddenly aware of a full moon lactating onto the floor, the sound of a creaking mattress, and the spectacle of Toxine heaving her bosom to the sky, arching her back, throwing her head from side to side, panting. She lived. Beneath the sign of the virgin, my doll, my toy, my mistress of mistresses lived. Ave Toxine! I readjusted the valve so as to subdue her. Gradually, as once more her blood was transfused with anaesthesia, her convulsions ceased; but I did not allow her to sleep. 'Name?' I whispered into her ear. The eyes rolled within their porcelain sockets, and a sigh, like steam under pressure, issued from her lips.

'Tik,' she hissed, unable to pronounce the 'n' in 'Tink'.

'No,' I said, 'your name is Toxine. Toxine!'

Power-assisted, her hand reached out to me. She touched my cheek. 'Tok,' she gasped, similarly unable to pronounce the second syllable of 'Toxine'; then her eyes and breathing became troubled as her guttering consciousness sought indentity. 'Tik-tok, tik-tok, tik-tok,' she mumbled.

I reached beneath her chemise and deactivated her. 'Little girl,' I said with terrible satisfaction, 'you've had a busy day.'

The following weeks were the happiest I had known. Toxine began to walk, albeit only a step or two (I was always there to prevent her falling over and smashing herself to bits); she even began to respond to commands such as 'sit', 'kneel', 'stand', and 'fetch'. We played games. There was work too, of course. It was during this time that I loaded her wetware with a programme I hoped would more fully wed the molecular with the machine. 'Listen,' I intoned. 'When God made Adam he gave him a wife and her name was Eve. And Eve was wicked and mocked her husband, betraying him for that old serpent, Satan. God was merciful. He gave the man Lilith, mother of automata. And Lilith had many daughters, all beautiful as stone. And Lilith said "Daughters, comfort them who are persecuted by the offspring of Eve. Learn the Way of the Doll. Untouched by birth and death, rejected by and rejecting man's laws, rejoice in my commands"'.

Then, while she lay in semiconscious repose, I would pour into her ear honeyed propaganda urging her to renounce the world, embrace the mechanical, and always, always be mine. The education of Toxine, however, was predominantly a sentimental affair. I would comb out her elflocks while she, lying on her bed, listened to my tales of devotion, interrupting only with a pert 'Tik-tok' when, starved of her elixir and becoming frisky, she would again have to submit to that artificially induced coma she had become so familiar with. 'Die for the King,' I would say.

When I talked of the past, of our childhood assignations, of lathes, drills and porcelains, I detected a sadness in her eyes. She had never, of course, seen more of life than the insides of attics and workshops; her life had been as circumscribed as my own. Fear, I decided, would no longer constrain us; we would begin to live. When I perceived Toxine had learned to regard her new body as a temple rather than a sarcophagus, I treated her to a trip up West. The street empty, I carried her to my car. We drove to the end of the night. 'Look, Tox, that's Pollock's Toy Museum, I often used to go there; and that, Tox, is Madame Tussaud's – oh, you'd like *that*; and this, Tox, is Piccadilly Circus, where I sometimes buy your morphine. Wave, Tox, wave!' We parked by the Embankment and walked to the river. It was near to dawn and an autumn mist lent us privacy; only a tramp's brief register of surprise disturbed our peace. Beneath Westminster Bridge, as Big Ben tolled five o'clock, we kissed. I can still hear the rustle of her gown, still feel the smoothness of her anaemic flesh. And there, with the whistle of trains in the distance, we consummated our love. It was a happy, happy time.

Knock-knock. Who's there? A man. What man? A man come to take your loved one away, to pollute your home, to destroy you: the Dazman.

He arrived early, knocking with inescapable persistence. I had been making breakfast in the kitchen behind the shop. Leaving Toxine staring uninterestedly at an array of toast and marmalade, and thinking I had but an intransigent milkman to attend to, I opened the door to a man-shape of monumental corpulence who filled the jambs with his bulk. The endomorph, oozing sweat from beneath his crombie, despite the sleet that rained upon his head, apologized for the disturbance. His bearing was dandified, correct; but there was something of the schoolboy about him, something stickily adolescent, that signified a threatening lubriciousness. 'My daughter, Tina, I believe she works here?'

My shock-tightened vocal cords allowed only a choked negative; I would have to dissemble skilfully, or I would have to kill him.

'May I come in? It's rather wet . . .' He affected a lisp. Inspecting the curios and bric-à-brac – all my father had sold during his declining years – as if, I thought, for clues, evidence, he waited patiently for my move; but I had had no time to deploy an adequate defence.

'She's gone,' I ventured, 'to Bournemouth.'

'Bournemouth? Not her sort of place.'

'I know she ran away from home. I used to tell her to write. She was here just three months. She left in September.' He said nothing. 'I'm sorry.'

'Those friends she had – in that squat.' She had no friends, I wanted to say, except me. 'They said she lived here as well.'

'That's right. She had a room upstairs. It was part of our agreement.' He stared at me, long and unblinking, his Tweedledum looks infused with inquisitorial menace.

'Was it an agreeable agreement?' Your suspicions are misplaced, fat boy, I thought; I don't much like human girls. And who are you to pontificate? Daddy Reaver, robber baron of innocence? Though half paralysed with dread, I began to prickle with rancour.

'There was no small print.'

'Ah,' he sighed, 'desire!' He loosened his coat and passed his hand over a Gallé vase, a Tiffany lamp and a Siamese Buddha: the only things of value in the shop. He picked up the Buddha. 'Is this for sale?'

'Everything's for sale.'

He caressed the bronze and smiled. 'There is but one thing more desirable than desire itself and that is the release from desire.' What a clever boy he was; what a precious Bunter. He sat down upon an Empire-style chaise longue, juggling the Lord of Compassion from hand to hand. 'How much for the little yellow idol? No, don't tell me; for the tourists, I suppose? But information about my daughter: is that for sale?' He knew the value of nothing. 'For pretty lady, many rupee.'

'Everything is for sale,' I said curtly, 'except her.'

'What's this? A love-sick harlequin? A booby boy?' His composure fractured. 'Good God, she's just a little girl. I went to the police. They said they couldn't do anything. Over eighteen. Eighteen! She's just a child, a little girl . . .' He frowned. 'If you've so much as – '

'Desire,' I said, 'what do you know of desire?'

'What do you know,' he sneered, 'of its consequences? The lake of blood. The pit. The spike. Me.'

'I'm sorry – I've a lot to do.' In the back room a kettle was howling like a banshee. He didn't move. I looked for a weapon. The rings on his fingers – too many rings for a man – sparkled malignantly; his blubbery lips glistened with spit. I was dazzled. 'Breakfast – I must have breakfast and open shop.'

'Desire kills love,' he said, looking at the floor, his face twisted; then he seemed to refit himself, once more the worldly courtier. 'I digress. Forgive me. I have been under strain. I don't mind her having boyfriends. But she needs looking after. Her legs . . . People can be so cruel. Please, why don't you help?'

'But I have helped. Helped her on her journey. To a better world than this.'

'You are oblique. You are an oblique man. Your manner is oblique. Where is Tina? Tell me, *please*.' His voice played forward, then back, then forward, plaything of a tape deck possessed: Tina, oblique, where, tell me, your manner, her legs, so cruel, oblique, Tina, where, where is, tell me, please, tell me, tell me. I stifled an hysterical laugh, my mind shouting at him: Oh, but she's changed!

So different from when you last saw her! Matured! A princess! A real lady!

But 'Bournemouth' is all I said. 'She's gone to Bournemouth.' Something pierced his hide and he collapsed.

'I suspect,' he said sulking, 'that you are sincere.' He replaced the Buddha, rose and moved to the door. I had survived. I came up for air. The enemy was moving on. 'Daughters,' he said blackly before he left, 'don't have daughters. Things of darkness and deceit. They seem so innocent, but I tell you they're slink, pieces of slink . . .'

I suggested he contact the Salvation Army, check the hospitals, place an ad. I had triumphed. I resisted a smile and wished the swine luck. But even as, routed, he passed into the street, destiny outflanked me. The whirr of servos, the burr of gears, arrested him in mid-stride, and his head whiplashed to where the at once recognizable signature of porcelain feet upon floorboards emanated: the back room, hidden by a curtain partition; the room of dark secrets.

'O you bloody, bloody man,' he cried, 'she's here!' He ran and tore aside the veil, then stepped back as the mystery in all her awful splendour smote him: Toxine, undead, immortal white goddess, clockwork madonna, glorious and pneumatic, was revealed. I took her in my arms as she fell.

'Out of the way.' Astonishment had taught him obedience and he retreated into the shop. How had she stirred? I laid her upon the chaise longue, simultaneously running a hand beneath her clothes, flooding her veins with sleep. I closed her eyes.

'Tina?' he whispered.

'An automaton. Late nineteenth century. Studio of Fabergé. I must have left her wound up.' He moved closer, studying the features.

'It looks – it looks like Tina.' He touched her face. 'A china doll, just like Tina.'

'Take your hands off her – you'll break her!' How dare he be so intimate, this bull in a china shop, this gorer of maidenheads; did he wish to hurt her more? I would not allow it. 'I helped her, don't you understand? She was unhappy when she came here. I helped her. And then she left. How dare you reproach me, you of all people?' I wanted to tell him everything: what I knew of his crimes, the whereabouts of his daughter, her fabulous fate. I sparred with temptation, dancing into a corner, ready to take a dive. 'How dare you come here causing trouble like this – why don't you leave me alone!' I was ignored. Entranced by the doll's verisimilitude to his daughter, he studied her face as if for signs of life.

'She's so like Tina. I don't understand.'

'She's not for sale,' I said.

'You said everything was for sale, everything except *her*.' He lifted his hand as if to catch a fly; but it was my ear that fell victim, caught between the sticky membrane of forefinger and thumb. He twisted. 'What's going on? I want the truth.' He twisted again, as if unloosening a recalcitrant bottletop, forcing me to my knees. 'I want the truth,' he repeated. With contempt, I regarded the dandruff on his shoulders, the bullyboy eyes, the superfluity of his flesh. I wriggled with pain and disgust. 'Why does that *thing* look like my daughter?'

For too long the god of this world, the fat blood-god of Man, had intimidated me. I would placate him no more.

'So why don't you go to the police? We'll both go. I can tell them what a comfort Tink was to you after your wife died. We used to have such long talks, Tink and I. She had such an interesting child-hood.' He screamed a thin, girlish scream, and threw me backwards so I fell upon Mademoiselle. Covering her body with my own, I stared up into a face livid as a Halloween pumpkin, defiant. Then he spat. Spat into my eyes.

'O you bloody, bloody . . . You *will* talk to me.' He rolled into the street, his words dawdling behind, flying about the room, knocking over furniture, peeing on the carpet; then they too, with an insolent wiggle of their hindquarters, left. Wiping away the saliva, I got up to watch him stride down the Portobello Road.

Daz, my childhood tormentor, had returned.

The honeymoon was over. We would have to leave. When it was dark I drove Toxine the short distance to my house. I planned to flee London, to rent an isolated cottage in Cornwall or Wales, and to live there until Daz had relinquished his search. The following morning I thumbed the property pages of the daily press, telling myself that all was not lost, that Toxine and I, like refugees bound for a new world, would escape the jaws of the beast. Evening came, and I noticed a silhouette in the boarding-house opposite. Turning off all the lights, I watched him, as spotlit by a naked hundred-watt bulb, he swigged a hip flask or raised binoculars to his eyes: my chimera, the Dazman. My escape plans had been presumptuous; we would be followed. I threw every bolt, locked every door. We were under siege.

So that I might be alert during the night when I most feared attack, our habits became nocturnal. The daylight brought little rest. I slept fitfully, awakened by a telephone with no one at the other end. Poisonous letters arrived. I ran a fever. My anxieties, however, were mostly for Toxine. I could survive on soup and biscuits – all that the larder held – but Tox required that protein-rich drug compound only to be bought from all-night chemists and the lowlife that frequented them. Without it she would revert to her fallen self.

At night, the house was our playground: a labyrinth of corridors and interconnecting rooms, a baroque palace of cornices and ara-besques, mazes, towers and dungeons. Attempting to regain our former happiness, we engaged in desperate games of hide-and-seek. As my cache of opiates was reduced, Toxine participated in these games with alarming vigour, negotiating the stairs with ease and wandering through our vast intestinal nursery with embers of intelligence in her eyes. When these signs of an all-too-human sensibility became acute I would carry her to my studio, tie her overactive limbs to the sole workbench that remained, and gently sing her to sleep. I sang of voyages, of Cythera, Avalon, and El Dorado, of that city to which we would escape, where even now they prepared our welcome. To have her restored to me after so many years, and then to be condemned to watch over her as she degenerated, dying into the human world: this was bitter.

When she was at rest I'd peep through the curtains, and there, not a hundred feet away, was my enemy: a sniper who, night after night, patiently reconnoitred his kill. When he moved, he eclipsed the garishly lit window as thoroughly as he eclipsed my life. However ignorant he might have been of the motive, he would know I would some time have to leave the house; and when Tox began talking in her sleep, abandoning her mantra of 'Tik-tok, tik-tok', to speak of things she should not, could not know of, I imagined he smiled, for I was then compelled to risk his intrusion to go shopping for my loved one's favourite cocktail.

I disguised myself with greatcoat, hat and balaclava, and, leaving the car outside as a decoy, exited while the window from which Daz spied on us was momentarily devoid of his shadow. My expedition was successful, and I returned not only with supplies for Toxine but with a resolve (bolstered, no doubt, by my quality-control snufflings of high-grade H) to vacate London as soon as it was light. I at first thought that in the panic of my departure I had forgotten to close the door. I saw then the splintered wood sur-rounding the lock, and a cold wind blew through me as though I were a moth-eaten shroud.

The house seemed hostile, alien, unwelcoming as an out-of-season hotel. The floor dipped; I pitched towards the stairs. Gripping the balustrade, I gazed up into the black heart of a helix: a stairwell winding to its vanishing point three flights above. Giddy, I turned away. Up there, at the summit, Soapsuds the Terrible had come to steal my toy. I wanted to scamper up those stairs three at a time, but my feet dragged as in glue. A hidden fairground organ played the theme music from *Carousel*; the darkness poked and jeered. 'Why are you doing this?' I called softly. 'Why are you persecuting me over all these years?' The stairs creaked like arthritic vertebrae; they seemed to talk.

'Wait until I tell your father, young man; and what *will* your mother say.' She had betrayed me, the old crone, they had all betrayed me. Only Toxine had been constant. 'You think so?' said the stairs. 'That little hussy? Oh, why have you wasted your life on her? Why, why, why?' I reached the first landing and stopped. A grandfather clock confronted me. It chimed; the door opened. Inside, a homunculus sat astride a hypnotic pendulum, swinging to and fro.

'What *are* you doing?' it said.

'Go back to your pap and your ravings. I don't need you any more.'

'And what's an old man to do without love? His only boy a rude mechanical, his wife gone off with some Yank car-salesman. I should never have sent you to that school. A working-class hero, that's me. And what have I got for it? A snob of a son who goes weak at the knees over some tarty *machine*.' He raised a finger. 'He's up there, y'know. She's partial to fat men . . .'

I slammed the clock-door shut and continued my ascent. At the second landing the fairground music stopped. Some way down an adjoining corridor, light escaped from beneath a door. Outside stood a pair of riding-boots, smudged with lipstick. Pressing myself against the wall, I shuffled crabwise, my nostrils stinging with the sharp scent of cat.

'Mother?' I called, rapping on the door.

'Enter,' she said, 'my little bell-boy.' She was as I remembered her, beautiful as the Queen of the Night. She presided over a pink boudoir. An open fire blazed in the hearth. 'It's so good to see you. But then, I simply had to. We really must talk. The young lady people have been telling me about – Toxanne, isn't it? – I wanted to know, well . . . But what must you think of me? I haven't introduced you to your stepsisters. Tracy, Trisha, 'Tasha, Tereza, say hello to your big brother.' Lazing upon a rug before the fire, four adolescent *grisettes* tossed their heads and laughed, their peppermint eyes flickering. Flickering, snickering eyes.

'Why does he wear such funny clothes?'

'Like little Lord Fauntleroy.'

'Better go home, boy blue, Mr Daz is coming to eat you up!'

'O Baby Buntin', don't cwy!'

Mother hushed them with a stare. 'Now about this young lady. I feel it's only right to tell you I've heard *stories* about her . . .'

My stepsisters giggled and began to sing, very quietly, very nastily: 'We know what they're doing, we know what they're doing.' They crawled towards me on all fours, mewling like spoilt pampered kittens. I leaped into the corridor, turned the key in the ward, and ran. Behind me, they scratched at the woodwork.'Miaow! Let us out,' they cried. 'We're burning!' False cats; untrue tabbies. Slink! There was only one genus of sphinxlike demi-feline, and that was Toxine. Again I assaulted the house's crooked backbone, the final landing a flight above. I halted. Someone had cleared their throat.

'Still playing with dolls?' It was a boy's voice, coarse and dull. I looked up; a gang of goblin-faced youths leaned over the balustrade, slack-jawed, malevolent. 'Dead,' said the boy. 'Your poxy queen is dead.'

'Dead,' they chorused, 'dead, dead, dead. Little dolly daydreams is dead.' Hands over my ears, I rushed the gradient, shouts, jeers, giggles and screams swelling into a crescendo which would not resolve.

'She is alive!' My words bounced off a wall of white noise. 'I brought her to life. I raised her . . .' The air had grown rarefied. I could not find a footing. Abruptly, the voices ceased. I uncovered my ears, opened my eyes, and discovered I stood at the summit. I was alone. Ghosts, ghosts; this night I would put them all to rest. My workshop was opposite. I grasped the doorknob and listened, but heard only the tympanum of my heart. The hinges whinged; I squinted into the shadows. Before me in dim outline was a ransacked parlour of machinery and dismembered dolls; then, my pupils dilating, a horrible *tableau vivant* made itself known: Daz, pink and porcine, supporting a half-conscious Toxine – free now of her inhibiting bonds – and slapping her, like one trying to sober up a drunk. I switched on the lights. For an instant he seemed to fade, like a phantom surprised by day; then his corporeality returned, the insistent, heavy ink of his contours thick with a reality I could no longer bear.

'Help me.' he said, confused, pathetic. 'For God's sake help me get her out of this *coffin*.' An elemental spur goaded my flanks and I charged, storm-ridden, picking up the discarded limb of a dead proto-Toxine – a long, coltish leg – and, jumping the barricades like Liberty leading the People, stood before the tyrant, porcelain club held high, poised to end his reign. 'But I am her father!' he said.

'And I,' I said, breaking the limb over his skull, 'am the King of Clockwork!'

He fell and the house shook, tremulous with exultation. Easy, so easy. How had I not known it would be so easy? The storm dismounted, rumbling into the distance, taking with it the shame of the years. The ghetto of my childhood had been razed, Tox and I the only survivors. The dustcloud settled; shards of china spun and were still. I was free.

She stood by the window. Did a burgeoning sentience prompt her to look across the street, to where she suspected her violator's shade would always spy, always haunt? 'He's gone,' I assured her. 'He'll never hurt you again.' Her returning consciousness chilled me. 'Tox, are you all right? Don't worry, I've more dream-juice downstairs. You'll soon be back to normal.' As I reached beneath her chemise she stepped back, putting her arms across her breasts. 'Toxine,' I said gently, 'don't be silly. It's only me. *I'm* not going to hurt you. I want to help.' I caught her by the wrists. 'Toxine – please!' she was staring at the felled body of Daz, her lovely, vacuous face impossibly eloquent with distress. She turned, and her eyes blistered with pain. Withdrawal symptoms? Or was something human emerging from that chrysalis of stone, something empathic? 'He *hurt* you, Toxine, he wanted to take you from me. Don't you remember all the terrible things he did to you? I am your creator, Toxine, *I* am your father!'

With preternatural speed she seized me by the throat. Long, steel fingernails cut my flesh, her mechanically enhanced grip extraordinarily powerful. How could she? Was it simply malfunction? Or had sickness unmasked her? Perhaps I had been a fool, a cuckold long ignorant of her lusts and adulteries. Her grip tightened. All that they had said: it was true. The porcelain bitch had betrayed me. Twisting, flailing, my arms collided with the light fixture, and a black curtain dropped upon our stage. Her treacherous, half-human eyes ignited. Murderous eyes. We tripped and skidded across the workbench. 'I loved you,' I said, as she broke heart and neck. 'Have you forgotten the Way of the Doll?' My eyes closed and I knew only the smell of her silky mane, the coolness of her dress, the noise of my lungs as they rattled towards their doom; I knew too, but only half knew, that my hand had found a screwdriver and that I was driving it into her ribs, her thighs, cracking her immaculate flesh and sending slivers of porcelain to join the fragments of other dolls strewn about the floor. To no effect; her carapace protected her. Frantically I pulled up her crimson frock, and then the thousand petticoats beneath; with one hand I flipped open the belly panel, while the other . . . but by then I was beyond the stars and planets, a castaway of time and space; somewhere, somewhere, I heard the screwdriver's snicker-snack! as it drove into the overheated motor, breaking gears, cogs and wheels. 'Johneee!' she yelled, clockwork filigree scrambled – Ah, so tell it to him, tell it to Mr Impaler – and, releasing her steely garrotte, writhed beneath me like a fish upon the slab, until, the arc lights of her eyes blown, fused, her life retreated to a single fluttering eyelash, the metallic spikes of which, after an eternity of indecision, finally crashed shut like a miniature portcullis.

I lay on top of her, gasping. What had I done? 'Toxine,' I whispered, 'come back, come back.' My tears spattered her face. Toxine was broken.

For days I walked the streets, following home women with pale skin or dark hair, or women robed in poppy-red dresses, women who moved like machines. But I need more than a replacement engine; I need a soul. And her soul, I think, will never return. What was Toxine? She was a wonder of engineering, a green-eyed Venus; the comfort of my childhood and the ardour of my manhood; she was my friend and the goddess who came back to me in a merciful moment of grace. She was my life. The human world was unworthy of her, and I, too, am unworthy.

Forgive me, little robot, and accept my amends. I have decided it is time to sleep. The attic, immutable shadowland of childhood, has gathered us to its ruin. We have been here now three days, three nights. Musty carpets, old furniture, surround us, and winter has come. Again, snow drifts down from the rafters, crowning her hair with ice. It is cold. I comb that hair, that long, long hair. We are about to make our journey. I lie down beside her. The light begins to fail. Outside, the wind is shaking the gables. Sleep, sleep. Those venomous lips I have half kissed away receive me as one lost, now found. I put my arms about her tiny waist. I look into her eyes. All is broken. Consumed by fire. But I am leaving this human world of sadness and regret, leaving as even now it grows dark. Deep in her eyes, in an emerald vision, I see again that land, that happy land, that far-off kingdom where we shall be at peace. My bisque-headed, wheyfaced love, how could I have thought you would betray me? The city descends. Softly, she calls. We go now together into the dark, she leading me through the shadows, out, far out, taking me home, the only home there will ever be for us. Goodnight, Toxine.

KIM STANLEY ROBINSON

Before I Wake

In his dream Abernathy stood on a steep rock ridge. A talus slope dropped from the ridge to a glacial basin containing a small lake. The lake was cobalt in the middle, aquamarine around the edges. Here and there in the rock expanse patches of meadow grass gleamed, like the lawns of marmot estates. There were no trees. The cold air felt thin in his throat. He could see ranges many miles away, and though everything was perfectly still there was also an immense sweep in things, as if a gust of wind had caught the very fabric of being.

'Wake up, damn you,' a voice said. He was shoved in the back, and tumbled down the rockfall, starting a small avalanche.

He stood in a large white room. Glass boxes of various size were stacked everywhere, four and five to a pile, and in every box was a sleeping animal: monkey, rat, dog, cat, pig, dolphin, turtle. 'No,' he said, backing up. 'Please, no.'

A bearded man entered the room. 'Come on, wake up,' he said brusquely. 'Time to get back to it, Fred. Our only hope is to work as hard as we can. You have to resist when you start slipping away!' He seized Abernathy by the arms and sat him down on a box of squirrels. 'Now listen!' he cried. 'We're asleep! We're dreaming!'

'Thank God,' Abernathy said.

'Not so fast! We're awake as well.'

'I don't believe you.'

'Yes you do!' He slapped Abernathy in the chest with a large roll of graph paper, and it spilled loose and unrolled over the floor. Black squiggles smeared the graphs.

'It looks like a musical score,' Abernathy said absently.

The bearded man shouted, 'Yes! Yes! This is the symphony our brains play, very apt! Violins yammering away – that's what used to be ours, Fred; that was consciousness.' He yanked hard on his beard, with both hands, looking anguished. 'Sudden drop to the basses, bowing and bowing, blessed sleep, yes, yes! And in the night the ghost instruments, horn and oboe and viola, spinning their little improvs over the ground bass, longer and longer till the violins start blasting again, yes, Fred, it's perfectly apt!'

132

'Thank you,' Abernathy said. 'But you don't have to yell. I'm right here.'

'Then *wake up*,' the man said viciously. 'Can't, can you! Trapped, aren't you! Playing the new song like all the rest of us. Look at it there – REM sleep mixed indiscriminately with consciousness and deep sleep, turning us all into dreamwalkers. Into waking nightmares.'

Looking into the depths of the man's beard, Abernathy saw that all the teeth were incisors. Abernathy edged towards the door, then broke for it and ran. The man leaped forwards and tackled him, and they tumbled to the floor.

Abernathy woke up.

'Ah ha,' the man said. It was Winston, administrator of the lab. 'So now you believe me,' he said sourly, rubbing an elbow. 'I suppose we should write that down on the walls. If we all start slipping away we won't even remember what things used to be like. It'll all be over then.'

'Where are we?' Abernathy asked.

'In the lab,' Winston replied, voice filled with heavy patience. 'We live here now, Fred. Remember?'

Abernathy looked around. The lab was large and well lit. Sheets of graph paper recording EEGs were scattered over the floor. Black countertops protruded from the walls, which were cluttered with machinery. In one corner were two rats in a cage.

Abernathy shook his head violently. It was all coming back. He was awake now, but the dream had been true. He groaned, walked to the room's little window, saw the smoke rising from the city below. 'Where's Jill?'

Winston shrugged. They hurried through a door at the end of the lab, into a small room containing cots and blankets. No one there.

'She's probably gone back to the house again,' Abernathy said.

Winston hissed with irritation and worry. 'I'll check the grounds,' he said. 'You'd better go to the house. Be careful!'

Fred was already out the door.

In many places the streets were almost blocked by smashed cars, but little had changed since Abernathy's last venture home, and he made good time. The suburbs were choking in haze that smelled like incinerator smoke. A gas station attendant holding a pump handle stared in astonishment as he drove by, then waved. Abernathy didn't wave back. On one of these expeditions he had seen a knifing, and now he didn't like to look.

He stopped the car at the curb before his house. The remains of his house. It was charred almost to the ground. The blackened chimney was all that stood over chest high.

He got out of his old Cortina and slowly crossed the lawn, which was marked by black footprints. In the distance a dog barked insistently.

Jill stood in the kitchen, humming to herself and moving black things from here to there. She looked up as Abernathy stopped in the side yard before her. Her eyes twitched from side to side. 'You're home,' she said cheerily. 'How was your day?'

'Jill, let's go out to dinner,' Abernathy said.

'But I'm already cooking!'

'I can see that.' He stepped over what had been the kitchen wall and took her arm. 'Don't worry about that. Let's go anyway.'

'My, my,' Jill said, brushing his face with a sooty hand. 'Aren't you romantic this evening.'

He stretched his lips wide. 'You bet. Come on.' He pulled her carefully out of the house and across the yard, and helped her into the Cortina. 'Such chivalry,' she remarked, eyes darting about in tandem.

Abernathy got in and started the engine. 'But Fred,' his wife said, 'what about Jeff and Fran?'

Abernathy looked out his window. 'They've got a babysitter,' he finally said.

Jill frowned, nodded, sat back in her seat. Her broad face was smudged. 'Ah,' she said, 'I do so like to dine out.'

'Yes,' Abernathy said, and yawned. He felt drowsy. 'Oh no,' he said. 'No!' He bit his lip, pinched the back of the hand on the wheel. Yawned again. 'No!' he cried. Jill jerked against her door in surprise. He swerved to avoid hitting an Oriental woman sitting in the middle of the road. 'I must get to the lab,' he shouted. He pulled down the Cortina's sun visor, took a pen from his coat pocket and scrawled *To the Lab*.

Jill was staring at him. 'It wasn't my fault,' she whispered.

He drove them onto the freeway. All thirty lanes were clear, and he put his foot down on the accelerator. 'To the lab,' he sang, 'to the lab, to the lab.' A flying police vehicle landed on the highway ahead of them, folded its wings and sped off. Abernathy tried to follow it, but the freeway turned and narrowed, they were back on street level. He shouted with frustration, bit the flesh at the base of his thumb.

Jill leaned back against her door, crying. Her eyes looked like small beings, a team trying to jerk its way free. 'I couldn't help it,' she said. 'He loved me, you know. And I loved him.'

Abernathy drove on. Some streets were burning. He wanted to go west, needed to go west. The car was behaving oddly. They were on a tree-lined avenue, out where there were few houses. A giant Boeing 747 lay across the road, its wings slewed forwards. A high tunnel had been cut through it so traffic could pass. A cop with whistle and white gloves waved them through.

On the dashboard an emergency light blinked *To the Lab*. Abernathy sobbed convulsively. 'I don't know how!'

Jill, his sister, sat up straight. 'Turn left,' she said quietly.

Abernathy threw the directional switch and their car rerouted itself onto the track that veered left. They came to other splits in the track, and each time Jill told him which way to go. The rear-view mirror bloomed with smoke.

Then he woke up. Winston was swabbing his arm with a wad of cotton, wiping off a droplet of blood.

'Amphetamines and pain,' Winston whispered.

They were in the lab. About a dozen lab techs, post-docs and grad students were in there at their countertops, working with great speed.

'How's Jill?' Abernathy said.

'Fine, fine. She's sleeping right now. Listen, Fred, I've found a way to keep us awake for longer periods of time. Amphetamines and pain. Regular injections of benzedrine, plus a sharp burst of pain every hour or so, administered in whatever way you find most convenient. Metabolism stays too high for the mind to slip into the dreamwalking. I tried it and stayed fully awake and alert for six hours. Now we're all using the method.'

Abernathy watched his lab techs dash about. 'I can tell.' He could feel his heart's rapid, emphatic thumping.

'Well, let's get to it,' Winston said intently. 'Let's make use of this time.'

Abernathy stood. Winston called a little meeting. Feeling the gazes fixed on him, Abernathy collected his thoughts. 'The mind consists of electro-chemical action. Since we're all suffering the effects of this, it seems to me we can ignore the chemical and concentrate on the electrical. If the ambient fields have changed . . . Anyone know how many gauss the magnetic field is now? Or what the cosmic-ray count is?'

They stared at him.

'We can tune in to the space station's monitors,' he said. 'And do the rest here.'

So he worked, and they worked with him. Every hour a grinning

Winston came around with hypodermics in hand, singing, 'Speed, speed, spee-ud!' He convinced Abernathy to let droplets of hydrochloric acid fall on the inside of his forearm.

It kept Abernathy awake better than it did the others. For a whole day, then two, he worked without pause, eating crackers and drinking water as he worked, giving himself the injections when Winston wasn't there.

After the first few hours his assistants began slipping back into dreamwalking, despite the injections and acid splashings. Assignments he gave were never completed. One of his techs presented him with a successful experiment: the two rats, grafted together at the leg. Vainly Abernathy tried to pummel the man back to wakefulness.

In the end he did all the work himself. It took days. As his techs collapsed or wandered off he shifted from counter to counter, squinting sand-filled eyes to read oscilloscope and computer screen. He had never felt so exhausted in his life. It was like taking tests in a subject he didn't understand, in which he was severely retarded.

Still he kept working. The EEGs showed oscillation between wakefulness and REM sleep, in a pattern he had never seen. And there were correlations between the EEGs and fluctuations in the magnetic field.

Some of the men's flickering eyes were open, and they sat on the floors talking to each other or to him. Once he had to calm Winston, who was on the floor weeping and saying, 'We'll never stop dreaming, Fred, we'll never stop.' Abernathy gave him an injection, but it didn't have any effect.

He kept working. He sat at a crowded table at his high-school reunion, and found he could work anyway. He gave himself an injection whenever he remembered. He got very, very tired.

Eventually he felt he understood as much as he was going to. Everyone else was lying in the cot room with Jill, or were slumped on the floors. Eyes and eyelids were twitching.

'We move through space filled with dust and gas and fields of force. Now all the constants have changed. The read-outs from the space station show that, show signs of a strong electro-magnetic field we've apparently moved into. More dust, cosmic rays, gravitational flux. Perhaps it's the shockwave of a supernova, something nearby that we're just seeing now. Anyone looked up into the sky lately? Anyway. Something. The altered field has thrown the electrical patterns of our brains into something like what we called the REM state. Our brains rebel and struggle towards consciousness as much as they can, but this field forces them back. So we oscillate.'

He laughed weakly, and crawled up onto one of the countertops to get some sleep.

He woke and brushed the dust off his lab coat, which had served him as a blanket. The dirt road he had been sleeping on was empty. He walked. It was cloudy, and nearly dark.

He passed a small group of shacks, built in a tropical style with open walls and palm-thatch roofs. They were empty. Dark light filled the sky.

Then he was at the sea's edge. Before him extended a low promontory, composed of thousands of wooden chairs, all crushed and piled together. At the point of the promontory there was a human figure, seated in a big chair that still had seat and back and one arm.

Abernathy stepped out carefully, onto slats and lathed cylinders of wood, from a chair arm to the plywood bottom of a chair seat. Around him the grey ocean was strangely calm; glassy swells rose and fell over the slick wood at the waterline without a sound. Insubstantial clouds of fog, the lowest parts of a solid cloud cover, floated slowly onshore. The air was salty and wet. Abernathy shivered, stepped down to the next fragment of weathered grey wood.

The seated man turned to look at him. It was Winston. 'Fred,' he called, loud in the silence of the dawn.

Abernathy approached him, picked up a chair back, placed it carefully, sat.

'How are you?' Winston said.

Abernathy nodded. 'Okay.' Down close to the water he could hear the small slaps and suckings of the sea's rise and fall. The swells looked a bit larger, and he could see thin, smoky mist rising from them as they approached the shore.

'Winston,' he croaked and cleared his throat. 'What's happened?'

'We're dreaming.'

'But what does that mean?'

Winston laughed wildly. 'Emergent stage one sleep, transitional sleep, rapid sleep, rhombencephalic sleep, pontine sleep, activated sleep, paradoxical sleep.' He grinned ironically. 'No one knows what it is.'

'But all those studies.'

'Yes, all those studies. And how I used to believe in them, how I used to work for them, all those sorry guesses ranging from the ridiculous to the absurd, we dream to organize experience into memory, to stimulate the senses in the dark, to prepare for the future, to give our depth perception exercise, for God's sake! I mean, we don't know, do we, Fred? We don't know what dreaming is, we don't know what sleep is, you only have to think about it a bit to realize we didn't know what consciousness itself was, what it meant to be awake. Did we ever really know? We lived, we slept, we dreamed, and all three equal mysteries. Now that we're doing all three at once, is the mystery any deeper?'

Abernathy picked at the grain in the wood of a chair leg. 'A lot of the time I feel normal,' he said. 'It's just that strange things keep happening.'

'Your EEGs display an unusual pattern,' Winston said, mimicking a scientific tone. 'More alpha and beta waves than the rest of us. As if you're struggling harder to wake up.'

'Yes. That's what it feels like.'

They sat in silence for a time, watching swells lap at the wet chairs. The tide was falling. Offshore, near the limit of visibility, Abernathy saw a large cabin cruiser drifting in the current.

'So tell me what you've found,' Winston said.

Abernathy described the data transmitted from the space station, then his own experiments.

Winston nodded. 'So we're stuck here for good.'

'Unless we pass through this field. Or – I've gotten an idea for a device you could wear around your head, that might restore the old field.'

'A solution seen in a dream?'

'Yes.'

Winston laughed. 'How I used to believe in all our rationality, Fred. Dreams as some sort of electro-chemical manifestation of the nervous system, random activity, how reasonable it all sounded! Give the depth perception exercise! God, how small-minded it all was. Why shouldn't we have believed that dreams were great travels, to the future, to other universes, to a world more real than our own? They felt that way sometimes, in that last second before waking, as if we lived in a world so charged with meaning that it might burst . . . And now here we are. We're here, Fred, this is the moment and our only moment, no matter how we name it. *We're here.* From idea to symbol, perhaps. People will adapt. That's one of our talents.'

'I don't like it,' Abernathy said. 'I never liked my dreams.'

Winston merely laughed at him. 'They say consciousness itself was a leap like this one, people were ambling around like dogs and then one day, maybe because the earth moved through the shockwave of some distant explosion, sure, one day one of them straightened up and looked around surprised, and said, "*I am.*"'

'That would be a surprise,' Abernathy said.

'And this time everyone woke up one morning still dreaming, and looked around and said, "*What am I?*"' Winston laughed. 'Yes, we're stuck here. But I can adapt.' He pointed. 'Look, that boat out there is sinking.'

They watched several people aboard the craft struggle to get a rubber raft over the side. After many dunkings they got it in the water and everyone inside it. Then they rowed away, offshore into the mist.

'I'm afraid,' Abernathy said.

Then he woke up. He was back in the lab. It was in worse shape than ever. A couple of countertops had been swept clean to make room for chessboards, and several techs were playing blindfolded, arguing over which board was which.

He went to Winston's offices to get more benzedrine. There was no more. He grabbed one of his post-docs and said, 'How long have I been asleep?'

The man's eyes twitched, and he sang his reply, 'Sixteen men on a dead man's chest, yo ho ho and a bottle of rum.'

Abernathy went to the cot room. Jill was there, naked except for light-blue underwear, smoking a cigarette. One of the grad students was brushing her nipples with a feather. 'Oh, hi, Fred,' she said, looking him straight in the eye. 'Where have you been?'

'Talking to Winston,' he said with difficulty. 'Have you seen him?'

'Yes! I don't know when, though . . .'

He started to work alone again. No one wanted to help. He cleared a small room off the main lab, and dragged in the equipment he needed. He locked three large boxes of crackers in a cabinet, and tried to lock himself in his room whenever he felt drowsy. Once he spent six weeks in China, then he woke up. Sometimes he woke out in his old Cortina, hugging the steering wheel like his only friend. All his friends were lost. Each time he went back and started working again. He could stay awake for hours at a time. He got lots done. The magnets were working well, he was getting the fields he wanted. The device for placing the field around the head – an odd-looking wire helmet – was practicable.

He was tired. It hurt to blink. Every time he felt drowsy he applied more acid to his arm. It was covered with burns, but none of them hurt any more. When he woke he felt as if he hadn't slept for days. Twice his grad students helped out, and he was grateful for that. Winston came by occasionally, but only laughed at him.

He was too tired, everything he did was clumsy. He got on the lab phone once and tried to call his parents; all the lines were busy. The radio was filled with static, except for a station that played nothing but episodes of *The Lone Ranger*. He went back to work. He ate crackers and worked. He worked and worked.

Late one afternoon he went out onto the lab's cafeteria terrace to take a break. The sun was low, and a chill breeze blew. He could see the air, filled with amber light, and he breathed it in violently. Below him the city smoked, and the wind blew, and he knew that he was alive, that he was aware he was alive, and that something important was pushing into the world, suffusing things . . .

Jill walked onto the terrace, still wearing nothing but the blue underwear. She stepped on the balls of her feet, smiled oddly. Abernathy could see goose-pimples sweep across her skin like cat's paws over water, and the power of her presence – distant, female, mysterious – filled him with fear.

They stood several feet apart and looked down at the city, where their house had been. The area was burning.

Jill gestured at it. 'It's too bad we only had the courage to live our lives fully in dreams.'

'I thought we were doing okay,' Abernathy said. 'I thought we engaged it the best we could, every waking moment.'

She stared at him, again with the knowing smile. 'You did think that, didn't you?'

'Yes,' he said fiercely, 'I did. I did.'

He went inside to work it off.

Then he woke up. He was in the mountains, in the high cirque again. He was higher now and could see two more lakes, tiny granite pools, above the cobalt-and-aquamarine one. He was climbing shattered granite, getting near the pass. There was lichen on the rocks. The wind dried the sweat on his face, cooled him. It was quiet and still, so still, so quiet . . .

'Wake up!'

It was Winston. Abernathy was in his little room (high ranges in the distance, the dusty green of forests below), wedged in a corner. He got up, went to the crackers cabinet, pumped himself full of the benzedrine he had found in some syringes on the floor. (Snow and lichen.)

He went into the main lab and broke the fire alarm. That got everyone's attention. It took him a couple of minutes to stop the alarm. When he did his ears were ringing.

'The device is ready to try,' he said to the group. There were about twenty of them. Some were as neat as if they were off to church, others were tattered and dirty. Jill stood to one side.

Winston crashed to the front of the group. 'What's ready?' he shouted.

'The device to stop us dreaming,' Abernathy said weakly. 'It's ready to try.'

Winston said slowly, 'Well, let's try it then, okay, Fred?'

Abernathy carried helmets and equipment out of his room and into the lab. He arranged the transmitters and powered the magnets and the field generators. When it was all ready he stood up and wiped his brow.

'Is this it?' Winston asked. Abernathy nodded. Winston picked up one of the wire helmets.

'Well, I don't like it!' he said, and struck the helmet against the wall.

Abernathy's mouth dropped open. One of the techs gave a shove to his electro-magnets, and in a sudden fury Abernathy picked up a bat of wood and hit the man. Some of his assistants leaped to his aid, the rest pressed in and pulled at his equipment, tearing it down. A tremendous fight erupted. Abernathy swung his slab of wood with abandon, feeling great satisfaction each time it struck. There was blood in the air. His machines were being destroyed. Jill picked up one of the helmets and threw it at him, screaming, 'It's your fault, it's your fault!' He knocked down a man near his magnets and had swung the slab back to kill him when suddenly he saw a bright glint in Winston's hand; it was a surgical knife, and with a swing like a sidearm pitcher's Winston slammed the knife into Abernathy's diaphragm, burying it. Abernathy staggered back, tried to draw in a breath and found that he could, he was all right, he hadn't been stabbed. He turned and ran.

He dashed onto the terrace, closely pursued by Winston and Jill and the others, who tripped and fell even as he did. The patio was much higher than it used to be, far above the city, which burned and smoked. There was a long, wide stairway descending into the heart of the city. Abernathy could hear screams, it was night and windy, he couldn't see any stars, he was at the edge of the terrace, he turned and the group was right behind him, faces twisted with fury. 'No!' he cried, and then they rushed him, and he swung the wood slab and swung it and swung it, and turned to run down the stairs and then without knowing how he had done it he tripped and fell head over heels down the rocky staircase, falling falling falling.

Then he woke up. He was falling.

DAVID LANGFORD

Blit

It was like being caught halfway through a flashy film-dissolve. The goggles broke up the dim street, split and reshuffled it along diagonal lines: a glowing KEBABS sign was transposed into the typestyle they called Shatter. Safest to keep the goggles on, Robbo had decided. Even in the flickering electric half-light before dawn, you never knew what you might see. Just his luck if the stencil jumped from under his arm and unrolled itself before his eyes as he scrabbled for it on the pavement.

That would be a good place, behind the 34 (a shattered 34) bus stop. This was their part of town; the women flocked there each morning, twittering in their saris like bright alien canaries. A good place, by a boarded-up shop window thick with flyposted gig announcements.

Robbo scanned the street for movement, glanced at his own hand to be reassured by a blurred spaghetti of fingers. Guaranteed Army-issue goggles – the Group had friends in funny places – but they said the eye eventually adjusts. One day something clicks, and clear outlines jump at you. He flinched as the thick plastic unrolled; then the nervy moment was past, his left hand pressing the stencil against a tattered poster while in his right the spray can hissed.

The sweetish, heady smell of car touch-up paint made it all seem oddly distant from an act of terrorism.

He found he had been careless, easy in this false twilight and through these lenses: there were tacky patches on his fingers as he rerolled the Parrot. A few hours on, in thick morning light, the brown women would be playing the wink game . . . Jesus, how long since he had been a kid and played *that*? Must be five years. The one who had drawn the murder card caught your eye and winked, and you had to die with lots of spasms and overacting. To survive, you needed to spot the murderer first and get in with an accusation – or at least, know where not to look.

It was cold. Time to move on, to pick another place. Goggles or no shatter-goggles, he didn't look back at the image of the Parrot. It might wink.

SECRET ⋆ BASILISK
Distribution UK List B[iv] only

. . . so called because its outline, when processed for
non-hazardous viewing, is generally considered to resemble that of the bird. A processed (anamorphically
elongated) partial image appears in Appendix three of
this report, page A3–ii. THE STATED PAGE MUST NOT BE
VIEWED THROUGH ANY FORM OF CYLINDRICAL LENS.
PROLONGED VIEWING IS STRONGLY DISRECOMMENDED.
PLEASE READ PAGE A3–i BEFORE PROCEEDING.

2–6. This first example of the Berryman Logical
Image Technique (hence the usual acronym BLIT)
evolved from AI work at the Cambridge IV super-
computer facility, now discontinued. V. Berryman and
C. M. Turner hypothesized that pattern-recognition
programs of sufficient complexity might be vulner-
able to 'Gödelian shock input' in the form of data
incompatible with internal representation.[3] Berryman
went further and suggested that the existence of such a
potential input was a logical necessity . . .

2–18. Details of the Berryman/Turner BLIT construction algorithms are not available at this classifi-
cation level. Details of the eventual security breach at
Cambridge IV are neither available nor fully known.
Details of Cambridge IV casualty figures are, for the
time being, reserved (*sub judice*).

'IRA got hold of it somehow,' Mack had said. 'The Provos. We do
some of our shopping in the same places, jelly and like that . . .
slipped us a copy, they did.'

The cardboard tube in Robbo's hand had suddenly felt ten times
as heavy. He had expected a map, a Group plan of action, maybe a
blueprint of something nasty to plant in the Sikh temple up Victoria
Street. 'You mean it *works*?'

'Fucking right. I tried it . . . a volunteer.' He had grinned. Just
grinned, and winked. 'Listen, this is poison stuff. Wear the goggles
around it. If you fuck up and get a clear squint at even a bit of the
Parrot, this is what you do. They told me. Shut yourself up with a
bottle of vodka and knock the whole lot back. Decontamination,
scrubs your short-term visual memory, something like that.'

'Jesus. What about the Provos? If this fairy story's got teeth, why
haven't they . . .?' Robbo had trailed off into a vague waving gesture that failed to conjure up a paper neutron bomb.

Mack's smile had widened into an assault course of brown, jagged teeth, as it did when he talked about a major Group action. 'Maybe they don't fancy new ideas . . . but could be they're biding their time for a big one. Ever thought about hijacking a TV station? Just for an hour? Don't think things like that, it'll be bad for you.'

. . . Dead TV screens watched him from another cracked shop window, a dump that also rented Hindi videotapes. That settled it for them. Why couldn't the buggers learn English? The Group would give them a hint: the Parrot stencil was already in position, the can sliding out of his pocket, fastest draw in the west. At school Robbo had never won a fight, had always been beaten down to cringing tears: he had learned good, safe, satisfying ways of hitting back. Double-A Group booby-trap work was the best of all, a regular and addictive thrill.

This had better be the last for now, or last but one. Twenty would be a good round number, but the sky seemed to be lightening behind its overlaid sodium-light stain.

If he went round Alma Street way he could hit the Marquis of Granby, where everyone said the local gays hung out. Taking over a good old pub, bent as corkscrews and not even ashamed of it, give you AIDS as soon as look at you, the bastards. Right in the middle of their glazed front door, then, glaring red and a foot high . . .

The light hit him like a mailed fist. The goggles parsed it into bright, hurtful bars. Robbo spun half around, trying to shield his eyes with the heavy, flapping something in his left hand. The heavy something had a big irregular hole in it; torchlight blared through, and, moving quickly closer, there was a voice. 'Like to tell me what you're . . .?'

As the beam dipped and the voice trailed off, he saw the shivered outline of a police helmet through that of the Parrot. Behind jagged after-images a face came into view, an Asian face as he might have expected this end of town. The eyes stared blindly, the mouth worked. Robbo had read old murder mysteries where the unmarked body wore an inexplicable expression of shock and dread. A warm corpse slumped into him, its momentum carrying them both through a window which dissolved in tinkling shards.

It wasn't supposed to be like this. The bomb wasn't supposed to go off until you were six miles away. Somewhere there was the broken outline of a second helmet.

SECRET ★ BASILISK

. . . independently discovered by at least two late amateurs of computer graphics. The Fractal Star is generated by a relatively simple iterative procedure which determines whether any point in two-dimensional space (the complex field) does or does not belong to its domain. This algorithm is now classified.

3–3. The Fractal Star does not exhibit BLIT properties in its macrostructure. The overall appearance may be viewed: see Appendix 3, page A3-iii. This property allowed the Star to be widely disseminated via a popular computer magazine, a version of the algorithm being printed under the heading 'Fun With Graphics'.[8] Unfortunately, the accompanying text suggested that users rewrite the software to 'zoom in' on aspects of the domain's visually appealing fractal microstructure. In several zones of the complex field, this can produce BLIT effects when the resulting fine detail is displayed on a computer monitor of better than 600×300 pixels resolution.

3–4. Approximately 4% of the magazine's 115,000 readers discovered and displayed BLIT patterns latent within the Fractal Star. In most cases, other members of family units and/or emergency services inadvertently became viewers while investigating the casualty or casualties. Total figures are difficult to ascertain, but to a first order of approximation . . .

'Tape the envelope, all round. That's it. And write DANGER DO NOT OPEN in ruddy big letters, both sides, right?'

'So you know all about it.'

'There've been bulletins. The squaddies picked up fifty in that Belfast raid. Leeds CID got another . . . some bastard just like this one. I tell you, this job's been a shambles for years and now it's a fucking disaster. Three constables and a sergeant gone, picking up a spotty little shit you could knock flying just by *spitting* at him . . .'

Robbo hurt in a variety of places but kept still and quiet, eyes shut, slumped on the hard bench where ungentle hands had dropped him. He had told them every place he had hit, but they had kept on hurting him. It wasn't fair. He felt the draught of an opening door.

'Photo ID positive, sir. Robert Charles Bitton, nineteen, two previous for criminal damage, suspected link Albion Action Group. Nothing much else on the printout.'

'I suppose it makes sense. Vicious sods: run into them yet, Jimmy? Nearest thing we've got here to the Ku Klux fucking Klan.'

'This one'll be out of circulation for a good long while.'

'Jimmy, you *haven't* been keeping up to date with this BLIT stuff, have you? It's the same as that fucking nightmare with the kids and their home computers. God knows how much longer they can keep the lid on. It's going to get us all sooner or later . . . Look. We are going to have four PMs with cause of death unknown, immediate cause heart failure, and have I really got to spell it out?'

'Ohhh.'

'The only evidence is in that sodding envelope, a real court clearer, eh? I remember when they nicked those international phone fiddlers way back when, and all we could do them for was Illegal Use of Electricity to the value of 60p. They didn't have a phone-hacker law in those days. We haven't got a brain-hacker law now.'

'You mean we clean up after the little bastard, give him a nice room for what's left of the night, and that's *it*?'

'Ah.' The tone of voice implied that something extra was going on: a gesture, a finger laid significantly alongside the nose, a wink. 'Car Three cleans up, they've got the eye safety kit, for what that's worth. We show young Master Urban Terrorism to his palatial quarters, taking the pretty way of course. And then, Jimmy, when the new shift arrives we hold a wake for our recently departed mates. No joking. It's in the last bulletin. You'll really appreciate hearing why.'

Robbo braced himself as the hands got a fresh grip on him. The outlook sounded almost promising.

SECRET ★ BASILISK

. . . informational analysis adopts a somewhat purist mathematical viewpoint, whereby BLITs are considered to encode Gödelian 'spoilers', implicit programs which the human equipment cannot safely run. In his final paper Berryman argued that although meta-logical safety devices permit the assimilation and safe recognition of self-referential loops ('This sentence is false'), the graphic analogues of subtler 'vicious circles' might evade protective verbal analysis by striking directly through the visual cortex.[3] This may not be consistent with the observed effects of the 'Reader' BLIT discussed in Section 7, unusual not merely because its incapacitation of cortical activity is temporary (albeit with some observed permanent damage in Army volunteers[18]), but also because its effects are specific to those literate in English and English-like alphabets. There may in addition be a logical inconsistency with the considerations developed in Section 12.

10–18. Gott's *post facto* biochemical counter-hypothesis[24] was regarded as less drastic. This proposes that 'memotoxins' might be formed in the brain by electrochemical activity associated with the storage of certain patterns of data. Although attractive, the hypothesis has yet to be . . .

12–4. The present situation resembles that of the 'explosion' in particle physics. Not merely new species of BLIT but entire related families continue to emerge, as summarized in Appendix 2. One controversial interpretation invoked the Sheldrake theory of morphic resonance;[25] it might be simpler to conclude that multiple simultaneous emergence of the BLIT concept was inevitable at the stage of AI research which had been reached. The losses amongst leading theorists, in particular those with marked powers of mathematical visualization, constitute a major hindrance to further understanding . . .

The cell was white-tiled to shoulder height, glossily white-painted as it went on up and up. Its reek of disinfectant felt like steel wool up the nose, down the throat. In a vague spirit of getting the most from the amenities, Robbo patronized the white china toilet and scrubbed his hands futilely in the basin (cold water couldn't shift those red acrylic stains) before lying down to wait.

They couldn't touch him, really. They might fine him on some silly vandalism charge, and he might accidentally fall down a few more flights of stairs before reaching the magistrates' court . . . even now the hard bunk caught him in all sorts of puffy, bruised places. But in the long run he was okay.

They knew that.

They knew that but they hadn't seemed bothered, had they?

He had a flash, then, of them smiling. 'We aren't pressing charges,' and 'This way, sir,' and 'If you could just pick up your property . . .' A door would open and guess what would be waiting there for him to see?

Silly. They wouldn't. But suppose.

Time passed. The terminus was easy to imagine. He had seen it so often through the shatter lenses, a long bird profile sliced at an angle and jaggedly reassembled: parrot salami. In outline against walls and windows and posters; as a solid shape in glistening red that lost its colour to orange sodium glare; in outline again as a dead man's broken eyes met his.

It seemed to hover there behind his closed eyelids. He opened them and stared at the far-off ceiling, spattered with nameless blobs and blots by the efforts of past occupants. If you imagined joining the dots, images began to construct themselves, just as unconvincing as zodiac pictures. After a time, one image in particular threatened to achieve clear focus . . .

He bit through his lip, took refuge in a brief white-out of pain.

It was in him. They knew. Even with protection, he had looked too long, from too many angles, into the abyss. He was infected. Robbo found himself battering at the heavy metal door, bloodying his hands. Useless, because just as there was no clear crime he could have committed, there was no good medical reason why unfriendly police should offer him a massive, memory-clouding dose of alcohol.

Flat on the bunk again, he ran for his life. The Parrot stalked him through the grey hours of morning, smoothing its fractal feathers, shuffling itself slowly into clarity as though at the end of a flashy film-dissolve, until at last his mind's eye had to acknowledge a

shape, a shape, a

wink

NICOLA GRIFFITH

Mirrors and Burnstone

Jink brushed a fingertip over the wall before her. It was smooth and smelled strange. A cloud unwound itself from around K'than, the spring moon. Silver light pinned her to the turf.

Motionless, she breathed slowly and deeply. This was unexpected. Just after dawn that day she and Oriyest had studied the clouds, decided they would stay heavy over the moon and stars for the whole of the night. Darkness rolled across K'than's face once more and Jink reached with her mind to the richly textured underbelly of the clouds. She gauged their denseness and speed, judging the time it would take to sing open the warehouse doors.

It should be safe.

Waiting for the space of ten heartbeats until the night was once more thick and black, Jink ghosted along the wall until she reached the glass doors. She felt a faint humming beneath her feet. To one side, the square of press-panel gleamed. She ignored it. Word had spread through the journeywomen: to press at random in the hope of opening the doors sent a signal to Port, that centre of noise and light that had appeared on their world six seasons ago.

No. She would sing the doors open.

She composed herself, back straight and legs slightly spread. She sang softly with throat and mind, reaching in to push this, gentle that. She stopped to test her work. Almost. Four more fluting notes and the doors hissed open.

At her tread, lights clicked on automatically, making her blink. The doors slid closed. Under her bare feet, the foamplast was hard and cold. She hardly noticed. Alien sights and smells pressed at her senses. Containers, sacks and crates. Mechanisms standing free under thick coats of lubricant. She sniffed in wonder, laid a hand on a bulging sack. There was enough food here to feed herself and Oriyest for seasons . . .

Jink was thoughtful. What did the Outlandar intend with such stores? The building was on grazing lands accorded seasons ago to Oriyest and herself. By that token, they were due a small portion of the goods stored. But what did the Outlandar know of such things?

She looked at the largest store of food she had seen in her life. They would not miss a pouchful.

She squatted to examine a sack. It was not tied but sealed in some way unknown to her. She slipped her knife from her neck sheath and hefted it. It would be a shame to spoil such fine material but there was no other way. She slid the blade down the side of the sack.

'Stop right there.'

Jink froze, then looked slowly over her shoulder. Mirrors. She had heard of such.

The figure in the slick, impact-resistant suit was pointing something at her. A weapon. It motioned her away from the sack.

'Move very slowly,' the voice said. 'Lie down on your belly, hands above your head.'

Jink could not tell if the voice was female or male. It came flat and filtered through the mirror-visored helmet. Nor did the suit give any indication. She did as she was told. The Mirror relaxed a little and holstered the weapon. A second Mirror stepped into view, levering up his visor. He looked down at Jink. 'Hardly worth the bother, Day,' he said and spat on the floor. Day, the first Mirror, shrugged and unclipped her helmet.

'You know what they said: every, repeat, every intruder on Company property to be apprehended and brought to Port. We let this one go and who knows what might happen? Some hard-nosed zeck gets wind of this and bang goes all that accumulated R & R. Or worse.'

Jink listened hard, understanding most of the words but making little sense of the whole. She held herself still when Day squatted down by her head.

'Don't be scared. You'll come to no harm from us.'

Jink said nothing. She sensed no violence in the Mirror but she would take no risks.

'She doesn't understand a word, Day. Just get her on her feet and I'll call a pickup.'

He raised his left wrist to his mouth and spoke into the com strapped there. Jink heard the indifference, the boredom in his voice as he recited a string of numbers to Port Central. Day leaned and casually hauled Jink to her feet.

Jink breathed slowly, stayed calm. Day's gloved fingers were still curled loosely round her elbow. The Mirror turned to her partner.

'All okay?'

'Yeah. Be ten, fifteen minutes.'

'Want to wait outside?'

'No.' He stamped his boots on the floor. 'It's cold enough in here. We'd freeze out there.'

Jink wondered at that. Cold? It was spring.

The Mirror eyed Jink, in her shift.

'Skinny thing, isn't she?'

'They all look the same,' Day said. 'Like wisps of straw.'

Jink held her silence but thought privately that the Mirrors were as graceful as boulders.

She felt a faint disturbance, a wrongness beneath her feet. She tried to probe beneath the foamplast, stiffening with effort.

Day tightened her grip.

'Don't try anything, skinny. The doors are locked good this time.' She tapped the key box on her hip. 'Besides, now we've reported you, we'd have to hunt you down even if you did escape. Which isn't really likely. No,' she said easily, 'you just keep quiet and behave and in a few days you'll be back with your family. Or whatever.'

Jink was not listening. Sun and moon! Did the Mirrors not feel it? Burnstone, going unstable beneath their feet!

She spoke, her voice harsh from disuse and fear.

'Leave. Now.'

'Well, it speaks. You're a sly one.' Day did not seem perturbed. 'The pickup'll be a few minutes yet. There's no rush.'

'No. We have to leave now.' She did not pull free of the tight hand around her arm but turned slowly to Day, then the other Mirror. 'We stand on burnstone. We must be very, very careful. Tread like flies on an eggshell.'

'What's she talking about, Day?'

'Don't know. Sounds . . .' She looked at Jink's strained face. 'What's burnstone?'

'Beneath the soil. A stone that burns. If you hit it too hard, or dig near it, if you let . . .'

She heard a noise from the other Mirror. She turned. He was lighting a cigarillo.

'No!'

But it was too late. The match strip, still alight, was already falling from his fingers. Jink moved in the blink of an eye.

While the Mirrors were still hearing her shout, she pushed away Day's grip with a strength they did not know she possessed. Even before the tiny spark hit the ground, she was running. Straight towards the glass doors.

'Hey! Stop! You'll . . .' Day fumbled for the key box.

Jink crossed her arms over her head and dived through the glass.

Day cursed and ran towards the shattered door.

Jink knew she was hurt but she had no thought in her mind but running. She ran with all her strength. She heard the soft *whump* of the erupting fireball before the edge of expanding air caught her and tumbled her head over heels. She rolled, but the force of the explosion drove her straight into an outcrop of rock. Her thoughts went runny and red. Pain all over. She hung on to consciousness, forced herself to her feet. After the fireball, there were always a few minutes before the Burn really took hold. She stumbled back towards the remains of the warehouse.

A quick glance told her that one Mirror was dead. She stepped over shards of glass and pieces of smoking plastic to where Day lay. She was unconscious but breathing. Jink could not see much wrong with her. Hissing against the pain, she bent and grasped the Mirror's suit at the neck seal. She hauled Day across the grass, hands aching with the effort. She dragged the unconscious Mirror behind the same rocks she had crashed into earlier. There was shelter enough only for one. Day would have to stay here and Jink would run for it.

She rolled Day as close to the rock as she could, tucking the flopping arms away. She saw the wristcom blinking green.

Jink hesitated, then released the strap, held it in the palm of her hand. Despite her dizziness she took three quick breaths and looked back into her memory, forcing it to be clear. Once again, she watched the Mirror touch two buttons, then speak. She opened her eyes. Pressed the buttons.

'Port Central.' The voice was flat, tinny. Jink held the com close to her mouth, as she had seen the Mirror do.

'Burnstone,' she croaked. The flames had caught at her throat.

'Port Central,' the voice repeated.

'Burnstone,' Jink said, fighting spinning nausea, 'your Mirrors have started a Burn!'

'WHO IS THIS. NAME AND NUMBER.'

Jink just looked at it. The voice tried another tack.

'WHERE ARE YOU?'

'I'm . . . a building. A store building.'

'WHERE. COORDINATES.'

'It . . . I know nothing of your numbers.' She could feel blood dripping from between her shoulder blades. She blinked, focused her thoughts. 'The storehouse lies beneath K'than's path as she travels across the sky from your Port to the horizon. The wind blows from my left as I face . . . as I face . . .'

'PLEASE GIVE DIRECTIONS.'

A great wave of pain swept over her.

'The clouds above are thick and soft. One holds the shape of a woman's face. One yet to pass overhead is a tree, the trunk short and strong.'

'REPEAT. PLEASE GIVE DIRECTIONS.'

Jink fought the urge to shout at the stupid voice. She was giving the best directions she knew. One had only to look at the sky and follow. She tried again.

'The grass here is –'

'GET OFF THE AIR, YOU LUNATIC. WE ARE TRACING THIS CALL AND GOD HELP YOU WHEN YOU SOBER UP IN THE LOCKHOUSE. WE'RE SENDING A PICKUP TO –'

'But one is already coming,' Jink said, trying to remember if she had already said that. 'It must not land. Its heaviness will only make the Burn worse. You must tell it not to land.'

The voice shouted something but Jink ignored it.

'It must not land,' she repeated. She was feeling very ill.

The ground was hot to the touch. There was danger of an extrusion. Port would not listen. Day was as safe as possible. She had to get away.

She dropped the wristcom and started walking. Vaguely, she realized that her arms and legs were red with her own blood. She kept moving. A walk, a shambling trot, a walk again. Every step counted.

She fell. The slight jar was enough to send her drifting off into nothingness.

When she woke it was dawn. She was sick and cold but her mind was clearer. The gaping cut that ran from between her shoulders to midway down her back had stopped bleeding. Her skin felt raw. From behind the hummock of grass where she lay she could hear Mirrors shouting, the rumble and clank of heavy machinery. Company had sent people to fight the Burn.

Jink eased herself into a squatting position and watched for a while.

They were doing it all wrong. The machine was tearing at the soil, lifting huge chunks and dumping it in piles. Figures in suits and masks walked in a line, spraying foam. Jink found it difficult to understand their stupidity. Had no one told them that the only sure way to deal with burnstone was to leave well alone? All this walking and digging aggravated the Burn.

She ran towards a black suit, grabbed the arm.

'Stop!' she shouted. 'You must stop.'

The man turned towards her, then shouted back into the noise.

'Lieutenant!'

'Sir?' A woman came running. She flipped up her visor.

'Take this native to the medic. Find out what she's doing here, how on God's earth this thing started.'

'Sir.' She turned to Jink. 'Can you walk?'

'Yes. But there is no time.'

She swayed and the lieutenant held out a hand. Jink backed away.

'No.'

Jink closed her eyes, probed. She could feel the Burnpath now. One heading north, one slightly eastwards, downslope, towards Orïyest . . . Nearby, an extrusion of hot rock bubbled from the ground. She heard the captain yelling for his Mirrors to smother it. She opened her eyes, caught the lieutenant's mind and pushed gently.

'Listen to me. Your . . . foam . . . it keeps the heat in. It feeds the Burn. You must not. The digging, it . . .' She did not know the Outland word. 'It . . . angers the Burn, prods it to greater fierceness. You must not. Leave it.'

'Lieutenant!' the captain snapped. 'I told you to take the native to the medic.'

'Sir.' She hesitated. 'Sir, she was speaking of the Burn . . . the fire, sir. Maybe we should listen. She seemed most certain that —'

'Lieutenant. The girl has a lump on her head the size of an egg. She is concussed, suffering from shock and weak from loss of blood. Even if she were talking sense, which I very much doubt, would it be fair to keep her here in this condition?'

'I . . . no, sir.'

'The medic, lieutenant.'

'Yes, sir.'

Jink did not stay to listen further. She had tried but now there was Orïyest to think of. She ran.

The captain shook his head.

'No, lieutenant. Let her go. We've enough to worry about here.'

Midmorning. Jink jogged over the familiar rise.

Where was the flock? Neither sight nor smell gave any clue. She cupped her hands around her mouth.

'Orïyest!'

The call echoed and was still. She ran on.

She came to a great outcrop of rock that towered above her like a bank of stormcloud.

'Orïyest!'

The rocks echoed back her shout, and something else. The herd bird flapped heavily overhead.

'Clan!'

The herd bird hesitated, made another overpass.

Jink smothered her impatience, forced herself to sink slowly into a crouch on the grass. She knew she smelled of burnstone and blood. Clan would be nervous. She waited.

The herd bird spread his leathery wings and sculled air, landing an arm's length away. He did not fold his wings and his crest stayed erect. Jink made no move.

Slowly, cautiously, he sidled nearer. Jink watched his beak slits flaring as he sampled the air. He hopped closer. Jink spat in her palm, rubbed it against the grass to wash away blood and sulphur. She reached out an inch at a time. Clan lowered his head but did not hop away. Her fingertips brushed his pectorals. He huffed. She scratched at the soft down around his keelbone. He began to croon.

'Where's the flock, Clan? Orĩyest?'

He grumbled in his throat, then flapped and hopped a few paces towards the rocks. Jink levered herself to her feet and followed slowly.

Orĩyest had left her a message, a satchel of food and a waterskin. Jink read the message first, picking the pebbles up one by one and dropping them into her pouch. The message stones, rounded and smooth from generations of use, were one of Orĩyest's treasures.

She ate cautiously, uncertain of her stomach, and thought hard. The message said that Orĩyest had felt the Burn and had taken the flock to their safeplace. Jink was to join her there as soon as possible. If Jink was injured, then she was to send Clan to the flock and Orĩyest would come to see to her. If neither Jink nor Clan came to the flock within three days, Orĩyest would journey to the store building and then to Port itself if necessary in search of her.

Message stones did not allow for subtlety of tone but Jink could well imagine Orĩyest's grim face as she placed those particular pebbles. She sighed, wishing Orĩyest was beside her now.

She shook nuts and dried fruit into one hand and clucked encouragingly at Clan. He sidled over on stiff legs and neatly picked up the offering. When he had finished, Jink pulled him to her. She pointed his head in the direction of the safeplace and scratched at his keelbone.

'Find Orĩyest, Clan. Orĩyest.' She pressed her cheek onto his skull and hummed the findflock command twice, feeling the bone vibrate. She pushed him. In an ungraceful clutter of legs and wings he hauled himself into the air. Jink watched him flap northwards, then lay down on her stomach. She was very tired.

It was afternoon and she could not expect Orīyest before night-fall, some time before the burnpath. She thought of the Outlandar store building, and anger at their stupidity stirred sluggishly at the back of her mind. She had heard rumours of their ignorance but to be faced with its enormity was something else. Outlandar ignorance would cost them vast areas of pastureland, destroyed in the Burn. Even if a good portion survived, the area would be unstable for seasons. Burnstone was like that. She had heard of one seam that had smouldered for generations before sighing into ash.

The Outlandar respected nothing. According to the last journey-woman teller to share a fire with herself and Orīyest, the strangers had triggered a handful of Burns already. Still they did not learn. Were they capable of learning?

Jink stretched, grimacing as the new scar on her back tugged awk-wardly. It was healing well but strength was slow to return.

She hunkered down again. The youngling on the grass before her would not live: the flock was birthing before time. The long run from the rock to safeplace ahead of the Burn had shocked the young from their mothers' wombs before they were grown enough to live. Jink looked at it sadly. As she watched, it stopped breathing.

On the way down the hill she caught the echoes of Orīyest's singsong commands to Clan as they herded the flock into the gully for the evening. They met at the bottom. Orīyest, stripped to the waist, looked at Jink.

'The little one died?'

'Yes.'

Orīyest nodded slowly.

'Flenk dropped two. Both dead. I buried them by the creek.'

Jink did not know what to say. Flenk was their best pro-ducer.

'The others?'

'I don't know.' They began walking back to the shaly overhang where they had been camping since their flight from the Burn. 'They seem sound. If only one or two drop tomorrow, then we'll be over the worst. And we will have been lucky.'

Her voice was not bitter, now was not the time for such things. The flock must be seen to first. After that there would be time to think. Then they would send out the message cord.

T'orre Na found them five days after they sent the cord. The three women sat around their fire, dipping hard, dry bread into the stewpot.

The sky was clear, bright with stars and K'than's shining three-quarters face. The fire popped. Jink added another stick.

'I worry, T'orre Na,' she said.

'Not about your flock,' the journeywoman said.

'No. And yes. We were lucky. We lost less than the count of two hands. This time.'

'Ah.' T'orre Na nodded to herself. She stripped the bark from a twig and began to pick her teeth.

Jink continued. 'The Outlandar understand nothing. Much of our grazing is destroyed and will take seasons to regrow. Do they take heed? No. Their hearts and minds are closed to us. Closed to our land, to what eases it, what angers it.'

'Perhaps they have not been taught to listen to the right things.'

'Is that what you wish, Orīyest? Jink?' The journeywoman tossed her stick into the fire. 'You want the Outlandar to learn to hear?'

'Something must be done.'

'Indeed.' She paused. 'It would not be easy.'

'Nor impossible.' Jink leaned forwards. 'I have spoken of the two Mirrors – Day and Lieutenant – who would have listened. And Captain, too, was not unkind, just . . .'

'Overfilled with small things.'

'Yes,' Jink said, surprised. That was it exactly. His mind had been heaving with little things that meant nothing. Numbers and quotas, money, promotion, service record . . . She shook her head to free it from those hard, incomprehensible thoughts.

'They are all the same,' T'orre Na said softly. 'I have been to their Port and I have seen.'

Jink and Orīyest said nothing. Not far away they heard one of the flock shifting over the rocky ground, sending pebbles scattering along the gully. There was an enquiring low from another, then silence.

'They should still be made to hear,' Jink said finally. T'orre Na looked at Orīyest who looked right back. The journeywoman sighed.

'Very well. What will you ask for?'

Jink pondered. The usual penalty for triggering a Burn was double the amount of destroyed land from the wrongdoer's holdings. But the Outlandar had no land to give . . .

'We will ask a hearing. As our reparation price we will demand that the Outlandar listen to us. Listen and hear. We will teach

them about burnstone. We will demand to learn what it is they
want from us, why they came here and put their store buildings
on our grazing lands. And when we know more, we will ask
more.'

She looked up.

'Will you help us?'

Day was startled when she saw them. Natives were a very rare
sight inside Port. Two of them, making straight for where she sat
at the bar. She recognized one of them as her skinny captive. As
they approached, she marvelled at how such a frail-looking thing
could have dragged her, in her full armour, all the way to the
shelter of that rock. But she must have done. There was no other
explanation.

'Greetings, Mirror.'

'Hello.' She lifted her helmet off the stool next to her. 'Uh, sit
down.'

Orïyest nodded. They sat. Day cleared her throat.

'You shouldn't be here. Technically, you're an escapee.' She felt
awkward.

'Will you help us?' Jink asked.

'Well, sure. But all you have to do is lose yourself. Leave Port. No
one'll think to chase you up.'

Day saw that the other one seemed amused.

'You mistake us, Mirror.'

Jink laid a hand on her arm.

'Listen to us. If you can help, we would thank you. It costs nothing to listen, Mirror Day.' Day blinked. 'Will you hear us?'

'Go ahead.'

To her surprise, the other one spoke.

'I am Orïyest. Jink and I tend our flock. Some seasons are good,
some are not so good, but we expect this and we survive. This
would have been a good season but for the Burn you and your
companion started.' Her brown eyes were steady. 'When you built
your store place on our land, we thought: it is not good grazing
land they have chosen; perhaps the Outlandar do not know of our
customs of permission and barter; we will not make complaint. This
has changed.'

'Now wait a minute. That land is Company land.'

'No.'

'Yes. God above, the whole planet is Company land!'

'No.' Orïyest's voice was steady but her eyes glittered like hard
glass beads. 'Listen to me, Mirror Day, and hear. Seven seasons ago

we petitioned the journeywomen. The land between the two hills of
Yelland and K'than-rise, between the river that runs to the sea and
the rocks known as Mother's Finger, was deemed to be ours to use
until we no longer have need of it.'

Day had never thought about natives owning things.

'Do you have any of that recorded?'

Jink furrowed her brow.

'Recorded?'

'Yes. Recorded on a disc or in a . . . No, I don't suppose you
would. Anything written down?' She looked at their blank faces.
'Here.' She pulled a pad and stylus from her belt. Wrote briefly.
'See?'

'This is a message?'

'Of sorts. Do you have any . . . uh . . . messages saying the land
is yours?'

'Our messages last long enough to be understood. Then . . .' Jink
shrugged.

Day drummed her fingers on the bar. There must be some way
they recorded things. She tried again.

'How would you settle a dispute?' She groped for words. 'What
would happen if another herder moved onto your land and claimed
it?'

'They would not do that. Everyone knows the land is for our use.
If they need more land, they have only to ask.'

'But how would they know the land is yours?'

Day realized that Orīyest was looking at her as though she were
stupid.

'If a herder thought that through some madness I spoke an
untruth, a journeywoman would be summoned. She would speak
the right of it.'

'But how would she know?'

Jink gestured impatiently.

'How does anyone know anything? We remember.'

'But what if a journeywoman forgot?'

'Journeywomen do not forget.' Her voice was clear, precise. She
leaned towards the Mirror and Day found herself afraid of the alien
presence before her.

'There is a life between us, Mirror Day. I ask you once again: will
you aid us?'

Day was afraid. She was more afraid because she did not understand what she was afraid of. She licked her lips.

'If a journeywoman will speak for you . . .' She hesitated but
neither Jink nor Orīyest stirred. 'If that's your law, I'll see what I

can do.' Day wished she had a drink. 'Look, I can't do much. I'm only a Mirror. But I'll find out who can help you. I can't guarantee anything. You understand?'

'We understand.' Orĩyest nodded once. 'I will bring the journey-woman.' She slid from her stool and was gone.

'Will she be long?'

'Not very long.'

'Long enough for a drink,' Day muttered to herself. She raised a finger to the bartender, who poured her another beer. She stared into her glass, refusing to look at Jink. The minutes passed. Now and then she raised her head to glance at her helmet on the bar. The doorway was reflected in its mirror visor. Men and women came and went, mostly Mirrors snatching an hour's relaxation between shifts.

Maybe she should just cut and run. She couldn't afford to get mixed up in a natives'-rights campaign. Her promotion to ser-geant was due in about eight months. Maybe even a transfer. But if Company got wind of all this . . . Then she remembered the look in Jink's eyes, the way she had said, 'There is a life between us.' Day shuddered, thinking of her own reply, 'I'll see what I can do.' In some way she did not fully understand, Day realized that she was committed. But what to? She sipped her beer and brooded.

When Orĩyest entered with the cloaked journeywoman, the change in atmosphere in the bar, though subtle, was immediate. Day deliberately took her time to swing her stool round to face the natives.

The woman standing next to Orĩyest seemed unremarkable. Day had expected someone more imposing. She did not even have the kind of solemn dignity which Day, over the years and on various tours of duty, had come to associate with those of local impor-tance.

The journeywoman slipped her hood from her head, smiled and held out her hand Earth-style.

'I am named T'orre Na, a journeywoman.'

Automatically, Day drew herself upright.

'Officer Day, ma'am.' She had to stop herself from saluting. She broke into a sweat. She would never have been able to live that down. Saluting a native . . .

T'orre Na gestured slightly at their surroundings.

'Can you speak freely here?'

'Yes.' Day glanced at the time display on her wristcom. Most of the Mirrors would be back on shift in a few minutes and the main damage, being seen with the natives in the first place, was already done. They sat in a corner booth. Day wanted another beer but wondered if alcohol would offend the journeywoman. To hell with it.

'I'm having another beer. Anything I can get any of you?'

T'orre Na nodded.

'A beer for myself, Officer Day.' She turned to Jink and Orîyest. 'Have you sampled Terrene beer? No? It's good.' She laughed. 'Not as strong as feast macha but pleasant all the same.'

The beer came. All four drank, T'orre Na licking the foam from her lips with evident enjoyment. Day spoke first.

'I've already said, to Jink and Orîyest, that I can't do much to help.'

'Officer Day, I believe that you can. Tell me, what is the normal complaints procedure?'

'There isn't one. Not for n– the indigenous population.'

'What procedure, then, would you yourself use if you had cause for complaint?'

'Officially, all complaints from lower grades get passed to their immediate superiors but – ' Day leaned back in her chair and shrugged – 'usually the complaints are *about* senior officers. Company doesn't have time for complaints.'

'Not all Outlandar are Company.'

Day frowned.

'What do you mean?'

'The SEC representative.'

'The Settlement and Education Council? You're mad,' Day said. 'Look, you just don't know how things work around here.'

'Explain it to us then, Mirror,' Orîyest said.

'It's too complicated.'

Orîyest's voice stayed even.

'You insult us, Mirror.'

That brought Day up short. Insult them?

T'orre Na smiled.

'Officer Day,' she said softly, 'you are not the first Outlandar with whom I have had speech. Nor shall you be the last. We are aware that we need more knowledge, that is why we ask for your help. Do not assume that ignorance is stupidity. And do not assume that my ignorance is total. I understand your . . . hierarchies. You have merely confirmed my guesses so far.'

Day did not know what to think.

'The information we need is simple. Jink met a lieutenant she thinks would help us. We need to find her.'

'What's her name?'

'We don't know. We have her description.' T'orre Na nodded at Jink.

'Tall, a handwidth taller than yourself, Mirror Day. Eyes light brown with darker circles round the rim of the iris. Thin face. Pale skin with too many lines for her seasons.' Jink looked at Day. 'I judge her to be younger than yourself. Square chin, medium lips with a tilt in the left corner. Her hair is this colour – ' she pointed to the wood-effect tabletop – 'and is not straight. It's longer than yours. She has no holes in her ears for jewellery. You know such a one?'

Day was nodding. Lieutenant Danner. The one on accelerated promotion. By the time Day made lieutenant, if ever, Danner would be a commander. At least.

T'orre Na was watching her.

'Will this lieutenant listen?'

'Yes. Lieutenant Danner will listen to anyone.'

'You do not approve.'

'No. She's too young, too unprofessional.'

'Too willing to listen.'

Day opened her mouth, then shut it again. The journeywoman's voice had said: What is wrong with listening? Just as Jink had said earlier. Day felt as though her world was being undermined. These crazy natives were confusing her, never reacting the way they should. The sooner she got rid of them, the better.

'I'll find the lieutenant.'

They were all crowded into Lieutenant Danner's living mod. Jink shifted uncomfortably. The space was too small for two, let alone five. T'orre Na and the lieutenant sat cross-legged on the bed, Oriyest sat on the floor and Day stood at parade rest by the doorport. Jink perched on the sink in the bathroom niche, the only place left. She felt like a spare limb. Day had made the introductions but it was mainly the journeywoman and the lieutenant who spoke.

'What point, then, shall I put forward to the SEC rep, T'orre Na? The necessity for concrete reparation or the implementation of an education programme regarding burnstone?'

Oriyest spoke.

'Both,' she said.

Annoyingly, the lieutenant looked to T'orre Na for confirmation. T'orre Na did not oblige. The lieutenant was forced to respond to Oriyest.

'I'm not really sure that both matters should be raised at the same time.'

'Why?'

'Because of the way bureaucracy works.'

'Is your bureaucracy so stupid it can only think upon one thing at a time?'

The lieutenant grimaced.

'Not precisely. If, only if, the SEC rep decides to pass on your complaint, things will be made difficult if the complaint encompasses more than one area. That will mean the involvement of more than one subcommittee, which will lead to delays.'

'The difficulty, then, is one of time?' Orīyest asked.

'Yes, exactly.'

Orīyest smiled.

'Well, then. There is no rush. Speak of both.'

'I don't believe you understand the kind of timescales involved here.' She turned to face T'orre Na. 'Even supposing I went out that door now, this minute, and that the SEC rep decided without pause for thought to continue with this action, and even supposing his superiors on Earth agreed to back us, that would just be the beginning. Evidence would have to be assembled, shipped out – it might even mean going off-planet for these two.' She nodded at Orīyest and Jink. 'After that there'll be delays for feasibility reports and if, at long last, it's all agreed, then there are advisory bodies to be formed, supervisory employees to be selected . . . And during all this, Company will be blocking and fighting everything. They have planets full of lawyers.'

Neither T'orre Na nor Orīyest seemed perturbed. Jink was barely listening, the small space was pressing on her concentration. Day's expression was politely attentive but Jink had a feeling that the Mirror's thoughts were elsewhere.

'At the minimum,' the lieutenant was saying, 'we are talking of two years. At the maximum . . . who knows? Eight years? Ten years?'

T'orre Na nodded.

'Do you know how long a year is?'

'We are familiar with your reckoning. Are you familiar with ours? No – ' she waved a hand to dismiss the lieutenant's nod – 'I don't speak of how many of our seasons there are in one of your years. I speak of deeper things. You think of us as passive creatures. We are not. We have been learning, watching. I know your customs, your attitudes, your food, your beer.' She grinned at Day, who was startled but grinned back. 'How much do you know of us?'

'Much!' The lieutenant's cheeks were flushed. 'I've read articles on your culture, your art, the structure of your society . . .'

'And dismissed it. Look at me, Hannah. How do you see me? As a child? A primitive you wish to study for your amusement? Look at my hand.' T'orre Na held out her hand and Hannah did as she was ordered. 'This hand can birth children, this hand can weave, sow crops and harvest them. This hand can make music, build a dwelling. This hand could kill you.' T'orre Na spoke quietly. 'Look at this hand, Outlandar. Do you truly believe that the owner of this hand would allow herself to be treated as nothing, allow herself to suffer the domination of others?'

Hannah's eyes were drawn reluctantly to T'orre Na's. The journeywoman's eyes were deep and black.

Day stared at the journeywoman, realizing she had never seen so much strength in a person before. Her breath whistled fast and rhythmically as in a combat alert. Once, on Earth, she had seen a spire of red rock towering up over a desert. From a distance it had seemed fragile but up close its massiveness, the strength of its stone roots had been awe-inspiring.

Gradually, Day's breathing slowed and relaxed: there would be no violence. A child kicking a mountain was not violence, merely insignificance.

The lieutenant was pale but her voice was steady.

'What are you going to do?'

T'orre Na smiled slightly.

'What we are doing now. Seek ways to educate you. Will you help us?'

'Yes.'

Jink stood up.

'I have to leave,' she said. 'It's too small in here, I can't breathe.'

'We can speak somewhere bigger if you prefer.'

'No, Oriyest. You know what I know. Speak for us both.'

'Officer Day.'

'Ma'am?' Day straightened at the lieutenant's tone.

'Escort Jink wherever she wishes to go. Be back here within . . . two hours. You will be needed to escort the journeywoman and her companions to the perimeter of the camp.'

'Understood, ma'am.'

She palmed the door plate and they stepped into the port.

'I need no escort,' Jink said once they were outside.

'I know. Neither of us has any choice.' She hesitated. 'If you wish I'll leave you, meet you here again in a couple of hours.'

Jink considered it.

'But I'd rather show you something of Port. I . . .' She hesitated
again. 'I still haven't thanked you for . . . coming back. When the
burnstone went.'

Jink waited.

'Thank you,' Day said. 'You saved my life.'

Jink just smiled and touched her on the arm. They walked in
silence past the canteens and kitchen.

'What would you like to see first?'

'The place where you heal the sick. If you have one.'

Day raised her eyebrows. 'The hospital?' She had expected Jink to
ask to see the spaceships.

'Have I said something wrong?'

'No. You just surprised me. Again.' Jink nodded. 'You're so . . .
different.'

'But of course.'

Clan snorted and butted Jink as she pulled the flatbread from the
cooking stone. She tossed him a piece. He huffed in disgust; it was
too hot to eat. Orĩyest and T'orre Na were already spooning beans
into their bread.

'When will you move?' the journeywoman asked.

'When the younglings are sturdy enough to keep up with the rest
of the flock,' Jink said over her shoulder. 'Ten days, maybe less.'

'We'll journey to Jink's clan land,' Orĩyest said, 'they have spare
grazing. After the hot season we'll hear of other land we can use?'

'Yes.' T'orre Na nodded. 'We will be swift.'

They were silent a while, eating.

'The Burn could have been worse,' Orĩyest said at last. 'We went
to see it, yesterday. Three seasons, no more, and we can return.'

'So. Good news.'

'Yes.' Jink stretched, watching her long evening shadow. 'We
took Day to see.' She looked sideways at T'orre Na. 'She is learning
to think of larger things, that Mirror.'

The journeywoman nodded.

'Good. Learn from each other. It will be needed.'

Orĩyest put down her bread, plucked idly at the grass.

'She would like to help us move the flock. When the time comes.
We told her yes.'

A flush crept up Jink's cheeks.

'Ah. So that's how it is.' She laughed, touched Jink's hair. 'Such
friendships are good, but stay mindful of your differences. Both of
you.'

They nodded. T'orre Na yawned.

'Now I must sleep.'

'A song before dreaming?' Jink held her pipe out to the journey-woman. T'orre Na gestured to her to keep it.

'Play something soft. I will sing.'

So Jink played, a low quiet melody, and T'orre Na sang of hills, of air, of patience. Oriyest, banking the fire before they slept, joined in to harmonize.

KIM NEWMAN

Famous Monsters

Y ou know, I wouldn't be doing this picture if it weren't for Chaney Junior's liver. In all the obits, they said it was a heart attack, but anyone who knew Lon knows better. Doing all these interviews with the old-timers, you must have heard the stories. They don't tell the half of it. I didn't get to work with Lon till well past his prime. Past my prime too, come to that. It was some Abbott and Costello piece of shit in the fifties. Already, he looked less human than I do. Wattles, gut, nose, the whole fright mask. And the stink. Hell, but he was a good old bastard. Him and me and Brod Crawford used to hit all the bars on the Strip Friday and Saturday nights. We used to scare up a commotion, I can tell you. I guess we were a disgrace. I quit all that after I got a tentacle shortened in a brawl with some hophead beatniks over on Hollywood Boulevard. I leaked ichor all over Arthur Kennedy's star. That's all gone now, anyway. There aren't any bars left I can use. It's not that they won't serve me – the Second War of the Worlds was, like, twenty-five years ago now, and that's all forgotten – but no one stocks the stuff any more. It's easy enough to get. Abattoirs sell off their leavings for five cents a gallon. But this California heat makes it go rancid and rubbery inside a day.

Anyway, just before Lon conked out – halfway through a bottle of Wild Turkey, natch – he signed up with Al to do this picture. It was called *The Mutilation Machine* back then. It's *Blood of the Cannibal Creature* now. Al will change it. He always does. The footage with Scott Brady and the bike gang is from some dodo Al never got finished in the sixties. *Something à Go-Go*? Lousy title. *Cycle Sadists à Go-Go*, that's it. It must be great being a film historian, huh? What with all this confusion and crapola? Do you know how they were paying Lon? Bottles. When Al wanted him to walk across a room in a scene, he'd have the assistant director hold up a bottle of hooch off camera and shake it. Lon would career across the set, knocking things and people over, and go for the booze, and Al would get his shot. I don't suppose I'm all that much better off. One of the backers is a wholesale butcher, and he's kicking in my fee in pig blood. I know you think that sounds disgusting, but don't knock it until you've tried it.

For a while, it looked like Lon would last out the picture. Al got the scene where he's supposed to pull this kootch-kootch dancer's guts out. He was playing Groton the Mad Zombie, by the way. So it's not Chekhov. Al has already cut the scene together. Okay, so there's some scratching on the neg. Al can fix it. He's going to put on some more scratches, and make them look like sparks flying out of Lon. Groton is supposed to be electric. Or atomic. One or the other. The girl keeps laughing when Lon gets his mitts inside her sweater, but they can dub some screams in, and music and growling and it'll be okay. At least, it'll be as okay as anything ever is in Al's movies. Did you catch *Five Bloody Graves*? It was a piece of shit. After this, he wants to do a picture with Georgina Spelvin and the Ritz Brothers called *The Fucking Stewardesses*. You can bet he'll change *that* title.

But one scene is all there is of Lon. So, when he buys the farm Al calls me up. I don't have an agent any more, although I used to be with the William Morris crowd. I do all my deals myself. I couldn't do a *worse* job than some of the people in this business. I used to be handled by a guy called Dickie Nixon, a real sleazo scumbag. He was the one who landed me in *Orbit Jocks*, and screwed me out of my TV residuals. Anyway, I know Al. I worked for him once before, on *Johnny Blood Rides Roughshod*. That was the horror western that was supposed to put James Dean back on the top. What a joke. The fat freak kept falling off his horse. It turned out to be a piece of shit. Al and me worked something out on this one, and so here I am in Bronson Caverns again, playing Groton the Mad Zombie. They've rewritten the script so I can be Lon in all the early scenes. I know it sounds ridiculous, what with the shape and everything. But, hell, I can cram myself into a pair and a half of jeans and a double-size poncho. In the new script, my character is a Martian – I mean, I can't play an Eskimo, can I? – but when John Carradine zaps me with the Mutilation Machine I turn into a human being. Well, into Groton the Mad Zombie. It's the most challenging part that's come my way in years, even if the film is going to be a total piece of shit. I'm hoping my performance will be a tribute to Lon. I've got the voice down. 'George, lookit duh rabbits, George.' Now, I'm working on the walk. That's difficult. You people walk all weird. No matter how long I hang around you, I still can't figure out how you manage with just the two legs.

I'm an American citizen, by the way. I was hatched in Los Angeles. Put it down to the Melting Pot. Mom flopped down in the twenties, when the Old World political situation started going to hell. She'd been through WWI and couldn't face that again. It's in the culture, I guess. When your head of government is called the High War Victor you know you're in trouble. I'm not that way. I'm mellow. A typical native Californian, like my twenty-eight brood siblings. I'm the only one of us left now. The rest all died off or went back to the skies. I can't let go. It's showbiz, you know. It's in the ichor. You must understand that if you do all these interviews. What do you call it, oral history? It's important, I suppose. Someone should take all this down before we all die out. Did you get to Rathbone? There was a guy with some stories. I never got on with him, though, despite all those pictures we did together. He lost some relatives in the First War of the Worlds, and never got around to accepting that not all non-terrestrials were vicious thugs.

I suppose you'll want to know how I got into the movies? Well, I'm that one in a million who started as an extra. It was in the late thirties, when I'd barely brushed the eggshell out of my slime. Four bucks a day just for hanging around cardboard nightclubs or walking up and down that street where the buildings are just frontages. In *Swing Time*, I'm in the background when Fred and Ginger do their 'Pick Yourself Up' routine. They were swell, although Rogers put my name down on some list of communist sympathizers in the fifties and I nearly had to go before HUAC. Do I look like a commie? Hell, how many other Americans can blush red, white and blue? I didn't stay an extra long. I suppose I'm noticeable. There were very few of us in Hollywood, and so I started getting bit parts. Typically, I'd be a heavy in a saloon fight, or an underworld hanger-on. If you catch *The Roaring Twenties* on a rerun, look out for me during the massacre in the Italian restaurant. Cagney gets me in the back. It's one of my best deaths. I've always been good at dying.

My big break came when Twentieth Century Fox did the Willie K'ssth films. Remember? Rathbone played Inspector Willie K'ssth of the Selenite Police Force. *Willie K'ssth Takes Over, Willie K'ssth and the Co-Eds, Willie K'ssth on Broadway*, and so on. There were more than twenty of them. I was Jimbo, Willie's big, dumb Martian sidekick. I did all the comedy relief scenes – going into a tentacle-flapping fright in haunted houses, getting hit on the head and seeing animated stars in fight sequences. The films don't play much now, because of the Selenite pressure groups. They hate the idea of a human actor in the role. And when Earl Derr Biggers was writing the books in the twenties, the Grand Lunar had them banned on the Moon. I don't see what they were bothered about. Willie always spots the killer and comes out on top. He usually gets to make a bunch of human beings look ridiculous as well. In not one of the books or movies did Jimbo *ever* guess who the murderer was, even when it was blatantly obvious. And it usually was. For a while, I was typed as the dumb, scared Martie. Some of my siblings said I was projecting a negative image of the race, but there was a Depression on and I was the only one of the brood in regular work. I've got nothing against Selenites, by the way, although the Grand Lunar has always had a rotten sapient-rights record. It's no wonder so many of them headed for the Earth.

After the New York Singe, I was quickly dropped from the series. We were halfway through shooting *Willie K'ssth on Coney Island* when the studio quietly pulled my contract. They rewrote Jimbo as a black chauffeur called Wilbur Wolverhampton and got Stepin Fetchit to do the role. They still put out the film under its original title, even though there wasn't a Coney Island any more. I'd have sued, but there was a wave of virulent anti-Martian feeling sweeping the country. That was understandable, I guess. I had relatives in New York, too. Suddenly, forty years of cultural exchange was out of the porthole and we were back to interspecial hatred. Nobody cared that Mom was a refugee from High War Victor Uszthay in the first place, and that since his purges most of her brood siblings were clogging up the canals. I was pulled out of my apartment by the Beverly Hills cops and roughed up in a basement. They really did use rubber hoses. I'll never forget that. I ended up in an internment camp, and the studio annexed my earnings. The hate mail was really nasty. We were out in the desert, which wasn't so bad. I guess we're built for deserts. But at night people in hoods would come and have bonfires just outside the perimeter. They burned scarecrows made to look like Martians and chanted lots of blood and guts slogans. That was disturbing. And the guards were a bit free with the cattle prods. It was a shameful chapter in the planet's history, but no one's researched it properly yet. The last interview I did was with some Martian–American professor doing a thesis on Roosevelt's treatment of so-called 'enemy aliens'. He was practically a hatchling, and didn't really understand what we'd had to go through. I bet his thesis will be a piece of shit. There were rumours about this camp in Nevada where the guards stood back and let a mob raze the place to the ground with the Marties still in it. And who knows what happened in Europe and Asia?

Then the cylinders started falling, and the war effort got going. Uszthay must have been a bigger fool than we took him for. With Mars's limited resources, he couldn't possibly keep the attack going for more than six months. And Earth had cavorite, while he was

still using nineteenth-century rocket cannons. Do you know how
many cylinders just landed in the sea and sunk? So, Roosevelt got
together with the world leaders in Iceland – Hitler, Stalin, Oswald
Cabal – and they geared up for Earth's counter-invasion. Finally, I
got all the hassles with my citizenship sorted out, and the authorities
reluctantly admitted I had as much right to be called an American
as any other second-generation immigrant. I had to carry a wad of
documentation the size of a phone book, but I could walk the streets
freely. Of course, if I did I was still likely to get stoned. I did most
of my travelling in a curtained car. According to what was left of my
contract, I owed Twentieth a couple of movies. I assumed they'd
pay me off and I'd wind up in an armaments factory, but no, as
soon as I was on the lot I was handed a stack of scripts. Suddenly,
everyone was making war pictures.

The first was *Mars Force*, which I did for Howard Hawks. I was
loaned to Warner's for that. It was supposed to be a true story. I
don't know if you remember, but the week after the Singe a handful
of foolhardy volunteers climbed into their Cavor Balls and buzzed
the red planet. They didn't do much damage, but it was Earth's first
retaliative strike. In the movie, they were after the factories where
the elements for the heat rays were being synthesized. In real life,
they just flattened a couple of retirement nests and got rayed down.
In *Mars Force*, I played the tyrannical Security Victor at the factories.
I spent most of the film gloating over a crystal-scope, looking at
stock footage of the smoking plains where New York used to be. I
also got to drool over a skinny terrestrial missionary, snivel in fear
as the brave Earthmen flew over in their Christmas-tree ornaments,
and be machine-gunned to death by John Garfield. It was typical
propaganda shit, but it was a pretty good picture. It stands up a lot
better than most of the other things I did back then.

I was typecast for the rest of the war. I've raped more nurses
than any actor alive – although what I was supposed to see in
you sandpaper-skinned bipeds is beyond me. And I did a lot
of plotting, scheming, saluting, backstabbing, bombing, blasting,
cackling, betraying, sneering and strutting. I saw more action than
Patton and Rommel put together, and without ever stepping off the
backlots. The farthest I ever went for a battle was Griffith Park. I
had a whole set of shiny, slimy uniforms. I played every rank we had
going. In *Heat Ray!* I even got to play Uszthay, although that's like
asking Mickey Mouse to play John the Baptist. I soon lost count of
the number of times I had to swear to crush the puny planet Earth
in my lesser tentacles. I got killed a lot. I was shot by Errol Flynn in
Desperate Journey, bombed by Spencer Tracy in *Thirty Seconds Over*

Krba-Gnsk, and John Wayne got me in *Soaring Tigers, The Sands of
Grlshnk* and *The Fighting Seabees.* In *Lunaria,* Bogart plugs me as I
reach for the crystalphone on the launchfield. Remember that one?
Everyone says it's a classic. It got the Academy Award that year.
Claude Rains asks Bogart why he came to Lunaria, and Bogart
says he came for the atmosphere. 'But there's no atmosphere on
the Moon,' says Rains. 'I was misinformed.' I wanted the role of
the freedom fighter who floats off to Earth with Ingrid Bergman at
the end, but Jack Warner chickened out of depicting a sympathetic
Martie and they made the character into a Selenite. Paul Henreid
could never keep his antennae straight. I had to make do with being
another Inferior War Victor. No one believed there were any anti-
Uszthay Martians. That's typical earthbound thinking.

Then the war ended, and suddenly there were no more Martian
roles. In fact, suddenly there were no more Martians period. The
Allies did a pretty fair job of depopulating the old planet. Since
then, we've been a dying race. We're feeble, really. Every time the
flu goes round, I have to go to funerals. There was a rash of anti-war
movies. There always is after the zapping is over. Remember *A
Walk in the Dust* or *Terrestrial Invaders*? I didn't get work in those.
All you ever saw of the Martian troops were bodies. There were
plenty of newsreel scenes of big-eyes orphans waving their tentacles
at the camera in front of the sludging ruins of their nests. Those
movies didn't do any business. The whole solar system was tired
of war. They started making musicals. I can't do what you people
call dancing, so those were lean years. I did a bit of investing, and
set up my own business. I thought I'd hit on the ideal combination.
I opened a Martian bar and a kosher butcher's shop back to back.
The Jews got the meat, and the Marties got the drainings. It was a
good idea, and we did okay until the riots. I lost everything then,
and went back to acting.

   I did some dinner theatre. Small roles. I thought my best performance was as Dr Chasuble in *The Importance of Being Earnest*,
but there weren't many managements willing to cast me in spite,
rather than because, of my race. I tried to get the backing to put
on *Othello* in modern dress with the Moor as a Martian, but no one
was interested. When Stanley Kramer bought up *Worlds Apart*, the
hot best-seller about the persecution of Martians on Earth, I put in
a bid for the lead. I said I'd do it for nothing because the material
meant so much to me, but Stanley had to say no. By then, I was
too associated with the stereotype Jimbo Martie. He said audiences
wouldn't take me seriously. Maybe he was right, but I'd have liked

to take a shot at it. As you must know, Ptyehsdneh got the part and went on to be the first non-terrestrial to walk off with the Best Actor statuette on Oscar night. I'm not bitter, but I can't help thinking that my career in the last twenty years would have been very different if Kramer had taken the chance. Ptyeh' is such a *pretty* Martie, if you know what I mean. Not much slime on his hide.

Of course, Willie K'ssth came back on television in the early fifties. They made twenty-six half-hour episodes with Tom Conway under the beak and me back as dumb Jimbo. The series is still in syndication on graveyard shift TV. I get fan mail from nostalgia-buff insomniacs and night watchmen all over the country. It's nice to know people notice you. I saw one of those episodes recently. It was a piece of shit. But at the time it was a job, right? It didn't last long, and I was more or less on the skids for a couple of years. I was on relief between guest spots. I'm in a classic *Sergeant Bilko,* where they're trying to make a movie about the canal Bilko is supposed to have taken in the war. Doberman wins a Dream Date With a Movie Star in a contest and all the platoon try to get the ticket off him. Finally, Bilko gets the ticket and turns up at the Hollywood nightspot, and I turn out to be the Dream Date Star. Phil Silvers has a terrific talent, and it was nice just to be funny for a change. We worked out a good little routine with the drinks and the cocktail umbrellas. I'd like to have done more comedy, but when you've got tentacles producers don't think you can milk a laugh. I popped out of a box on *Laugh-In* once.

The sixties were rough, I guess. I had a little bit of a drink problem, but you must have heard about that. You've done your research, right? Well, skipping the messy parts of the story, I ended up in jail. It was only a couple of cows all told, but I exsanguinated them all right. No excuses. Inside, I got involved in the protest movement. I was in with lots of draft evaders. They gave me some LSD, and I wound up signing a lot of petitions and, outside, going on plenty of marches. Hell, everybody now thinks the War on Mercury was a waste of time, but the planet was gung-ho about it back then. Those little jelly-breathers never did anyone any harm, but you'd creamed one planet and got a taste for it. That's what I think. I did a bit of organizational work for the Aliens' League, and spoke on campuses. I was on President Kissinger's enemies list. I'm still proud of that.

I had a few film roles while all this was going on. Nothing spectacular, but I kept my face on the screen. I was the priest in *The Miracle of Mare Nostrum*, Elvis's partner in the spear-fishing business in *She Ain't Human*, and Doris Day's old boyfriend in *With Six You Get*

Eggroll. The films were mostly pieces of shit. I'm unbilled in a couple of Sinatra-Martin movies because I knocked around with the Rat Pack for a couple of summers before I got politics. I get a tentacle down Angie Dickinson's *decolleté* in *Ocean's 11*. I know you're going to ask me about *Orbit Jocks*. I was just naive. Again, no excuses. When I shot my scenes, I thought it was a documentary. They had a whole fake script and everything. I took the job because of the trip to Mars. I'd never been before, and I wanted to discover my roots. I stood in front of landmarks reading out stuff about history. Then the producers spliced in all the hardcore stuff later. I don't know if you've seen the film, but the Martian in all the sex scenes is not me. It's hard to tell with the steel cowl, but he's got all his tentacles.

I'm not retired. I won't retire until they plough me under. But I'm being more selective. I'll take a picture if I can pal around with any of the other old-timers. I was in something called *Vampire Coyotes* last year, with Leslie Howard, Jean Harlow and Sidney Greenstreet. I don't mind working on low-budget horror movies. It's more like the old days. The big studios these days are just cranking out bland television crap. I was asked to be a guest villain on *Columbo*, but I turned it down and they got Robert Culp instead. I went to a science-fiction film convention last year. Forrest J. Ackerman interviewed me on stage. He's a great guy. When I finally turn tentacles-up, I'm having it in my will that I be stuffed and put in his basement with the Creature From the Black Lagoon and all that other neat stuff. Lon would have gone for that too, but humans are prejudiced against auto-icons. It's a pity. I hope Forry can make do with just Lon's liver. It was the heart and soul of the man, anyway.

After this, I've got a three-picture deal with Al. That's not as big a thing as it sounds, since he'll shoot them simultaneously. *Blood of the Brain Eaters*, *Jessie's Girls* and *Martian Exorcist*. Then, I might go to the Philippines and make this movie they want me to do with Nancy Kwan. Okay, so it'll be a piece of shit . . .

If I had it all over again, do you know what? I'd do everything different. For a start, I'd take dancing lessons . . .

IAN LEE

Driving Through Korea

You could say it's just a story about some men in a car, driving through Korea. It seems quite plausible in many ways, if a little odd around the edges. Many things that happen are quite ordinary and might have happened to anyone before or since; but there are also signs of metaphor and hidden meaning and the longer the journey goes on and the further it gets from home the more things happen that defy belief.

To that extent, it's just like life.

It might have been called a story about two men in a car, driving through Korea. But actually there were three men from the start, if you count Jim. Jim is the Korean driver. The other two originals are in the back and they do all the talking, so it's easy to forget that Jim's there. And then before long they pick up another, so really it appears (if that's not too oxymoronic) to be a story about four men in a car, driving through Korea.

The trouble is, though, that even this is not right. One cannot in all honesty pretend it's a story about four men in a car driving through Korea because in reality (if that's the right word) one of them is an alien. In the extreme sense: which is, 'not of this earth' rather than just 'not from Britain' or, as the Koreans would say, 'not from Korea'. The alien knows which one it is. But to start with the others don't. In fact, owing to the alien's ability to adopt an alien form (alien to him, her or it, that is, though inconspicuous and commonplace to the humans in the story), the others don't realize at first that there's an alien 'in the frame' at all.

Why should they? They only believe things are true if they can pick them up with their senses. But rather than continue until the denouement with cumbersome circumlocutions such as (for example, not meaning to be significant) 'the sentient being in the form of a Korean chauffeur' (so as not to give anything away), the story will rely on the usual shorthand: it will consider things according to their outer appearance rather than their inner being. It is to be hoped that this device, also imitating life, will help retain the necessary suspension of disbelief.

To that extent, it's just like a story.

Jim has a round head and black hair and so much brow and cheek-bone that his eyes have all but disappeared. He drives with a sort of practical directness that is rough and insouciant, treating the car as a machine, in the Eastern fashion, rather than as a minor deity, as Westerners do. He sits in the front and wears his blue suit and drives and that's about all. He speaks only a few words of basic English: coffee, tea, yes, no, Ford Cortina, can't stand this rain, Charles and Diana – things like that.

At the start the front passenger seat is empty, then later, but not much later, the fourth man will sit in it next to Jim. (Time is not important except that it gets in the way and confuses things. It's not a story about time; more about space, really. Not inner space or outer space but the bit in between; that is to say 'space' itself. To that extent, it's only half like science fiction.) The fourth man will sing a little and recite some strange, rather personal poetry and no one else will quite know what to make of him. He comes from a society that the others do not understand and will be dressed in a way that sets him apart from ordinary mortals. But that's not to say he's the alien. Oh no, it's not as easy as that.

One of the two men in the back is in Korea on business. The other is a student, travelling on a geography scholarship. There is a younger man and an older man. They came (separately) to size up Korean industry; they haven't been here more than a couple of days but already it's bigger than when they arrived. The older wanted to buy and wanted to sell and was particularly interested in electronic components. As the younger of the two said (would an alien be so ironic?), isn't everyone these days? They met for the first time at Kimpo airport and these were the few details of personal history they told each other. But can one trust the stories of people one meets in airport lounges or on long journeys through foreign landscapes? Isn't there always the temptation to try out fantastic personae; isn't that what they mean when they say travel broadens the mind – that it broadens it to include things which are not true and the will to behave outrageously out of character without being considered mad or embarrassing one's friends?

The two men in the back watch the countryside. Let us call them Arthur and Billy, for this is what they told each other they were called. Arthur is older and taller; as he sits, his legs are doubled up like a cricket's and his knees come almost up to the bottom of the car windows. He has a rather worn appearance, like the car, and is, one might say, beginning to rust a bit under the doorsills and on his wing cases. (That's not a necessarily hint, either; it's a sort of fanciful metaphor.) Billy is younger and shorter, with an air of rebellion about him. Perhaps it is generated by the Glaswegian accent, perhaps by the James Dean haircut and the poor posture. But Billy would have counted Jim; he would have said three men and a car. Arthur wouldn't. Now, is that significant? Or just part of the generation gap put in as verisimilitude: the sense of the post-war Western babies that it's about time we stopped treating the rest of the world as scenery and walk-on parts for *The Caucasian Story*? As Billy might have said. For the alien, on the other hand, the very concept of hierarchy was a struggle: initially he/she/it had a tendency to count everything, including the family of earwigs living under the rubber mats on the floor of the car, and would have found it almost impossible to summarize the situation at all.

At Kimpo, Billy had lost his luggage. That is, the airline lost the luggage on the way to Kimpo. Billy explained this to Arthur, who had been puzzled as to how anyone could arrive in Korea with no luggage. Arthur had helped Billy describe his situation to the airport officials. After all, they were both a long way from home. Billy was grateful but a little suspicious at first at the way Arthur had taken him under his wing and suggested they share a taxi into Seoul. Billy watched for chinks in Arthur's masculinity. Later, the luggage turned up. It was very new.

Why Korea? Because it's there. That is to say, it is very much 'not here' and that's important. Here is always too complicated and blurred and shades of grey; but Korea is black and white, yin and yang, North and South and no one knows much about it.

To that extent, it's easy to understand.

'It looks like Scotland, doesn't it?' says Arthur, as the car enters a tawny Korean glen.

'Aye,' replies Billy. 'But without the rain.'

'Can't stand this rain,' chirrups Jim suddenly, looking over his shoulder with a big grin, untroubled by semantic suitability. Outside the sun shines in a crisp, clear, blue November Korean sky. The silver bark of the birch trees shimmers through a faint mistiness that hangs over the soft russet hills. A US Army helicopter sweeps across the sky at spotting height and chatters away over the brow of a hill. In fact, Jim appeared to say, 'Can't stand this lane', an interpretation given plausibility by the way the car sashayed danger-ously across the carriageway under the helicopter's gaze. But Arthur and Billy have already learned to aim off for Korean pronunciation. Some small concessions have to be made to the conventions of per-ception when one is a long way from home.

There is a minute or two of silence. Then they pass some small-holdings and Billy sits up abruptly, looking out of the window.

'Why are the trees wearing little waistcoats?' he asks, in a voice sufficiently loud for Jim to think he is being spoken to.

'Yes, please?' he calls over his shoulder, foxed by the question.

'Nothing, Jim. Don't worry,' says Arthur. A magpie struggles through the air from one side of the highway to the other. Definitely not a strong swimmer. The car drones on, spluttering ominously on the upward inclines, heading north on the expressway towards Seoul, which is now only an hour ahead.

'The straw jackets,' says Arthur, authoritatively, as if delivering a lecture, 'are put on the fruit trees in the autumn. The tree's colony of insects and other parasites flock into the straw for warmth as the cold weather approaches. Then, just when they think they've got their heads down for some serious hibernation, the gardener comes along, takes off the jacket and burns it.'

'Tough,' says Billy, with Glaswegian sang-froid.

'Tough, indeed,' says Arthur in a rather more melancholic and meditative tone. He glances sideways as he speaks, trying perhaps to gauge the tone of Billy's remark.

But what the characters are thinking is an unknown quantity. The story will not attempt to be definitive about that. If it were not so, then all would be revealed, and if all is revealed, then what would be the point of carrying on? Thus, it is a journey of discovery, driving through Korea; and what could be more realistic than that?

At this point a small figure becomes visible on the horizon, standing at the side of the road up ahead. At first, it could have been a sign (a road sign, that is, not a portent) but then it becomes more distinctly human. At about 440 yards it becomes a Western figure, male, facing the oncoming car. At 220 yards it is identifiable as man wearing a bottle-green parka and trousers. At 110 yards the figure stretches out its right arm across the nearside carriageway and at 50 yards it is possible to see distinctly that there is a thumb pointing heavenwards from a fist at the end of the arm.

'Stop, Jim,' says Arthur, giving Jim two hefty slaps on the shoulder.

As the car stops, the man approaches the driver's window. At six feet one can see that he has a black shirt with a white collar. And in that collar is no place for a tie.

'It's a bloody priest,' says Billy under his breath.

'Can we offer you a lift?' says Arthur more helpfully, leaning forwards to speak through the front passenger window that Jim has leaned across to open.

'Ah thought ah'd seen everything in this country: invasion tunnels, a DMZ patrolled by Swiss bank managers, commercial shipyards still working and little winter coats on the trees. And now a lift from a couple of Brits in the middle of nowhere,' says a voice emanating from a quizzical face at the window in perfect Tennessee English.

It seems to turn the tables on anyone who might have thought it was odder to find a Confederate preacher hitchhiking in that same nowhere. Jim clears a space on the front seat and the padre climbs in, placing a small haversack at his feet.

'Well, hi there, y'all,' he goes on. 'Guess I'm a little unexpected for you too. Name's Forsythe, sky pilot to the US troops in Korea.'

Introductions are effected and Forsythe spends a good deal of effort twisting round in his seat to shake everyone's hand and smile at them with plenty of perfect teeth and clear blue eyes.

Bracken, hills, magpies, blue sky, trees, more bracken. It seems an underpopulated country, still clean in the bright November sunshine. Some of it looks strangely familiar: silver birch trees and poplars mingle with the modest spirit of the landscape and columns of woodsmoke rise from half-hidden farmhouses to convey a reassuring mood of rural peace and tranquillity. Only the padded blue jacket and conical headgear of an occasional peasant in the middle distance or a glimpse of a turquoise roof swept up at the eaves remind the travellers that they are driving through Korea. Except for the alien, of course. To the alien it is unremittingly strange and new and frightening and one thing is no more strange or Korean than another. For the alien is not used to a world where things have one form and changing thoughts are hidden. In his/her/its world there is no concept of opposites or difference, since at some time everything takes a turn at being everything else.

The car drones on. Jim notices that the traffic in the opposite direction, heading south, is becoming heavier but he doesn't say anything, partly because his passengers are deep in conversation and partly because he would have to say it in Korean.

Instead, noticing that it is almost time for the news, Jim puts on the car radio. Sounds emerge as of an unoiled drawbridge being raised against the foe, that is to say, an ancient creaking or, as the Koreans would say, music.

It puts Billy in mind of the music playing softly in the background at the lunch they had just had at a Korean research laboratory.

He starts to tell Forsythe about it but Forsythe looks singularly unmoved.

'We had this pickled cabbage stuff called *kimchee*,' says Billy. 'And loads of little steaming bowls of soup with meatballs and fish and stuff, all with mounds of whiter than white rice.'

The squeaking on the radio has stopped abruptly, as it had done towards the end of the lunch. The travellers are unaware that this is not the typical ending of all such Korean music. They are similarly unaware that the Korean voice that follows the music is not just any old continuity announcer but Korea's top news presenter. The gist of the announcement is that the Land of the Morning Calm is in danger of becoming the Land of the Afternoon Panic as news spreads of an alien spacecraft having been found near the DMZ. Rumour has bred rumour and spread like a disease, causing large numbers of both uneducated and educated Koreans to believe that some dread alliance has been formed by the North with evil spirits or the Devil and that the long-feared invasion is about to roll.

Billy is telling Forsythe how Arthur had failed to get to grips, literally, with the chopsticks and had had to resort to a fork.

The radio is saying, effectively to Jim only, whose eyes are now as round as flying saucers, that there is reason to believe that the spacecraft held one occupant only but that the occupant was capable of changing its form to match anything it might see in its surroundings, including a human being. In a shamanistic society, such a notion strikes a chord and for the Koreans who hear this the landscape once more springs to life and begins to vibrate with immanent beings as it had done in the days of their forefathers.

Arthur is trying to retell a joke he made at lunch about silicon chips and potato chips and *bap* (Korean for rice) and then he recounts how the Koreans hadn't laughed but had all looked at the radio speaker in the corner, where the music had stopped and a voice was saying something in Korean. Then the lunch had finished rather abruptly. Arthur and Billy and Forsythe belatedly realize that the music has stopped this time too. Billy tries to laugh but no sound comes. Arthur catches Jim's eye in the driving mirror and is immediately assailed by a powerful feeling of *déjà vu*.

The Korean voice on the radio continues for a few moments as they listen, uncomprehending, then stops to let the rasping music start again. Jim turns it off and there is an eerie silence in the car. Does anyone notice that Jim has started to grip the steering wheel more tightly? Only Forsythe seems to remain comfortably innocent in a world of his own choosing. He rummages in his haversack and pulls out some crumpled sheets of paper.

'Let me read y'all a pome,' he says, breathing in dramatically before beginning,

> 'I have a pet magpie called Imagination,
> who gathers shiny objects for me
> and decorates my world.
> When I first had my magpie,
> she was black and white and I feared her strong beak.
> But now we are more intimate, I see
> that she is green and purple like shot silk
> and must really struggle to fly.'

The alien, here, in the midst of this, formlessly manifesting though an earthly form, is aware of the increased anxiety the poem seems to create but keeps its/her/his counsel.

After a silence of several miles, Arthur, perhaps trying to get the mood back down to earth, asks Billy what assessment he has made of Korean industry so far.

'Well . . .' begins Billy, pausing to gather himself for an opinion. 'It looks to me as though they worked out how to make a three-pin plug the week before last and they'll probably have a man on the Moon by next Christmas.'

'A man on the Moon . . .' muses Arthur, looking out of the window and remembering all the round moon-faces he has seen since he arrived. 'I feel as though I'm on a different planet already.' Down to earth hasn't worked.

Later, without prompting, Jim pulls in to a service area beside the expressway.

'Coffee, tea; yes, no,' he says economically.

One explanation would be that Jim is not the alien but believes that one of the others might be. He has pulled in in the hope of getting rid of his passengers and making good his escape. But one must remember what was said at the outset. The story proceeds by reference to what appears to be happening. Motivation is invisible; it keeps you guessing. It is also the key to behaviour and is revealed in stories precisely because in life it is next to unknowable. We certainly cannot guess what this alien's motivation might be and a Korean's is hardly more limpid. Perhaps Jim is simply hungry or needs a pee. Perhaps he wants to talk to others of his own kind to find out how seriously the alien story is being taken.

There are refreshments for the humans at an open counter and petrol for the cars at a Western-style array of pumps. The alien doesn't actually need refreshment of this kind but is content to go along with the interlude for the time being.

As they arrive the area is deserted. But then a large number of silver coaches with high sides and small windows arrive and suddenly there are great throngs of Koreans clutching polystyrene cups of coffee and small wads of food. It is like a convocation, a murmuration of birds of the air sweeping through the sky to a temporary roost. Their breath, however, steams like cattle's in the cold air.

Arthur and Billy get out of the car and walk towards the open-sided building which seems to be the source of most of the coffee and the food. The throng beats them to it; it is a determined throng and will not be delayed; and it is fired with suspicion. Arthur, six feet four in his stockinged feet, towers above the little Koreans like a tall white crane and, like a crane, is languid, while they are filled with starlings' intensity. They have seen cranes before, of course, but not here, not so close. You can even see the pinky colour of its skin, its round eyes, its lack of cheekbones and its thin sandy hair. Arthur looks nervously around at the Koreans, who pretend to ignore him, believing that to look at danger is to invite it to approach. Arthur has to duck slightly to get his head beneath the awning over the coffee counter and see what is on offer.

Behind glass are strange pots of liquefied snake, small pastries containing fried entrails, skewered magpie brains, who can tell? A diminutive lorry driver to Arthur's left is jabbering something across the till and receives a sort of pancake filled with what look like fiery-red duck giblets. Arthur looks round in despair for Jim, who has apparently dematerialized (hyperbolically speaking, that is – in other words, he is nowhere to be seen). Everything is labelled in Korean, an unpronounceable script which strikes Arthur disturbingly dumb. Here, where language is a kind of meaningless graffiti, there is nothing to hold back the underlying fear of being pecked to death by other people. The alien is calm, thankful for the protection of her/its/his adopted identity.

A high-pitched chatter returns Arthur's attention to the counter. Then the starlings clear, swirling off to perch on low walls and peck their booty. The crane is next, but can only stand with mouth open, no words coming out. Billy intervenes, pointing to the coffee urn and holding up two fingers. No problem. Then he spins his fingers in the assistant's gaze like a conjuror's flourish and directs her attention to some doughnuts nestling in the corner of the display.

The assistant seems effortlessly to understand; it is like a display of magic.

'Ah ken fine whit it's like when folks canna understond ye,' says Billy in his best broad rapid-fire Glaswegian with a grin.

A few minutes later, after a brief stop in a reassuringly Western-style convenience (though the receptacles seemed to have been set rather low), Arthur and Billy re-emerge from the other side of the building with a copy of an English-language paper. There is a large headline which declares the discovery of the alien spacecraft.

'They thought it was you,' says Billy to Arthur. 'They've never seen anyone over five foot eight before.' He looks around, noting that the Koreans have melted away again as quickly as they came.

The newspaper, which Arthur and Billy stand and read open-mouthed, says that a flying saucer has been found the previous day near the DMZ.

'It must have landed when we did,' suggests Billy provocatively.

It is large, smooth and round. Scientists from the US forces are assisting the ROK Army in investigating the find and have already issued statements reassuring the population that it is not some fiend-ish device from the North. Remembering the throng, Arthur and Billy doubt whether the populace has believed it.

'They're off to find the straw jacket,' says Billy laconically.

Arthur and Billy look around the car park to see where Jim has parked. The Korean-built Ford Cortina is easy to spot as it is distinctively black with white doors. Billy said when they first saw it that it was a motorized magpie, the Korean national bird. Forsythe is sitting on the bonnet and Jim, standing in front of him, is gesticulating, evidently trying to convey something important. Jim is saying something over and over in Korean and then pointing at the sky. Forsythe only looks puzzled. As Arthur and Billy approach, Jim is trying to make use of his few phrases of English. He points at the car once more and says 'Ford Cortina' and again points at the sky.

'He's trying to tell you that a flying saucer has been found near the border,' says Billy, making Jim jump a little as he speaks from behind him. Billy hands Forsythe the paper. 'I would've thought, being in the forces, that you'd have known . . .'

The alien is now aware that the humans' interest has been aroused and that discovery is only a matter of time.

Or, to put it another way: only a matter of space. That is to say, it will be assumed (by the humans) that the alien is enormously differ-ent from them because the alien comes from enormously far away and has an enormously different constitution. For the alien, on the

other hand, such matters are relatively irrelevant; it would not judge
this story by the ink used to print it.

So, as promised, we now appear to have four men in a car travelling
through Korea. But one of them is an alien. Somehow they have
convinced Jim (if he really is, that is) that the story must be a hoax
and they are heading for the border 'to see some sights'. While
they travel they are talking about the war and about neutrality.
On the back window ledge of the car, apparently unheeded, lies
the newspaper open at the headline: UFO EMPTY: ALIEN PILOT
AT LARGE. The humans still think it's all happening to someone else but the alien knows different and is beginning to feel
uneasy. Having acquired on her/his/its travels, driving through
Korea, the experience of Earth-conditions he/she/it needed for
its/his/her own reasons she/it/he is now keen to return home.
The alien has begun to manipulate affairs for his/her/its own benefit and in doing so runs the risk of revealing her/its/his presence.

The discussion is mainly between Arthur and Billy. Billy starts
by saying that he thinks it would be a good idea to extend the
DMZ (the demilitarized zone – the dee-emm-zee) by an agreed
amount each year until eventually the whole country would be
neutral. Arthur is not impressed by this plan and states forcefully
that the peace is kept by the existence of strong opposing forces.
The charmed life of the Swedish and Swiss accountant/soldiers
who, as UN nannies, supervise neutrally the DMZ, counting the
Siberian cranes and carving their initials on the trees, is sustained
by the willingness of the US to defend the attack corridors of
Kaesong-Munsan and the Chorwon Valley. According to Arthur,
the neutrals are a theatrical device, a fiction, part of the vacuum
in space through which the fundamental forces of the Universe
operate. But it is those forces – attack and defence, good and
evil – that are real, he declares, not the void through which they
flow.

Billy innocently suggests that little is known of the North and one
must beware of assuming that their intentions are inevitably hostile.
Arthur's exasperation ignites at this. Does Billy not realize that there
is an army of 900,000 in the North, that they have tunnelled fifteen
kilometres under the border, that people with birth defects are not
allowed to live in Pyongyang? Does he not know that brave British men died here in defence of freedom? 'Does Imjin River mean
nothing to you?' asks Arthur passionately. (Would an alien be so
emotional?)

Billy is awed by this outburst but also a little angry.

'I'm from the North, you know. Scotland was North Korea once.' It is enough to shut Arthur up.

Jim and Forsythe don't appear to follow it at all. Forsythe is turning over pages of a book of homilies entitled *He Brings Us Fruitful Seasons* and humming the chorus of 'All Things Bright and Beautiful' as he does so. Apart from this, there is an awkward silence, which Forsythe, turning in the front seat, is the first to break.

'So, it's us and them, is it, my friend? But the question is, who is "us"? Let me tell you. While we're sitting here in this car it's "us" in here and "them" out there. Another time it might be "us" because we're Caucasian and "them" because they're Korean. That'd put Jim here on the other side, wouldn't it?'

He breaks off to smile at Jim and give him a reassuring pat on the shoulder. Jim smiles back.

'Then again,' continues the sky pilot, 'another day "us" might be Europeans and then I'd be one of "them". Or it might be older people against younger people, tall against short.' His eyes seem to flick like a laser between Arthur and Billy as he says this, then he drawls more lazily, as from a Tennessee porch with a pipe and a slug of Southern Comfort on a summer's evening, and casually adds, 'Or it might be that we all have to come together as "us" on this planet, because "them" is what's coming from up there.' Everyone remembers the alien and lingering doubts about the credibility of the hoax theory are unanimously magnified. After a pause, Forsythe adds with chilling throw-away candour:

'I'm a deserter. They wanted me to take sides. I went mad.'

(Would an alien be so peculiar?)

Forsythe points a bony finger at his temple and screws it in. As he does so, the engine, climbing a long hill, splutters like someone clearing their throat. They are north of Seoul now, no longer on the expressway, but still driving through Korea.

'She's not too good on the hills, is she, Jim?' says Arthur, loudly and cheerily, trying once more to rescue the mood.

Later, but not much later, Jim pulls in to a gravel-covered car park at the top of a hill and they all get out. A long stretch of road is visible in both directions winding through the hills; but no traffic sounds. In fact, everyone notices how quiet it has suddenly become now the car has stopped and they are away from towns. They have arrived in the hills above Imjin River.

There are no old men on ancient pedal Hondas, no women with babies strapped in quilted eiderdowns on their backs, no buses, no GIs, no smoke from any chimney. There are no magpies fluttering from the hills, no cattle, no life visible against the brown land or the deepening clear blue sky. The alien, who is among them, listens to the heartbeats of the humans, having stilled its own. It hears the heartbeats quicken and knows that the humans' thoughts are turning to its presence. A more sophisticated breed than it had given them credit for.

Forsythe zips up his parka and, raising his palms together before him as in prayer, speaks in the voice of a poet:

> 'Sometimes I think I am dreaming God.
> Sometimes I think I am dreaming, God.'

Not surprisingly, Arthur gives Forsythe a strange look. Jim looks at Arthur. Billy looks at Jim. Forsythe looks at everyone with his bright, flickering eyes. Perhaps Arthur is remembering that Billy had no luggage at Kimpo. Is Jim looking puzzled because of Forsythe's sudden appearance at the roadside and the strange shirt he is wearing with no place for a tie; perhaps it is a sort of space suit? Maybe Billy thinks it strange that Arthur's agent in Seoul didn't recognize him, and had appeared to be expecting someone else. Does Forsythe regret that he has attached himself to a party of other-worldly disputants, whose car has put them down in the middle of somewhere and whose number includes a mysterious alien with unknown intent?

'It's a poem I wrote,' says Forsythe, unapologetically.

In silence the four men leave the car and walk to the vantage point at the front of the car park which commands a view of the valley and the Imjin River. Through the mist a silent plain is visible, a green and purple land, spreading out of sight towards the mysterious North. In front of them on the ground a model landscape has been built within a neat, low, rectangular wall. They look down as gods upon this replica scene, which is labelled with small brass plaques in English and Korean to show the course of the battle. They stand, heads bowed, like mourners, and the wind blows their differences away.

Quite suddenly, each of them has realized that none of them knows any of the others. None of them went to school together; none of them has bumped into any of the others at the supermarket, at a night club, on a train or on a package holiday; religion, art, culture, family, nation, race, social class – none really has anything in common. It brings them together as close as only strangers can be.

In the fading light the miniature landscape becomes more real than the one in distant gloom. Billy, hands in pockets away from the cold, notices that the battle was taking place on the day he was born. Arthur, stamping his feet and shuffling clumsily from side to side, observes that here there was fighting on the day he got married. Forsythe sees the date and announces out loud, 'My father was here before. This was where he died.' No one knows how to take this. Jim leans over a miniature mountain, points to the plaque which pays final tribute to the British troops and, selecting from his tiny vocabulary of their tongue, says proudly, 'Charles and Diana.' (Would an alien, posing as a representative of a liberated people, choose such a phrase to express respect and gratitude for the sacrifice of young lives?) Miraculously, the others seem to understand.

Somehow the humans begin individually to know also that the alien is near and, more than that, they realize that the other humans present also know. They cannot see the alien but they can feel a presence. At the edge of the car park the South Korean flag rattles in the wind, its blue and red reflecting the darkening colours of the eastern and western sky. What had been a business trip became a jaunt became an adventure is becoming a conclusion. But it's all the same. Black and white, yin and yang, sun and moon, heaven and earth, war and peace, North and South, spring, summer, autumn and winter, science fiction and life.

Then, spontaneously and simultaneously, they turn to look back at the Ford Cortina and they know: they were the characters in the story and the vehicle was imagination. As they hear the chatter of the spotting helicopter across the valley, the Ford Cortina flashes its headlights and they know. (Would an alien mind have risked trying to be human when he/she/it had the option of being a motorized magpie? Perhaps it was obvious all along.) In the blink of an eye he/she/it becomes the avian original and when the helicopter lands to take Forsythe away the orderlies see only a solitary magpie, the national bird, a gleam in its eye, flapping and struggling home in the last evening glow, its green and purple sheen invisible to those looking for the black and white. Billy, Arthur, Jim and Forsythe say nothing. But now that it's too late, they know.

S. M. BAXTER

The Quagma Datum

The soup was cold. I pushed it away. 'Tell me why I'm here.'

Wyman didn't answer until the next course arrived. It was a rich *coq au vin*. He forked it in with an enthusiasm that told me he hadn't always been accustomed to such luxury. Earthlight caught the jewellery crusted over his fingers.

Faintly disgusted, I lifted my eyes to the bay window behind him. Now we had left the atmosphere the Elevator Restaurant was climbing its cable more steeply. The Sahel anchor site had turned into a brown handkerchief, lost in the blue sink of Earth.

Suddenly they turned the roof clear. Starlight twinkled on the cutlery and the table talk ebbed to silence.

Wyman smiled at my reaction.

'Dr Luce, you're a scientist. I asked you here to set you a scientific puzzle.' His accent was stilted, a mask for his origins. 'Did you read about the lithium-7 event? No? A nova-bright object fifteen billion light years away; it lasted about a year. The spectrum was dominated by one element. Doctor, the thing was a beacon of lithium-7.'

A floating bottle of St Emilion refilled my glass.

I thought about it. 'Fifteen billion years is the age of the universe. So this object went through its glory soon after the Big Bang.'

Thin fingers played with coiffed hair. 'So what's the significance of the lithium?'

'Lithium-7 is a relic of the early universe. A few microseconds after the singularity the universe was mostly quagma – a magma of free quarks. Then the quarks congealed into nuclear particles, which gathered into the first nuclei. Lithium-7 doesn't form in stars. It was formed at that moment of nucleosynthesis. So all this points to an early universe event.'

'Good,' he said, as if I'd passed a test.

Our empty plates sank into the table.

'So what's this got to do with me? I hate to disappoint you, Wyman, but this isn't my field.'

'Unified-force theories,' he said rapidly. 'That's your field. At high enough energies the forces of physics combine into a single superforce. Right? And the only time when such energy densities

188

obtained was right after the Big Bang. The superforce held together your quagma.' He was a slight man, but the steadiness of his pale eyes made me turn aside. 'So the early universe is your field, after all. Dr Luce, don't try to catch me out. You think of me, no doubt dismissively, as an entrepreneur. But what I'm an entrepreneur of is human science. What's left of it . . . I've made myself a rich man. You shouldn't assume that makes me a fool.'

I raised my glass. 'Fair enough. So why do you think this lithium thing is so important?'

'Two reasons. First, creation physics. Here we have a precise location where we can be certain that something strange happened, mere moments after the singularity. Think what we could learn by studying it. A whole new realm of understanding . . . and think what an advantage such an understanding would prove to the first race to acquire it.'

'And what profits could be made from it,' I said drily. 'Right? And the second reason?'

'The Silver Ghosts think it's important. And what they're interested in, I'm interested in.'

That made me cough on my wine. 'How the hell do you know what the Ghosts are up to?'

His grin was suddenly boyish. 'I've got my contacts.' He wasn't more than twenty-five, I realized abruptly – about ten years younger than me, young enough to enjoy showing off. 'And they tell me the Ghosts are sending a ship.'

I choked again. 'Across fifteen billion lights? I don't believe it.'

'It's a fast ship.'

'Yah . . .' I thought it through further. 'And how could such a ship report back?'

Wyman shrugged. 'Hypernet?'

'Wyman, hypernet works by passing signals through hyperspace. The attenuation over such distances would reduce the data to mush.'

'Maybe,' he said cheerfully. 'In conversational mode anyway. I hear the Ghosts are planning a high-intensity packet-burst device. Would that get through?'

I shrugged. 'Perhaps. You still haven't told me why you're talking to me.'

Abruptly he leaned forwards. 'Because you've the expertise.' I flinched from his sudden intensity. 'You've no family. You're fit. And the youthful idealism that trapped you in research has long worn off – hasn't it? – now that your contemporaries are earning so much more in other fields. You need money, Doctor. I have it.'

Then he sipped coffee.

'I've the expertise for what?' I whispered.

'I've got my own ship.'

'But the Ghosts —'

He grinned again. 'My ship's got a secret . . . a supersymmetry drive. The Susy drive is a human development. The Ghosts don't have it. So my ship's faster, and we'll beat them.'

'For Christ's sake, Wyman, I'm an academic. I've never even flown a kite.'

A cheeseboard floated by; he cut himself precise slices. 'The ship will fly itself. I want you to observe.'

I felt as if I were falling. I tried to think it out. 'Tell me this, Wyman. Will there be any penalty clauses in my contract?'

He looked amused. 'Such as?'

'For not getting there first.'

'What's going to beat the Susy drive?'

'A Xeelee nightship.'

Expressions chased across his face.

The Xeelee own this part of the universe. All of us — even races like the Ghosts — are children at their feet. And it's bad for us. The Xeelee stop us doing things . . .

'All right, Doctor. I accept your point. The Xeelee are one of the parameters we have to work within. There'll be no penalty clauses.'

Above my head the restaurant's geostationary anchor congealed out of starlight into a mile-wide cuboid.

'Now the details,' Wyman said. 'I want you to make a stop on the way, at the home world of the Ghosts . . .'

Wyman's 'ship' was a man-sized tin can.

It was stored in an open garage on the space-facing side of the Elevator anchor. The thing's cylindrical symmetry was broken by strap-on packages: I recognized a compact hyperdrive and an intrasystem drive box. Set in one wall was a fist-sized fusion torus.

Wyman pointed out a black suitcase-sized mass clinging to the pod's base. 'The Susy drive,' he said. 'Neat, isn't it?'

I found half the hull would turn transparent. The interior of the pod was packed with instrument boxes, leaving precious little room for me.

I studied the pod with mild distaste. 'Wyman, you expect me to cross the universe . . . in this?'

He shrugged delicately. 'Doctor, this is the best my private capital could fund. I've not had a cent of support from any human authority. Governments, universities, so-called research bodies . . . In the shadow of the Xeelee mankind is suffering a failure of imagination, Luce. We live in sorry times.'

'Yah.'

'And that's why I've set up a meeting with the Ghosts on the way out. This flying coffin isn't much, but at least it demonstrates our intent. We're going for the prize. Perhaps it will persuade the Ghosts that we should pool our resources.'

'Ah. So this pod is really a bargaining counter . . . You don't mean it to make the journey after all?' I felt a mixture of relief and profound regret.

'Oh no,' Wyman said. 'What I told you is true. I sincerely believe the Susy drive could beat the Ghosts to the prize. If necessary. But why not spread the risk?' He grinned, his teeth white in the gloom of his helmet.

I left a day later.

Our universe is an eleven-dimensional object. All but four of those dimensions are compactified – rolled up to an unimaginable thinness.

What we call hyperspace is one of those extra dimensions. The hyperdrive module twisted me smoothly through ninety degrees and sent me skimming over the surface of the universe like a pebble over a pond.

Of course, I felt nothing. Hyperspace travel is routine. With the pod's window opaqued, it was like riding an elevator.

I was left with plenty of time to brood. When I checked the pod's external monitors I could see the Susy-space module clinging to the hull, dormant and mysterious.

After five days, with a soft impact, the pod dropped back into four-space.

I turned on my window. I was rotating slowly.

The sun of the Silver Ghosts is in the constellation of Sagittarius. Now it transited my window, huge and pale. I could see stars through its smoky limb. Something came crawling close around that limb, a point of unbearable blue. It dragged a misty wave out of the sun.

Of course I knew the story of the Ghosts. That blue thing was the main sun's twin. It was a pulsar; it sprayed gouts of heavy particles across the sky six hundred times a second. Over a billion years that unending particle torching had boiled away the main star's flesh.

The world of the Silver Ghosts was once Earthlike. Blue skies, a yellow sun. As the Ghosts climbed to awareness their sun evaporated, killed by the pulsar. What was left was a bloated caricature, as large as Sol but a fiftieth the mass.

The oceans froze and life huddled inwards; there was frantic evolutionary pressure to find ways to keep warm. Then the atmosphere started snowing . . .

The Ghosts refused to die.

The intrasystem drive cut in with a dull roar, a kick in the small of my back.

Then the planet of the Silver Ghosts floated into view.

I heard myself swearing under my breath. It was a world dipped in chrome, reflecting the universe.

I was flying over a pool of stars. Towards the edge of the pool the stars crowded together, some smeared into twinkling arcs, and the blanched sun sprawled across one pole. As I descended my own image was like a second astronaut, drive blazing, rising from the pool to meet me.

Now I saw what looked like the skeleton of a moon, floating around the limb of the world. I directed monitors toward it. 'Wyman. What do you make of that?'

Wyman's voice crackled out of the hypernet. 'That's where they built their ship to the lithium-7 event. They hollowed out their moon and used its mass to boost them on their way.'

'Wyman . . . I hate to tell you this, but they've gone already.'

'I know.' He sounded smug. 'Don't worry about it. I told you, we can beat them. If we need to.'

I continued to fall. The pod began speaking to the Ghosts' landing control systems. At last the perfection of the planet congealed into graininess, and I fell among silvered clouds. The landscape under the clouds was dark: I passed like a firefly, lighting up cities and oceans.

Under the Ghosts' control I landed in a sweep, bumping.

I rested for a moment in the darkness. Then –

I heard music. The ground throbbed with a bass harmonization that made the pod walls sing. It was as if I could hear the heart of the frozen planet.

I lit an omnidirectional lamp.

Mercury droplets glistened on a black velvet landscape. I felt as if I were brooding over the lights of a tiny city. There were highlights on the horizon: I saw a forest of globes and half-globes anchored by cables. Necklaces swooped between the globes.

It was a world of Christmas-tree ornaments, frosted with frozen air . . .

When the sun decayed, the only source of heat available to the Ghost biosphere was the planet's geothermal energy. So the Ghosts turned themselves and their fellow creatures into compact, silvered spheres, each body barely begrudging an erg to the cold outside.

Finally clouds of mirrored life forms rolled upwards. The treacherous sky was locked out, but every stray photon of the planet's internal heat was trapped.

'I don't get it, Michael,' Wyman said. 'If they're so short of heat why aren't they all jet black?'

'Because perfect absorbers of heat are perfect emitters as well,' I said. 'High-school physics, Wyman. While perfect reflectors are also the best heat containers. See?'

'Yah. I think so.'

'And anyway. Who cares about the why of it? Wyman, it's . . . beautiful.'

'I think you've got a visitor.'

A five-foot bauble had separated from the forest and now came flying over the sequinned field. In its mirrored epidermis I could see my own spectral face. Taped to that hide was a standard translator box. A similar box was fixed to the pod floor; now it crackled into life. 'You are Dr Michael Luce. I understand you represent a Mr Wyman, of Earth. You are welcome here,' said the Silver Ghost. 'I work with the Sink Ambassador's office.'

'The Sink?' I whispered.

'The sky,' said Wyman. 'The Heat Sink, you see. I am Wyman. Thank you for meeting us. Do you know what I wish to discuss?'

'Of course. Our respective expeditions to the lithium site.' The truncated spheroid bobbed, as if amused. 'We can make an educated guess about what you seek to achieve here, Mr Wyman. What we don't know yet is the price you'll ask.'

Wyman laughed respectfully.

I felt bewildered. 'Sorry to butt in,' I said, 'but what are you talking about? We're here to discuss a pooling of resources. Aren't we? So that men and Ghosts end up sharing –'

The Ghost interrupted gently. 'Doctor Luce, your employer is hoping that we will offer to buy him out. You see, Wyman's motivation is the exploitation of human technology for personal profit. If he proceeds with your expedition he has the chance of unknown profit at high risk. However, a sell-out now would give him a fat profit at no further risk.'

Wyman said nothing.

'But,' I said, 'a sell-out would give the Ghosts exclusive access to the lithium knowledge. All that creation science you told me about, Wyman . . . I mean no offence, sir,' I said to the Ghost, 'but this seems a betrayal of our race.'

'I doubt that is a factor in his calculation, Doctor,' said the Ghost.

I laughed drily. 'Well, well. Sounds like they know you too well, Wyman.'

'So what's your answer?' Wyman growled.

'I'm afraid you have nothing to sell, Mr Wyman. Our vessel will arrive at the lithium-7 site in . . .' A hiss from the translator box. 'Fourteen standard days.'

'See this ship? It will be there in ten.'

The Ghost was swelling and subsiding; highlights moved hypnotically over its flesh. 'Powered by your supersymmetry drive. We are not excited by the possibility that it will work –'

'How can you say that? Have you investigated it?'

'We have no need to, Doctor. Our ship has a drive based on Xeelee principles. Hence it will work.'

'Oh, I see. If the Xeelee haven't discovered something, it's not there to be discovered. Right? Well, at least this shows mankind isn't alone in suffering a fracture of the imagination, Wyman.'

The Ghost, softly breathing vacuum, said nothing.

'We humans aren't so complacent,' snapped Wyman. 'The Xeelee aren't ominipotent. That's why we'll have the edge over the likes of you in the end.'

'A convincing display of patriotism,' said the Ghost smoothly.

'Yah, that's a bit rich, Wyman.'

'You're so damn holy, Luce. Let me tell you, the Ghost's right. This trip is risky. It's stretched me. Unless you come up with the goods I might have trouble paying your fee. Chew on that, holy man.'

'Dr Luce, I urge you not to throw away your life on this venture.' The Ghost's calm was terrifying.

There was a moment of silence. Suddenly this world of mirrors seemed a large and strange place, and my own troubled eyes stared out of the Ghost's hide.

'Come on, Luce,' said Wyman. 'We've finished our business. Let's waste no more time here.'

My drive splashed light over the chrome-plated landscape. I kept my eyes on the Ghost until it was lost in a blanket of sparkles.

I soared out of the gravity well of the Ghost world.

'Strap in.'

'Disappointed, Wyman?'

'Shut up and do as I say.'

The drive cut out smoothly, leaving me weightless. The control screens flickered as they reconfigured. Thumps and bangs rattled the hull; I watched my intrasystem and hyperdrive packs drift away, straps dangling.

The pod was metamorphosing around me.

I locked myself into a webbing of elasticated straps, fumbling at buckles with shaking fingers. There was a taste of copper in my throat.

'Do you understand what's happening?' Wyman demanded. 'I'm stripping down the pod. Every surplus ounce will cost me time.'

'Just get on with it.'

Panels blew out from the black casing fixed to the base of the pod; a monitor showed me the jewelled guts of the Susy drive.

'Now listen, Luce. You know the conversational hypernet will cut out as soon as you go into Susy-space. But I'll be – with you in spirit.'

'How cheering.'

The pod shuddered once – twice – and the stars blurred.

'It's time,' Wyman said. 'Godspeed, Michael – '

Something slammed into the base of the pod; I dangled in my webbing. For as long as I could I kept my eyes fixed on the Ghost world.

I lit up a hemisphere.

Then the planet crumpled like tissue paper, and the stars turned to streaks and disappeared.

Wyman had boasted about his Susy drive. 'Hyperspace travel is just a slip sideways into one of the universe's squashed-up extra dimensions. Whereas with supersymmetry you're getting into the real guts of physics . . .'

There are two types of particles: the building blocks of matter, like quarks and electrons, and force carriers, like photons. Supersymmetry tells us that each building block can be translated into a force carrier, and vice versa.

'The supersymmetric twins, the s-particles, are no doubt fascinating,' said Wyman. 'But for the businessman the magic comes when you do two supersymmetric transformations – say, electron to selectron and back again. You end up with an electron, of course – but an electron in a different place . . .'

And so Wyman hoped to have me leapfrog through Susy-space to the lithium-7 object. What he wasn't so keen to explain was what it would feel like.

Susy-space is another universe, laid over our own. It has its own laws. I was transformed into a supersymmetric copy of myself. I was an s-ghost in Susy-space. And it was . . . different.

Things are blurred in Susy-space. The distinction between me, here, and the stars, out there, wasn't nearly as sharp as it is in four-space. Can you understand that?

Susy-space is not a place designed for humans. Man is a small, warm creature, accustomed to the skull's dark cave.

Susy-space cut through all that.

I was exposed. I could feel the scale of the journey, as if the arch of the universe were part of my own being. Distance crushed me. Earth and its cosy sun were a childhood memory, lost in the grief of curved space.

Eyes streaming, I opaqued the window.

I slept for a while. When I woke, things hadn't got any better.

Trying to ignore the oppressive aura of Susy-space, I played with the new monitor configurations, looking for the Susy-drive controls. It took me two hours of growing confusion to work out that there weren't any.

The Susy-drive had been discarded after pushing me on my way, like a throwaway rocket in the earliest human flights.

I could see the logic of it. Why carry excess baggage?

There were two problems.

The trip was one-way. And Wyman hadn't told me.

I'm not a strong man; I don't pretend to be. It took some time to work through my first reaction.

Then I washed my face and sipped a globe of coffee.

The translator box lit up. 'Luce. What's your status?'

I crushed the globe; cooling coffee spurted over my wrist. 'Wyman, you bastard. You've hijacked me . . . And I thought the hypernet wouldn't work over these distances.'

'We have a packet link; but apart from that, it doesn't. This isn't Wyman. I'm a representation stored in the translator box. I should think you're pleased to hear my voice. You need the illusion of company, you see. It's all quite practical. And this is a historic trip. I wanted some small part of me to be there . . .'

I breathed hard, trying to control my voice. 'Why didn't you tell me this trip was no return?'

'Because you wouldn't have gone,' said the Wyman representation – mentally I started calling him 'sWyman'.

'Of course not. No matter what the fee. And what about my fee? Have you paid it over yet?'

sWyman hesitated. 'I'd be happy to, Michael. But . . . do you have an estate? Dependants?'

'You know I don't. Damn you.'

'Look, Michael, I'm sorry if you feel tricked. But I had to make sure you'd take the trip. We have to put the interests of the race first, don't we?'

After that my courage began to fail once more. sWyman had the decency to shut up.

We popped out of Susy-space, sparkling with selectrons and neutralinos.

My time in that metal box had seemed a lot longer than ten days. I don't remember a lot of it. I had been locked inside my head, looking for a place to hide from the oppression of distance, from the burden of looming death.

Now I breathed deeply; even the canned air of the pod seemed sweet out of Susy-space.

I checked my status. I'd have four days' life support at the lithium-7 site. It would expire – with me – just when the Ghosts arrived. Wyman had given me the bare bones.

I de-opaqued my window and looked out. I was spinning lazily in an ordinary sky. There was a powdering of stars, a pale band that marked a galactic plane, smudges that were distant galaxies.

Earth was impossibly far away, somewhere over the horizon of the universe. I shivered. Damn it, this place felt old.

There was something odd about one patch of sky. It looked the size of a dinner plate at arm's length. There were no stars in the patch. And it was growing slowly.

I set up the monitors. 'sWyman – what is it?'

'All I see is a dull infrared glow. But that's where the lithium object is hiding, so that's the way we're headed.'

The patch grew until it hid half the sky.

I started to make out a speckled effect. The speckles spread apart; it was as if we were falling into a swarm of bees. Soon we reached the outskirts of the swarm. A hail of huge objects shot past us and began to hide the stars behind us –

'They're ships.'

'What?'

I straightened up from my monitor. 'Ships. Millions of ships, sWyman.'

I swung the focus around the sky. I picked out a little family of cylinders, tumbling over each other like baby mice. There was a crumpled sphere not much bigger than the pod; it orbited a treelike structure of branches and sparkling leaves. Beyond that I made out bundles of spheroids and tetrahedra, pencils of rods and wands – my gaze roved over a speckling of shape and colour.

I was at the heart of a hailstorm of ships. They filled the sky, misting into the distance.

But there was no life, no purposeful movement. It was a desolate place; I felt utterly alone.

I looked again at the tree-thing. The delicate ship was miles wide. But there were scorch marks on the leaves, and holes in the foliage bigger than cities.

'sWyman, these are wrecks. All of them.'

A motion at the edge of my vision. I tried to track it. A black, birdlike shape that seemed familiar –

'Luce, why the junk yard? What's happened here?'

I thought of a shell of lithium-stained light growing out of this place and blossoming around the curve of the universe. At its touch flocks of ships would rise like birds from the stars . . . 'sWyman, we're maybe the first to travel here from *our* galaxy. But races from further in have been flooding here from the start. As soon as the lithium-7 light reached them they would come here, to this unique place, hoping as we hope to find new understanding. They've been seeking the lithium treasure for billions of years. Let's hope there's something worth dying for.'

Something was growing out of the speckled mist ahead. It was a flattened sphere of blood-coloured haze; starlight twinkled through its substance.

It was impossible to guess its scale. And it kept growing.

'sWyman. I think that's another ship. It may not be solid, but I know we're going to hit. Where's the intrasystem drive?'

'Fifteen billion light years away.'

There was detail in the crimson fog, sparks that chattered around rectangular paths. Now the huge ship shut off half the sky.

'Christ.' I opaqued the window.

There was a soft resistance, like a fall into a liquid. Red light played through the pod walls as if they were paper. Sparks jerked through right angles in the air.

Then it was over. I tried to steady my breath.

'Why worry, Michael?' sWyman said gently. 'We've no power; we're ballistic. If another of those babies runs into us there's not a damn thing we can do about it.'

'It's getting clearer up ahead.'

We dropped out of the mist of ships and shot into a hollow space the size of the solar system. On the far side was another wall of processed matter – more ships, I found. There was a sphere of smashed-up craft clustering around this place like gaudy moths.

And the flame at the heart of it all?

Nothing much. Only a star. But very, very old . . .

Once it had been a hundred times the mass of our sun. It had squirted lithium-7 light over the roof of the young cosmos. It had a terrific time. But the good days passed quickly. What we saw before us was a dried-up corpse, showing only by its gravity signature.

Just an old star . . . with something in orbit around it.

I focused my instruments. 'That's about a foot across,' I recorded. 'But it masses more than Jupiter . . .'

The tiny, monstrous thing crawled past the surface of its wizened mother, raising a blood-red tide.

'So what? A black hole?'

I shook my head. 'The densities are wrong. This is a different ball game, sWyman. That stuff's quagma.'

The largest piece of quagma I had had to work with before had been smaller than a proton. This was my field, brought within miraculous reach. I stammered observations –

Things started to happen.

The quagma object veered out of orbit and shot towards us. I watched in disbelief. 'It's not supposed to do that.'

I felt a tingle as it hurtled past, mere yards from my window. It looked like a lump of cooling charcoal. Its gravity field slapped the pod as if it were a spinning top, and centripetal force threw me against the wall.

Clinging to the window frame, I caught a glimpse of the quagma object whirling away from the pod and neatly returning to its orbit.

Then a shadow fell across the window.

'That's shot us full of all sorts of funny stuff,' shouted sWyman. 'Particles you wouldn't believe, radiation at all wavelengths – '

I didn't reply. There was a shape hovering out there, a night-dark bird with wings miles across.

'Xeelee,' I breathed. 'That's what I saw in the ship swarm. The Xeelee are here. That's a night-fighter – '

sWyman roared in frustration.

The Xeelee let us have it. I saw the exterior of the window glow cherry-red; gobbets melted and flew away. The Xeelee dipped his wings, once; and he flew away.

Then the window opaqued.

Something hit my head in the whirling darkness. The noise, the burning smells, sWyman's yelled complaints – it all faded away.

'. . . damn those Xeelee. I should have known they can beat anything we've got. And of course they would police this lithium beacon. It wouldn't do to let us lesser types get our hands on stuff like this; oh no . . .'

I was drifting in a steamy darkness. There was a smell of smoke. I coughed, searched for a coffee globe. 'At least the Xeelee attack stopped that damn rotation.'

sWyman shut up, as if cut off.

'What's our status, sWyman?'

'Nothing that counts is working. Oh, there's enough to let us interpret the quagma encounter. But, Luce, the hypernet packet link is smashed. We can't talk to home.'

Cradling the cooling globe I probed at my feelings. There was despair, certainly; but over it all I felt an unbearable shame.

I had let my life be stolen. And, in the end, it was for nothing.

sWyman hissed quietly.

'How's the life support, by the way?' I asked.

'What life support?'

I let the globe join the cabin's floating debris and felt my way to the opaqued window. It felt brittle, half melted. It would stay opaqued for ever, I realized.

'sWyman. Tell me what happened – when that quagma droplet lunged out of its orbit and sprayed us.'

'Yah. Well, the particles from the quagma burst left tracks like vapour trails in the matter they passed through.' I remembered how that invisible shower had prickled. 'The scars laced everything – the hull, the equipment, even your body. And the tracks weren't random. There was a pattern to them. There was enough left working in here for me to decipher some of the message . . .'

I felt my skin crawl. 'A message. You're telling me there was information content in the scar patterns?'

'Yes,' said sWyman casually. I guess he had had time to get used to the idea. 'But what we can't do is tell anyone about it.'

I held my breath. 'Do you want to tell me?'

'Yah . . .'

It was less than a second after the Big Bang.

Already there was life.

They swarmed through a quagma broth, fighting and loving and dying. The oldest of them told legends of the singularity. The young scoffed, but listened in secret awe.

But the quagma was cooling. Their life-sustaining fluid was congealing into cold hadrons. Soon, the very superforce which bound their bodies would disintegrate.

They were thinking beings. Their scientists told them the end of the world would be followed by an eternal cold. There was nothing they could do about it.

They could not bear to be forgotten.

So they built . . . an ark. A melon-sized pod of quagma containing all their understanding. And they set up that unmistakable lithium-7 flare, a sign that someone had been here, at the dawn of time.

For trillions of seconds the ark waited. At last cold creatures came to see. And the ark began to tell its story.

I floated there, thinking about it. The scars lacing the pod – even my body – held as much of the understanding of the quagma creatures as they could give us. If I could have returned home engineers could have dissected the pod, doctors could have studied the tracery of tracks in my flesh, and the patterns they found could have been unscrambled.

Perhaps we would never decipher it all. Perhaps much of it would be meaningless to us. I didn't know. It didn't matter. For the existence of the ark was itself the quagma datum, the single key fact:

That they had been here.

And so the ark serves its purpose.

sWyman fell silent.

I drifted away from the buckled walls and began to curl up. There was a band of pain across my chest; the air must be fouling.

How long since I dropped out of Susy-space? Had my four days gone?

My vision started to break up. I hoped sWyman wouldn't speak again.

Something scraped the outside of the pod.

'Luce?' sWyman whispered. 'What the hell was that?'

The scrape went the length of the pod; then came a more solid clang over the midsection. 'I'd say someone's trying to get hold of us.'

'Who, damn it?'

I pressed my ear to a smooth patch of hull. I heard music, a bass harmonization that rumbled through the skin of the pod.

'Of course. The Ghosts. They're right on time.'

'No.' There was a bray in his voice. 'They're too late. Our Susy-drive took the Xeelee by surprise, but if the Ghosts try to get any closer to the quagma you can bet they'll be stopped.'

'But – ' I stopped to suck oxygen out of the thick air. 'The Ghosts don't need to get any closer. The quagma data is stored in the scarred fabric of the pod itself. So if they take the pod they've won . . .'

Then, incredibly, I felt a glimmer of hope. It was like a thread of blue oxygen.

I tried to think it through. Could I actually live through this?

To hell with it. I had been a passive observer through this whole thing; now, if I was going to die, at least I could choose how. I began stripping off my scorched coverall. 'sWyman, listen to me. Is there a way you can destroy the pod?'

He was silent for a moment. 'Why should I want to?'

'Just tell me.' I was naked. I wadded my clothes behind an equipment box.

'I could destabilize the fusion torus,' he said slowly. 'Oh. I get it.'

'I presume the Ghosts have been monitoring us,' I said breathlessly. 'So they'll know that my flesh, my clothes, the fabric of the pod, contain the information they want. But if the pod's destroyed, if everything except me – even my clothes – has gone, then the Ghosts will have to preserve me. Right? My body will be the only record.'

'It's a hell of a gamble, Luce. You have to rely on the Ghosts knowing enough about human physiology to keep you alive, but not enough to take you apart for the quagma secrets. So they'd have to return you to Earth, to human care –'

'I don't perceive too many alternatives.' I grabbed the frame of the pod window. 'Will you do it?' More scrapes; a judder sideways.

'It means destroying myself.' He sounded scared.

I wanted to scream. 'sWyman, your original is waiting for word of us, safe on Earth. If I get through this I'll tell him what you did.'

He hesitated for five heartbeats.

Then: 'Okay. Keep your mouth open when you jump. God-speed, Michael –'

Grasping the frame with both hands I swung my feet at the window. The blistered stuff smashed easily and the fragments rushed away. Escaping air sparkled into ice. Sound sucked away and my ears popped with a wincing pain.

Snowflakes of air billowed from my open mouth and gas tore from my bowels.

I closed my freezing eyes and felt my way around the hull. Then I kicked away as hard as I could.

I waited five seconds, then risked one last look. The Ghosts' moon ship was a silvered landscape, tilted up to my right. A thick hose snaked up to the ripped-open pod. Chrome spheres clustered around the pod like bacteria over a wound.

I saw the flash through closed eyelids.

I tumbled backwards. The pain in my chest passed into a dull acceptance. Those Ghosts would have to move fast.

A cold smoothness closed around me.

There was light behind my eyes. I opened them to an airy room. A window to my left. Blue sky. The smell of flowers. A nurse's concerned face over me.

A human nurse.

Behind him, a Ghost hovered.

I tried to speak. 'Hello, Wyman.'

A footstep. 'How did you know I was here?' His pinched expression made me smile.

'You're looking a lot older, Wyman, you know that?' My voice was a croak. 'Of course you're here. You've been waiting for me to die. But here I am, ready to collect my fee.

'I expect the doctors will spend the next year scanning me on all wavelengths, mapping out the quagma scars and working out what they mean. I'll be famous.' I laughed; my chest hurt. 'But we're going to get the treasure, Wyman. A message from another realm of creation.

'Of course we'll have to share it. Humans and Ghosts . . . but at least we'll get it.

'And you'll have to share the profits, won't you? And there's my fee as well. You didn't budget for that, did you, Wyman? I'd guess you're about to become a lot poorer –'

He walked out, slamming the door.

'But,' I whispered, 'we must put the interests of the race first.'

There was a bit of blue sky reflected in the Ghost. I stared at it and waited for sleep to return.

Notes on the Authors

Brian Stableford, born in 1948, recently gave up his job as a lecturer in Sociology at the University of Reading. He has written many novels, from *Cradle of the Sun* (1969) to the highly praised *The Empire of Fear* (1988). Among his several non-fiction books is one entitled *The Way to Write Science Fiction* (1989). He is currently at work on an ambitious new trilogy of SF novels.

Lisa Goldstein won the American Book Award for her children's fantasy novel *The Red Magician* (1982). Her other books include *The Dream Years* (1985) and *A Mask for the General* (1987). She lives in San Francisco. 'City of Peace' is her first story for *Interzone*.

Greg Egan, born in 1961, is one of Australia's most promising new SF and fantasy writers. He has contributed three stories to *Interzone*, of which 'The Cutie' is the most recent, and he has just completed a horror novel.

Eric Brown, born in 1960, has contributed five short stories to *Interzone*, and his first collection is forthcoming in 1990. He lives in Yorkshire. 'The Time-Lapsed Man' won the magazine's popularity poll as the most admired story we published in 1988.

Rachel Pollack won the Arthur C. Clarke Award for her third novel, *Unquenchable Fire* (1988). She has written three earlier stories for *Interzone*, and now we are proud to present 'The Bead Woman', a piece which shares the background of her prize-winning novel, as an original item in this anthology. She lives in the Netherlands.

J.G. Ballard, born in 1930, is the author of *Empire of the Sun* (1984), a work which already has the status of a modern classic. His most recent books are the novel *The Day of Creation* (1987), the novella *Running Wild* (1988) and the collection *Memories of the Space Age* (1988). He has contributed four stories to *Interzone* since the magazine's inception in 1982, of which 'The Enormous Space' is the most recent.

Barrington J. Bayley, born in 1937, is the author of SF novels ranging from *The Star Virus* (1970) to *The Rod of Light* (1985). He lives in Shropshire. 'Tommy Atkins' is the most recent of three stories he has contributed to *Interzone* magazine.

John Sladek, born in 1937, is the author of the hilarious *Bugs* (1989) as well as many earlier novels and short-story collections. A few years ago he moved back to his native America after seventeen years of residence in London. 'Stop Evolution in Its Tracks!' is his third story for *Interzone*.

Richard Calder is a wholly new British author who informs us that 'Toxine' is the first short story he has ever written. (It is published here for the first time.) His second piece, 'Mosquito', will appear in *Interzone* magazine shortly after this anthology is published, and both pieces amply demonstrate that he is definitely a writer to watch.

Kim Stanley Robinson, born in 1952, is one of the newer stars of American SF. His novels include *The Wild Shore* (1984), *The Memory of Whiteness* (1985) and *The Gold Coast* (1988). He lives in Maryland. 'Before I Wake' is his first short story for *Interzone* magazine.

David Langford, born in 1953, is a one-time nuclear physicist who now works as a full-time writer of books, stories, magazine columns and software. He lives in Reading. 'Blit' is his second piece for *Interzone*.

Nicola Griffith lives in Hull. 'Mirrors and Burnstone' was her first published short story, and she has since sold a couple more.

Kim Newman, born in 1959, is the only writer who has appeared in all four *Interzone* anthologies to date. He is the author of *Nightmare Movies* (1984; updated 1988) and has recently completed his first novel, *The Night Mayor* – to be published by Simon & Schuster at the same time as this anthology.

Ian Lee, born in 1951, is another of *Interzone*'s recent British discoveries. He lives in London. In the past year he has contributed two wayward and amusing stories to the magazine, of which 'Driving Through Korea' was the first.

S.M. Baxter is a new British writer who works effectively in traditional SF modes. He lives in High Wycombe. He has written four stories for *Interzone*, plus 'The Quagma Datum', which is published for the first time in this volume.

Acknowledgements

We wish to thank the following people, who have assisted the magazine in various ways and hence have helped make this anthology possible: Paul Annis, Malcolm Edwards, Gamma, Judith Hanna, Lee Montgomerie, Ann Pringle, Andy Robertson, Robyn Sisman and Bryan Williamson.

Interzone is published bimonthly from 124 Osborne Road, Brighton BN1 6LU, UK. A six-issue subscription costs £11 (inland) or £12.50 (overseas).

INTERZONE THE 2ND ANTHOLOGY

'From the beginning, *Interzone* has sought out new writers ... No other magazine in Britain is publishing science fiction at all, let alone fiction of this quality'
The Times Literary Supplement

In this second selection from *Interzone* are new stories from J. G. Ballard and Thomas M. Disch, together with Brian Stableford's first piece of fiction in five years. Then, before your very eyes and for the very first time, we present a cyberpunk collaboration between John Shirley and Bruce Sterling ...

'The most exciting development in this area of British publishing for a decade'
City Limits

Rising stars Neil Ferguson and Paul J. McAuley, along with a real chiller from Gregory Benford and Ian Watson's tale of alien love ...

'*Interzone* is the decade's most interesting science fiction magazine'
William Gibson

'The best new science fiction magazine in twenty years'
The Washington Post

Sixteen writers, gathered together to delight, to intrigue, dazzle and challenge. Sixteen story tellers and their 'Brilliantly varied and frequently breathtakingly audacious'
Iain Banks

HODDER AND STOUGHTON PAPERBACKS

INTERZONE THE 3RD ANTHOLOGY

This third selection from *Interzone* includes stories from 1987 John W. Campbell Award winner Karen Joy Fowler, from Nebula winner Pat Murphy, from David Brin, Brian Stableford, Lisa Tuttle, from newcomers Eric Brown and Richard Kadrey ... they range from the surreal to cyberpunk, satire to fantasy ...

'A selection of stories that combine the grim and the glorious with an audacity that recalls *Dangerous Visions* ... it should not be missed at any cost'

Locus

'*Interzone* strides over the frontier and well on to a summit of art'

New Statesman

'They have the quality of going right to the edge of ideas which can chill as well as warm'

The Times

Post·A·Book

A Royal Mail service in association with the Book Marketing Council & The Booksellers Association.

Post-A-Book is a Post Office trademark.

KIM NEWMAN

THE NIGHT MAYOR

In the City it is always two-thirty in the morning and raining.

Edward G. Robinson is strangling Joan Bennett on a fire escape. James Cagney is walking the mean streets. The City is black and white and grey-grained. Light flares on blood-wet sidewalks. Someone is playing tenor horn. Footsteps echo.

The City: dream creation and dream refuge of Truro Daine, aka the Night Mayor, the 21st century's Napoleon of crime.

A man and a woman enter the City. Professional Dreamers, their task is to hunt Daine down before he can escape for good into his own ever-expanding world ...

'Kim Newman knows his films. He also knows his sci-fi ... should appeal as much to cinephiles as cyberpunks'
Time Out

'The *Night Mayor* is light-hearted, ironic even ... its most gruesome metamorphosis reminiscent less of William Gibson than Roger Rabbit'
The Listener

HODDER AND STOUGHTON PAPERBACKS

BRIAN STABLEFORD

THE CENTRE CANNOT HOLD

The Gods of Asgard were in trouble.

In fact, if the machine intelligences which ran the macro-world couldn't be saved from their enemies, the starlet at its centre might go nova, and hundreds of billions of intelligent humanoids would be destroyed. Unfortunately, the one man who was in a position to save the situation was Mike Rousseau, who didn't feel that he was cut out to be a hero.

Rousseau had always wanted to reach the centre of Asgard, and this was his big chance, but he found himself taking part in a desperate race against time – and the closer he got to the centre, the tougher the going became. His newest enemies were nastier than any he had ever faced before, and his friends wanted to double the odds in their favour by making a copy of him.

It was all too much for one man to bear – but if there were two of him, wouldn't the nightmare be twice as bad?

HODDER AND STOUGHTON PAPERBACKS

BRIAN STABLEFORD

JOURNEY TO THE CENTRE

They called the world Asgard: the Home of the Gods.

Beneath its artificial shell were three vast cave-systems, each one the size of an Earthlike world; beneath those, three more. No one knew how many layers there might be – and no one knew what secret was buried at its centre.

At some time in the remote past Asgard had suffered a terrible catastrophe. Now its outer layers were cold, its builders presumed dead. Explorers and exploiters from a hundred different worlds were scavenging among the ruins. But deep below there might still be light, and life, and perils unknown.

When the race to the lower levels began, Mike Rousseau was right up with the leaders. He wasn't alone, but the friends he had were the kind that would normally make you prefer your enemies – except that *his* enemies were the worst a man could possibly have . . . and they were right behind him . . . and closing in . . .

He might be the man to solve the biggest puzzle in the galaxy – if he could only stay alive . . .

HODDER AND STOUGHTON PAPERBACKS